Stagecoach to Liberty

Stagecoach to Liberty

Montana Gold Series

By

Janalyn Voigt

Stagecoach to Liberty
Published by Mountain Brook Ink
White Salmon, WA U.S.A.

The website addresses shown in this book are not intended in any way to be or imply an endorsement on the part of Mountain Brook Ink, nor do we vouch for their content.

This story is a work of fiction. All characters and events are the product of the author's imagination other than those stated in the author notes as based on historical characters. Any other resemblance to any person, living or dead, is coincidental.

Scripture quotations are taken from the King James Version of the Bible. Public domain.

ISBN 9781-943959-51-8

The Team: Miralee Ferrell, Susan K Marlow, Nikki Wright, Cindy Jackson
Cover Design: Indie Cover Design, Lynnette Bonner Designer

Mountain Brook Ink is an inspirational publisher offering fiction you can believe in.
Printed in the United States of America

Reader Bonuses

Read the stories behind this story, try recipes from its pages, and learn more about the author here: www.janalynvoigt.com/stagecoach-to-liberty-readers

Dedication

To my mischievous, adventurous, and adorable daughter, Jessica. Thanks for teaching me to parent.

Acknowledgments

Working with such a talented bunch of people to perfect Stagecoach to Liberty has been a blessing.

Miralee Ferrell, my estimable publisher deserves a place at the top of this list. Her commitment to quality is a gift to readers and authors alike. Generous in her praise but determined when calling for a correction, she gave this story the polish it needed.

Editor Barbara Scott brought her vast knowledge of story to bear when helping shape Stagecoach to Liberty in its initial stages. She was a joy to work with.

Susan Marlow's keen mind and attention to detail vastly improved this story. She is a gifted editor.

Many thanks to those who proofread the book and offered advice from a reader's perspective.

I must compliment Lynnette Bonner, the talented cover designer who made working on the cover fun.

Sarah Joy Freese, my agent at Wordserve Literary, encouraged me to write this story. Her unwavering loyalty and support mean a great deal.

I must thank my family for pitching in at home and allowing me time alone to write and edit this book. My husband, John Voigt, serves as my sounding board, advisor, and greatest fan.

Creating a publishable book takes a village.

CHAPTER ONE

Independence, Missouri, April 1867

ELSA MEIER GRIPPED THE RAILING ON the riverboat's hurricane deck and stared at the city beyond the dock. Independence shone in the afternoon sun, a sprawling metropolis with wide streets plied by wagons, riders on horseback, and carriages. The waterfront bustled with activity, and the excitement she always felt in a port thrummed the air. She'd come a long way from her family's cottage in rural Germany to land in such a place. Hopefully, fortune awaited her in America, or at least enough money to send home to help her mother and the young ones.

She sighed. Leaving had been a hard decision, but she'd made it for her family. If only Peter had taken it better, she wouldn't have this pang in her stomach. His reaction still mystified and troubled her. She had no taste for hurting another person, and especially not someone who had expressed the tenderest of sentiments for her.

"Come along." Alicia Peabody tugged her arm. Her words sounded impatient, but she softened them with a smile.

Alicia's white teeth and creamy complexion were only part of her beauty. She reminded Elsa of the porcelain dolls she'd begged for as a child after seeing them displayed in a store window. That was before she'd grown old enough to realize that no amount of pleading could divert money for such a luxury from her parents' constant struggle to fill their children's bellies and keep shoes on their feet.

Grateful for the distraction, Elsa picked up her valise and joined the other young women traveling with the Peabodys. Red-haired Adele Wargel, who had been her neighbor, grinned at her. "You were daydreaming." She spoke in German.

"I suppose so," Elsa answered in the same language.

Adele walked beside her as the small group turned toward the stairs. "Thinking of Peter?"

Elsa lowered her voice. "I can't figure out why he thought we were promised."

Adele laughed. "Maybe it was the way you flirted with him during that sleigh ride at Christmas."

"Oh, that." Elsa frowned. "I won't deny that I admired him, but it went no further. I have no idea how he came to the wrong conclusion."

"Truly?" Adele's eyes danced.

Elsa arched an eyebrow. "A person might expect to remember something so important. No, Peter chose to believe what he wished. I'm only sorry he's hurting."

The breeze off the water whisked strands of hair into Adele's blue eyes. She clawed them away. "From the sound of it, Peter broke his own heart. I wouldn't worry about that one. He needs humbling, if you want my opinion."

Ida Henkel, a tall, blonde girl who had lived across town, looked back at the head of the stairs. "What are you two gossiping about?"

Adele shrugged. "Nothing much."

"English please, ladies!" Alicia's voice held a miffed note. For the past month, she'd forced them to speak only English while tutoring them in the language. Elsa had the advantage. Her beloved Papa, an Englishman, had taught her from childhood to speak his native tongue. "And you'd better keep up with the rest of us. We don't want to make Mr. Peabody wait."

Ida rolled her eyes and turned down the stairs behind Alicia.

Adele moved closer to Elsa. "I'm beginning to wish I hadn't signed that contract."

Elsa could offer no reassurances since she shared the same feeling. She pulled in a breath and mustered a reply for them both. "It's too late for second thoughts. We'll have to make the best of things." She squared her shoulders and followed the others.

At the foot of the stairs, Miles Peabody waited with ill-concealed impatience. Alicia and her brother were both blond, but there the resemblance ended. Miles was elegant and handsome but lacked Alicia's fine features.

The two differed in other ways. Even in the short time Elsa had known Miles, she'd become familiar with his peculiar habits. One in particular annoyed her. While Alicia always met her eyes when Elsa spoke to her, Miles glanced away as if neither Elsa nor anything she could say were worth his time.

Miles watched his sister approach with a smile that didn't include Elsa or any of the other women in his charge. He picked up the twin valises at his feet and tipped his head toward the gangplank, which was thick with passengers. "Shall we?"

He had not behaved so dismissively when persuading Elsa to sign a contract to perform for miners in a gold-rush town. He and Alicia had approached after seeing her play the hurdy-gurdy and dance to draw attention to the brooms her family made. Other girls from her village had come home from entertaining the crowds in Frankfurt with their wares all sold, so she'd decided to try it. She'd been happy to help *Mutter* put food on the table more often but hadn't earned enough for her own keep. Miles and Alicia offering to pay her passage to America if she signed their contract had seemed a godsend.

Elsa treaded with her newfound companions down the gangplank, wondering if she'd made a mistake in coming. Miles guided them across the street and turned aside toward the entrance of a brick building with a sign that read "The Hotel Imperial."

Inside the lobby, Adele halted, causing Elsa to bump into her. "Are we really staying in such a grand place?" Adele whispered in an awed voice.

Elsa could understand her feeling. Dark paneling, plush carpeting, and a prism-bedecked chandelier proclaimed this hotel a fine establishment.

"Only for the night." Alicia lowered her voice. "You'll double up and avoid room service. Make the most of the chance to sleep in a bed, ladies. You won't see another until we reach Salt Lake City."

Bry stretched and pulled back the chintz curtains at her bedroom window. In the early morning, with the sky washed clean from the night rains and the river bathed in soft light, she could believe in a world where miracles happened. The new school for Indian children would do more good than harm. The town of Liberty, local settlers, and ranch would stay safe from attack. Her brother Con still lived and would return.

She rested her head on the pane and blew out a breath. "God, please watch over my brother." Tears dampened her cheeks.

The door behind her opened, and boots thumped the carpet. She straightened, but her husband must have noticed her moment of sorrow.

"Come here, you." Nick enfolded her in his arms. He didn't ask what troubled her, having comforted her often enough to know.

She sheltered against her husband and poured out her grief, then dried her eyes with the back of her hand. "How much longer must we wait to find out what happened to Con?"

Nick kissed the top of her head. "As long as it takes."

She turned in her husband's arms and lifted her face to gaze into the warmth of his eyes. "You always know how to comfort me. What would I do without you?"

A smile dented the corners of his mouth. "God willing, you won't have to find out." He smoothed her cheek, then lowered his head for a kiss that brought her thoroughly awake. "I love you, Mrs. Laramie."

She laughed. "That's best, since we're married."

His eyes gleamed. "I need no reminder of that."

"I hope you don't mind being stuck with me." She treated him to a flirtatious glance.

He tightened his arms. "Look at me like that again, and I'll settle your mind on the matter."

She smiled but refrained from taking his invitation. That was not easy with passion emphasizing the dark handsomeness of her half-Cheyenne husband. "I have a thousand things to do today."

"Shouldn't your husband find a place at the top of that list?" He nuzzled her neck.

"Of course." She walked her fingers up his chest. "Don't *you* have a list?"

Nick captured Bry's hand and kissed each of her fingers in turn. "Mine can wait." He claimed her lips in a caress that left her breathless, but then released her. "I came to tell you that your brother Rob is back from Liberty."

She smiled. "He's remembered to tear himself away from Maisey, has he?"

Although Rob wouldn't admit it, he was clearly smitten with Bry's friend. Since the thaw, he had traveled to Liberty often to help build a cabin for Maisey, who taught children from the local tribes in the new Indian school.

"He'll be in after he tends his horse. Seems like he has something on his mind. He wants to talk to you particularly."

Bry's forehead puckered. "What about, I wonder?"

"You'll find out, I'm sure." He gave her a wolfish smile. "Dress yourself, woman, and meet us downstairs."

With Nick's footfalls dwindling down the hallway, Bry topped her linen chemise with a soft dress made of green wool. Remembering Con's disparaging remarks about the unflattering widow's weeds she'd worn as a servant in Boston brought a smile to her face. He'd thereafter lavished clothing on her.

Bry's smile vanished. After being kidnapped by the Cheyenne, she'd lost the trunk Con had bought her. She'd been forced to start over in so many ways, including her wardrobe. Almost a year later, memories still plagued her, the worst being when Con took an arrow and fell from his horse.

Pushing her thoughts away, she went downstairs and found Rob pacing in the parlor. Against walls papered in beige with a brown fleur-de-lis pattern, her brother seemed utterly masculine and, after his journey, rather unkempt. The ginger hair, so like Da's, lifted in peaks, and red shot the whites of his blue eyes.

Nick watched Rob from one of the leather armchairs scattered throughout the room. "It's good to have you home, brother of mine." Bry sank into a blue cushioned chair across a small table from her husband. "What brings you so early in the day?"

A sheepish look crossed Rob's face. "I left Shane's house later than planned. It seemed best to make camp before sunset instead of pushing on. I figured you wouldn't want me barging in at midnight."

"Very sensible." Nick saluted him with his coffee mug. "Night travel holds too many dangers."

"Yes, well. I almost came then anyway." Rob ran a hand through his hair, a habit that probably explained its rumpled state. "I made a decision while on the road, and it presses my mind."

Bry exchanged a glance with Nick. From the determined expression on Rob's face, she could guess what he meant to do. "Oh?"

Rob plunked into the chair across from her. "It's late enough in spring that I should make it to Fort Sedgwick." His voice shook with eagerness.

Bry pulled in air. "I'd feel better if you waited for summer. Why go at a time of year at risk for avalanches?" What with Indian unrest, road agents, natural disasters, and predatory animals, many perils faced a lone traveler in the wilderness. Taking more chances than necessary made no sense to her.

Rob jumped to his feet and began pacing again. "We've already waited too long. If I'd gone after Con sooner, I might have found him before the snow set in. I don't want to make the same mistake twice."

Bry put a hand to her stomach to soothe its churning. She hated that Rob was right. *Please, God. Don't let me lose two brothers.*

The man called Reilly stood outside the Fitzgerald homestead as light ebbed from the sky. Why did the reluctance to enter take hold of him? He should welcome an evening spent in the company of the family that had taken him in after the accident stole his memory. Finley had felt responsible, since it was his freight wagon that threw Reilly when it overturned.

Reilly shook his head. Whatever the cause, he couldn't deny the feeling that he belonged elsewhere.

The lighted window framed Keira, the oldest of the Fitzgerald daughters. Black-haired and lovely, she possessed blue eyes put in, as the saying went, with a sooty finger. Whatever she was talking about lit her face with excitement, but then Keira always embraced life with enthusiasm.

He should go in. At the back door, he stamped the mud from his boots and reached for the knob.

The world slid away, and he stood in another location, reaching for a different doorknob. A brisk wind shook the cottonwoods behind him, and a mourning dove raised its lament above the rushing leaves. He paused and glanced around with a feeling of pride. He'd built this ranch from nothing but love for the Bitterroot Valley.

A dog barked, returning Reilly to the present. He closed his eyes and tried to bring back the memory. Hope quickened his breathing, but the wisp of memory was gone. Reilly took a moment to compose himself. He didn't want to explain what had happened to anyone, not when he needed time to absorb it himself. His hand shook as he turned the doorknob and went inside.

CHAPTER TWO

ELSA'S FEET SANK INTO THE RED carpet in the corridor that ran down the main corridor of Salt Lake City's Grand Hotel. Dark wainscoting topped by ornate molding gave way to wallpaper patterned in flocked burgundy medallions on a red background. Golden cages encircled glass globes at intervals along the wall. The lamps would later light patrons to their rooms.

Dusty and bedraggled after more than a week of stagecoach travel, Elsa felt like a street urchin amid such elegance. She made sure to keep the case of her hurdy-gurdy from banging into the wall. In her other hand she carried the worn valise her mother had insisted she take. It had belonged to her father.

Mutter could never have Papa back alive again, but his belongings remained. Elsa had seen her mother run gentle fingers over a scarf he'd worn, the Bible he'd cherished, and his beloved fedora.

Elsa hadn't wanted to take even this small part of Papa away, but the small reminder of her loving father soothed her as a foreigner in a strange land. When Papa had carried this valise on business trips, she'd been too young to wonder if he ever felt homesick for his family. Gripped by that very emotion, she could appreciate her father's sacrifice.

She walked with the other women in a huddle behind Miles. Alicia brought up the rear, as if keeping watch to prevent their escape. Elsa cast a glance back at her and was awarded a frown. Alicia had seemed sweet at their first meeting, but after the ship departed for America, she'd become bossier each passing day.

"Hurry up, ladies." Impatience overlaid Alicia's voice. "Find your rooms."

Ida, walking beside Elsa, rolled her eyes but held her tongue. Anything they said would carry down the hallway.

Laughter caught in Elsa's throat. She coughed instead.

Adele, on Elsa's other side, patted her back. "Are you all right?" She scanned her face with an anxious look.

"Yes, of course," Elsa hastened to reassure her. Of them all, Adele seemed least able to adapt to change. She'd remained hidden on the ship and spoken little throughout the stagecoach journey. Elsa gave her a bolstering smile. "Just think. Tonight we'll sleep in a real bed."

"I'm glad to share a room with you." Adele's gaze clung to hers. "In so large a hotel, I'd lose my way trying to find the stairs."

Elsa laughed. "What makes you think I won't?"

Ida glared across Elsa at Adele. "Try not to be such a frightened goose."

"That's not fair," Adele protested.

Elsa frowned. "Leave Adele alone, Ida. Can't you see that she's tired and upset?"

"Quiet down." Alicia turned back, her face red.

Elsa wondered if she meant to strike them. Alicia divided her gaze equally among them all. "Remember to practice your English and try to show some manners. Create a disturbance, and you'll have us thrown out."

Adele hung her head. "Sorry, Miss Peabody."

Ida gave Elsa a haughty look, then followed the others down the hall.

Ida and the four other hurdy-gurdy girls turned aside into their rooms. Elsa was grateful when they reached the door that corresponded to the numbers on the key Alicia had given her.

"Once the porter brings your trunks, wash and change." Alicia's crisp command followed them through the doorway. "Then come up to the penthouse suite."

Small but not cramped, the beige and pale-blue room created a soothing effect that should suit them both. Elsa released a sigh and lowered her valise to the carpet while she searched for a safe place for her instrument. On impulse, she laid the case on the bed nearest the door and unsnapped the clasps.

Reaching inside, Elsa picked up the hurdy-gurdy Papa had brought home for her when she was ten. Its sturdy wooden body felt comforting in her hands. She ran her fingers lightly over the strings but refrained from turning the crank that spun the rosined wheel to give voice to the instrument.

Elsa sighed and put the hurdy-gurdy away, then propped her case against the wall in a corner where it wasn't likely to fall. Safeguarding the instrument had become a habit. She valued its worth in much more than coin.

Adele placed her own case in the opposite corner. "Do you think anyone will object if I play?"

"You probably shouldn't risk it." Regret laced Elsa's voice. She would miss caressing music from the strings, especially before lying down to sleep.

"Do you care if I take the bed closest to the window?"

"Go ahead."

"Thank you. I always slept by the window at home." Tears welled into her blue eyes and threatened to spill.

"Did you notice the view?" Elsa tried a distraction. "Those are such lovely mountains."

Adele went to look out the window. "They make me wish for home."

"I know." Her delight in the view gone, Elsa dropped onto the bed. "What do you suppose it will be like" —she hugged her pillow—"living in a gold-rush town?"

Adele shuddered. "I don't want to think about it."

"It might not be bad. We'll be able to sing and play, after all."

A knock came, and Elsa answered the door.

Two porters stood outside with a laden trolley. "Let's see, yes. Here are yours." They carried in the girls' trunks and stood awkwardly until Elsa remembered the tip. She closed the door behind them.

Adele turned away from the window. "Why do you think she wants us to come to the penthouse?"

Elsa shrugged. "To feed us supper without parading the six of us through a restaurant?"

"That makes sense." Adele swung her valise onto her bed. "I'm not sure I can bring myself to eat."

"Try your best." Elsa could sympathize. Her own stomach wasn't feeling so well. After the train trip to Hamburg, followed by ten days at sea and another rail journey, then a riverboat ride, being on solid ground felt dizzying. Elsa glanced in the mirror above the carved washstand and grimaced. She looked rumpled, annoyed, and exhausted. A number of locks had escaped their pins, allowing curly auburn wisps to float about her head. Her gray eyes held a mutinous expression. Even her clothing refused to obey. Her lace collar had gone awry, and the blouse that had been ironed and white this morning showed wrinkles and stains. She squinted with the mild headache that afflicted her and wished she could climb into bed and sleep.

She sighed and pulled her gaze away from her reflection. "We'd better hurry or Alicia will come looking for us."

Washed and changed, they left the sanctuary of their room. Despite Adele's fears, they found not only the stairs but also an elevator. Adele refused to enter the movable room but changed her mind at Elsa's insistence. Outfitted with paneling, benches, and a gilt chandelier, the elevator glided upward. A short while later, Elsa knocked on the carved oak door of the penthouse suite.

Alicia opened the door wearing a blue silk gown. Her golden hair shone as brightly as her eyes. She looked, Elsa decided with a touch of annoyance, fresh and beautiful.

Alicia frowned. "You're late. The others are already here." She ran her gaze over them and stepped back.

Elsa walked through the doorway with Adele at her heels. Oak paneling, a chandelier dripping with prisms, and a gilt mirror graced the tiled entrance. Alicia led the way past double doors that opened into a parlor. They trailed her down a short hallway, through an archway, and into the dining room.

Tall windows commanded a view of the river. In the countryside beyond, rooftops gave way to clustered trees and undergrowth interspersed with carpets of spring grass. The wild beauty seen from this vantage point sent a thrill through Elsa. Soon she would travel to a point farther west than she could see from these windows.

The sense of someone watching drew Elsa around. She met the unwavering gaze of eyes so dark she couldn't see their pupils. They belonged to a man seated with the others at the table. His reddish-brown hair reminded Elsa of the foxes she had seen crouching outside her family's henhouse. Something she couldn't name about this man warned her that, in a similar way, he waited to pounce on unwary prey. She pulled in air, ready to announce a headache and the need to lie down.

Adele made a small, distressed sound beside her, and Elsa abandoned the idea of escape. For her friend's sake, she would remain.

"Here are the last two of our hurdy-gurdy girls, Atticus."

Miles waved his hand. "All are lovely, as I'm sure you will agree."

Alicia touched Elsa's back. "Sit down and we'll begin our supper."

Atticus watched Elsa take her seat. "What is your name?"

She started at being singled out. "Elsa Meier."

"You have the same hypnotic eyes as Ada Menken. Give you brown hair instead of auburn, and you'd be her very image. Have you heard of Ada?"

Elsa shook her head and looked down at her plate. "I've never met anyone by that name."

Miles and Alicia laughed. The other women exchanged mystified glances.

"You wouldn't have to meet Ada to know who she is." Atticus's voice thrummed with enthusiasm. "I saw her in *Mezippa* when she came to San Francisco. She was magnificent, and of course I fell in love with her. Everyone did."

Elsa risked a glance at Atticus, whose lips were curved in an adoring smile. "Is Ada a performer?"

"She's an actress, and a good one." He scanned her face. "Your hair is a different color, or I'd swear you are her."

"We all have a *doppelgänger* somewhere in the world." A tremor ran through Elsa's voice, despite her effort to keep her tone light.

"If Ada returns to the West, I'll take you to meet her."

Elsa needed a moment to regain command of her voice. "I don't understand."

Atticus glanced at Miles. "I want Elsa, along with the others I've chosen."

Alicia smirked. "Mr. Merrick is in town on other business, but when he and Miles chanced to meet in the lobby, he agreed to dine with us."

Miles looked directly at Elsa for the first time since she'd signed her contract. "I promised he could choose the girls he wants for his dancehall."

"I have other business in town before I can return to Virginia City." Atticus appraised Elsa in a way that made her face heat. "We'll leave for Virginia City in two days' time."

Shane walked along the path from the barn, his thoughts heavy as the dark clouds threatening rain. Bill Drury had closed his eyes in death an hour ago, another victim of the fever ravaging town. He'd left a bewildered widow and five children crying for a father who would not answer them in this life.

Shane shook his head. He'd held himself together for the family's sake, saving his grief for the ride home, during which he discussed matters with the Lord. It wasn't the first time he'd done so, and he doubted it would be the last. He relied on Archibald's night vision and sure-footedness to carry them home through the cold and dark. The new widow had been too distraught to offer Shane a bed, and he preferred his own anyway.

The hour was late. He didn't expect his household to be awake, but a light shone through the kitchen window. He knocked at the back door and called out his name. Leaving his family alone at night was not Shane's favorite duty, and he insisted America lock the house in his absence.

Not that he had to persuade her. His wife never mentioned uneasiness at being left alone—sometimes for days—while he attended his flock. He could guess that it wasn't easy for her. Weddings, burials, and births all needed his attention. Shane's congregation had crops to till, barns to raise, and fences to mend. When life became too difficult, they asked for help.

He didn't begrudge them the time, but it meant leaving his own family to fend without him. He was thankful for a good flock however. When America came down with the fever, members of his congregation had brought food and taken care of his children.

The bolt thudded, and the door creaked. America, in her chemise and wrapped in a shawl, stood in the opening with the light spilling around her. He dropped a kiss on her golden head. "I hope you didn't wait up for me. I could have slept in the barn."

She clasped her arms around him. "I didn't want that. Besides, I couldn't sleep."

"Why not?"

"I'm a silly woman, that's why. I should have more faith that God will keep you in your travels."

He pulled her more closely against him, enjoying her warmth after the coolness of night. "'I hate to put you to the worry."

She laughed, a soft sound that sent a thrill through him. "I put myself to the worry. I wish I could trust more."

"I feel the same when I leave you and the children. Don't think it's any easier for me to sacrifice for the Lord's work."

He thought of Rob going off to find Con, alone. Shane had always been close to Con, and he would have preferred to go along to search for his cousin. With a funeral on Sunday and the new widow's crops to plant, however, he needed to remain in Liberty.

Keeping her arms around his neck, America leaned back to gaze into his eyes. Her own were deep and mysterious in the lantern light. "I will always love you, no matter what."

"And I, you." He lowered his lips to hers and tasted the salt of tears. Had she been crying? He suspected that she hid the depth of her feelings to spare him.

He would not burden her with his own sorrows.

Reilly slammed the axe down, cleaving the log in two. He paused for breath before tackling the next piece of firewood. The pile he'd chopped littered the ground. He ran a hand over his shoulder, which still pained him. Finley said his wound looked like he'd taken an arrow. Reilly had no memory of receiving the injury.

Pacer, the Fitzgerald dog—who had acquired his name for obvious reasons—had clearly worn himself out walking back and forth while guarding Reilly's labors. The red coonhound sprawled in the sun with sides heaving. He periodically rattled out a snore.

Reilly smiled and lifted another log onto the chopping block.

"Here you are. I wondered." Keira came around the corner behind the barn. She wore her black hair up as befitted her womanhood beneath the bonnet that protected her fair skin from the harsh sun. "I thought you went fishing."

"Good morning." Reilly smiled a greeting. "I decided the harder task should come first."

"If you're not careful, you'll sound like a preacher." Her dimples showed, belying her frown. "Or maybe a school teacher."

"Oh, I fully intend to fish, but a man should earn his keep."

"Fishing is for food." Her eyes sparkled.

He laughed. "Indeed it is, as I've proven before and will again." He brought the axe down in a clean stroke, then looked back at her. "What did you want with me?"

She lifted a shoulder. "Nothing much, really. Just to talk."

Her tone rang false, but which was the half-truth? That she wanted nothing much from him or that she only wanted to talk? Either way, he gave her his full attention. "Something on your mind?"

She glanced about, then jutted her chin in that peculiar way she had when getting into mischief. "It's such a fine day. Can I not draw you away for a walk beside the river?" Tears glossed Keira's eyes, and she turned her head away.

About to refuse on the grounds that strolling fell into the same category as fishing, he changed his mind. Had something gone amiss at the barn dance Friday night? Come to think of it, she'd been quiet since then.

Reilly laid the axe aside. "All right." He stepped onto the path to the river, not entirely convinced he'd made the best choice in joining her. He determined to make this as short as possible.

She caught up. "Could you go a little slower?"

"Sorry." He shortened his stride.

Keira walked beside him on the dirt path that skirted the field before it disappeared into the brush lining the Snake River. The foliage and grasses glowed green this early in spring, and the wind-ruffled river swelled its banks. Water scented the breeze that brushed his face.

A pheasant burst from cover with a rasping call.

Keira cried out and grasped his arm. "My word, but that startled me."

He gave her a gentle smile. "Your thoughts lay elsewhere, I suppose."

"If you're going on about Tom Dougal again—"

"I wasn't, actually."

"Why do I doubt that?"

Reilly watched the pheasant wing above the river and out of sight. "I've no idea."

All right, he *had* teased her about their besotted neighbor a time or two. She hadn't seemed to mind, despite her protests, until now. He scanned her flushed face. "He didn't misbehave at the dance, did he?"

She crossed her arms. "Of course not, as you would know if you'd stayed."

He shrugged. "I'm not much for crowds." It was more than that, but Keira didn't need to know how alone he felt in a gathering. Although the community welcomed him, he couldn't escape the feeling of intruding among them.

"Tom asked me to marry him."

"Did he now?" Reilly hid his delight at the news, certain she wouldn't find it flattering. The two would make a good match. Tom Dougal was the steady sort of man able to stabilize a high-strung woman like Keira.

"I told him no."

He blinked. "Why would you do such a thing?"

She glanced away. "I love someone else."

"Are you certain? I thought Tom made quite an impression on you."

"Honestly!" Her nostrils flared. "I know my own mind."

"The mind is not the heart."

She stamped her foot. "I don't care about a turn of phrase."

"This one matters quite a lot."

Keira glared at him. "I know the man I want."

He hesitated, choosing his words. "How does this person feel about you?"

She moved closer and tilted her face toward his. "That's what I've come to find out."

Reilly stared at her. "You can't mean me."

"Why not?" She thrust her lower lip into a pout.

"I'm too old for you, to start with."

"How can you say that when you don't *know* how old you are?"

He sighed, guessing how the rest of this conversation would go. "It's obvious. I'm a man fully grown, and you've barely come of age."

"I don't care about that, and Da doesn't either."

"'You've discussed this with your father?"

She lowered her gaze. "No, but I've heard him say that he'd welcome you as a son."

"That's kind of him, but I'm sure he meant it differently."

Her eyelashes, clumped with tears, swept upward. "He'd be pleased. You know he would."

He shook his head. "You need a man with more patience than I possess."

"I love you, Reilly." She flung her arms around his neck.

He gently disengaged himself and stepped backward. "I'm sorry."

Keira stared at him with stricken eyes, her chest heaving. "Do you care nothing at all for me?"

"I'm not unfeeling."

"Then why?" Her tears spilled over.

With her eyes shining and passion on her face, Keira had never looked more beautiful. It occurred to Reilly that she'd wept from the outset of their meeting, as if suspecting the truth herself.

The thought gave him the push he needed to resist her charms. "It won't work, more's the pity."

"You can't know that."

"Have you considered that I don't even know my real name, or whether I have a wife and family awaiting my return? I must assume, for honor's sake, that I do." He shook his head. "I have no future until I know my past."

Keira gazed at him, a tragic expression on her face. "I will wait for you to discover your identity."

"Don't put yourself on the shelf for me. What if I never remember who I am?"

"Then I will endure this life as best I can."

He touched her cheek. "I am flattered to have aroused such devotion in one so tender, but we would never suit." He left the bald fact to hang between them.

Circumstances might change, but dispositions never could. He and Keira would soon burn out, whereas Tom's quiet manner would soothe her dramatic nature and steady her through the trials of life.

Reilly wouldn't dream of robbing Keira of the full life she deserved. As for him, the yearning to be elsewhere wouldn't leave him alone.

CHAPTER THREE

Birdsong brightened Elsa's spirits as she strolled into the hotel garden beside Alicia. The brick walkway glistened from a recent rain shower, but the wrought-iron bench where Alicia invited her to sit felt dry. In the fountain before them, the statue of a beautiful woman in flowing garments poured water from a jar. The spray misted toward them and caught the sun in shifting rainbows.

Elsa released her breath on a sigh. She hadn't realized until this moment of quiet the toll that leaving home, family, and country had extracted from her.

Alicia tilted her head toward the sun. "I sometimes wonder what it would be like to have musical talent like yours."

"Music has always been a part of me," Elsa replied. "My mother told me that even as a small child I kept a melody on my lips."

Alicia glanced sideways. "Will you sing for me now?"

Elsa hid her surprise. Surely Alicia hadn't brought her to the garden to listen to her sing but to lecture her for her reaction last night at dinner. Her dismay at the idea of going anywhere with Atticus Merrick must have been obvious. The thought made her shudder. Perhaps she could appeal to Alicia to send her somewhere else.

She had no instrument but nodded and launched into "In Stiller Nacht," a folksong with a haunting melody that suited her mood.

"In a quiet night,
In the first watch
A voice began to complain.
The night wind,
Sweet and gentle,
Carried the sound to me.

"From bitter sorrow
And sadness
My heart melted away.
The little flowers,
With pure tears,
I watered them all.

"The beautiful moon
Wants to set,
For sorrow not wanting to shine anymore.
The little stars
Their sparkling streak,
They want to cry with me."

Caught up in the sadness of the song, Elsa sat with her hands in her lap, staring into the falling water. *What will become of me in Virginia City?* Before leaving Germany, coming to America had seemed a grand adventure. Now she wished she'd never left home.

"No birds singing
Nor joyful sound
Can be heard in the air.
The wild animals,
Also grieving with me,

In rocks and crevices.

"Wherever I go,
Wherever I turn my eyes,
My worries will follow me,
Haunting me 'til the end,
Hidden deep in the heart.

"The beautiful moon
Wants to set,
For sorrow not wanting to shine anymore,
The little stars
Their sparkling streak,
They want to cry with me."

"Beautiful," Atticus Merrick spoke from behind her.

Elsa sprang from the bench in alarm. "I didn't hear you there."

"No need to rise." His gaze slid past Elsa to Alicia, and he gave a slight nod.

Alicia stood and gestured to the bench she'd vacated. "Won't you sit here, Mr. Merrick?" She smiled at Elsa. "I'll return in a moment. I'd like a closer look at a flower I spotted earlier."

Elsa gave Alicia the skeptical look she deserved. A child could see through her lie. Alicia had brought her to the garden not out of kindness but to trick her into Atticus's company. *Perhaps this vile man had arranged the encounter.*

She frowned. It made no sense that he would want to meet like this. He would choose a more private setting if he intended to take liberties. There was no need for him to persuade her to go with him to Virginia City. She had no choice but to abide by her contract. It was difficult to believe that this man, who had shown himself insensitive to a woman's finer feelings, would care to soothe her nerves.

Atticus stood before her, well-groomed in a striped suit and vest set off by an elegant cravat. He removed his bowler hat and placed it under his arm, his red hair catching fire in the sun.

Elsa surrendered her hand to him and managed a nod. There was no point antagonizing a man whose presence she would have to endure. He gestured to the bench, and she sank back down. "I didn't expect to see you today." Her voice emerged breathlessly.

"I concluded my business early." He lowered himself onto the bench beside her. "What a pleasant day we have, wouldn't you agree?"

"Spring always makes me glad." She relaxed, thankful for the neutral subject.

He fixed his dark-eyed gaze on her. "You are even more lovely with the sunlight turning your hair red-gold."

She looked away. "Thank you for the compliment." Her words sounded stilted. Bright streams cascaded from the statue's water jar to the splash of falling water. The breeze she had welcomed before now made her shiver.

"You seem cold." He scooted closer. "Would you like my jacket?"

She shifted away. "No, thank you."

He placed his arm on the bench behind her. "At least let me warm you."

She jumped to her feet. "Forgive me, but I need to check on my friend. Adele was prostrated by a headache when I left her."

"Stay a moment." Atticus's hand closed around her wrist. He tugged her down beside him. "I would like you to come with me willingly."

She tried to pull away, but he held her fast. Her heart thudded. "Mr. Merrick, you must release me."

"You have utterly captivated me." His voice turned husky. "I only want to please you."

"If you don't stop, I will call for help."

"Do you plan to summon Miss Peabody?" Amusement laced his words, but he let go of her wrist. "There's no need to sound the alarm. I came to reassure you. I'll treat you well."

She jumped up. "I'm sorry, but I don't want to go with you. I'll ask Mr. Peabody to free me from my contract."

Atticus straightened his cravat. "He'll take a dim view of that idea, considering he paid your passage to America."

Elsa heaved in air. Did this man know everything about her? "I'll return his money." She spoke bravely even as her hope faded.

"Elsa, be reasonable." Atticus advanced toward her with the look of a man calming a wild beast. "Even if Miles agreed, he would want immediate payment. I don't think you have that kind of money."

"I will go to debtor's prison if I must." Determined not to let him touch her again, she backed away.

His eyes widened. "Watch yourself!"

The edge of the fountain thumped the back of Elsa's legs. She flailed and twisted on the way down. Water closed over her head, and she barely stopped herself from drawing it into her lungs. She struggled to sit up, but her sodden clothing and the stabbing pain in her ankle hindered every effort.

Atticus grasped her wrist and hauled her, dripping, from the fountain.

"What have you done?" Alicia's startled cry rang out.

"She fell into the fountain." Atticus's answer rumbled through Elsa, for he held her against his chest.

"You've ruined your dress. I doubt those moss stains will come out."

Elsa summoned her voice. "My ankle hurts."

Atticus lowered Elsa to the brick pavers. He removed his coat and draped it over her prone body. "Don't move, darling." Atticus looked up at Alicia. "Stay with her while I go for the doctor." He stood and strode away.

"Foolish girl." Alicia shook her head. "Now look what you've done."

Smokey, the Fitzgeralds' spotted grey draft horse, clomped behind Reilly. The barn hove into view around a bend, the last embers of daylight smoldering on the horizon behind it. He'd worked long and hard since talking with Keira two days ago, partly to avoid her but also to think. Decisions came easier to him while moving.

He led Smokey into the grooming stall and picked up the curry comb. The horse's coat smoothed under his care. He picked at several burrs tangled in the thick mane. With light fading inside the barn, he looked up for a lantern.

"Thought I might find you here." Finley appeared in the doorway carrying a lantern. Sturdy muscles compensated for his compact stature. He radiated energy, even after a hard day's labor about the homestead. Keira's enthusiasm for life matched her father's, and it wasn't hard to figure out how she came by her black hair and blue eyes. "Looking for this?" Finley thumped the lantern down on top of a barrel near the stall.

Reilly straightened. "'Twould come in handy."

Finley pulled a box of matches from his pocket. "Mrs. Fitzgerald sent me to remind you it's suppertime. She's made the shepherd's pie you favor."

He smiled. "I can't say no to such a feast. Tell her I'll be in shortly."

"Abide with me a moment." Finley struck a match and touched it to the lamp wick. The flame sputtered and grew, while the sharp scents of kerosene and sulfur mingled. "I want a word with you."

"Of course." Reilly went back to picking burrs.

"Keira's been moping for days now, ever since she came back from a walk with you in fact. Any idea what troubles her?"

Reilly laid aside the curry comb and considered how best to phrase his reply. He'd leave out Tom's proposal, which was Keira's news to tell. "She invited me to come courting."

Finley's brows went up. "Oh, did she?"

"I refused her offer."

"Are you certain? I wouldn't mind having you in the family."

"Thank you for saying that, but it's impossible. For all I know, I'm obligated elsewhere."

"Yes, yes, I can see that." Finley rubbed the back of his neck. "I should have realized this might happen. Bringing you home might have been a mistake." He shook his head. "Sorry, Reilly. I didn't mean that the way it sounded."

"No, you're right. I'm grateful for all you've done for me, but I should leave."

"Don't be daft, man. Where would you go?"

"I've remembered something from my past." Reilly picked up the curry comb and turned to tackle the last of the burrs.

"Have you?" Finley moved closer. "That's wonderful."

"'Twas only a glimmer, mind you, but enough to tell me where to search. I may own a ranch in the Bitterroot Valley."

Finley whistled. "That's a lot of territory. Any idea *where* in the valley?"

"None, except that the ranch stands on a rise above the river."

"That's something, anyway. If you don't find it, what will you do?"

"I don't know, but the thought of striking out for the Bitterroot Valley has taken hold. I can't let fear stop me. I might have lived at the ranch a long time ago and may not own it any longer. Even so, seeking my past is better than waiting on the vagaries of memory to reveal it."

Finley crossed his arms on the ledge of the stall's half-door. "I don't blame you for wanting answers, but I hate to say goodbye. I've grown fond of you."

Reilly straightened. "I feel the same about you. It doesn't have to be goodbye forever. I'll send word once I'm settled, wherever that may be. I'd welcome a visit from you, should the fancy strike."

"I'd like that." Finley picked up the lantern. "Now, come inside before dinner gets cold. Afterward, we can tell the family where you're headed."

Reilly put aside the curry comb and took up Smokey's reins. "I'd like to give Keira the news myself, if that's all right."

"She might take it better from you." Finley opened a stall door and stood back while Reilly led the grey out of the grooming stall and into another for the night. They started for the house together.

Finley clasped Reilly's shoulders. "I hope you know that if it doesn't work out, you have a home here."

"Thank you." Reilly smiled, although he knew that was no longer true. Being around Keira had become awkward and would remain so. He had a man's desires, and Keira had grown into an attractive young woman. Resisting the tempting lips she had pressed to his had not been easy.

He was glad—for her sake and his own—that he had restrained himself. A part of him wished that marrying Keira would work out. How easy it would be to give in to her wishes!

But that would cheat her plus one other—the person who had ceased to exist at Reilly's birth. He would make it his mission to find that man of mystery and return his life to him.

Light fell across Elsa's closed eyelids, rousing her from her drowsing state. She sat up, squinting in confusion until her surroundings became familiar. She remembered now.

Unsatisfied with the doctor's diagnosis of a sprained ankle, Atticus had demanded she be admitted to the hospital for observation. Alicia had been less than happy about the arrangement. For once, Elsa agreed with Alicia, although she suspected their reasons differed. Alicia railed about the fact that Elsa hadn't gone off to Virginia City with Atticus, at least until Miles looked in. He pulled Alicia aside and murmured near her ear.

Elsa strained to hear. *Mutter* had taught her never to eavesdrop, but she thought her mother might overlook this trespass. Try as she might, she couldn't catch Miles's words. The pain medication blurred her thoughts, and she shut her eyes.

She awakened to find Miles gone. Alicia, seated in the chair beside Elsa's bed, seemed in a better mood and no longer complained, a worrisome fact. In the short time she'd known the woman, Elsa had become adept at detecting when Alicia was up to something. She feared what Alicia's talkativeness might mask this time.

A mad plan presented itself. Elsa would pretend to take her medicine and then slip out when no one was looking. She could exchange her hospital gown for her clothing, which hanging cleaned and pressed in the closet. It would be difficult, but she could hobble about using the crutch the nurse had leaned against the wall beside her bed.

Elsa repressed her guilt at running away from Miles and Alicia, but it might be her only chance to avoid debtor's prison. She only needed a little time to pay Miles for her passage.

Maybe she could find a way to make money playing her hurdy-gurdy. Alicia had brought it from the hotel. She'd informed Elsa that they'd given up her room at the hotel. Adele had gone off to work in a dancehall. Alicia had asked the porter to move Elsa's trunk and valise to her own rooms.

A pang went through Elsa at this news. She would lose everything she owned but the clothes in the closet, her hurdy-gurdy, and the necklace she'd been wearing when she fell into the fountain. Elsa lifted her chin, resolving not to let the prospect of losing her possessions stop her.

Elsa cupped her hand around the small weight of the emerald pendant set in gold filigree. It could fetch a tidy sum, but she hated to part with a family heirloom and her mother's gift to her.

No. She couldn't bring herself to sacrifice this link to her family. She must call upon her strength of will and find another way to raise money.

Alicia gave Elsa a bright smile. "The doctor stopped by while you were sleeping. He's agreed that you can leave in the morning. Isn't that wonderful? I'm sure you'll be glad to see the last of this place."

"True, but I thought he wanted me to stay longer."

"Miles persuaded him that we can look after you, since

you'll be off your feet while on the stagecoach."

"What stagecoach?"

"The one going to Virginia City, of course. Did you hit your head when you went into that fountain? Mr. Merrick is determined that we should bring you. He's paid for us to follow him. You should be honored that a man of wealth and position has taken such a shine to you."

Elsa felt a number of things in this moment, but *honored* was not among them.

"Mr. Merrick mentioned that you said something about refusing him. It's only natural to feel nervous, but I'm certain you will come to appreciate his attentions." She leaned close and touched Elsa's pendant. "How did a peasant like you come by such a lovely piece?"

Elsa swallowed, horrified that she'd forgotten to hide the gem beneath the neck of her gown. "My family was not always poor."

"Interesting." Alicia's tone indicated her disbelief.

Elsa tucked the pendant inside her hospital gown and opened her mouth to convince Alicia of the truth. Realizing the pointlessness of trying to persuade the woman about anything, she remained silent. What did it matter anyway? In a few hours she would make her escape.

Alicia wasn't the only one with something up her sleeve.

CHAPTER FOUR

Maisey breathed in the scent of Phoebe's hair, still damp from her bath. Her sleeping five-year-old daughter snuggled against her with a soft sigh.

Evening was Maisey's favorite time. With her duties done for the day, she could cradle her small daughter in the rocking chair Shane and America had given her. Maisey held Phoebe closer, remembering when she'd wondered if she would ever hold her again. And yet God in his mercy had seen fit to return this precious child to her arms.

Doc Mather and his wife had cared for Phoebe well during Maisey's Indian captivity. They'd believed the child theirs, but later returned her upon learning Maisey was alive. The sorrow on Mrs. Mather's face had wrenched Maisey's heart. She'd urged Rob to take her and Phoebe to Hell Gate to visit the Mathers, and they stopped by whenever they drove through the area. That wasn't often, especially of late.

Red Cloud's War in the East set the settlers' and tribal members' nerves on edge. It impacted the Liberty School for Indians, as well. Attendance plunged after the massacre of Captain Fetterman and his men outside Fort Phil Kearney.

The Sioux and Arapaho objected to the Bozeman Road, which gave miners easier access to search for gold in Montana. Although, the route cut through tribal hunting grounds, Red Cloud might have signed the treaty to allow safe passage if not for the seven hundred soldiers Colonel Carrington had lined up to ensure his cooperation. That had angered him into refusing.

Maisey rose and carried Phoebe to the small bed Rob had made for her. "Good night, sweet girl," she whispered, brushing a kiss on her brow. She gazed at her sleeping child's face, hoping that by the time she grew up, these Indian troubles would have blown over like a summer storm.

Maisey covered Phoebe with the child's prized possession—the quilt the Mathers had wrapped her in when they brought her back. She tucked the quilt lightly around Phoebe to avoid waking her. Once disturbed, her daughter's lively mind would find it hard to return to sleep.

She loved Phoebe but also knew her well. The child's curiosity and mischievous nature had almost gotten her killed in a buffalo stampede during the journey west. Had it really been almost two years since that event? It seemed so much longer. Thankfully, Phoebe had been spared.

Maisey shook her head. She still wasn't over Natty's death. A fourteen-year-old cut down in the bloom of life seemed too cruel. Maisey would always remember with gratitude the girl who had lost her life while protecting Phoebe.

She slipped out of her daughter's bedroom and went to look out the kitchen window. Sunsets came later and later these days, with spring claiming the countryside. The sun hung low in the sky, a fireball that would soon descend behind the mountains. Sunset blushed the wildflowers that swayed with the grasses, among them Indian paintbrush, butter-and-egg flower, and lupine. Maisey favored the delicate purple petals of the bitterroot flower best.

She sighed. The town of Liberty had accepted her. She didn't want for company, living on the Hayes' property in a cabin near Emma Duncan, the schoolteacher. She wasn't lonely in certain ways, but in others . . .

Remembering Avery, she let teardrops fall to her cheeks.

She had loved her husband deeply. Seeing him killed by an arrow in his chest still gave her nightmares. The memory shadowed her waking hours. She had lost her husband, and her life would never be the same again.

A lone rider passed on the dusky road by the schoolhouse. The pulse pounded in Maisey's throat, but then she realized her mistake. A trick of the light made him look like Rob returning home, but he hadn't been gone long enough.

Maisey wrinkled her brow. Her feelings for Rob confused her. She enjoyed his company and looked forward to his visits. However, the longing for his companionship and—if she was honest—his touch seemed disloyal to her husband's memory. She sighed. Perhaps a person was only granted one great love in life, and Avery had been hers.

She let the curtain fall and turned away from the window. *No use pining over a man who'd set his heart on going away to seek his fortune.* Remembering her five-year-old daughter asleep in her bed, Maisy knew where her own heart lay.

Keira stood at the edge of the river with her back to Reilly, by all appearances fascinated by a flock of geese lifting off the river. She heaved a breath in a way that made Reilly suspect she was crying. He resisted the urge to comfort her with an embrace. She wouldn't welcome his touch. That his words had wounded her was clear by the way she flinched.

He opened his mouth, but then closed it without speaking. He had nothing to say that would not hurt her more. All he could do was wait for her to speak.

"But I don't understand. *Why* must you go?" Keira's voice

wavered on a shrill note. "There's no need for you to leave."

"Keira—" Reilly broke off, struck again by his inability to ease her unhappiness. It went against the grain to see a woman suffer on his account. He'd hoped to make parting easier for her but delivering the news himself had been a mistake. He didn't believe for a moment that her heart was broken. He'd merely wounded her feminine pride.

Keira probably didn't know the difference between the two.

She swung around, her chin jutting. "Don't use that maddening tone on me, Reilly. You're giving up, and I don't like you for it."

"Careful, now. You don't want to say anything you'll regret."

She made a derisive sound that in one less delicate would be taken for a snort.

"You're upset." He spoke quickly to forestall the brewing storm of her anger. "One day you'll thank me, I promise." As soon as the words left his lips, he knew their folly. No woman wanted such a high-handed declaration, and especially not from a man scorning her affections.

Her eyes narrowed. "You're a vile, detestable man! I'm sorry I ever thought myself in love with you."

Reilly restrained himself from smiling. Keira reminded him of a barn cat spitting and hissing after a drenching in the rain. "I hope someday you'll remember me with more charity."

Her nostrils flared. "I'm *glad* you're going away."

"Given the way you feel about me, it's just as well we decided not to court."

She stared at him. Her mouth worked, making inarticulate noises, then she shoved past him and bolted toward the house.

Reilly frowned, not comfortable with Keira running into the house in such a state. She was, after all, Finley's daughter. He was an outsider. Hopefully Finley would understand his intention to let Keira down gently.

If Reilly harbored any doubts about the wisdom of rejecting Keira's overtures, their conversation had settled them. Keira's parents favored her. Some might call her spoiled. That must be why she couldn't conceive that his own feelings didn't match those she'd imagined. Thankfully, he'd resisted kissing her when she'd offered. If he'd taken advantage of the moment, he'd have been hard pressed to leave her with only a telling off.

He picked up a smooth pebble and turned it over. The stone glistened in the sun and warmed his hand. He hauled back and flung the rock across the river with a gesture acquired from long practice.

The stone skipped three times before sinking. Ripples radiated across the surface, a lingering reminder. When and where had he learned to do that?

He needed to know.

Elsa opened her eyes with a sense of despair. Last night she'd poured the prescribed draught into the chamber pot when the nurse's back was turned but while waiting to make her escape, had fallen asleep.

She could have slipped away during the night without incident. With morning light filtering through the drawn curtains, the opportunity was lost. Tears trembled on Elsa's eyelashes and overflowed onto her cheeks. She had been so sure about her ability to escape. When she refused to go along with Miles's plan for her, he would probably have her thrown into debtor's prison.

She couldn't let that happen.

Elsa caught the faint sound of voices and sat up with renewed determination. The nurses were beginning their rounds, but she still might have time to make a break for freedom. After pushing the covers back, she winced at her ankle. The bandage hid the bruising but not its swelling.

She shifted toward the edge of the hospital bed and let out a yelp, paying the cost of skipping her medication. The worst of her pain had abated, but her injured ankle throbbed.

The room spun. Elsa waited until it righted itself. She stared with longing at her crutch, out of reach against the wall. Reaching it would be her first test.

Elsa braced herself against the edge of the nightstand and levered to her feet. The table rolled on its wheels, and her water glass crashed to the floor. Water mixed with glass shards splattered her feet. She held her breath and listened.

No voices raised in response, nor did any feet come running.

She leaned out and grasped her crutch. Elsa pushed the worst shards away with its tip, then maneuvered across the room to the closet.

Elsa dressed herself with jaw set and heart racing. It took longer than expected. She couldn't fit her swollen ankle into her lace-up boot, so she tied the strings together and dangled the spare shoe from one arm. Ready at last, she blew out a relieved breath. She had only to collect her hurdy-gurdy.

The water hadn't quite reached her instrument case, thankfully. Leaning on her crutch, she bent to pick it up. The crutch slipped in the water, and Elsa cried out before slamming into the floor.

The door thudded open. Footsteps thumped toward her. Hands turned her over.

Elsa gasped. "What are *you* doing here?"

"I came to collect you." Miles lifted Elsa to her feet. "You're being discharged today. If the hospital staff hurries, we'll have time to catch the next stagecoach out of town."

Elsa took a deep breath. "I'm not going with you."

An amused light entered Miles' eyes. "Oh? And where do you plan to go?"

"I have no idea, but not anywhere with you."

Miles arched an eyebrow. "You are under contract."

"I need no reminder of that. I intend to break our agreement, but I promise to pay you back for my passage."

"Is that so?" Miles frowned. "You had better prepare to pay me back with interest, and that won't be cheap. The longer you wait, the more it will cost."

The wind went out of Elsa. "Won't you give me a little time?"

Miles crossed his arms. "You took my money without hesitation, eager to come to America. Now you want to delay giving it back. Does that seem fair?"

She lowered her gaze. "I'm sorry."

"Sorry is not good enough. If you can't come up with the cash, your mother will have to."

Elsa's head snapped up. "You can't do that!"

"You think not? I'm due to return to Germany for another shipment of young ladies. I'm sure I remember her address."

The nurse looked in. Her gaze swept Elsa, Miles, and the mess on the floor. "Is everything all right?" She frowned. "It's early for visitors yet."

Miles treated the woman to his most charming smile. "Elsa had a little accident, I'm afraid. It's a good thing I arrived when I did to help her. Be careful. There's glass everywhere."

"Oh, my goodness! I'll see to it." The nurse withdrew.

Miles looked back to Elsa. "I came to escort you to the stagecoach station, but it appears your mind is made up."

Elsa glanced away. She would not let shame and harm fall on her mother. "I will come with you."

"Wise girl." Miles spoke in quiet triumph. He helped her back into bed, where she waited for the doctor to release her.

Elsa left the hospital with mixed feelings. Miles would not put her into debtor's prison, but he'd entrapped her all the same. She wanted to shrink away but accepted his help into the waiting carriage. A lump formed in her throat. If only Adele rode beside her. She hadn't realized how easing her friend's fears had distracted her from her own. Elsa's last sight of Adele was with her lying in bed, a washcloth over her eyes. Tension must have brought on her migraine. Elsa frowned. "What has become of Adele?"

Miles glanced everywhere but at her. "She's gone to a different dancehall from you."

"Where?"

"What does it matter? You probably won't see one another again." Leaving her in the carriage, he stepped back into the hotel.

Elsa swallowed against tears. She wouldn't give him the satisfaction of witnessing her tears. Porters soon appeared and loaded their trunks into the boot. Miles returned with Alicia, who climbed into the carriage looking well rested. She glanced at Elsa but offered no greeting.

Miles leaned out. "To the stagecoach station, and hurry."

The carriage jerked then fell into a swaying rhythm. The stagecoach arrived at the station right as a man with a rifle climbed into the driving box beside the driver.

"Wait!" Miles's call rang above the sounds of jingling harnesses and snorting horses.

The driver nodded. "Make it quick."

Miles hurried into the station to pay their fare, leaving the coachman to help Alicia and Elsa from the carriage. Elsa hobbled, using her crutch, behind Alicia.

A lean man wearing soldier's regalia jumped down from the stagecoach and rushed past Alicia to Elsa. "Please allow me to introduce myself. I am First Sergeant Robert Hartwell of the US Cavalry, on my way to my station at Fort Hall. I noticed your difficulty. May I assist you?"

Elsa smiled in relief. "Thank you."

To her unending surprise, the young sergeant swung her up in his arms. He carried her into the stagecoach and deposited her beside Alicia on the seat facing forward. He sank into a seat across from them.

Miles joined them an instant before the stagecoach pulled out.

A man in striped trousers, starched shirt, satin vest, and a cravat sat beside the sergeant. He looked like he'd stepped out of a catalogue. Why would so elegant a personage travel into the Wild West? Elsa's brow furrowed at the small mystery. She might never know the answer, for he kept his shoulder turned and said little.

Seated on the soldier's other side, a man wearing thick-lensed spectacles clutched a satchel. Between bouts of chatter about topics of interest only to himself, he littered them with suspicious glances, as if he expected them to steal his valise.

What might it contain? Did the man guard the map to a lost mine? A rare artifact? Bank notes? Perhaps the satchel held none of those but a last gift from the mother he would never see again.

Sergeant Hartwell continued to watch Elsa throughout the journey.

Her annoyance at becoming the object of the soldier's

attention gave way to speculation. Perhaps she should ask him to help her get away from Miles and Alicia when they reached the fort later today.

The thought died a quick death. *Why am I still hoping to escape?*

It was useless. If she failed to cooperate with Miles, he would make good on his threats. She didn't trust him or his methods to extract payment from her mother. What if he threatened to take her younger sister, Hilda, when he returned to America?

The stagecoach hit a bump, jarring Elsa from her imaginings. She yelped in pain.

Alicia pulled a flask from her reticule. "Take your medicine."

Elsa swallowed a mouthful and made a face. She resisted the urge to vomit. This sickly-sweet taste differed from the draught the hospital had given her. Why had the doctor changed prescriptions?

The man with the valise smiled. "May is such a nice month for a wedding, don't you think?" He spoke without addressing any one person, neatly avoiding his lack of introductions to the ladies.

Miles curled his lip at the man and exchanged a glance with Alicia, who sat on Elsa's other side. Miles and Alicia had placed her between them, supposedly for support, but Elsa couldn't help feeling trapped between jailers.

"I'm looking forward to meeting my future sister-in-law." The man leaned forward and pulled in a breath.

Elsa stared at him in alarm. He was going to drone on endlessly, she could tell. She swallowed, her throat dry, while the sound of the man's voice cut in and out. She turned to Alicia, watching with a strange expression on her face. Alicia's face blurred.

Elsa blinked to bring her surroundings into focus, but to no avail. Her heartbeat quickened as understanding dawned. *They drugged me.*

Her thoughts faded, and the mists of unconsciousness closed over her.

CHAPTER FIVE

OUTSIDE FORT HALL'S LIVERY, REILLY CLASPED Finley's shoulder and pushed words past the lump in his throat. "Thanks for everything."

Finley's mouth lifted in his crooked smile. "'Twas the least I could do." He cleared his throat and looked away. "You'll be missed."

"Likewise." Carrying his satchel, Reilly joined the passengers queuing for the stagecoach that would carry him north into Montana Territory. A uniformed soldier jumped to the ground and helped the ladies board before striking out for the trading post. Reilly stepped inside the coach and wrinkled his nose at the reek of unwashed bodies. The leather curtains were lowered, no doubt against the dust to come.

Squinting from the dimness after the sunlit town square, Reilly took a seat. His eyes focused to reveal an auburn-haired beauty wedged between two fair-haired companions across from him. A bandage wrapped one of her feet.

The woman didn't stir, and her eyes remained closed. That she managed to sleep with the driver shouting about mailbags and baggage hinted at the influence of pain medications. How had she sustained her injury?

None of my business. The thought countered his sudden urge to interfere. The young woman seemed helpless and stricken, a state that stirred his masculine instincts to protect. Surely, that was the only reason for his reaction.

Watching her face in repose fascinated Reilly, but he pulled his gaze away from her out of respect. He'd never met a woman who would welcome being watched in an unguarded moment. How he knew this, he couldn't say, but he had no doubt of its truth.

The blonde woman beside the beauty stared shamelessly at Reilly. He could flatter himself that she admired him if she didn't look so familiar. Did she recognize him? He waited, but she said nothing.

Reilly had seen the man who accompanied the two women before. He was certain.

He smiled in the face of the man's hostility. "Good afternoon. Forgive me, but have we met? I'm recovering from amnesia, but I think I might know you."

The man pinpointed him with his gaze, and Reilly could have sworn recognition lit his eyes. "I doubt I'd spend time with an *Irishman.*"

"My mistake." Reilly let the matter drop. "I should introduce myself. I'm Reilly . . . Fitzgerald." Finley wouldn't mind lending Reilly his last name.

The blonde woman's eyes widened, and she exchanged a glance with the man. He nodded at Reilly but withheld his name.

Snubbed, Reilly sank back against the leather upholstery and exchanged a glance with the nervous-looking fellow beside him. The man clutched a valise and wore thick-lensed spectacles. His actions announced to all and sundry that the bag contained his worldly wealth.

"Pleased to meet you." He gave Reilly a limp handshake. "My name is Silas Warner. I'm on my way to my brother in Deer Lodge. He's the barber. He doesn't know I'm coming. I thought I'd surprise him after he sent me a letter telling me he's getting hitched. I've had a hankering to see the West, so I figured" —he shrugged—"why not?"

Reilly smiled, then glanced beyond him to a well-dressed gentleman. The man looked up from his pocket watch, assessed Reilly with a glance, then stared at the leather curtain beside him as if gazing out the window.

The sleeping beauty was going to prove a distraction. Reilly looked away from her only to find himself entangled in the blonde woman's gaze. Ending the contact abruptly, he met her male companion's glare.

Reilly folded his arms and settled down for a long journey.

Rob tied his horse to the hitching post in front of Chrisman's store and glanced around before going inside. Bannack basked in the spring sunshine, a welcome change from the overnight rain that had muddied the streets.

His boots thumped against the rough boardwalk. Tall doors inset with glass panes admitted him to Bannack's unofficial news bureau and social center. No flames leaped in the hearth on so fine a day, but a group of men— miners, most of them— sat around the wide fireplace, a habit likely carried over from the winter.

A red-bearded man moved the black knight poised on a chessboard over a wooden barrel. Murmurs of approval and protest rose. The man's opponent scowled at him but then broke into a grin. "You won me again, I reckon."

Another man took his place, and a new game began, much to the delight of those watching.

George Chrisman, jotting in a ledger at the counter, glanced over his spectacles. He straightened with a smile for Rob. "I haven't seen you since last year's cattle drive. Did you bring more beef?"

Rob shook his head. "Not this time."

"How are things at Con's ranch?"

"My sister, Bryanna, is married now."

"I heard." Chrisman would have also heard that Bry's new husband was half Cheyenne, but his expression gave no clue to his thoughts. "Have you heard anything about your brother?" he asked Rob.

The room quieted. Rob glanced at the men about the fireplace, who must be straining their ears. By now everyone in Bannack knew about his brother's disappearance. Con had lived in Bannack and served as one of its deputies. It was natural that the town's residents would wonder what happened to him.

If only Rob had good news to give. "I was hoping Con had returned to Bannack."

Chrisman shook his head, a look of regret on his face. "Sorry, Rob. I haven't seen him since he went East to bring home his family."

"I was afraid you'd say as much, but I had to check." Rob eased his shoulders, stiff after the long ride. "I'm setting out to search for him."

Chrisman arched a brow. "There's still snow in the passes."

"I know that, but I have to try."

Chrisman nodded. "Be careful."

"I will." Rob started for the door, then turned back. "If you see Con before I do, tell him Bry's at the ranch and worried sick."

"Of course." Chrisman frowned at a purple stain his fountain pen had leaked on his knuckles.

Rob nodded to the men around the fireplace, went outside, and climbed into the saddle. He rode to his brother's cabin, which he located from Cousin Shane's description.

His horse's hooves crunched gravel on the approach to the abandoned building, which watched him with sightless eyes. Any lingering hope that he would find Con here died in his chest, but he swung down anyway.

The knob turned in his hand, and the door swayed open. Light filtered through a window on the far. He stepped inside.

So, this is the cabin Con built in Bannack.

It seemed smaller than the tales Shane told of it. Rob sank onto one of the benches at the scarred oak table and placed his hands on the rough wood. He'd wondered for years where his brother had gone after he left home. The West seemed so big, and yet in this tiny place Con had gone about the daily tasks of life. His brother must have sat on this very bench while taking his meals.

A lump rose in Rob's throat. Tears pricked his eyes. Left behind with their father in the slums of Manhattan, Rob had despised Con for abandoning them. Now he understood his brother's reasons. If Con had not gone West, he'd never have returned to free the brother and sister he'd left behind from poverty.

Where are you, Con? The silent cry wrenched from his soul.

Silence deadened the air.

While claiming his fortune, Con must have endured hardship, discouragement, and danger. Shane related horrific stories about the hanging of Sheriff Plummer alongside two of his deputies. Some folks said the vigilantes had lynched an innocent man, but others declared justice served. The truth might never be known, for those who could reveal it had taken up permanent residence on Boot Hill.

Finding no answers, Rob headed back to town.

Bannack's past was notorious. The town still gave pause to any sensible person riding down the street at dusk. Rob was no exception. Music throbbed from saloons and dance halls, and the stench of rotgut whiskey wafted to him. The demon substance lured men to perform foolish and evil acts.

Rob would rent a room for the night, then start for Virginia City and the cabin Con had built on his claim. Rob had a greater chance of finding his brother there, but he doubted that solving the mystery of Con's disappearance would be so easy.

A monster chased Elsa in and out of restless dreams. She jerked awake with a gasp and fought to free herself, but its arms tightened around her.

"What's wrong with her, Miles?" Alicia's distant voice sounded annoyed.

"She's dreaming." Miles's words penetrated the thick fog surrounding Elsa.

The monster shook her.

Elsa screamed.

A moan answered her.

"Wake up, Elsa!" Alicia's command penetrated the fog surrounding her.

Elsa cracked her eyes open, and Alicia's face swam into view. "The monster—"

"Monsters aren't real," Miles asserted in a matter-of-fact voice.

Elsa struggled to leave the nightmare behind. A dull ache pounded behind her eyes, and her stomach felt hollow. "Why is the room rocking?"

"We're on the stagecoach, remember?" Alicia snapped.

"Yes, of course." Elsa sat up straighter. How could she have forgotten? They'd drugged her, no doubt to prevent any chance of her leaving them at Fort Hall.

A glance at the seat across from her confirmed that she had slept through the stop. Sergeant Hartwell was gone, and in his place sat a dark-haired stranger. Rugged features, a cleft chin, and green eyes combined to make him the most stunning man she'd ever seen. Their gazes met, and she caught her breath. The man staring back at her looked as thunderstruck as she felt.

Aware she was gaping, Elsa pulled her gaze away. Her cheeks flamed.

The leather curtains were rolled up. Elsa peered through the window opening in the door. They'd climbed into the mountains, and the view stretched a long way. So did the drop below the road, she imagined, although she couldn't see it fully.

Stagecoaches did not have glass windows, Miles had explained to Alicia earlier. They would break when the stage tossed about on rough roads. This left passengers the choice of traveling in dimness or braving the elements. In early spring, the conditions were easier to take, although rain could slow progress while the horses strained, and the wheels hurled mud.

The sun burned above the horizon. Brilliant colors lit the sky. Elsa couldn't tell whether it was morning or nightfall. It suddenly mattered very much to know. "What time is it?"

She asked the question of Alicia, but the well-dressed man abandoned his reserve to consult his pocket watch. "Six o'clock." He snapped the case shut with a flourish.

"In the evening?"

Alicia jeered her with laughter. "It's morning."

The newest passenger gave Alicia an assessing look, then smiled at Elsa. "Daybreak and sunset look much alike." His Irish lilt made for pleasant listening.

"No one invited you to address my ward." Miles shifted

forward in his seat. "See that you refrain from doing so again."

Elsa frowned. Miles had cut off Sergeant Hartwell's attempts to talk to her during the long trip yesterday as well. If he succeeded in keeping her from conversation, this journey would become even more tedious. She wouldn't argue in public, but she didn't like Miles calling her "his ward." He had no more power over her than the contract granted. How she wished she'd never signed that document. It stood like an insurmountable wall between herself and liberty.

The course of Elsa's life had been dictated first by the pecking order within her village, then by poverty. By coming to America, she had hoped to better herself.

What a foolish dream. If such a thing as *freedom* existed, it did not belong to her.

CHAPTER SIX

ELSA LIFTED HER HEAD FROM ALICIA'S shoulder, where it had fallen while she slept. Alicia stirred and sat up out of a slouch.

Miles smiled. "That was a long nap."

"It's a wonder I slept at all, what with this stagecoach bouncing like a newborn calf." Alicia poked at her hair in a futile attempt to restore order.

She shouldn't have worried, Elsa decided. Even with wisps straying from her chignon to float about her head, Alicia managed to look beautiful.

Scowling, Alicia peered out the window. "Where are we?"

Miles shrugged. "Somewhere between the last swing station and the next."

"How close to Bannack City have we come?" Alicia enunciated her words, making her annoyance clear.

Miles smirked, as if pleased to have irritated her. "The driver tells me we'll reach it soon. From there, it's another day to Virginia City."

"I'll be glad to put this trip behind us." Alicia pulled the flask out of her reticule. "Elsa, it's time for another dose of your medicine."

"I don't want it." She shrank away from Alicia but bumped into Miles.

"Take your medicine." Miles's voice brooked no argument.

Alicia pressed the flask to Elsa's lips. Cloying liquid poured into her mouth, forcing her to swallow or choke. She clamped her lips shut and pushed the flask away. A trickle ran down her neck and beneath her collar.

"Let me do it." Miles rapped out the words.

"She's had enough." Alicia sounded smug.

Elsa could have wept. "Please, I need water."

Miles produced a canteen. Elsa drank in greedy gulps and returned it with reluctance. Miles stroked her forehead. "There, there. You'll be out of pain soon."

Elsa looked away from his cold stare and into a pair of green eyes fringed by dark lashes. Was it her imagination, or did a silent communication pass between herself and the stranger?

The drug deadened Elsa's thoughts and returned her to darkness.

Reilly set his jaw as the light faded from Elsa's eyes. Her lids drifted shut, and her mouth slackened in sleep. The urge to wrest her from her companions and shelter her in his arms took hold of him. He ought to have stopped them from forcing medicine on her, might have done so if he hadn't been taken by surprise.

"She didn't want the medicine." Irritation roughed his voice. "You shouldn't have forced it on her."

Miles gave him a hard look. "Mind your own business, *Irish*."

There it was again, that flash of connection not quite memory. Reilly had heard this slur before—in exactly that tone—but such insults came with being Irish.

He returned stare for stare. "Mistreat a woman in front of me, and you *make* it my business."

"I reckon it's mine too . . ." Silas's face turned red, and he sank against the seat. "Mostly."

"They're concerned, Miles." Alicia smiled. "That's understandable, since they don't know the whole story."

Miles gave a quick nod. "My ward needs the medicine to keep her mind from wandering."

Silas's eyes widened. "You mean she's crazy?"

"I wouldn't go so far as to say that." Alicia shot Miles a sharp look.

"Elsa is given to fits of passion." Miles shook his head. "Without the medicine, she might harm someone. As you can see, she's injured herself."

A frightened look came into the eyes of the gentleman sitting next to Silas. "Why have you brought a madwoman on the stage? We must inform the driver to put you off at the earliest opportunity."

Miles furrowed his brow. "I assure you that, properly medicated, Elsa is quite docile. I can testify that she's recovering. In fact, she's nearly well."

This seemed to mollify Silas, who settled against the seatback.

The gentleman did not yield so easily. "The driver should know."

"Yes, of course, but there's no hurry." Miles glanced at his fingernails with a bored expression. "Elsa should sleep soundly all night."

Reilly wasn't sure he believed any of this. Miles's story seemed to shift to suit his whim. During Elsa's brief period of wakefulness, she'd seemed rational. Before the sedative took hold, she'd gazed at him with the look of a cornered doe.

In that instant, Reilly had given Elsa his silent pledge to protect her, and he meant to keep it. "How often do you plan to sedate her? If you don't allow her to eat, she'll waste away."

Miles's jaw tensed, but Alicia spoke before he could. "Don't worry about Miss Meier. She's under a doctor's orders."

Short of calling her a liar, Reilly had to accept her claim, at least on the surface. Watching Miles and Alicia exchange a secretive glance, he drew his own conclusions. Something was wrong. What, he didn't know, but he wouldn't rest until he found out.

He pinned Miles with a stare. "How did you acquire a foreign ward?"

Miles sniffed. "I refuse to answer such a nosy inquiry."

Reilly rubbed his chin. "I just wonder, given your dislike for immigrants, why you would assume the care of one."

Miles curled his hands into fists. "Never question me again."

"Why don't we talk about something else?" Silas squeaked.

Reilly held Miles's gaze until the man's hands relaxed.

Silas blew out a breath. "Yes, sir. May is a grand month for a wedding."

Reilly jerked awake as he slammed into the stagecoach wall. He thrust himself away from the leather-covered padding that had spared him injury. He hadn't slept much due to the stagecoach's bouncing, but he must have finally dropped off from utter exhaustion. The driver navigated the bad stretch of road, and Reilly clutched the leather strap beside him. In the muted light slanting through the small windows beside the door, he made out his fellow passengers. They peered back at him, bleary-eyed. The constant rattling of the stagecoach made sleep nearly impossible. They all suffered from the lack, except Elsa, who still slumbered.

"Good morning," Silas greeted him with a smile. "Bannack shouldn't be far off."

Reilly rolled up the curtain beside him and strapped it into place. "That's good news. It means we're closer to leaving this stage."

"This isn't my favorite way to travel," Silas agreed. "Thank heavens we'll be stopping for a couple of hours in Bannack for repairs."

"Hopefully we'll have time for a decent meal."

Silas nodded. "I'd welcome food myself. It will be nice to walk about for longer than the ten minutes they allow at swing stations."

The stagecoach slowed. The road broadened beside a creek. Houses rose on either side. They passed through a cottonwood grove and crossed a bridge. A turn brought them into the main part of town.

"Bannack!" The driver slowed the horses.

"Wake up." Miles shook Elsa until she opened her eyes.

The expression on her face made Reilly want to push Miles away from her. "Stop that. Can't you see that you're frightening her?"

Miles gave him a belligerent look. "I'll not take correction from a bog-trotter."

"Please." Alicia reached across Elsa to touch Miles's arm. "Can't we get off this abominable conveyance?"

His expression softened. "Of course." He stood and pulled Elsa to her feet. He frowned as she sagged. "I'd rather not have to carry you, but if I must . . ." He hoisted her upward.

Reilly stepped down from the stagecoach and into the mud. He turned back to Miles, who was having trouble negotiating the steps. "Give her to me."

Miles shook his head. "Stand back. The driver can assist me."

"He's busy with the horses."

Miles glanced about. "Someone else, then."

Reilly tightened his jaw. "There's no one free."

Alicia came up behind Miles. "I *insist* that you let me off this stage."

"All right." Miles lowered Elsa into Reilly's arms.

Elsa weighed next to nothing, a fact that increased Reilly's desire to protect her. He gazed into her hazel eyes. "You need feeding." He squashed the urge to stride off with her while Miles was assisting Alicia from the stagecoach.

Elsa frowned. "Thank you, but I can walk if you'll put me down. Where is my crutch?"

"Here." Miles retrieved it from the open boot.

Reilly hesitated. Elsa looked injured and weak, not like someone who should walk on her own. After seeing her ordered around by her companions, however, he had no desire to do the same. He lowered her to the boardwalk and supported her while she balanced.

Alicia latched onto Miles' arm. "Escort me?"

Miles glanced over her head at Reilly. "There's no need for you to remain with us."

Reilly tamped down a burst of annoyance. "But Miss Meier—"

"My ward can walk with the aid of her crutch."

Reilly withdrew his hand from Elsa's arm. He was glad to see her standing, although she looked a little wobbly. "Let me walk alongside you, at least."

She sent a Her glance skittered toward Miles. "Thank you, but I can manage." Even while she refused, her eyes pleaded with Reilly.

Reilly wished he understood what she needed from him. "As you wish." He stepped away.

Elsa hobbled down the boardwalk behind Miles and Alicia.

Silas, clutching his valise, came to stand next to Reilly. "Do you think she's crazy?"

Reilly shrugged. "I'm no doctor." He had instincts, however, and they suggested that Elsa's reactions would be logical if he only knew all the facts.

He decided then and there that he would make it his business to find them out.

Miles and Alicia crossed the muddy street and turned to wait. Elsa stepped off the boardwalk into the mud.

Her stumbling made Reilly bite his lip. When he could endure it no longer, he caught up to her. "May I assist you?"

"I'm fine, really." Her strained expression belied her words. She took another step and went flailing.

Reilly reached for her in time to prevent her fall. He swung her into his arms without asking permission this time. A man could only take so much. Standing by while a defenseless woman struggled went against the grain.

Miles, for once, did not protest. He watched silently as Reilly carried Elsa across the street.

Elsa's eyes shone with unshed tears. "Thank you for your kindness, but I don't need more help."

"As you wish." He set her down on the boardwalk and tipped his Stetson.

Elsa hobbled after Miles and Alicia, who turned into a two-story, white-frame structure. A sign suspended by chains above the porch read "Merrick Hotel."

"Looks like a good place to find a meal."

Reilly jumped. He didn't like Silas's way of sneaking up on him. Images of gang members creeping up flashed before his mind's eye. He pulled in a breath as one more part of his past slid into place. In the slum where he'd once lived, he'd fought to survive.

"That it does." Grateful for a reason to follow Elsa, Reilly turned toward the hotel entrance.

Reilly, with Silas beside him, followed the chink of dishes past the bored-looking man at the front desk and a pair of batwing saloon doors. In the dining room, he looked around in puzzlement. A dozen guests sat at unadorned oak tables, but Elsa, Miles, and Alicia were nowhere in sight.

He tapped Silas on the shoulder. "I'll be back."

Silas's surprised expression gave way to a look of understanding, and he nodded.

Reilly strode out to the lobby and approached the desk.

"What can I do for you?" the clerk asked.

"I'm looking for my friend, a fair-haired man. He's with two women, one blonde, and the other with copper hair."

The man's gaze sharpened. "A friend, you say?"

"Yes." Reilly stood square and endured the man's scrutiny.

"What's his name?"

"Miles."

The clerk nodded. "The Peabodys checked in with their ward ten minutes ago. I doubt they'll want visitors. They seemed tired, coming off that stage."

Reilly smiled. "I'll check back later then."

"Suit yourself."

He rejoined Silas, seated before a heaping plate of biscuits and gravy.

"Did you find them?" Silas spoke with his mouth full.

Reilly sank down across from him. "They've either checked into rooms to rest or have abandoned the stagecoach altogether."

"Not surprised." Silas swigged a huge gulp of coffee. "That blonde gal looked mighty fed up."

"Maybe so." Reilly had other guesses. With the stagecoach passengers—himself in particular—asking too many questions about Elsa, her companions no doubt wanted distance.

Well, they won't get rid of me so easily. His mind made up, Reilly wandered over to serve himself at the buffet.

Later, with his belly full and Silas bent over a second helping, Reilly strode outside.

Bannack had the wide streets and low-slung buildings of a typical western town. Residences jumbled together with businesses on this street, much finer than Reilly had expected.

He started down the boardwalk, and his steps slowed. This place rang a bell. *I've been here before.* How else would he know what the barber shop looked like inside without entering it?

Reilly continued down the boardwalk, away from the main part of town. He halted in front of a certain cabin. He *knew* this place! Picking up his pace, Reilly walked toward the cabin.

Spotty memories clustered in his mind. He'd cooked in what passed for a kitchen, read a tattered copy of *Uncle Tom's Cabin* at the table, and slept under this roof many a night.

He had lived here.

The door creaked open beneath his hand, and he walked inside. Daylight slotted through the cabin's rough-hewn wall slats. He had thrown the lumber up quickly, in a hurry to pan for gold, never taking time to caulk the gaps between boards.

Reilly had lived here . . . with someone else. He strained at the memory of a face but couldn't recall the man's name or identity. He shook his head in frustration, but then urged himself toward patience.

No good would come of trying to force memories to return. He'd learned that long ago, and it hadn't changed since. No matter. He'd gained ground by coming here.

Reilly closed the door and turned toward town, where surely someone could tell him his real name.

Elsa peered around the room. The furnishings were humbler than Alicia preferred, but for a western town, the brass bed and plain rosewood dresser and armoire were probably fancy. A cot was set up for her at the foot of the brass bed where Alicia would sleep. Miles had taken a room with an adjoining closed door.

Alicia turned from the wash basin, dabbing the moist skin above her chemise with a towel. She swept a glance over Elsa. "Wash up. You look a mess."

Elsa hurried to obey.

Alicia pulled a dress from the wardrobe. "I'm glad to be off that horrid stagecoach. We'll have a couple of days before we have to climb into one again."

Elsa's thoughts went into turmoil. Why would they stop here rather than remain with the stagecoach? Miles and Alicia had drugged her to prevent her from leaving them. It made no sense that they'd risk her escaping during a long stay in Bannack.

Her feverish thoughts brought on a headache, so she gave up the effort. Whatever the reason, she was grateful for a reprieve. Elsa's stomach fluttered. She would never again see the handsome stranger who might have helped her.

Alicia picked up a brush and brushed her hair with even strokes. "They should bring up breakfast soon."

Of course they would order room service to keep her away from other diners. From their disdainful attitudes, Miles and

Alicia couldn't wait to see the last of her. Upon reaching Virginia City, they would part ways. Elsa couldn't feel sorry about that, but she would exchange their company for that of Atticus Merrick.

I can't go through with it.

The quiet certainty filled Elsa with a sense of peace. Come what may, she couldn't cast aside her decency and self-respect, not even to spare her mother or sister. She must find another way. Meanwhile, she had to escape.

They wouldn't trust her alone, but Elsa couldn't picture Alicia spending the next couple of days stuck in a hotel room with her, either. The solution brought heat rushing into her cheeks. Miles and Alicia thought they could bully her, but she would teach them they couldn't. She had changed since coming to America. Miles and Alicia had changed her, forcing her to leave behind the frightened girl they'd pushed around.

When they tried to drug her again, she'd be ready.

CHAPTER SEVEN

Reilly pushed open the door of Bannack's mercantile and immediately underwent scrutiny from a group of men gathered around the fireplace. He nodded to them, watching for signs of recognition.

He didn't have to wait long.

A grizzled man dressed in the rough clothes of a miner stared at him. "Well, I'll be blamed—"

"Where have you been all this time?" The man next to the miner scowled, but then broke into a grin.

A man wearing red suspenders laughed. "Look what the cat drug in!"

"Con Walsh!" another crowed. "We thought you'd died."

Reilly stood transfixed. *My name is Con Walsh.* Past and present tangled together in his mind, a snarl that unraveled a little more each moment.

He'd left Bannack to avoid the same fate as Deputy Dillingham, murdered for defying the local gang of road agents. After paying his respects to the honest deputy at his grave he'd fled Virginia City. Guilt by association was more than enough evidence for the vigilantes back then, and he'd narrowly avoided a hangman's noose.

Relocating to Deer Lodge Valley had brought out his love for ranching. He'd learned the ropes as a ranch hand before claiming his own land in the Bitterroot Valley.

"It's a long story," he answered simply. "I lost my memory, but it's coming back."

"That so?" A man wearing spectacles came out from behind the counter. He looked familiar, but Reilly—*no*, Con—searched for the man's name in vain. "Too bad you missed your brother. Rob was here looking for you only a few days ago. He told me to send you to the ranch. Your sister very much wants to see you."

"Bryanna?" His sister's name rolled off his tongue. He was worried about her, but why?

The helplessness of watching her capture by Indians returned to haunt him. How had she escaped? "Is she all right?"

The man nodded. "I'd say so."

Reilly felt the tension drain from him. "I'll go to her."

He would, right after he took care of another matter. A painted warrior hadn't ridden off with Elsa, but he suspected she was no less a prisoner. He couldn't leave her without knowing the truth.

"Elsa, take your medicine." Alicia held out the flask. In the light of the oil lamp on the dresser, the woman looked soft and sweet, but her tone said otherwise.

Elsa finished plaiting her hair and turned from the dresser mirror. "I'd rather not."

"Don't be difficult." Alicia scowled. "It does you good."

"It makes me sleep too much."

"What does that matter, since it's bedtime?" Alicia tapped her foot, a sure sign her temper was on the rise.

Elsa held firm. "It gives me bad dreams and then I'm groggy when I wake."

"Nevertheless, I must insist you take it." Alicia poured the amber liquid into a glass and extended it to her.

Elsa crossed her arms. "I don't need it. My ankle doesn't pain me much."

"You are not completely mended. Now, will you take your medicine, or do I need to call for Miles?"

Irritation rushed through Elsa. "I know you've been drugging me."

Alicia's eyes widened, then narrowed. "I'm sure I don't know what you're talking about."

"Stop pretending. A child could guess what you're doing. Well, no more. Don't think I won't tell Atticus how you treated me."

Alicia flinched.

She must fear Atticus. The knowledge bolstered Elsa and renewed her desire to avoid the man.

"All right." Alicia thumped the flask down on the dresser. "But if you show any sign of strain, I'll give you no choice."

Elsa stretched out on the cot with a sense of relief. It hadn't been easy, but she'd won this battle of wills. She could plan her escape with a clear mind. She would try to slip away tonight.

Elsa wasn't sure where to go for help in this town. Watching the stagecoach from the window as it drove away had been hard to bear. She shouldn't have placed her hope in a stranger's kindness. He would continue on his journey and soon forget all about her.

Alicia blew out the oil lamp, and the bedsprings creaked. She sighed and turned over. Her breaths deepened, then she broke into a soft snore.

Elsa startled awake and sat up, heart pounding. The nightmare lost its grip on her, and her panic slid away. She waited for Alicia's scolding, certain she'd woken her, but heard nothing.

Morning light softened the dimity curtains. Elsa groaned inwardly. Instead of escaping, she'd fallen asleep. She should have realized that exhaustion from the stagecoach ride and the lingering effects of the drug they'd given her would combine to put her out.

She'd have to wait until tonight to escape. Maybe by then she would figure out where to go.

Con sat up in the rope bed and rubbed sleep from his eyes. He'd slept soundly. Using the dingy light that penetrated the dust layered on the windows, he crossed to the door and flung it open.

Chill morning air poured into the cabin. Con breathed deeply, savoring its crispness. Birds sang fiercely, as if desperate to usher in a new day. He envied the feathered creatures, flying about at will and playing among the branches.

Yet, even a bird had its troubles. He'd seen a tiny creature lying dead alongside the road yesterday. He didn't recognize it as a sparrow until he drew closer. A Scripture came to mind in that instant. "Are not two sparrows sold for a farthing? and one of them shall not fall on the ground without your Father. But the very hairs of your head are all numbered. Fear ye not therefore, ye are of more value than many sparrows."

Con had committed that passage to memory at some long-ago point. He must have needed a reminder of God's love. His mouth quirked. If he didn't watch himself, he'd turn into a preacher like Shane.

Shane. One more piece of the puzzle of his past slid into place. A face appeared in his mind's eye, and he laughed. How had he forgotten Shane Hayes, his foolhardy-but-brave cousin given to rushing in where angels feared to tread? He'd lost count of the times Shane had almost gotten himself killed while trying to save the lost sheep of Bannack. Con had built the other rope bed in his cabin for whenever Shane's preaching circuit brought him to Bannack. They'd argued a time or two, but only out of concern for one another.

Memories flooded Con. In the years since Shane had moved to the Bitterroot Valley to establish a church, he'd mellowed into a fine man-of-the-cloth and a good husband and father. Con hadn't been sure his cousin's marriage to America Reed would take place, but now he couldn't imagine the two apart.

Love ought to be like that. Con felt sure of it, although he knew little about that tender emotion. After loving and losing a girl in his youth, he'd decided never to marry. He didn't feel that way any longer. Maybe someday he'd find a woman to anchor him the way America did Shane.

His thoughts turned to Elsa. Hopefully she would wake up refreshed after spending a peaceful night. *Look after her, will You?* After lifting the silent prayer, he sat down on a bench to pull on his boots . . . and paused.

Sometimes the Good Lord could use a helping hand.

Elsa ignored Alicia, slathering huckleberry jam on her toast while seated beside Miles across the table. Musing out the window beside her, an image of the green-eyed stranger from the stagecoach rose in Elsa's thoughts. She sighed. The man was gone from her life but still managed to plague her idle moments.

"Don't pick at your food."

Elsa jumped at Alicia's sharp tone and jerked her mind onto the present. Her cheeks flaming, she straightened in her ladderback chair and picked up her fork. Food didn't appeal to her, but it would take strength to carry out her plan.

Miles glanced at Elsa, then turned to Alicia. "You look contented."

Alicia sipped from a porcelain tea cup painted with pink roses. "I'm happy to be anywhere but on that infernal conveyance that brought us here."

Miles showed his white teeth in a smile. "Don't make yourself too comfortable. We head out on tomorrow's stage."

"I'd rather not think about that." Alicia pouted. "They forgot my breakfast steak."

"I noticed and requested they send one up. Beef costs a pretty penny in this town, I'll have you know."

Elsa took a mouthful of hash-brown potatoes and let her gaze wander out the window once more. She must not fail. Unless she escaped tonight, tomorrow's stagecoach ride would carry her to Virginia City and—she shuddered—to Atticus Merrick.

A man walking between the hotel and the next building caught her attention through the window pane. Even in the shadow, he seemed familiar. When he stepped into the sunlight, Elsa held her breath. She'd assumed the stranger had left town, but there he stood, his face turned upward and his hat pushed back on his head. She shouldn't stare but couldn't pull her gaze away.

"What are you looking at?"

Alicia's question recalled Elsa, and she broke the contact. "Nothing."

"It didn't *seem* like nothing." Miles stood and peered out the window.

Elsa shrugged. "Someone was walking by, but he's gone now." It was true. The stranger had vanished while her head was turned.

Miles sat down, but Alicia watched her with narrowed eyes. After a moment, the woman lifted her tea cup and settled against her chair.

Elsa released her breath in relief. She'd rather not point out the stranger's presence in town, although it probably had nothing to do with her. If only she had taken the chance to tell him she was in trouble. Fear should not have stopped her.

Voices carried from below, then boots thumped the stairs. The sound grew louder until it stopped outside their room. A knock shook the door.

"That will be your steak." Miles scraped back his chair and strode to the door.

Alicia lifted a biscuit to her mouth and waved her free hand. "Send it back unless it's medium rare."

She continued talking, but Elsa had stopped listening. The green-eyed stranger—of medium build and with compact muscles—stood in the doorway, bristling with pent-up energy. He would do well in a fight, she decided. She ran an assessing glance over Miles, who might not.

"What are you doing here?" Miles looked ready to slam the door in the stranger's face.

"You paused your journey. Is anything amiss?"

"There's no reason for concern." Miles flicked a glance at Elsa. "We are quite well."

"Miles, invite Mr. Fitzgerald in." Alicia pushed her food away and rose with easy grace. "He's only being friendly."

"Thank you." The stranger stepped inside.

Miles blocked his path. "Mr. Fitzgerald is intruding."

The stranger gave a brief shake of his head. "That's not my real name. I've remembered a great many things since last we spoke. Allow me to introduce myself. I'm Con Walsh."

Miles ignored the hand Con extended. "Whatever your name, take yourself away at once. Or have you stayed behind to afflict us?"

Con stood taller. "I'll ignore your rude question for the ladies' sakes. My reasons for departing the stage in Bannack are my own. I'm glad I stopped, for I remembered myself here."

"Really?" Alicia flounced over and stood shamelessly close. "You must tell us what it's like to forget your own name."

A vein stood out in Miles's neck. "He won't be staying long enough." He glared at Con. "Whoever you are, if you don't leave, I'll send for the sheriff."

Con tensed into a posture that even Elsa, with her limited knowledge of fisticuffs, had no difficulty recognizing. She made a small sound in her throat.

Con eased out of his fighting stance and backed toward the door. "No need for that. I only came to see if you needed assistance." He rested his gaze on Elsa.

Warmth prickled her skin. If only she could tell him her troubles, but anything she said might lead to violence. She met his gaze and gave a slight nod. From the gleam in Con's eyes, he understood her meaning.

"I'll be going then." He walked through the doorway and vanished down the hallway.

Elsa stared after him, dumbstruck. She'd finally communicated her plight, and he'd abandoned her.

CHAPTER EIGHT

C ON KICKED A STONE OUT OF his way and crossed the street. Yesterday's mud lay in hardened ruts cut by wagons. Con passed the place where he'd pulled Elsa into his arms. Miles should never have forced her to cross the treacherous street on one crutch.

He shook his head. Elsa's faint nod settled his mind on one fact. She was a young woman in trouble. Now that she'd affirmed his suspicions, he would not stand by and allow her to suffer.

In his youth, he'd have taken Miles on then and there, and he couldn't deny that impulse now. He disregarded it. Sheriff Plummer's hanging had impressed him with the need to rely on law and order. Earlier he'd seen Matt Helmsley, wearing a sheriff's badge, come out of the office at the back of Chrisman's store.

Con knew Helmsley as an honest and fair man. He'd stake his life on it.

He stepped onto the boardwalk in front of Chrisman's store, his jaw tightening. He would seek law and order, but no matter what, he couldn't fail to protect Elsa.

A memory teased his thoughts. He'd met Miles and Alicia before, and not under favorable circumstances. If only he could remember where he'd met them.

A shadow rippled over Con, and he looked up. A red-tailed hawk spread black-tipped white wings overhead. Caught by the beauty of its flight, he watched the bird fly over the roof of the mercantile. The hawk must be headed to Grasshopper Creek for a fish dinner.

An image flashed before him—Miles shaking his fist and shouting for Con's arrest. Con had run with Bry across a boardwalk, not unlike the one on which he stood.

Ah, yes. Now he remembered.

He saw again Alicia drop her handkerchief and himself bend to retrieve it. He offered her the lacy scrap, but Miles rejected it as 'tainted.' Con withstood the man's personal taunts, but then Miles called his sister names.

Con understood why he would want to forget their meeting, but why did Miles pretend not to know him? Why did Alicia? Had the incident been so minor that they had forgotten it? More likely, they'd prevented him from stirring up trouble on the stagecoach.

One question remained. What were they up to with Elsa?

The answer didn't take much imagination. The hurdy-gurdy girls who played and danced for miners sometimes fell into prostitution.

He didn't like that possibility one bit.

Chrisman was waiting on a customer, so Con joined the miners around the store's fireplace. There were fewer gathered today, no doubt the effect of dry weather.

"Walsh, what are you still doing here?" The grizzled man dressed in what looked like the same brown-duck trousers and red-plaid shirt from yesterday bellowed good-naturedly. "Thought you'd hightail it for your ranch."

"I'd like to, Tim." Con inserted the man's name with a sense of triumph. He'd remembered it at the last instant. "I've something to take care of first."

The red-bearded man next to Tim had stopped speaking when Con came in, but now pulled in a breath. "Building a road through Sioux hunting grounds was asking for trouble."

"So what?" Jake Faraday demanded in his Missouri accent. "Them Injuns shouldn't have ambushed Captain Fetterman and his men like that."

Others murmured their agreement.

Con had heard of the shocking attack. Red Cloud, Crazy Horse, and High-Back-Bone, leaders from the Lakota Sioux, had lured Captain Fetterman from Fort Phil Kearney and over a rise. Fetterman and his eighty men were dead within half an hour. It had happened last December, but folks were still nervous, and for good reason.

"Never mind." A furrow indented the space between Tim's eyes. "Red Cloud's War shouldn't reach us here."

The customer went out the door, so Con approached the counter. "Good morning."

George Chrisman looked at him over his spectacles. "What do you need, Con?"

"A word with Helmsley. Is he in?" He glanced toward the closed door of the sheriff's office at the back of the store.

The shopkeeper's eyebrows went up. "Sorry, no. He came by this morning, then went out. He's somewhere around town."

"Thank you." Con wasn't pleased with the news, since it meant he'd have to walk the town over looking for Helmsley. "If he comes back, tell him I'm looking for him."

"I'll do that."

The men at the fireplace were discussing the acquisition of Alaska from the Russians, a purchase that opponents called "Seward's Folly" to mock Secretary of State William Seward. Most of the miners favored the move.

Con's search took him through the upper streets of town, then across the bridge that led across Grasshopper Creek to Yankee Flats. He stopped at the center of the span and sent up a simple prayer. *Help me, Lord.* Water glinting blue and brown wallowed between banks plush with spring grass. He'd slept well last night, lulled to sleep by the homey chorus from the creek's namesake creatures. A breeze smoothed his cheek as he turned to resume his quest.

He emerged from a stand of shushing cottonwood trees into a part of town built on level ground. Bannack residents loyal to the Union Army during the War Between the States had made their home here, while their southern-supporting neighbors had claimed higher ground. The barber had relocated his shop from Yankee Flats to Main Street due to his political leanings.

Hungry and ready to give up on finding Sheriff Helmsley, Con headed back.

The man he sought stood on the bridge. His posture told Con he was waiting for him. Dressed in trousers of jean cloth, a leather vest with a striped shirt, and a high-crowned Stetson hat, the lawman wore his badge with confidence.

Helmsley nodded. "Nice to find you hale and hearty."

"Thanks." Con gave him a wry smile. "I share your sentiment. Where have you been? I've looked all over town for you."

"Chrisman told me you wanted me, and Tim Mulligan saw you come this way." A couple of magpies chattered at one another in the cottonwoods, and the sheriff paused to watch them. "Funny birds. I've heard them mimic dogs barking." He turned to Con. "Care for something to drink and a bite of food?"

Skipping breakfast hadn't been a good idea. Con's stomach seemed bent on gnawing a hole in his belly. "Thank you." He fell into step beside Helmsley and retraced the path beyond the bridge.

The sheriff glanced sideways at him. "It's been a long time since I've seen you. I'd like the chance to catch up. Did you really lose your memory?"

"'Tis true."

"Do you have it back?"

Con considered the question. "Mostly."

"That must be a relief."

"I'd rather have it than not, except for certain memories that are better forgotten."

Helmsley laughed. "Too bad we can't pick and choose." He turned down a street and called over his shoulder. "Let's see what Mrs. Helmsley has made for the midday meal. Hopefully she'll forgive me for arriving late."

"And for bringing a guest with you unannounced?"

Helmsley waved a hand. "Never mind about that. She cooks enough to feed an army."

They reached a sprawling house surrounded by a picket fence. Helmsley unlatched the gate but with a hand to Con's shoulder, stopped him from going through. "Now tell me, what's on your mind?"

Con looked into his concerned face. "I think a woman in town is being forced to travel with a couple against her will. I believe they drug her to keep her quiet."

"*Think? Believe?*" Helmsley's brows drew together. "I'm not sure what I can do with opinions. Have you any proof?"

"No, but—"

"I'll check into the matter"—Helmsley released Con's shoulder—"but I have to warn you that it might not turn out how you'd like. Proof is what's needed. Will the woman in question confirm your suspicions?"

"I believe so." Con went through the opening, aware that he'd spoken with less confidence. Elsa had turned his help away before, after seeming to want it.

Helmsley latched the gate and joined him on the path. "If

what you say is true, I hope you're right."

Elsa breathed in the heady fragrance of French perfume. Why Alicia doused herself at bedtime remained a mystery. It seemed such a waste. Elsa settled on her cot as if ready for slumber. With little to do but listen to Alicia's complaints throughout the long day, she would have welcomed the oblivion of sleep.

She wouldn't allow herself that luxury until she reached safety. Where that might be, Elsa didn't know. The only plan she'd made involved hiding among the cottonwoods she'd glimpsed when she and Alicia stood outside on the balcony that extended over the hotel porch. She would go hungry but could drink from the creek and conceal herself among the trees.

Miles and Alicia probably wouldn't search for her long. Once they left town, Elsa could emerge and ask for assistance. Not every woman in this town was a fancy lady. She had seen a modestly dressed woman taking clothes down from a line across the street.

Alicia's silken hair rippled beneath her brush. The oil lamp bathed her face in warm light. Her neck arched gracefully above the swells of her breasts, only partially concealed by her chemise. She pouted into the mirror, her lips redder than usual, then laid down her brush. "You look pale, Elsa. I believe your injury must bother you."

Elsa's heartbeat picked up its pace. "No, it doesn't."

"You are one to hide your pain, I think." Alicia reached into her reticule and pulled out the dreaded flask. "Well, I don't intend to let you suffer."

"Then you will not try to give me that horrid substance."

Elsa sat up and enfolded her knees in the protective gesture she'd often used as a child after waking from a nightmare. *Mutter* had found her like that more than once and carried her to the soft bed she shared with Papa. Snug and warm between her parents, Elsa would always forget the monsters that plagued her dreams.

How she wished for her parent's love and protection now!

Alicia poured some of the liquid from the flask into a glass. "Stop being difficult."

Elsa lifted her head in defiance. "Is that what you call it when a person wants to be left alone?"

Alicia stared at her. "You are becoming more trouble than you're worth, Missy."

"Then I will not inflict you with my company any longer." Beyond caution, Elsa snapped out the words she most wanted to say.

"That's it." Alicia's nostrils flared. She rushed to the connecting door and pounded it with her fists. "Miles!"

Elsa bit her lip. Alicia wasn't the only one with a temper. Her own had goaded her into speaking when she should have remained silent. Now that she had determined to part ways with Alicia, every moment she spent in the woman's company became harder to endure.

The door swung open. Miles stood in the doorway, wearing a black and gold dressing gown. His hair shone in the lamplight as he stepped into their room. He flicked a glance between the two women. "What's wrong?"

"I tried to give Elsa her medicine." Alicia ground out her words.

Miles's gaze fastened on Elsa. "You will cooperate if you know what's good for you."

Elsa's cheeks warmed, and she pulled the bedclothes up to

cover her chemise. "All right." She didn't have to pretend to be frightened.

Miles's smile had never seemed more charming. "There's a good girl." He gestured with his head, and Alicia advanced on Elsa.

Elsa gave Alicia a chastened look and took the glass. She turned slightly away and lifted the rim to her lips. Tilting her head, she pretended to drink, while letting the draught slide out the side of her mouth and down her neck to soak into her chemise. She plunked the glass down and reclined, covering herself before they noticed her deception. Elsa closed her eyes and pretended to sleep.

"She's already out," Alicia purred. "Thank goodness."

"Why are you so happy about that, dear *sister*?"

"You know why and stop calling me that. I'm glad anytime I can stop pretending you're my brother."

Miles's laugh vibrated, low and seductive. The sound of kissing followed.

Elsa caught her breath but managed not to gasp. Her mother wouldn't have let her go with these people had she known they weren't what they appeared.

"Don't try smoothing me over." Alicia's voice had lost its edge. "If I have to watch her any longer, I'll go mad."

"Sorry it's fallen to you, but I can't chaperone a woman."

Alicia laughed. "That would be like the fox guarding the henhouse."

"Still angry with me about that saloon girl? After the way you threw yourself at Con Walsh today, you have nothing to reproach me about."

"He's very handsome." She giggled.

"Vixen!"

Elsa endured another romantic interlude. Finally, the

connecting door clicked shut. Muffled sounds reached her from behind it. She waited, gathering her courage. Laughter drifted from the hotel's saloon. She pushed back her covers and sat up. With her companions distracted, she would find no better time to escape.

Elsa picked up her crutch from beneath the bed, where she'd hidden it earlier. She pushed herself to her feet and dressed quickly. After buttoning her coat against the night air, she took up her hurdy-gurdy case and started for the door.

Her case thumped against the dresser. Elsa held her breath, waiting for Miles or Alicia to burst into the room. Time passed, but no one came. She slipped into the darkened hallway. Holding her breath, she passed Miles's room. The urge to run down the stairs shook her—impossible while balancing on a crutch and carrying an instrument. Her ankle wouldn't hold up on its own, although she could put her weight on it briefly.

The hotel desk stood empty. The clerk had probably retired for the night. She hobbled across the dimly-lit lobby, pursued by laughter and the reek of whiskey from the saloon behind its batwing oak doors. The windows in the front doors stared out into the night. She ached to reach them. Only a little farther, and she could hide herself in darkness. She set her case down and opened the front door, then picked up her instrument again.

Wood crashed against the wall behind her. A glance over her shoulder revealed two men swaying on their feet. The tallest wore brown clothes and a red kerchief, while the other was dressed in black.

"Hands off, Boone." The man in brown grinned at his companion. "Saw her first."

"Nah-uh." The other man laughed. "She's mine."

Elsa hurried onto the porch and skittered a glance about. She needed somewhere to hide, and fast. *But where?*

Boots thudded on the porch as the men caught up.

"Wha's the hurry, darlin'?" Boone breathed foul fumes into her face. He tilted his head toward the other man. "Come with me, won't you? I pay better than Billy."

"Gentlemen, you're mistaken—"

"Don't listen to him." Billy thrust between them. "I'm the one you want."

Elsa shook her head. "I'm not for sale." No matter how low she fell, she refused to stoop to that level.

Billy scowled. He grasped her upper arms, nearly throwing her off balance. Her instrument case thudded to the porch, and she barely held onto her crutch. "Don't be playin' with me, darlin'."

"You're hurting me." Elsa kept her voice low to avoid rousing the hotel. If that happened, she'd wind up back where she started.

"Come away." Boone pulled at Billy's arm. "I don't think she's a fancy woman after all."

Billy shook off his friend. "Why else would she go about on her own at night?" He pulled Elsa closer and nuzzled her neck. "Take me to your room, and I'll make it worth your while."

"Stop it!" Elsa forgot to be quiet. Her ankle hurt, her instrument might be damaged, and this drunken man had no right to touch her.

A gun lever clicked. "The lady wants to be left alone."

CHAPTER NINE

CON KEPT HIS GUN TRAINED ON Billy Hardin, the man giving Elsa the most grief. Boone Higgins raised his hands and stumbled backward, toward the open door. Con silently thanked the Good Lord that he'd been walking home from the Helmsley house when Elsa's protests called him from the shortcut that ran past the Merrick Hotel.

"Hands in the air, and step away from her." Con kept his voice low to avoid drawing Miles Peabody's attention. Why Elsa was outside by herself he didn't know, but this might give him a chance to talk to her alone. He wanted to make sure she would cooperate with Helmsley when he came calling first thing in the morning.

"Do it, Billy." Boone spoke loudly enough to raise the hotel. "Don't be stupid."

A light came on in the room Miles occupied. Con would have to end this quickly. "Do it now or regret it."

"Aw, don't shoot, Con." Billy moved away from Elsa and raised his hands. "See, I let her go."

"Keep on backing right through that doorway, and don't come out again."

"I'm doing it." Billy followed Boone into the hotel.

Con sighed his relief. He had no intention of shooting the miners, who must have tangled with a bottle of rotgut whiskey. Nor would he have risked a bullet ricocheting into the shaking woman next to him. He put an arm around her. "You're safe now."

Miles's voice rang out from upstairs.

Elsa gasped and clutched the front of Con's jacket. "I need to hide."

"Come with me." He took Elsa's instrument case and pulled her with him in the direction of the side steps. He helped Elsa down from the porch and guided her on the darkened path. She swung on her crutch so quickly that he restrained the urge to swing her into his arms. The last time he'd tried that hadn't turned out so well. They rounded the corner behind the hotel. just as voices rang out in front.

He hurried her along the short path that bent behind the saloon and followed the base of the hill past a row of cabins. Preferring his privacy, Con had built his cabin a little apart from the others beside a stand of aspen trees.

The cabin door gave under his hand. He struck a match, and the scent of sulphur infused the air. The lantern sputtered and flamed to life, making shadows jump.

Elsa stood inside the door, propped on her crutch, her eyes wide.

He gestured to a bench at the table. "Sit down."

"What is this place?" Her voice came out barely above a whisper.

He gave her a reassuring smile. "My cabin."

If anything, her eyes widened more. "It's not proper for me to be alone with a man in his home."

"I'm afraid it's necessary, but no one else needs to know."

She limped to the bench and sat down. "Thank you for saving me."

At the thought of what could have happened to her if he hadn't, Con's tension returned. He strode to the window and peered out. No one had followed. The ruckus Miles had raised appeared to be contained at the hotel and was already dying down.

Well, good.

He'd keep watch for a while, just in case. Miles knew of Con's interest in Elsa but not about his cabin. Billy and Boone had seen him with Elsa but probably wouldn't remember anything in the morning. Helmsley knew of his concern too, but Con doubted betrayal would come from that direction. As long as they kept quiet, Elsa would remain safe under his protection.

He lit the stove to warm the place, then tidied Shane's old rope bed for her. Later, he would sleep in the tiny separate room. Hopefully, that would quiet her qualms. He didn't want to compromise her reputation, but he could think of no better solution for tonight.

Elsa looked drowsy-eyed when he sat across from her at the table, but he needed to understand what he was involved in. "Tell me your story."

She gazed at him for a moment with unreadable eyes, then nodded. "Miles and Alicia Peabody brought me from Germany. I signed their contract to play my hurdy-gurdy, sing, and dance for the miners. But I didn't understand what they would expect from me."

Con listened without interrupting.

"They were taking me—" Her voice strangled off, and she heaved in a breath. "They were taking me to Atticus Merrick. He especially likes me." Her face took on color, and she looked down at the tabletop. "I think he wants me for his mistress."

Con jumped to his feet and gripped the rough window sill. He didn't doubt that the owner of the Merrick Hotel would buy a woman against her will. "That doesn't have to happen."

"I ran away to avoid it." She shook her head. "I won't go back to my companions. Miles and Alicia are not brother and sister, as they pretend."

"I suspected as much."

"I'm not sure whether those are even their real names."

Con came around and rested his hands lightly on her shoulders. "I won't let them hurt you anymore."

She glanced up with a look of trusting innocence. "Thank you."

Con mumbled something and turned away. She must have family in Germany. He ought to ship her straight back to them. The fact that he didn't want to had nothing to do with anything.

America's tea cup clattered into its saucer. Maisey Wilcox, seated across the oak table in her kitchen, jumped and lifted a startled face. America shook her head. "That's the third time I've asked you the same question."

"Sorry." Maisey put down her cup, which she'd held without drinking from for several minutes. "I was thinking."

"I could tell. What's on your mind?" America asked, although she thought she knew the answer. Ever since Rob Walsh had ridden out to look for his brother, Maisey's attention had been hard to claim.

Maisey bit her lip. "I can't help but wonder how Rob is faring."

"I'd like the answer to that too."

"He had such high hopes when he left. I'd hate to see them dashed."

"For all our sakes, let's not anticipate the worst." The window above the sink framed a blue sky dotted with gray clouds. Storms had soaked the area of late, but America had thought them blown over.

Maisey pulled her gaze from America's face. "Your cousin's disappearance must be hard to take."

"Yes, for both of us. Shane is especially close with Con, and I grew fond of him when I lived in Virginia City. I've always suspected—but he'll never admit—that Con pretended an interest in me to inspire Shane to court me himself." America laughed. "If so, it worked."

Maisey joined in her laughter. "Your cousin sounds like a character."

"That's a fair assessment. Con knows how to have fun, but there's a side he keeps hidden from all but a few."

Maisey's face grew pensive. "Rob is the same."

"Must be a family trait. Bry keeps to herself, as well." America frowned. "Con's return seems less likely the longer we wait, but we still hope for it."

"I can't imagine what you and Shane have gone through."

"It's not been easy." America picked up her cup and cradled its warmth in her hands. "My husband is beside himself with the longing to join Rob."

Maisey's brown eyes widened. "Will he go?"

"I suppose so." America schooled her expression into neutral lines, but her heart obeyed less easily. She didn't want Shane to go off on what might prove a foolhardy expedition.

Impulsive as ever and eager to search for his brother, Rob had left too early in the season for safe travel through the passes. She only hoped he had the sense to turn around if the need arose. She said none of this to Maisey, who already worried too much about Rob.

It wasn't hard to figure out the feelings between the pair. America, of all people, knew how hard surrendering to love could be, but Rob and Maisey would both be better off to admit the truth.

She worried about Maisey. Her friend at times seemed mired in gloom. Maisey had suffered a great deal when she and Bry had fallen into the hands of the Cheyenne. How did a person recover from seeing her husband slain before her eyes? If that wasn't bad enough, circumstances had parted her from her young daughter without Maisey knowing whether the child lived.

America knew something about suffering, but she also knew of the soul's resilience. Five-year-old Phoebe's return had brought a new spark to her mother. The same age as her own sweet Liberty, Phoebe was a mischievous sprite who had captured America's heart.

The poor child's separation from her mother, a plight not uncommon on the Oregon Trail, had ended when the carriage drew up and the Mathers returned Phoebe to her mother. America would never forget the joy on Maisey's face when she realized her daughter remained alive.

Boots stomped on the back porch, and the door opened, sending a rectangle of sunlight across the kitchen floorboards. Shane stood in the doorway, so handsome that America's heart beat faster. Three years after their marriage, gazing on him still sent a thrill through her stomach.

America rose and went to her husband. He embraced her and dropped a kiss on the top of her head. "The last of the spring crops went in today, at least the ones our congregation needed help with."

America knew what that meant, although she didn't want to voice it. The time had come for Shane to leave. She touched her stomach, already swelling with their third child. It would be so easy to keep him here with her.

A sigh parted her lips. She couldn't take the choice from the man she loved.

Rob camped along Alder Creek on the outskirts of Virginia City. He would wait for daylight to look for Con's claim. He didn't trust his ability to find it, although Shane had drawn a map. Lines on paper didn't always translate well into actual places.

His fire crackled to life, contained in a ring of stones. While his coffee percolated, he sat on a log and gnawed elk jerky. He'd picked a spot near a group of miners for company, but far enough away for privacy. "Forty Mile City" they called the tents and cabins that sprang up along Alder Creek after the discovery of gold. That was four years ago, and the communities birthed by the Alder Stampede were in full swing. Although the gold had slowed a bit, Alder Creek could still reward the diligent.

The excitement of a mining camp always pulled at Rob. He'd made up his mind to seek his own fortune, rather than rely on Con's wealth to sustain him. That would be true whether or not his brother lived. A man needed to make his own way in the world.

Maisey's face rose before him as he'd last seen it, with lips parted and eyes wide. He frowned. Upsetting her brought him no joy. She'd seemed distracted and unsettled by his leaving. Maybe he should have stayed away after helping Shane build her cabin, instead of finding reasons to spend time with her. He'd encouraged her to rely on his company, but he didn't want her to miss him when he sought his fortune elsewhere.

Well, at least not too much.

Rob couldn't deny that he liked the interest Maisey showed in him. It was too late to harden his heart against her, but that didn't matter. He wouldn't settle down with a wife until he had something that wasn't borrowed from his brother to offer her.

With the stars shining in a clear sky, he spread his rubber blanket on the ground rather than rigging it overhead with the ropes that had secured his bedroll. Lying on his back, he flung his hand over his forehead and gazed into the heavenly lights. How small he felt in creation, too unimportant for the Almighty to care about. Talking to God never came easy, but he was overdue.

Dear Lord, finding my brother seems impossible to me, but I know it isn't too much for you. Wherever Con is tonight, keep him safe.

Elsa sat up with a cry. She stared about her, willing herself to have courage. Something, whether in her dream world or the real one, had woken her to a sense of peril.

An owl hooted, and she glanced toward the window above the cabin sink. Had an intruder imitated the bird call? The grayness of a moonlit night lurked beyond the panes, but nothing more. Her uneasiness lingered, and she turned her head to gaze about the dim cabin.

Two shadows crept toward Con's bedroom, and a dark figure bent over her.

She hauled in the breath to scream.

A hand clamped over her mouth. "You don't want to do that," Miles murmured in her ear.

She twisted and shoved at him, but to no avail.

"There's a girl, take your medicine." He shifted his hand and covered her nose, then pressed a flask to her mouth so firmly the rim ground her lip against her teeth.

Con's voice called out in challenge, followed by the sick

sound of flesh slapping flesh.

Elsa's head spun with the need to breathe. She opened her mouth, and the foul-tasting liquid poured in. Forced to swallow, she gasped in air when he pulled the flask away.

A crash from the other room turned her head. "What are they doing to him?"

"Beating him within an inch of his life, if I have my way."

"*No!*" Elsa tried to stand but the pain in her ankle kept her from putting her foot down. She fell sideways.

Miles caught and lifted her. "Don't concern yourself about that bog-trotter, Elsa. Not when a man like Atticus Merrick waits for you."

CHAPTER TEN

"Con, wake up!"

Helmsley's voice dragged Con to the surface of what felt like a murky pond. He pried one eye open but the other remained closed.

The sheriff's concerned face hovered above him. "What happened to *you*?"

"Boone and Billy."

Helmsley wrapped an arm around Con's back and propped him up on the floor, where he'd landed after the last punch. "What bone did those two good-for-nothings have to pick with you?"

"They didn't say, but I could guess."

The sheriff squinted in the sunlight falling through the open door. "Have anything to do with that German woman?"

"They didn't like my standing up for her."

Helmsley whistled. "No wonder they left town this morning."

"Where's Miss Meier?" If they'd taken Elsa, Con would chew up the countryside until he found her.

"She's not with them." The sheriff laid a restraining hand against his chest. "She left on the stage to Virginia City with that couple you told me about."

Con scowled. "Why would she do that?" He staggered to his feet with only a little help from Helmsley.

"That's what I've been asking myself. Trouble is, she wasn't awake. Made me think of your story about those two drugging her, so I asked questions."

Con held onto the table for support. "And?"

Helmsley shook his head. "I couldn't find a reason to detain them."

"Couldn't you have invented one?" Con jerked out the words, then reminded himself that Sheriff Helmsley didn't know everything Elsa had told him. His mouth felt dry, so he reached for the water pitcher on the table. It crashed to the floor.

"Careful there." Helmsley reached out to him. "Maybe you'd better sit down."

Con pulled away. "If you want to help, find me a horse."

"You're not fit to ride anywhere."

"I'm sturdy enough, and you know it."

Helmsley avoided his gaze. "I'm not sure you should go after them."

Con stared at him in disbelief. "Why would you say that?"

"Miles Peabody showed me a letter from a Doctor Weiss in Germany." Helmsley paused, his mouth working.

"Let me guess—"

"It stated that Elsa Meier is his lunatic cousin for whom he has authority to dispense medication."

"I don't care what some trumped-up—"

"It bears the seal of the Idelmar Institution in Wiesbaden."

Con tensed. "Miles either faked that letter or bribed someone to write it."

Helmsley gave a quick shake of his head. "With no proof of wrongdoing, I had to let them go."

"But I told you what was going on."

"Once again, your opinion does not qualify as evidence."

"Elsa fears that the Peabodys are taking her to Atticus Merrick to become his mistress."

Helmsley shook his head. "I can't arrest anyone on the basis of someone's fears."

Con gave up on convincing the sheriff. The letter seemed to have swayed him, and Helmsley couldn't move past his prejudices. The pain in Con's gut made him want to curl into a fetal position, but he started for the open doorway. He'd almost reached it when his legs gave out. He crashed to the floor, moaning.

Helmsley propped him up.

"Find me a horse." Con spoke between gasps, his teeth gritted.

"Not today, Con. If I can't get you to rest any other way, I'll lock you up for disorderly conduct."

Con clutched his stomach, panting in pain. "You win, but I'm riding out tomorrow."

"Suit yourself." Helmsley sighed. "I sure hope she's worth all this trouble."

Reluctant to stir from the warmth of his bedroll, Rob kept his eyes closed and drifted in and out of slumber. Dawn soon broke across the sky, and he gave up trying to sleep. He crawled from his bedroll, built a fire and made coffee, then packed his sparse belongings.

The road took him in the direction of Virginia City. Birds sang in a frenzied chorus, and the scent of wildflowers drifted to him as he traveled down the green lane. His spirits lifted with the last of the darkness, and he pressed onward with renewed zeal. He would find his brother or hear word of him, whether in this city or somewhere else.

He shouldn't have feared not finding Con's old mining

cabin, for he came upon it readily. A giant cottonwood tree stood as a sentinel on the path, exactly like Shane's map indicated. He darted glances about while passing under its shadow. The cabin hunched on a bank above the creek, with mist rising in lazy spirals off the water. No smoke curled from the chimney. The windows stared at him with dead eyes.

Rob dismounted and left his horse to graze the lush grass while he tried the door. It creaked open on rusty hinges. He stepped inside, struck at once by the odor of dust and disuse. Wavering light reflected off the creek's surface and shone in the window above the kitchen counter.

Once inside, Rob searched for a note or some other clue to his brother's whereabouts. He picked up an unopened flour sack from the floor and thumped it onto the table. Tins and bottles lay tumbled on the shelves or scattered across the kitchen counter. Broken crockery strewed the floor. Rumpled linens spilled over the rope bed in the sleeping room.

Con had always been neat and tidy. He would not have left his cabin in this state. His brother must have been rushed, or an intruder had made a mess of the abandoned place.

Rob turned and went outside. Disappointment choked his throat. His brother wasn't here. After the long trip, he needed a rest. He would ask after Con in town, then ride out in the morning.

Shane tilted America's face to the light, revealing the marks of tears. He traced his thumb over her cheek, as if to erase his wife's suffering. "I'll be careful."

She lifted her chin in the way he loved best, for it told him that she accepted and owned the sacrifices of a preacher's wife. "Mind that you do." Adopting an Irish accent, she gave him a look that made him wish he didn't have to ride away.

He grinned and lowered his mouth to hers for a kiss that left his feelings in no doubt. She clung to him, then slowly let go. He ran a finger along her jawline. "Lock the door every night while I'm away."

"Of course." She spoke with confidence, but the shadows lurking in her amber eyes told him that staying alone on the edge of town wasn't easy.

"If you have the slightest worry, don't hesitate to tell the neighbors. The Buckthorns have promised to take you in, if need be, while I'm away."

America nodded the way she always did when he left. Shane kissed her trembling lips one last time for good measure, then bent to say goodbye to Liberty and Seth. Liberty begged for a horsey ride, and he gave her one. Seth clung to his mother's skirts but came forward to shake his father's hand.

Shane stepped into Archibald's saddle and tilted his hat to shade out the sun. With a wave to his family, he left them behind.

This trip was the same as countless others he'd taken, but not in all ways. Shane normally carried less food, content to rely on his hunting skills to provide. That would take more time than he could afford, starting out days behind Rob.

He knew his cousin planned to look for Con in Bannack and Virginia City before heading east. It gave Shane a chance to catch up with him, but he'd have to push his horse. He patted Archibald's neck. "Extra oats for your trouble, old boy."

The crossroads loomed ahead. Shane turned east beyond the serviceberry bushes that lined the way. The sunshine sent shadows racing along the ground beside his horse. Grass, green from the spring rains, waved on the banks of the Bitterroot River. The waterway winked in and out of sight until the road pulled beside it for a time. The breeze coming off the water brought a fresh scent that revived him.

He would spend the night at Con's ranch, then head out before dawn. His thoughts turned to America, who would sleep alone in their bed tonight. *Lord, keep her safe.*

Shane had learned to cope with constant peril as a circuit preacher. Even so, he added a similar prayer for himself.

Con peered out the barred window of his jailhouse. Helmsley was nowhere in sight. Con pounded his hand against the sturdy log wall. When the good sheriff returned, he would give him a piece of his mind.

Helmsley shifted further down in Con's estimate, already low after the lawman had failed to intervene for Elsa. Miles could be convincing, but Helmsley should have been less trusting.

The sheriff had prevented Con from riding out for two days now. With Elsa in trouble, that was unacceptable. He paced his small cell until his strength wore out and he collapsed onto the cot. The pain in Con's belly was mending fast, but he needed to conserve his strength to go after Elsa.

Assuming Helmsley ever lets me go.

With nothing to do but worry and fret, Con drifted in and out of sleep.

A familiar voice roused him. Con lurched to his feet, clanking with every movement. The jailhouse contained no cells, but chains locked to manacles secured his ankles. The heavy iron links attached to eyebolts embedded in the floor. He wrapped his hands around the window bars. "Helmsley, let me out of here!"

The sheriff came into view, carrying a basket that no doubt contained Con's supper. He opened the door and stepped inside.

"Did you hear me?" Con shouted.

"Of course I did." Helmsley pushed his hat back. "Me and anyone else this side of town."

"Let me go."

"I can't do that yet, Con, for reasons you already know."

Con groaned. "It takes a lot of nerve to lock a man up without cause."

Helmsley didn't look at him. "You disturbed the peace."

"*What*? By insisting on going after Miss Meier? There isn't a judge in the territory who would convict me."

The sheriff shook his head. "I'm not going to haul you before a judge."

"Why would you, after stretching the truth like you did?"

"I didn't. You disturbed *my* peace. You're bothering it now, in fact."

Con gritted his teeth. "I'm trying to reason with you."

"Oh, really? Seems more like bellowing."

"We both know you mean to delay me from riding out of town."

Helmsley grinned. "That's a happy result, I'll admit. You can be hot-headed, if you didn't notice."

Con had heard that complaint from his sister often enough. He wouldn't give Helmsley joy by admitting it, though. "If you cherish peace and quiet so much, why keep me here?"

"Because you're not in a fit state to meddle in other folks' affairs."

"What if I've come to think of them as my own?"

"I was afraid of that. Forget her, Con. She's tetched."

"You don't know that for certain."

"Why would you want to put it to the test?" Helmsley shook his head. "Never mind, I know why. She's pretty."

Con couldn't explain in a way Helmsley would believe—or that he himself could understand—but he felt as if he knew Elsa. She was a gentle dove caught in a cat's jaws -- wounded but not beyond rescue.

Con scratched at the scar from his arrow wound, and his mind wandered into the past. The injury had puzzled him during his bout of amnesia. How could he have forgotten receiving it? At the time, he had been too weak to do more than crawl out of harm's way. After fainting, he'd come to with searchers calling his name. If not for Nick Laramie's drag sled hauling him to the wagon camp for medical attention, Con would not be alive now.

Helmsley shoved the basket at Con, and his thoughts returned to the present. "Here."

Con took his meal but didn't respond. It came to him that rescuing Elsa would be a lot like going back in time and saving himself. He lifted the red-gingham napkin and discovered an ample slice of meat pie, a portion of vegetables that looked reconstituted, a cup of applesauce, and a pale drink in a jar.

He bit into the pie and took a swig of vinegar lemonade, then challenged Helmsley with a look. "You can't keep me locked up forever."

Helmsley sighed. "I'll release you tomorrow."

A mourning dove sobbed in the cottonwood tree, a melancholy sound that brought a lump to Rob's throat. The light, diminished at this hour, glowed with a yellowish hue behind the blackened trees. Beyond Con's cabin, Alder Creek rushed between its banks, adding a low murmur to the dove's lament.

Rob's inquiries had gone as expected. No one he'd spoken with in Virginia City had seen Con since he'd gone east. Shoulders slumped, he followed the path back to the cabin. He had taken to the road with high hopes, but also with the knowledge that he might not find his brother alive.

But I have to go on. He'd pass the night in Con's cabin, then start for the passes in the morning. There was nothing worse than an untold story, an unsolved mystery, or a lost family member. Con's disappearance imposed all three on those who loved him.

Rob's thoughts drifted into the past. He should have welcomed Con more warmly when he arrived at their tenement in the Manhattan slum to escort his family to his ranch. Con showing up out of the blue after an absence of several years was a shock. Their brother had missed Bry's marriage to Ian, the husband who had widowed her. He'd also missed their father's death.

That last omission rankled Rob the most, forcing him to push past his resentment to go to Con's ranch. With the wisdom of hindsight, Rob saw that he had his brother to thank for a decision that had changed him for the better. He would go forward from here, never backward.

The cabin door stood like a sentinel guarding secrets, and he approached it with a sense of unease. It somehow looked different from his earlier visit. Night shadows crouched in the twilight, like wolves ready to spring.

Rob let himself inside and struck a match to find his lantern.

Sulphur clogged his throat, but the small flame that flared, however briefly, brought courage. He fumbled with the lantern, and soon its friendly light glowed throughout the cabin.

The damp air chilled his bones. He lit a fire in the stove from the scant supply of split logs in the wood box. He would fill it in the morning, ready should his brother return.

After a quick meal of beans and corn cakes, Rob did his best to restore a semblance of order. It was the least he could do to honor his fastidious brother. Much later, he bedded down in Con's rope bed. With the creek swishing outside, he closed his eyes and let the mourning dove's lament lull him to sleep.

Restless dreams disturbed his slumber. Con ran ahead of him in a forest, but Rob couldn't catch up. He heard Maisey weeping nearby but couldn't find her in the mist. He came upon Bry lying close to death—

A hand on his shoulder shook him awake.

Rob started and reached for his gun. His hand slid into an empty holster.

A trigger clicked. "Looking for this?"

A dark figure limned by the moonlight falling through the window challenged him.

Rob squinted but couldn't make out features. "Who are you?"

"I was fixin' to ask *you* that. What are you doing on my claim?"

Rob's thoughts grew to fever pitch. Had he entered the wrong cabin by mistake?

No. Shane had drawn the map well, and the large cottonwood was unmistakable. Hadn't his lantern been waiting on the table where he'd left it? "I don't know who you are, mister, but this is my brother's cabin."

"Maybe it used to be." The intruder slammed the gun butt

against Rob's head with a *thunk*.

Rob tensed to fight back, but blackness crowded the edges of sight, and the intruder's last words came from far away.

"It's mine now."

CHAPTER ELEVEN

SUDDEN COLD SHOCKED ROB AWAKE. WATER closed over his head, and he barely resisted the instinct to draw breath. The current carried him downstream. He bumped the creek bed, then thrust upward. He gasped sweet air into his lungs. A grassy bank slid by above him.

An undertow sucked him downward. Rob fought free, scraping against submerged rocks. He surfaced and swam diagonally to the bank, where he grasped at clumps of grass and other vegetation leaning into the water. The water tugged him onward.

His arm hooked something. The current dragged at him, but he kept hold of the submerged root that had stopped him. He pulled himself toward the bank and heaved upward but fell back panting. It was all he could do to hang on.

He tried again. Blackness pressed Rob's vision, and he slipped into the water. He clung once more to the root, but his fingers were cramping. In seconds, he'd be swept away. With the strength of desperation, he hauled himself partway out of the water.

Another kind of current pulled him into the depths of darkness . . .

Rob opened his eyes. Shivers wracked his body, regardless of the sun shining down on him. Ignoring the pain in his head and the urge to vomit, he heaved himself fully onto the creek bank. He moaned and fell onto the soft ground beneath the tree.

Rob woke to ribbons of sunlight slanting low across the

water. The serrated leaves of an alder tree waved above him. The tree's shade had shifted to cover him while he slept.

Rob sat up, gritting his teeth against the pain. A crane fly whirred past his ear and hovered above the creek before moving downstream. A breeze whipped through the grass and ruffled Rob's hair. With nothing to do but think, he frowned at his foolhardiness. Challenging the claim jumper had been a mistake. The man must have thrown him in the creek to drown.

Rob had no intention of obliging the claim jumper by dying. If he wanted to live, though, he needed to walk – in a moment. Right now he needed to lean against the tree and closed his eyes to shut out the world's spinning.

"Are you all right?" A red-bearded man stood over him.

Rob squinted to see the man better. He'd raised his brows, and creases marked his forehead. Dressed in brown duck pants and a red flannel shirt, he was probably a miner. "I'm injured."

The miner gave a swift nod. "I saw Tate Weatherby try to kill you. That claim jumper took a horse from the stable at the cabin and lit out. I came looking for you. 'Course, I thought I'd be burying a body." He narrowed his eyes. "Who are you, anyway? What were you doing on that claim?"

"I'm Rob Walsh, and that's my brother's property"

The man broke into a grin. "You're Con's brother? Haven't seen him for quite a spell. I'm his nearest neighbor, Cecil Brown." The miner examined him from clear, gray eyes. "Where do you hurt?"

Rob touched the sore place on his crown. "I have quite a lump on my head."

"May I?" The man's fingers probed Rob's scalp. "I don't think it's anything to worry about, but you never know with these things. Better to play it safe and let someone watch over you tonight."

"That's not possible." Rob gritted his teeth at the pain. "I'm traveling alone."

"I can put you up if you don't mind sharing my slapped-together cabin. It's better than sleeping on the ground out in the open, and I'll be there to keep an eye on you."

"Thanks." Rob struggled to rise.

Cecil pulled Rob to his feet and threw an arm around his shoulders. "Let's get you patched up."

"I hope you show enough sense to stay put until you're mended." Helmsley turned the key, and the second manacle clanked to the jailhouse floor.

"Don't think on it, and you'll be a happier man." Con rubbed his ankles, chafed by the manacles during his constant pacing. He'd never much liked tight places and had spent entirely too much time in this one.

Helmsley gave him a look that showed he knew exactly what Con had in mind. "Be careful, will you? For my sake?"

Con inched a little closer toward forgiving the man. Helmsley's tactics might have been wrong, but his concern seemed genuine. Con twisted his lips in a rueful smile. "I can't recall the word *careful* ever guiding my life."

Helmsley grunted. "You'd be better off."

The sheriff stepped aside to let him out of the tiny building, but Con went to look out the window a final time. Partway up the gulch stood the gallows, the only view the jailhouse afforded.

Helmsley came up behind him. "Funny how things happen. Sheriff Plummer built those gallows, only to be lynched on them."

Con faced him. "Some say that the vigilantes became more of a problem than the crimes they wanted to cure."

Helmsley shrugged. "Any time untrained folks take the law into their own hands, there's bound to be trouble. The miners' committee demanded that the vigilantes leave town a couple months ago. They promised to return any offenses five-fold."

Con shuddered. "I'm not sorry to leave this place."

Helmsley gave a swift nod. "Can't say as I blame you."

Con went out the door and headed for the livery stable. It would take two days to reach Virginia City.

Elsa would have arrived by now. At the thought, he picked up his pace.

Elsa opened her eyes and blinked until the room shifted into focus. She was lying in a four-poster bed hung with a fringed canopy of gold satin. A gilded cherub graced the mirror above a vanity with a cushioned, velvet seat. The washstand stood in one corner beside a tri-fold dressing screen. The screen panels depicted a mansion, complete with swans and stone stairs.

Cream-colored curtains lay open in folds across a window that reached to the high ceiling. Dark wood paneling adorned the walls. Paintings of the same woman in different poses hung from the picture rail that circled the room.

Elsa shivered. Each likeness watched her with a compelling gaze similar to Atticus's description of that actress he favored, Ada Mencken.

Miles and Alicia must have brought her to Virginia City, collected whatever payment Atticus offered, and were on their way out of town.

Well, good riddance.

Outside the grilled window, a stand of cottonwoods shadowed the lonely road. What had happened to Con the night Miles took her from his cabin? Elsa winced at the memory of the sounds she'd heard. She hoped he remained alive. If the two people who'd slipped into his room had killed him, she would forever blame herself. Why should Con suffer when she alone had landed herself in this predicament? From now on, she would rely only on herself for deliverance and avoid causing harm to anyone else.

She searched the paintings for the resemblance to herself that Atticus mentioned. She and Ada each had plump lips and deep-set eyes. Elsa's eyes, however, were not dark like Ada's but hazel. Ada's face curved in soft lines that her own lacked, a result of going hungry too often.

In Germany, Elsa had always held back at meals and allowed her younger brothers and sisters to take most of the food. She'd hidden her discomfort from *Mutter*. In America, she could eat her fill, at least when she was not missing meals while sleeping off that wretched drug.

The thought of food stirred Elsa's appetite, but she had no idea when she might dine again. She swung her legs out of bed and reached for her crutch, leaning against the wall. She opened the closet, hoping to find her clothes.

Light from a high window centered in the outer wall fell over an array of fine clothing in rich fabrics and colors. Her own simple dress, made from brown linsey-woolsey, was nowhere in sight. Hat boxes lined a shelf, with several pairs of shoes below that. She touched soft velvets, smooth silks, and fine wools, but then snatched her hand back.

Whoever owned these clothes would not appreciate her

handling them. The suspicion that Atticus had bought this wardrobe for *her* gnawed at Elsa's mind. Either way, she felt vulnerable standing barefoot in her chemise.

The *clip-clop* of hooves and rattle of harnesses outside decided her. She struggled into a red and blue plaid dress and brown kid boots that fit fairly well, once buttoned. Elsa pulled a coat from one of the closet hooks and hurried to the door.

The knob turned under her hand, but the door did not open. She tried yanking on the knob. The door shuddered but remained closed.

Footsteps belonging to more than one person drew closer outside her door.

Elsa shrank against the wall, chest heaving. She darted glances about, then spied the fireplace poker in its stand, the only available weapon. She hobbled toward it.

Metal grated on metal, the sound of a key turning.

Elsa wanted to weep. The poker seemed a poor defense. She didn't have sufficient strength to wield it, and her injured ankle might hinder her.

The door swung inward.

"Put that down." Miles took a step toward her.

"Don't come near me." Elsa raised the poker like a sword.

He halted. His gaze traveled from the poker to her face. "Well, well, the mouse has spirit, after all. I can almost understand what Atticus sees in her."

"Shut up, Miles." Alicia rushed into the room carrying a basket over her arm.

Elsa glared at him. "You kidnapped me."

Miles gave a smug smile. "I felt it my duty to remove you from a compromising situation."

"What did those men do to Mr. Walsh?"

He shrugged. "I neither know nor care."

She stared at him, rendered speechless, but then found her voice. "You're horrible."

"He's the one who gave them cause to pick a fight with him."

"How much did you pay them to beat him up?"

He smirked. "They'll be in whisky money for a while."

"That's enough!" The sharp cry drew Elsa's attention to Alicia. "You shouldn't joke, Miles. Can't you see Elsa is overwrought?" She lifted the basket. "We've brought you food."

Elsa shook her head, although the aroma of fried chicken made her knees weak. "I don't want *anything* from you."

"Be reasonable." Alicia started toward her. "You need nourishment."

"Go away." Elsa's voice wavered. She wanted to reject their offering, but she wouldn't regain her strength by refusing to eat.

Alicia sidled closer. "There's fried chicken, soda biscuits, baked beans, and even a jar of lemonade."

Elsa's chin quivered, and she lowered her weapon.

"I'll take that." Miles relieved her of the poker but didn't return it to the stand.

"Why are you still in town?" Elsa spat out the question.

Miles leaned a shoulder against the wall. "Don't worry. You'll see the last of us once Atticus comes back and pays us."

"He's away?" Hope lilted Elsa's voice.

"We must have passed him somewhere on the road. He's gone to Bannack. Too bad we didn't know he was headed there. It would have saved us the trouble of escorting you the rest of the way here." He pulled a chicken leg out of Alicia's basket and bit into it.

Alicia frowned at Miles, then smiled at Elsa. "You must be starved." She unpacked the contents of the basket onto a small table against the wall and sank into one of the lyre-back chairs that bracketed the table. "Come and eat."

"Escorting?" Elsa passed Miles on her way to the table. "Is that what you call it?"

He opened his mouth, but Alicia gave a brief shake of her head. She raised her eyebrows. "Don't you have something to do downstairs, Miles?"

"I suppose so." He pushed away from the wall. Instead of going to the door, though, he approached the table and stood over Elsa. "I have a word of advice for you, *Fräulein*."

She looked away. "I don't want it."

He lifted her chin until she met his gaze. "Don't cross Atticus. If you do, I promise you'll live to regret it." He strode to the doorway, then gave her a final glance before closing her into the room with Alicia.

Elsa's appetite deserted her, but she bit into a biscuit and chewed anyway. The food might have been sawdust for all she tasted of it. She put the biscuit down on a linen napkin and picked up her glass. "Where am I?"

Alicia's eyebrows shot up. "Haven't you guessed? This is Mr. Merrick's home in Virginia City. He'll come back from Bannack to find you waiting."

CHAPTER TWELVE

Shane rode into Bannack and dismounted in front of Chrisman's store. The usual gaggle of men chewed the fat around the fireplace. A few glanced up with surprised looks when he entered.

George Chrisman's spectacles magnified the widening of his eyes. He broke into a grin and came out from behind the counter. "It's been a long time, Preacher."

Shane crossed the floorboards to shake his hand. "Three years, in fact."

"Hard to believe, isn't it? What brings you to town?"

"I'm trying to catch up with my cousin Rob. How long ago did he come through town?"

Chrisman crossed his arms. "He stopped by a couple of days ago—three, I think—before going on to Virginia City."

"Thanks for the information. I'd better stable my horse." He started for the door.

"Wait!" Chrisman's voice halted him. "Don't you want to know about Con too?"

Shane whirled. "What about Con?"

"You and Rob both missed him. He came to town right after Rob left. He ran into trouble with the sheriff. It wasn't anything serious, but it did land him in jail for a couple of days. He rode out this morning headed for Virginia City, same as Rob."

Shane stared at the man, trying to credit what he'd said. "Con's . . . *alive*?"

"I'm sorry, Shane." Chrisman touched his arm. "I shouldn't

have blurted it out like that."

"Did he say where he's been all this time?"

"Not really. All I know is that he stepped off the stagecoach from Fort Hall."

Shane shook his head. "That's more than I knew a minute ago."

Chrisman walked with him to the door. "He mentioned having lost his memory."

"That would explain his long absence. Has he found it again?"

"I believe so, for the most part."

Shane glanced at the men around the fireplace, where all conversation had stopped. He moved closer to Chrisman and lowered his voice. "Then what's he doing in Virginia City? It's the last place Con would want to show his face."

Chrisman gave him a startled look. "You mean—"

"Con left his claim in a hurry for a reason."

Quick comprehension dawned on Chrisman's face. "He was one of Sheriff Plummer's deputies."

Shane nodded.

"I can't believe Con was one of the Innocents."

"He was never part of that gang of road agents," Shane hastened to explain. "Which was why he gave up his deputy badge. Con knew as much as Deputy Dillingham, God rest his soul."

"I thought he wanted to go with the rest of the miners who stampeded to Alder Gulch."

"He did, mostly. Con registered a claim in Virginia City and tried for a fresh start, but it wasn't far enough away for safety."

"I'd say not."

"Dillingham's murder by his fellow deputies, then the hanging of Sheriff Plummer and two of his men, settled Con's mind on the matter. My cousin was innocent of wrongdoing, but there's such a thing as guilt by association."

Chrisman nodded. "The vigilantes don't spare a man much time to explain himself. It's one reason the miners don't want them in Bannack anymore."

Shane shook his head. "With the Montana Vigilante headquarters in Virginia City, it makes no sense that Con would go there."

Chrisman glanced about, then moved nearer. "There's a woman. Her name is Elsa Meier, and I hear tell she's the prettiest lady we've seen hereabouts for a long while. From the way they say he acted, Con fell head over heels."

"Really?" Apart from Con's irritating display of interest in America, he'd shied away from women – the result of having his heart broken long ago. "I'd like to meet her."

"Go after your cousin, and I suspect you will." Chrisman pressed his lips together and said no more.

Shane decided against pressing the shopkeeper, not with the mercantile so silent and such nonchalant looks on the faces of those gathered there.

"That's what I aim to do." He touched his hat brim. "Good afternoon to you."

Shane wanted to push on, but with daylight fading and Archibald hanging his head, he would wait to ride out early in the morning. He stabled his horse in the livery, then turned his steps toward Con's cabin. He'd spend the night there for old time's sake.

The town that had been a thriving territorial capital clearly saw less industry these days. Shane recalled many boots pounding this boardwalk three years ago, but only a few walked it now. Grasshopper Creek ran along its course without throngs of miners panning on its banks. A wagon or horse could make its way down the once-teeming main street without encountering traffic.

Passing the Merrick Hotel brought memories crashing over him. He tasted again the bitter mud that filled his mouth after being thrown out of the hotel by Atticus. Virgil Henry wanted to shoot him, only to be stopped by America's protests. Shane smiled, recalling her indignation when he'd tried to protect her after Tendoy rode into town on his war pony.

The front door of the hotel opened. "Well, well. If it isn't Saint Preacher."

Shane didn't need to turn to know who had spoken. "Hello, Atticus."

"After abandoning your *sacred charges*, it takes nerve to show your face in Bannack again."

Shane clenched his teeth to resist being drawn into unwise words. He felt no need to explain himself, but Atticus was a soul in need of saving. Shane should remove any hindrance that might stand in the way.

By God's grace, he wouldn't fail in this duty. Shane lifted his head. "I merely transferred to a different area with another flock."

Atticus smirked. "Gave up, did you? Well, good riddance."

Shane held his temper. "I'm surprised you would trouble to keep this hotel, when your holdings in Virginia City must pay more."

"Maybe I'm fond of quiet." Atticus leaned against the door frame, his neutral expression slipping. He became, all at once, a world-weary man without a spark of hope to lighten the darkness of his soul.

Shane had to swallow before he could speak. "That's not a word anyone would have used for Bannack only a few years ago."

Atticus shrugged. "Times change."

"That they do," Shane murmured. This man had humiliated and pummeled him. Atticus had once beaten him so badly that he'd been bedridden. And yet, Shane could find it in himself to pity him.

He bid Atticus goodbye and continued on to Con's cabin, shaken by the realization. He'd allowed Atticus to defeat him due to his own shortcomings. He hadn't feared much in those days, except himself. After accidentally killing a man in the slums, he'd wanted nothing more to do with violence. It had taken several beatings and much soul searching to figure out that a man should defend himself and those he loved against usury.

Silence lay heavy on Con's cabin. Here he had broken the journey around his preaching circuit. He smiled, remembering how he and Con quibbled. It had always been so between them, yet with no lack of love. He supposed they were too much alike—impatient in different ways. Perhaps it was a family trait, for he saw it in Rob as well.

He frowned down at his old rope bed. The rumpled covers seemed out of place, with Con so tidy. He'd kept his bedroom door shut, but it hung open. Shane squinted. Bedding strewed the floor. He went through the doorway and halted inside the bedroom. The contents of Con's dresser had been pulled out of their drawers, and mirror shards scattered over the floor.

What had his cousin gotten himself into *this* time?

Con's horse stood fetlock-deep in the shallows at the edge of the Beaverhead River. Con gazed into shining waters that reflected a sky tinged by the first blush of sunset.

After today's hard ride, both he and his horse needed rest.

He would camp in this vast open valley between far-flung mountains in the shadow of a limestone monolith he recognized. The Shoshone had named Beaverhead Rock for its likeness to the head of its namesake creature. The formation reared above flat lands cut by waterways that snaked through the grasses at its feet. Clouds of geese and other fowl lifted above the surface or rode the currents, where fish jumped after hovering insects.

Con lifted his face to the breeze, and the wild wind flowed over him like the very breath of God. He would search for Elsa when he reached Virginia City tomorrow. He also wanted to see his claim.

Beyond that, he'd rather be anywhere else. The thought of showing his face in town didn't appeal. It had been several years since the lynching of Sheriff Plummer's deputies and other suspected members of the Innocents. Con could hope the vigilantes had short memories, at least where he was concerned.

The tasks before him seemed clear. He needed to find Elsa first of all, then figure out how to rescue her. This might prove difficult, considering that Atticus had sunk a lot of money into Virginia City.

He hobbled his horse for the night, spread his bedroll, and lay himself down to watch the sunset. A passage from the Bible drifted across his mind. "Take therefore no thought for the morrow: for the morrow shall take thought for the things of itself. Sufficient unto the day is the evil thereof."

Con would hold those words close tonight. Tomorrow he would face hardships, but tonight he slept under the stars in a place of beauty.

Rob leaned back in his chair and sipped the cooling coffee in his cup. He'd enjoyed the simple supper of fish stew and sourdough bread as well as Cecil's stories of life in a growing mining camp.

The miner's red hair and beard glowed in the light shed by a lantern strung above the scarred table. He pushed his plate aside with a sigh. "'Course, every claim around here is spoken for now. Ten thousand or more have piled into the area to seek their fortunes."

Rob frowned. "I guess I'll have to go elsewhere to pan for gold."

"Probably, unless you can use your brother's claim or somehow buy one. Unscrupulous folks, like the fellow you tangled with, move in on abandoned claims, but I wouldn't recommend that." He shook his head. "It's funny to think how this all started."

Rob sensed another story coming on.

Cecil folded his arms. "While prospecting in Yellowstone country, a miner from Bannack named Bill Fairweather and five of his friends fell into the hands of Crow Indians, and were instructed to leave the area. This they were anxious to do, so they took a shortcut home and camped in Alder Gulch. They wanted to buy tobacco and so panned for gold along the selfsame creek outside this cabin."

Cecil glanced around his home, little more than a gap-sided hovel, with pride gleaming in his eyes. "They found plenty."

Rob could imagine the excitement the men must have felt at their discovery. "They could have been rich as Croesus if they'd kept it to themselves. Why did they let on to so many others?"

Cecil smiled. "They didn't mean to. After they showed up in Bannack with gold to spare, folks caught on. They acquired quite a few fans. Every time one of them made a move, hopeful miners followed. They finally gave up and led the way to Alder Gulch. I was one of hundreds who filed up Hangman's Gulch on the way out of town in the Alder Stampede."

He chuckled. "We took every horse that could go and any ox that could shoulder a pack. Others followed on foot, carrying blankets with coffee pots, fry pans, picks, shovels, and all manner of equipment hanging from them."

"That must have been a sight to see."

"Indeed it was."

"When I return, I'd like to try my hand at mining."

Cecil raised his eyebrows. "I still think you should tell the sheriff what Tate did."

Rob considered the idea, yet again, and came to the same conclusion. "I've already lost two days. That would delay my departure even more."

Cecil's chair creaked back to stand on two legs. "I'll be sorry to see you go. Con used to visit, but since he left I don't get much company."

"If I come back this way, I'll stop by. Thanks for patching me up."

"Glad to. You leaving right away?"

Rob nodded. "Tomorrow."

"Are you sure you've mended enough? The ride into the mountains taxes a body."

Rob laid a hand over the bruised ribs Cecil had taped. "I'll be all right."

"I'd feel better if you waited for the snow to melt from the passes."

"I'm not going that way."

Cecil's chair legs thumped on the floor. "Have you thought this through?"

"If I'd done that, I'd never have left the ranch."

"The Bozeman road isn't the safest route these days. Why don't you travel to Fort Sedgwick by the southern route?"

"I planned to, but traveling through Sioux country seems

safer than risking the snow."

Cecil shook his head. "I can't decide if you're the bravest or most foolish man I've met."

"I can make it. A rider alone has a better chance of going undetected than a wagon train, and I can stop at the new forts along the road."

Cecil drained his coffee cup and thumped it down. "What's the hurry?"

Rob stared at him. "My brother is missing."

"Same as he was last summer, but I didn't see you looking for him then."

"We thought he might come home on his own. Then we had word he was alive, but he didn't come home. It wasn't easy to break away from minding his ranch and looking after my sister. I set out late in the season but had to turn back to wait for spring. It would be hard to tolerate another delay."

Cecil gave a nod. "You love your brother, that's clear."

"If anyone had to die, I'd rather it was me."

"Take the Bozeman Road, and you might get your wish." Cecil stood and stretched. "Sleep on it, why don't you?"

Rob shook his head. "I've made up my mind."

Cecil frowned. "Then I guess there's nothing more to say. Still, I wish you'd think of your brother."

"What do you mean? That's who I *am* thinking about."

"Is that right?" Cecil's gaze pierced him.

"Of course it is."

"Seems to me that if you want what's best for Con, you won't deprive him of a brother by trespassing into the Powder River Valley during Red Cloud's War."

Rob pushed back his chair. "Goodnight, Cecil."

America sat up in bed. What unearthly racket had woken her?

The yowling came again.

She hurried to her bedroom window, pulled aside the curtains, and peered across the moonlit yard toward the barn. Shane liked the half-wild cats that hid in the hay because they kept the rodents out of the barn, but America couldn't get used to their caterwauling.

These were probably only mating calls, but America wished they wouldn't raise such a ruckus with Shane gone. Living on the outskirts of town made their holding more vulnerable, as she had learned during last year's attack by Kicking Horse and his band of renegades.

About to let the curtain fall, she stiffened. The barn door hung partway open, but she'd shut it after feeding the horses

The door opened farther, and a long shadow stretched over the ground. Another shadow ran beside a figure outlined in moonlight crossing the yard to join the first. Both slipped inside.

America turned her head to look for other intruders. Horses tossed their heads, the feathers tied to their manes flying like ghosts in the moonlight. Heart pounding, she leaned against the wall and caught her breath. She had feared this very thing happening with Shane away. In the daytime such worries seemed nonsensical, but at night they gained merit.

She rushed down the hall, praying the commotion hadn't awakened the children. The door to Liberty's room creaked open beneath her hand. Her daughter, curled beneath the covers, never stirred. She checked Seth next. Her son had kicked off his bedclothes but otherwise slept peacefully. She covered him, then pulled the door closed. America turned toward the kitchen.

Time to take the gun down from its pegs above the back door.

Cradling the weapon, America crept to the kitchen window. The barn door remained ajar, and horses' squeals pierced the night. Anger shook through her at being robbed, but she did not venture out. She would not shoot another mortal to protect property. To save her children's lives, however, she wouldn't hesitate.

Two Indians emerged from the barn, leading her family's horses. Several others appeared but didn't follow down the road. Instead, they rounded the bend to vanish behind the barn. America hauled in a breath and gripped the rifle harder. The intruders could only have taken the path to the cabins where Maisey and the schoolteacher slept.

CHAPTER THIRTEEN

Maisey sheltered her daughter in her arms while glass shattered and furniture crashed outside the closet. Phoebe wrapped her arms around her mother's neck and pulled herself closer with a whimper. Maisey hushed her frightened child and tightened her grip on the rifle she'd taken from its pegs above the kitchen window.

Excited chatter sounded within the cabin, uttered in a tongue she recognized but did not speak. A translator came from Fort Owen every Saturday to help her teach in the Indian school, but Maisey had only a small grasp of the Salish language. How could they break in like this when she'd given so much to the tribe's children?

Footsteps neared, and Maisey held her breath. The closet door opened, pouring in light. The warrior holding the lantern that normally sat on her table aloft peered at her and Phoebe with bright interest.

War paint whitened his face except around the eyes. A black handprint covered his chin and mouth. He spoke in the Salish tongue, after which a second Indian joined him. The bonnet she'd left hanging to dry on a peg in the kitchen perched jauntily on the newcomer's head. Its delicate lace edge contrasted strangely with his solemn face.

"Get back." Maisey raised her rifle, but the weapon jumped in her shaking hands. She couldn't hold it still enough to aim.

The warrior with the handprint stepped back and barked a command. The Indian wearing her bonnet aimed his rifle at

Phoebe's head. The hand-printed warrior gestured for her to put down her weapon. Heart pounding, Maisey lowered the rifle. The hand-printed warrior snatched it out of her hands, then reached into the closet and tore her daughter out of her arms.

Phoebe wailed and reached for her mother.

"Please—" Maisey's voice choked off. Tears slid down her cheeks. This couldn't be happening. Not again! She'd lost her husband in an Indian attack. She couldn't bear to lose Phoebe too.

The bonneted warrior stepped backward and gestured with his head.

Maisey straightened and walked out of the closet. Past caring about the consequences, she reached toward her child. The warrior holding Phoebe jumped back, but then his face softened. He offered Phoebe for her to take.

Maisey cradled her sobbing child and resolved to survive this ordeal for both their sakes.

The hand-printed warrior, who seemed in charge, pointed to the kitchen and made eating motions with his hand. She stared at him, hardly crediting that the intruders might only be looking for something to eat.

The warrior pushed Maisey toward the stove. Despite her terror, she understood that he wanted her to cook for them. Fearing they would try to take Phoebe if they thought she might hinder her, Maisey nodded and put her daughter down.

Phoebe whimpered and clung to her skirts.

Moving mechanically, Maisey gathered ingredients to make sourdough flapjacks with bacon, the easiest meal her panicked mind could remember how to make.

Her hands weren't working right. She fumbled while opening the flour sack, dropped a spoon on the floor, and spilled molasses down her bodice. She heaved a sigh of relief when the first flapjacks poured onto the cast-iron griddle sizzling with bacon fat.

The front door slammed open. America came in pointing a rifle. She tossed her head. "Clear out."

The bonneted Indian swung his rifle barrel upward.

"Watch out!" Maisey pulled Phoebe closer.

Rifle fire blasted the air. The bonneted Indian howled and dropped his weapon. Clutching his bloodied hand, he ran from the cabin. The hand-printed warrior followed.

America rushed to the door and bolted it behind them. She swept a glance over Maisey. "Are you all right?"

Maisey lifted Phoebe into her arms and held her shuddering body tight. "Now I am. Thank you. Why did you come to help me?"

"I had to. I couldn't in good conscience leave you and Phoebe unprotected while I cowered in my house."

"What about Emma?"

I checked the schoolteacher's cabin first. Emma was all right but frightened and worried about you. I sent her to watch over Liberty and Seth." America snatched up a hot pad and pulled the smoking griddle from the stove. "You're burning breakfast."

Elsa gazed out the parlor window and onto the empty driveway outside Atticus's house. Soon, he would come back and seek her here. She put a hand on her churning stomach.

Alicia and Miles had released her from the confines of the bedroom, but Elsa had no doubt that if she wandered from their presence, one or both of them would follow her. If not for the mind-crushing boredom, she preferred imprisonment to constant monitoring

Alicia stood looking down at the piano positioned to catch the light from the window, her face absorbed. She ran a hand over the keys. "Elsa, do you play more than one instrument?"

Elsa didn't feel up to making idle conversation with Alicia, but the woman's interest seemed genuine. "My family had a piano once, but we had to sell it."

She had been fascinated by the instrument ever since she could reach the keys. She remembered *Mutter* plunking out melodies with adequate skill, and Papa praising her as if she could produce music like a master.

Elsa sighed. The piano was the first of their belongings sold to keep food on the table after Papa's death. Elsa had been grief-stricken over its loss. She'd kept her hurdy-gurdy because playing it while singing and dancing helped sell the brooms her family made.

Alicia lowered herself to the bench and began a haunting melody Elsa had never heard before. She listened, entranced, until the final chord faded away.

"What piece was that?" Elsa asked.

"I'm not surprised you haven't heard it." Alicia sat with her hands on the keys, more relaxed than Elsa had ever seen her. "'Beautiful Dreamer' is an American parlor song."

"I enjoyed it." Elsa smiled. "Did you learn to the piano as a child?"

Alicia perked up. "I did. The orphanage's headmistress insisted we all learn."

"You were raised in an orphanage?" Elsa tried to picture the pampered woman before her in such a setting.

Alicia shrugged. "A person has to grow up somewhere."

Elsa felt a pang of sympathy for her. Perhaps Alicia had turned out wrong due to her upbringing. "That can't have been easy."

"No." Alicia frowned. "I was taken from my mother, who couldn't afford to support me. When I turned thirteen, they put me on an orphan train West. I grew up fast." She shook her head. "Never mind. I can't think why I told you all that."

Miles glanced up from a newspaper emblazoned with *Tri-Weekly Post*. "You surprise me, Alicia. I didn't know you played."

She slanted a look at him. "There's a lot about me you don't know."

He shuffled his paper and went back to reading.

Elsa had never revealed that she guessed their secret, but they seemed no longer to care about hiding it. A brother would know whether his sister played the piano, and a sister would not tease her brother in such a way. Neither had there been any mention of a brother in her orphan story.

Alicia flounced into a Windsor chair upholstered in silk. "Isn't it time to ring for tea?" She gave Elsa a pointed look.

Elsa stood and reached for the cord on the wall that would summon the maid.

Miles looked at her over the top of his paper. "Living here is spoiling you, Alicia. How will I ever keep up after we leave?"

She smiled sweetly. "You can try."

Elsa could stand their flirtatiousness no longer. "I'll go and lie down until supper."

Miles followed her from the parlor and up the stairs. She turned to close her door, but he pushed past her.

"I want to be alone." Anger throbbed in her voice.

He watched her with the intensity of a cat cornering a mouse. "Atticus will have learned by now that we left Bannack for Virginia City. He should be back soon, maybe even tonight."

Elsa swallowed hard and pretended to look out the window

to hide her fear.

Taking her by the shoulders, Miles pulled her against him in an embrace that held no love. "If you hadn't been marked for Atticus, I'd have staked my claim by now."

His words startled her, especially after his apparent indifference. She jerked away from him. "Stop it."

Miles turned her around to face him and tilted her chin. The odor of the Scotch he'd drunk wafted her way. For a horrifying instant, she thought he would force a kiss on her. He stroked her cheek. "Be good to Atticus."

Anger flared through Elsa like a white-hot flame. She shoved against his chest, and he stumbled backward. "Never touch me again!"

He regained his balance with a scowl. "I've a mind to teach you a lesson, *Fräulein*."

"As you mentioned, Atticus will be home any minute." She glared at him despite her quaking.

"I wish him joy of you." Miles shut the door behind him with a bang.

CHAPTER FOURTEEN

Rob shook Cecil's hand outside the flimsy structure the miner called home. "Thank you for your hospitality."

"My pleasure." Cecil squinted against the morning sun and put up a hand to shield his eyes. "Since you're determined to go through with this, I'll wish you a safe journey."

"Thank you." Rob lifted into the saddle and touched the brim of his hat. He headed along the path to the turning onto Wallace Street, the main road through town. Storefronts bustling with activity lined the broad street on either side. He passed a residential district, then the town fell away.

On this fine spring day with the wide sky above him, massacres, marauding Indians, and soldiers seemed far away. Drifts of lupine, blue-flag, wild rose, and numerous other blossoms tumbled down hillsides dotted with quaking aspen, alder, cottonwood, and lodgepole pine. Lofty mountains, blued by distance, stood sentinel over the foothills at their feet.

The road curved northeast to flank the Madison River, which shone with the sky's reflected glory. The chestnut quarter horse from the livery nodded its head and swayed down the dirt track in front of a pack horse laden with supplies. The horses' hooves crushed pine needles blown into drifts across the road. The earthy scent mingled with the smell of sun-warmed grasses.

Rob stopped for lunch beside a creek that cascaded between rocks and into the river. The sound of falling water accompanied the twittering of birds. He ate his jerky and cornpone quickly, then started off again. The creak and sway of the saddle combined with the day's warmth to lull him, but he continued his journey until the quiet hour before nightfall. He camped on the banks of the Madison and lay in his bedroll listening to fish jump in the river.

Today's departure had taken longer than he'd wanted, but he'd make up for it tomorrow. The faster he traveled through Indian territory, the better. That meant long hours in the saddle and no time to hunt.

Morning saw Rob early upon the road. The wind had picked up in the night and now blustered down the river channel. He was glad to turn aside when the road trended due east. It took him toward the wide corridor between mountain ranges that would deliver him to the last place his brother had resided. Rob would start his search there at Fort Sedgwick. He'd go on to the ferry crossing, where the owner had told Bry's husband, Nick, that he remembered seeing Con.

Afternoon shadows lay long across the road before Con. With his horse flagging, he had considered stopping in Nevada City, but pressed on the additional two miles to Virginia City. He rubbed the sturdy neck beneath his hand and murmured a soft word. The grey's ears flicked backward, then pricked forward. Its hooves picked up their pace.

Con smiled. The horse deserved a clean stall and a bucket of oats. The stable he'd built behind his cabin had neither, so he would put the grey up in the livery for the night.

Virginia City, glowing with soft light, opened before him. He tied up to a hitching post in front of Daily's saloon, an establishment belonging to Atticus Merrick. The bartender who looked up from polishing a glass behind the counter was a man Con didn't recall meeting during his days in Virginia City.

But then, I spent next to no time in saloons.

His only visit to this one had ended when Shane rescued him from a spiked drink, a card sharp, and a fancy lady. He remembered little of the episode, or of divulging his closest secrets to his cousin, who had hauled him home.

Unfortunately, Con recalled every detail of his prostration the next day. He'd lost a lot of gold but had learned the wisdom of avoiding spirits and easy women. That knowledge had served him well in building a fortune selling beef to the mining camps.

Con slid onto a stool at the elaborately-paneled bar.

The barkeeper nodded to him. "What will you have?"

"Sarsaparilla."

The man appraised him, but without a word retrieved a brown bottle from a shelf behind the bar. While he poured the fizzy soda into a glass, Con familiarized himself with his surroundings. Oil lamps burned on either side of a mirror on the wall behind the bar. Above it hung the painting of a woman draped in soft garments and lying in a rose bower.

No one else sat at the counter this early, but a few miners lounged around a table toward the rear of the saloon. A row of booths upholstered in red leather lined the wall behind him.

The barkeeper plunked the soft drink in front of him.

Con gestured him closer and waited for the man to lean in before speaking. "I'm looking for information."

The barkeeper raised his eyebrows. "What's your question?"

"I'm looking for the new dance hall owned by Atticus Merrick."

"You want The Silk Stocking. It's down the street on the left."

"Thank you." Con took a long pull of his soda and sighed when it eased his parched throat.

"What business is it of yours, *Irish*?"

Con swiveled toward the familiar voice.

Miles' fair hair gleamed in the lamp light. In shirt sleeves and vest, he sat in one of the booths butted against the wall. His jacket and bowler hung from hooks on a nearby post.

Con scowled. Of all the people in Virginia City, why did he have to run into Miles? "That's my own concern."

Miles tipped his glass and drained its contents. "I'll have another."

The barkeeper moved to obey.

Con stepped down from his stool and strolled toward Miles. "It's well that I've found you here."

"I can't say the same." A guarded expression covered his face. "Judging by those bruises, someone else agrees with me."

Con had his suspicions about who was behind the attack in his cabin, but as Helmsley would point out, no evidence.

The barkeeper placed the amber drink at Miles's elbow and retreated.

Con leaned over and rested his hands on the table. "Let me deliver a warning to the wise."

A look of fear chased across Mile's face. "Stand back, I'm warning you." He picked up his drink with a shaking hand.

Con leaned closer. "If Miss Meier has come to harm, you'll answer to me."

Miles flicked his wrist. The contents of his glass splashed into Con's face.

Cupping his burning eyes, Con stumbled backward. A fist caught him in the stomach. He sprawled on the floor. Hands grasped the front of Con's leather jacket and jerked him close to his assailant.

Con's vision cleared enough to reveal a fist drawn back, ready to strike. He bucked to break the hold on his chest and twisted sideways.

The blow landed against the floor. Miles gave a cry of pain.

Con staggered to his feet, and Miles jumped up to face him. Panting, they squared off.

The barkeeper opened the door and made a sweeping gesture. "Take it outside, gentlemen."

Con rammed his opponent. The force of his charge carried them toward the door. Locked in an embrace, they wrestled for dominance.

"I said *outside*! Or I'll fetch the sheriff!"

With Miles's hand clamped around his throat, cutting off his air, Con disregarded the barkeeper's instructions.

"I've been wanting to do this for a long time," Miles ground out, his face near Con's.

Con freed a fist and slammed it into his opponent's stomach. Miles's hold on his throat slackened. Con broke free and rubbed his throat. He had to cough before speaking. "I'd say we have a score to settle."

Miles uncoiled like a snake and rammed his fist into Con's face.

Con staggered backward and fell through the open door onto the boardwalk. He scrambled to his knees.

Roaring, Miles barreled toward him.

At the last second, Con rolled out of harm's way.

Miles landed face down in the street, unmoving.

Con grabbed the back of his vest and flipped him over.

"Don't hit me!" Miles covered his face.

Con restrained the punch he'd been about to throw. He rose and stood over his opponent, dabbing blood from the corner of his mouth. "Next time you decide to have a man beat up—" He stopped to breathe. "Consider the possibility of him coming after you later."

"What's going on here?" The harsh voice came from behind Con.

A tall man with a handlebar moustache and a sheriff's badge pinned to his leather vest was hurrying down the boardwalk. Con squinted, trying to place him.

Miles struggled to his feet and touched his swollen face. "This man struck me."

"What happened here?" The sheriff called to the barkeeper, who stood in the doorway.

"Remember who you work for." Miles spat out the words.

"Nothing much." The barkeeper shrugged.

"That so?" The sheriff shook his head. "Doesn't look like nothing."

"My customers are waiting." The barkeeper went inside and closed the door.

The sheriff swept a glance over Con. "You're new in town, aren't you?"

Memories swarmed over Con. He'd seen this man riding with the vigilantes during the lynchings after Sheriff Plummer's hanging. "I just arrived."

The sheriff grunted. "Maybe you should think about continuing on your way."

Miles limped onto the boardwalk beside the sheriff. "You should lock him up."

The last thing Con needed was to wind up back in jail. "There's no need for that, Sheriff." He glared at Miles.

The sheriff nodded. "Keep it that way."

Con stumbled to his horse. It took a little effort, but he pulled himself into the saddle. He rode toward the livery, glad to leave the saloon behind. Neither time he'd darkened its door had turned out well.

After stabling his horse and washing in the pump outside the livery, he returned to Wallace Street and found The Silk Stocking. He stepped inside the posh dancehall, with its rich paneling, leather upholstery, and gilded lamps. A quick glance told Con that Elsa was not among the women in low-cut bodices and high skirts, who would dance with a miner for a dollar.

He wanted to feel relieved, but Elsa's absence from this place might mean Atticus wanted to keep her for himself.

When the post office opened tomorrow, he could ask the address of Atticus's private residence without rousing the townsfolk's suspicions. Meanwhile, after the long ride with a fight at its end, he needed food and rest. He'd stop for a meal then head for his cabin, where he could claim a good night's sleep under his own roof.

Back on Wallace Street, he stepped inside a restaurant he'd visited many times before. A woman with brown hair pinned at her nape was washing down a table. She didn't glance up. "Sorry, we're closed."

Con stayed put. "Is that all the welcome you give an old friend?"

She looked at him then, and her mouth gaped open. It took her a moment to speak. "Con Walsh! Is it really you?" She rushed to him.

Con enfolded her in his embrace, then held her at arm's length to gaze at her. She'd changed little in the intervening years, apart from growing lovelier. Marriage suited her. "Addie, it's good to see you."

She reached up, her fingers gentle on his face. "What happened to you?"

He touched the sore spot. "How bad is it?"

Nate Whalen looked out from the kitchen. "Hey now, that's

my woman." His grin belied the ferocity of his tone.

Con extricated himself from Addie and shook his friend's hand. "She's a fine one, and a good cook too." He gave Addie his most charming smile.

She laughed. "All right, you rogue, I'll feed you. But first come into the kitchen. Nate can break out the medicine kit."

Nate applied ointment to Con's cheek with silent intensity. He capped the ointment and stepped back. "Who did this?"

Con shrugged. "It's not important."

"You like to keep to yourself. I respect that." Nate folded his arms. "But self-sufficiency can be taken too far. You'll let me know if you need help?"

Con nodded. "Thank you." Despite Nate's offer, Con would never put a man with a wife depending on him at risk.

After partaking of Addie's buffalo chili and cornbread, Con set off for his cabin. He made his home in the Bitterroot Valley but would always have a fondness for this claim. He'd joined the stampede out of Bannack and settled here. After gaining and losing a fortune to Atticus and his card sharp, Con had applied himself to finding enough gold to settle elsewhere.

But part of his heart remained here.

Con followed the path on the outskirts of town slowly, savoring his moment of return. Shadows formed pools of darkness, but glimmers of moonlight shone through the tree leaves. Water burbled in the creek. A mourning dove sobbed in the big cottonwood tree.

The cabin stood black against the fading sky. He went inside, lit a match, and found a lantern he didn't recognize sitting on the table. Alarm took him back a step.

His match sputtered out even as another light flared.

Con reached for his gun and cocked the hammer.

A heavy body tackled him, and Con's finger slipped. His

gun went off, and the explosion spattered him with blood. The weight of his assailant carried Con down. His head struck the floor hard. He groaned.

The table crashed on top of them, and Con slipped into darkness.

CHAPTER FIFTEEN

ELSA WOKE FROM HER NAP, DRIFTED back toward sleep, but then jerked awake fully at the sound of clopping hooves. She threw aside her covers and stumbled to the window in time to catch sight of a rider on horseback rounding the corner of the house. She pulled on the first outfit she found in the closet and plucked shoes from the shelf.

A door opened and closed, and a deep voice murmured alongside Alicia's lighter tones.

Elsa spun about. She rammed her toes against the stepstool. It crashed to the floor. She blinked away tears and righted the stool. Clouds shifted in the sky outside the high window, penetrating its panes to light the wall. Atticus had neglected to put a grill in that window.

Elsa froze, captivated by an idea. If the shoe shelf would hold her, she might escape by the closet window. It would be a tight fit, since its purpose was to admit light, not allow a person to squeeze through. She'd have to leave her crutch behind, but her ankle hardly troubled her anymore. She itched to try, but right now the risk of discovery was too great.

A tap came at the bedroom door.

Elsa shrank against the wall inside the closet.

A metallic click signaled the key turning in the lock. The knob rattled and the hinges creaked.

She held her breath and caught the tread of light footsteps.

"Elsa?" Alicia sounded carefree.

"I'm here." Elsa emerged from the closet.

Alicia stood alone in the room. The door gaped open behind her. "Atticus is home." She smiled, as if expecting Elsa to rejoice in the news.

Elsa stared at Alicia. Had the wretched woman no idea what she and Miles had done?

"You may come down when you're ready."

She would never go down if they waited for that. How could she ever be *ready* to face Atticus? If she told him she didn't want to be with him, she doubted he would let her go. No, he must not suspect she wanted to escape. "Give me a moment, please."

"I'll wait." Alicia slid into one of the chairs at the table.

Elsa took her time putting on her shoes and pinning her hair into a twist at the back of her head. When she could delay no longer, she steeled herself to follow Alicia.

Atticus, seated on a settee in the parlor, watched her descend the stairs with the intent look of a cat toying with a cornered mouse. He rose as she entered and took her hand. "My dear, you are even lovelier than I remembered."

"Thank you." Elsa withdrew her hand and glanced away. Miles gazed at her from an overstuffed chair across from the piano. She returned her attention to Atticus. "Did you have a pleasant trip?"

"Not particularly, but the prize at its end makes the journey worthwhile."

A pink-cheeked servant brought a tea tray and withdrew.

Atticus gave Elsa an intimate smile. "Will you pour, my dear?"

She picked up the pot, but her hands shook. Tea slopped on the tray.

Atticus seemed not to notice her discomfort. He took the cup and plate of miniature cakes she extended to him. He gave her an appraising look. "Have you been comfortable here?"

"Yes, for the most part." She threw a glare at Miles.

Atticus drew his brows together. "If—"

"Miss Meier and I have discussed music." Alicia sipped her tea.

Elsa guessed that Alicia's claim—which was true to a certain extent—was a ploy to make Atticus think they had treated her well.

What would happen if I told him they drugged me?

The words trembled on her lips but remained unspoken. If Miles and Alicia were banished, she would be alone with Atticus. She shivered, suddenly glad of their company. Atticus had told her before her mishap at the hotel that he wanted her to come to him willingly. If so, he was doomed to disappointment.

They exchanged small talk, then the men fell into a discussion about politics. Atticus quaffed the last of his tea and thumped down his empty cup. "Thomas Meagher is putting together a militia against the Indians."

Miles shook his head. "Never trust an Irishman."

"Why President Jackson ever named that Irish rebel Montana's territorial governor is beyond me." Atticus folded his arms. "Never mind. We have a new governor now."

Miles leaned forward in his chair. "How will Red Cloud's War turn out, do you think?"

Elsa sat bored, and Alicia yawned behind her hand while the two men explored the possible outcomes of Red Cloud's War. The topic wasn't suitable for women, which was fine with Elsa. She was glad to remain silent.

The servant returned and announced supper, and they started for the dining room. "After you." Atticus put his hand behind Elsa's back in a courtly gesture that almost made her believe she could appeal to him for release. If only she could know for certain.

After supper, Alicia sat at the piano while Miles and Atticus quartered themselves in Atticus's office. Miles emerged later, a triumphant look on his face. Elsa suspected that Atticus had paid Miles handsomely for bringing her to him. The couple took their leave shortly afterward.

Alone in the lamp-lit parlor, Elsa wandered over to the piano. She plunked one of the keys, then another, and finally sat down. She ran her hands over the keyboard in a song she'd learned to play by rote as a child.

Atticus entered the room and stood behind Elsa. Her memory failed her, and her fingers stopped moving.

He put his hands on her shoulders. "Go on. That was lovely."

She shook her head. "I've forgotten the rest."

"I'll see that you have lessons."

Elsa stood up and stepped sideways, putting distance between them. She retrieved the hatpin she'd hidden in the waistband of her dress and held it in her palm. It wasn't much of a weapon, but she would use it to defend herself, if necessary. "I'll retire now." She blurted out the words.

"Certainly." Atticus moved nearer, the lamplight turning his curls mahogany. He raised her hand for his kiss. "Don't worry about being disturbed tonight. I wouldn't force you against your will."

She stared at him, unable to form words.

"Given time, I know you will come to admire me, as I do you." He touched her cheek. "You are a prize worth waiting for, and one I intend to win."

Cheeks burning, Elsa stumbled backward. She turned and fled the room. From the corner of her eye she saw Atticus watching from the base of the stairs. She hurried down the hall and into her bedroom and leaned against the closed door while her breathing slowed.

"Sweet dreams, Elsa." Atticus's voice carried to her from outside the room. A key grated in the lock.

Elsa's shoulders shook, and tears dampened her cheeks. If Atticus really wanted to allow her freedom of choice, he would not lock her in.

Rob mopped up the last of his beans with a hunk of johnnycake. "Thanks for supper."

Skip Crawley smiled. The light from his fire glinted in the miner's fair hair and deepened the grooves beside his mouth. "I'm glad you came across my camp."

"Me too. I'm grateful for a warm meal and the company of another person. Traveling these parts is a lonely business."

"There's good reason for that. Are you aware of the Indian trouble in the Powder River Valley?"

"Yes." Rob's coffee had grown tepid in his cup. He drank it anyway.

The miner squinted against the wood smoke. "If I'd known when I started what I know now, I wouldn't have taken the Bozeman Trail. No shortcut is worth a man's life."

Rob threw a twig into the fire and watched it catch. "I'll chance it."

Skip peered at him as if he'd lost his wits. "Why would you put your life in danger on purpose?"

"It's a long story, but my brother is missing. I'm searching for him."

"Sorry about your brother." Skip poked at the fire with a stick, sending sparks spitting upward. "Getting yourself killed won't help him none."

"Is it that bad?"

"I've been shot at and chased, and I was one of the lucky ones. It's going to get worse before long, what with the army gathering forces at the forts. I suggest you turn around."

"I've heard that advice before."

"And decided against it? Why?"

Rob flung out the dregs of his coffee. "Because going by the southern route to Fort Sedgwick would delay my journey and take me through the mountains in snow."

"That may be." Skip nodded. "But keep going this way and you're likely not to arrive at all."

The ticking of the grandfather clock on the landing, loud in the silence, was the only sound in the house. Hardly daring to breathe, Elsa slid back her covers and lowered her feet to the floor. She'd abandoned her crutch before going to bed, delighted that she could walk with only a slight limp. As long as she made it through the window without wrenching her ankle, she could manage.

Elsa touched her hurdy-gurdy with a pang of regret. She must leave it behind. She would have enough trouble putting herself through so small a window without trying to manage the case. Besides, her instrument might bang the siding and alert Atticus.

She struck a match to the oil lamp beside her bed and carried it as she walked quietly across the carpet. The closet door creaked open.

Elsa caught her breath and waited, poised to run back to bed.

Nothing stirred.

To avoid a betraying light beneath the bedroom door, Elsa closed herself in the closet. The door shut behind her with a quiet *click*. She placed the lamp on a high shelf then thrust her arms into the sleeves of her coat. Her ankle protested when she stepped up on the footstool. She steadied herself against the wall until it stopped wobbling.

With one foot on the low shelf that she had earlier cleared of shoes, she hauled herself upward. The little window swung outward as she perched on the ledge. The closet floor seemed a long way below, but one glance out the second-story window made her head spin.

Balancing precariously and fearful of discovery, Elsa took a moment to breathe. She would need steady nerves to climb down safely.

Grasping the makeshift rope she'd tied together from strips torn from her bedsheets, she secured it to several closet hooks and pushed it out the window. The soft *thud* against the house made her wince. Who might have heard that? She didn't take time to listen. Instead, she swung her legs out the opening and wiggled through the frame.

Elsa lowered herself down the rope. Praying her sweaty palms would not lose their grip and slip, she took care not to bump into the house. Hopefully, Atticus would remain deep in slumber until she was well away. Her arms ached, and her grasp on the rope slipped. She slid, her hands burning.

A knot near the ground stopped her fall. The rope wasn't quite long enough, and she dangled several feet off the ground. Her strength gave out, and she dropped. The impact jarred her into crying out. Thankfully, she'd landed on her good leg.

A dog barked beyond the cottonwood trees. Elsa froze, but the sound came no nearer. The cottonwoods shushed in the night breeze, and moisture weighted the air. A storm would soak her, but better that with freedom than the warm prison in which Atticus meant to trap her.

Limping, she started down the road that wound toward the lights of town. Voices, laughter, and music from the saloons and dancehalls rode the wind. *Does this town never sleep?* It was nearer morning than night.

Bypassing the businesses, Elsa followed a narrow street behind them. The ache in her leg increased, slowing and finally stopping her. She leaned against the side of a stable. A warm tear slipped down her wind-chilled cheek. If only she could go home to her mother's house in Germany! How simple the life she'd once led seemed to her now. She needed to find somewhere to hide before morning dawned and Atticus searched for her.

Elsa pushed off the wall and turned onto the main road. Away from the lights, shadows closed in, and her footsteps slowed for a different reason. She wished for the lamp left burning in the closet. If not for the light of the gibbous moon glazing the road, she might wander astray.

Only a little way ahead, water rushed where a bridge crossed a stream. Before reaching it, she came upon a path that veered off into trees lifting silvered arms against the sky.

She could have water to drink if she hid near the stream. The path probably followed it. She saw no houses nearby, but braving creatures of the wild was better than facing the two-legged predator bound to pursue her. She took the path.

Hooves thudded from behind, and she peered toward the sound. A horse and rider turned onto the path from the road. *Oh, no!* She had better conceal herself behind the grove of alders to the side of the path. Heart pounding, she hurried toward them.

Elsa's legs banged against something unyielding. Crying out, she extended her hands to break her fall. Pain stung her palms. She pushed herself up and turned to sit on the boulder she'd fallen across.

The time for escape was gone. A man wearing a dark hat with a wide brim rode toward her. He reined in his horse. "What have you done?" His lilting accent soothed her ears. He dismounted.

Struggling to her feet, Elsa put her foot down wrong and cried out in pain.

"Careful there." He steadied her with a hand on her arm. "You've hurt yourself."

She nodded. His hat shadowed his face, but his clerical collar shone in the moonlight. She sucked in a breath. "Are you a preacher?"

"Allow me to introduce myself. I'm Reverend Shane Hayes from Liberty Township. May I ask what you're doing by yourself in the dark this time of night?"

"My name is Elsa Meier." She bit her lip, hesitant to say more. After Con's beating, she had vowed not to involve anyone else in her troubles.

But what else can I do?

After the long, sleepless night, weariness dragged at Elsa, but she had nowhere to lay her head. Her stomach reminded her that it had been a long while since supper, but she had no food to give it. With her hurdy-gurdy, she might have earned enough to survive, but she'd left her instrument behind. She had thought of little else but freedom, without considering what she would do once she gained it.

The sad truth bore down on her. Her attempt to free herself

from poverty in the Land of Liberty had ended in failure. Poorer than when she'd left home, she was stranded in a foreign country, barely able to walk, and owned nothing but the clothes on her back.

Reverend Hayes had a kind face and a gentle manner that made him seem easy to trust. "Please help me."

"Of course." He smiled. "You only had to ask."

Elsa blinked away tears. "Thank you."

"What happened, if I may inquire?"

"I ran into a boulder. My leg hurts."

"May I look at it?"

She raised her skirt, her face heating at the immodesty. Blood oozed from a scrape below her knee. Reverend Hayes knelt and ran light fingers over her leg. "You have a nasty-looking wound but from what I can tell, no broken bones."

"That's good news." She lowered her skirt and picked a small rock from her palm.

"My cousin's cabin should have the means to fix you up. If I may lift you onto my horse's back, Archibald can carry you there for doctoring."

"Your cousin?" Elsa looked up in alarm. The more people who knew about her, the less likely she would remain hidden from Atticus.

"Perhaps you know him. Have you met Connor Walsh?"

"Con? I'm worried about him."

"You and many others."

"Is he all right?" She spilled the words in a rush.

Reverend Hayes gazed down the trail. "That's what I've come to find out."

CHAPTER SIXTEEN

CON WOKE WITH A THROBBING HEAD. He'd managed to drag himself from beneath the table and away from the body of the stranger who had jumped him, but he must have passed out again. How long Con had slept remained a mystery. The light coming in the kitchen window could belong to dusk or dawn.

He attempted to sit up but gasped and lay down. He could hope his ribs were bruised and not broken. Either way, he had to stand. Lying here injured and alone put his life in jeopardy.

Summoning all of his will power, Con ignored the pain and rolled to his knees. Darkness pressed at the edge of his vision. He waited for it to dispel before pushing to his feet.

The doorknob rattled.

Con froze. Was another intruder about to challenge him? He cast about for his gun. The barrel gleamed a small distance away. In his battered condition, he'd have a hard time reaching it in time. He tried anyway, thrusting toward the weapon with more zeal than precision. The ache in his head increased, and he cried out.

The cabin door burst open. "Con!"

Shane's call faded as Con fell back into darkness.

The splash of water roused Con, and he opened his eyes. Sunlight shone through his bedroom window, haloing Elsa's hair as she placed a damp cloth over his brow.

He smiled. "Have I gone to heaven, because here's an angel?"

Elsa's lips curved. "You're awake."

Con summoned his most roguish look. "I'll pretend to sleep again if you'll keep smiling at me like that."

Elsa blushed and averted her gaze.

Con grinned. Really, he shouldn't tease her, but it was hard to resist when such charming results rewarded his effort. The tension he read in her face sobered him. "What brought you here?"

"Miles and Alicia took me to Atticus Merrick's house, but I ran away. Atticus was out of town until yesterday. I couldn't—" She swallowed. "I decided not to accept his hospitality any longer."

"I'm glad of that." She'd left out parts of the story, that much was clear. But why?

"Early this morning I came across Reverend Hayes looking for you. We found you here." She gazed at him with wide eyes. "Did you shoot that man?"

"No, or at least not on purpose. He came out of the dark, and my gun went off when he barreled into me." He shook his head. "Poor fellow. He deserved a good thrashing for attacking me, but not death."

Elsa was watching him with a solemn expression. "Reverend Hayes thinks you surprised a claim jumper."

"He's probably right. Where *is* my cousin, anyway?"

She shuddered. "Burying the man."

"I'm sorry you had to see that." Con squeezed her arm. He had meant to comfort her, but his caress became something more. The yearning to explore her parted lips with his own seized him, and he cupped her cheek.

Elsa turned her head, nestling slightly against his hand.

Con pulled her toward him and felt her yield. He gazed into her eyes, inches from his own, drawn by her look of trust. Tugging her nearer, he felt her breath fan his face. Her eyes drifted shut, and he closed the gap between their lips.

Elsa sighed and surrendered to Con's kiss. She shouldn't allow this, especially not while at his bedside. However, the feelings he stirred in her made him hard to resist. His lips moved over hers with a feather-light touch that left her wanting more. She responded in kind, caught by the sweetness of the moment.

An ache awoke inside Elsa, a spark that touched the tinder of her soul. When she had kissed Peter during that village sleigh ride, her emotions had curled under like froth on the waves. The effects of Con's kiss would not vanish in a moment.

His lips slanted over hers more intently, and an unknown current threatened to drag her under. Elsa moaned.

Con broke away. "You're far too tempting." He smoothed her hair and released her.

Elsa turned from him and rose to look out the window. She scolded herself for making a compromising situation worse.

"Is something wrong?" Con's voice followed her.

"I'm tired," she answered with her back to him. "I didn't sleep much last night."

"Elsa, tell me what else is wrong."

"All right." She faced him. "No matter how low life takes me, I refuse to become the kind of woman who gives away her favors easily."

His eyebrows shot upward. "I never thought you would."

Chilled in the draft from the window, she wrapped her arms around herself. "This is my fault."

"I don't agree." Con shifted to sit up straighter but winced and gave up.

Elsa hurried to prop the pillows behind him. "I shouldn't be alone with you in this cabin."

He captured her hand and kissed it. "I can't think what else you could have done."

She pulled her hand from his grasp. "I shouldn't have stayed the night in your Bannack cabin, either."

"No one knows about that but us."

"Miles does. He kidnapped me that night." She shook her head. "And those horrible men who beat you also know."

Con tilted his head. "I didn't think of that."

"Why should you be troubled by this, when my reputation is already ruined?" She plunked into the chair by his bedside. "Atticus Merrick made sure of it."

Con fixed his green gaze on her. "Has he laid a hand on you?"

She shook her head. "He hasn't harmed me in body."

She seemed to have taken harm of some sort, but he would play along and wait for her to confide more. "That's a comfort, anyway." Con took her hand. "As to the rest, perhaps we can find a solution you can live with."

The shovel plunked into the hole at Shane's feet. He lifted another load of dirt and dropped it on the pile beside him. Digging a grave was never a happy event, but the day's warmth and a persistent fly made this task even more unpleasant. He finally finished digging, glad he'd made the effort. Every man should be tucked into the earthen bed to which he returned.

Ashes to ashes, dust to dust.

He loosened his clerical collar to cool his neck and gazed at the body of the dark-haired burly man lying in the shade of the big cottonwood. Would someone wonder what became of him? He must have had a mother, a father, perhaps brothers and sisters. Without knowing his identity, Shane had no way to notify his kin.

The man looked in his mid-thirties—the prime of life. He should have lived a long while more. Shane shook his head in silent regret at the ravages of a misled life.

A red-bearded man turned off the path. "Good day to you." Shane greeted the newcomer when he came within earshot.

"Likewise, Preacher." The man stared at the body. "I'm not surprised to find Tate Weatherby received his comeuppance."

"You know this person?" Shane mopped the perspiration from his brow with a bandana.

The man shrugged. "After a manner of speaking."

"I'm Reverend Shane Hayes." His hands were filthy from digging, so he refrained from offering a handshake.

"Name's Cecil Brown." The man's grey gaze fastened on Shane. "Who shot Tate?"

Shane could think of no good reason to name Con. "Mr. Weatherby died accidentally when a gun went off."

The man nodded. "While he was getting into mischief, no doubt."

Curiosity overcame Shane. "What do you know of this man?"

"Tate was a no-good claim jumper and thief."

"Even so, I'd like to let his relatives know he died."

Cecil's eyebrows shot upward. "His kin aren't the kind of

folks you'd want to tell such a thing. No, sir, not when a gunshot is involved."

"There was no foul play, except on his part. He tried to jump my cousin, Con."

"So, you're the preacher he told me about." Cecil beamed. "I forgot your name, but he had a powerful lot of good to say about you."

"Oh, really?" Shane took in the bemusing fact.

"I'm glad to hear Con is back. I'd like to say hello. Will I find him inside?"

"Yes, but lend a hand first, will you? I could use help shifting Tate."

Cecil grasped the dead man's feet while Shane took his arms. Together they dragged the body into the grave.

"I'm obliged." Shane nodded to the red-bearded miner.

"No bother. It's a good thing I came along. Shall I help you fill in the grave? I don't mind taking a turn with a shovel."

Shane smiled. "That's kind of you, but I can manage."

"All right, then. I'll wash up at the pump and go knock on the door."

Shane glanced from his own dirt-stained hands to the waiting shovel. It would be a while before he did the same. "I'll warn you that Con is pretty beaten up."

Shane had officiated at many funerals in his years as a preacher. None were sadder than those held for lonely deaths. He prayed for the man's loved ones, who would see him no more. He prayed for his cousin. Living with memories of the accident that had caused this death wouldn't be easy.

Shane was thankful he'd chosen to ride through the night to reach Virginia City on the last leg of the trip. Otherwise, he'd not have found Elsa, and Con would have had a harder time. Shane didn't doubt that his cousin's ability to survive, regardless. Con always landed on his feet, as he'd proven many times.

Shane shoveled a load of dirt over the body and swiveled to pick up another.

"Well, well, Saint Preacher. I find you wherever I go."

Shane stabbed the shovel into the ground and ran an assessing gaze over the man before him. Atticus Merrick stood with legs apart and hands behind his back, wearing elegant dress. He looked as if he'd never dug a hole in his life. Probably, he hadn't.

Shane ran a hand across his moist brow. "Do you have business here, Atticus?"

Atticus tilted his head. "What if I do?"

"Come out with it, then go on your way." Shane snapped out the words, driven beyond patience by the man's insolence.

Atticus took a step toward Shane. "Who are you burying?"

"A man who died by accident."

Atticus peered into the grave at the partially covered body. "Looks like someone shot him." He straightened. "Gunning a man down in cold blood is a hanging offense."

"It's a good thing no one's done that, then." Shane glared at Atticus. "If you have nothing more to discuss, perhaps you'll let me finish this duty."

"Not so fast." Atticus narrowed his eyes. "A young woman under my protection is missing. Her name is Elsa Meier."

Shane did his best not to betray his reaction. "What has that to do with me?"

Atticus shrugged. "I thought you might have information about her. She was seen heading this way late last night. So were you."

Shane doubted the story. Apart from those who would have consumed too much whiskey to remember, no one but he and Elsa had been about at that hour. He gave Atticus a pointed look.

"I'm afraid I can't help you."

"I'd hate to think you helped a mental patient escape her caretaker."

"Is that so?" Shane kept his voice neutral. He wasn't surprised Atticus would try to manipulate him. These were low tactics even for Atticus. His claim rang false. Elsa seemed quite rational, whereas Atticus's stability might well be in question.

"Have you come across Miss Meier?" Atticus ground out the question.

Shane shoveled another load of dirt into the grave. "Have a pleasant afternoon, Atticus."

Atticus glanced at the cabin as if ready to storm inside.

Shane stepped sideways to block him. "Try that, and you'll find me changed from the man who once let you bully him."

Atticus snorted. "Careful, Saint Preacher, or you'll lose your halo."

"I've made my peace with God," Shane's quiet words vibrated the air. "Have you?"

The veins in Atticus's neck stood out. His mouth worked but no words emerged. He turned on his heel and stomped away.

CHAPTER SEVENTEEN

ELSA SLID A PLATE OF *ROTKRAUT*, her favorite red cabbage dish, and potatoes in front of Con, where he sat at the table. She returned to the kitchen counter to retrieve the plates she'd dished up for herself and Reverend Hayes. She would have trouble calling him Shane, although he'd given her permission to do so.

"Supper smells wonderful." Con picked up his fork but put it down at a glance from Shane.

"Shall we give thanks?" Shane bowed his head.

Con followed suit.

Elsa folded her hands in her lap and closed her eyes while Shane blessed the food.

The preacher's gentle ways eased her fears. She'd been on edge ever since learning that Atticus had come looking for her. He even seemed to know where she might be found. She might not have guessed he'd come by, except that Con's reaction when Shane told him privately had given the news away.

She smiled. Con's personality was very different from Shane's, but each man possessed a deep faith in God. Abiding with them made her feel secure, despite all Atticus might do.

After the meal, Elsa carried their dishes into the kitchen, then took a moment to sit at the table with a cup of tea. With a fire blazing in the stove and the cousins engaged in lively conversation, she took a moment to think. She had allowed her own faith, once strong, to lapse after Papa's death. She admitted privately that she'd been holding a grudge against God.

She would no more.

God, please forgive me for not trusting You for my freedom. I tried to win it without You but made a mess of my life.

The heartfelt prayer bestowed her serenity. Elsa finished her tea and put on water to wash the dishes. The simple chore restored her. She could almost believe nothing bad could happen to her in this place.

Moving lights glowed from the direction of town. Hoofbeats pounded the air.

Elsa put a hand to her throat. *Something's wrong.*

Joining her at the window, Shane pulled aside the curtain and looked out. "We'd better leave."

Elsa hurried to support Con as he rose to his feet. He put an arm around her and shot a look at Shane. "Tell me what's wrong."

Shane hesitated before answering. "I'm not sure."

"You suspect something, though."

Shane peered out the window again. "At a guess, I'd say there's a posse headed this way."

"Atticus." Con made the name sound like a cuss word.

Shane gave a swift nod. "Likely so."

Elsa shifted away from Con. "He wants me, not you."

Con pulled her back. "Don't talk like that."

The hoofbeats grew louder. A minute later, a fist pounded the door. "Con, let me in."

Shane hurried to the door and wrenched it open. "Rob! I thought you were a couple of days down the trail."

"I turned back." A brown-haired man with a resemblance to both Con and Shane walked in.

"It's good to see you, Brother." Con's voice trembled.

Rob turned to him. "I'd say you're a little late coming home. Where have you been?"

"Now, *there's* a tale." Con stepped forward, and the two embraced.

Rob held Con at arm's length. "It looks like you came out worse in a fight with a mountain lion."

Con smiled. "That's another story."

"I'd love to hear them both, but we can't delay." Rob released him. "There's a vigilante mob forming in town. From what I heard, they're headed this way. Something about a murdered man and a kidnapped woman. They may also have brought up your association with Sheriff Plummer."

Shane let out a breath. "Atticus is stirring up trouble. We need to light out of here but being shy on horses makes escape difficult."

"I brought two." Rob looked out the kitchen window, then let the curtain fall. "We don't have much time."

"I'll saddle Archibald." Shane shrugged into his coat, took his hat from a hook by the door, and went outside.

Elsa peered out the window at the approaching lights. Swallowing against a dry throat, she hurried to the kitchen counter. "I'll bring food."

"No need." Rob shook his head. "I have supplies."

Con stood with painful slowness.

"Well, Brother." Rob moved to Con's side. "I've always admired your ability to get yourself out of scrapes. Let's see you do it this time."

Elsa put on her coat and went outside with Rob and Con. Last night's gibbous moon had rounded toward fullness and hung suspended above the cabin's stable. The pack mare pricked her ears and shifted when Elsa mounted.

"Easy, girl." She rubbed the mare's sleek neck. Hearing the thundering hooves and seeing lights moving in their direction, Elsa could well understand the mare's nervousness. If not for the solid presence of her three companions, she would have felt a similar desire to bolt.

With help from Shane and Rob, Con climbed into Archibald's saddle.

Shane stood back. "I hope you appreciate my giving up my horse for you, Cousin."

Con wrapped the reins around his hand. "I can't think why you did."

"Archibald knows how to keep a rider on his back. He's done it often enough for me."

Rob peered up at him. "Are you all right riding alone?"

"I've answered that twice already." Con smiled down at him. "Once for Shane, and once for Elsa. You, of all people, should know that I'm sturdy as my brother."

"You'll forgive my concern." Rob mounted his horse. "I've only just found you again."

"Perhaps you can discuss this later?" Shane spoke sharply.

Elsa turned her head. The lights had turned off the road and onto the path to Con's cabin.

Shane climbed into the saddle behind Rob.

Rob wheeled to face Elsa. "Make sure you keep up. Don't veer from the path unless you're forced to hide. You'll be safer that way." Rob turned his head to look at each of them in turn. "If we're separated, let's meet on the far side of Nevada City." He paused. "All right?"

Elsa's stomach churned. She wasn't sure where Nevada City was, but hopefully she wouldn't become separated from the men. She wished she could ride with one of them, but as the lightest, she'd been given the pack horse. Elsa had every intention of keeping up. Becoming separated would mean riding alone in the dark.

"Let's go." Rob's horse plunged down the path, away from

the road.

Con held back. He nodded to Elsa. "You first."

She opened her mouth to protest against Con bringing up the rear. What if his injury overcame him, and he fell? With the approaching hoofbeats louder and an unmovable expression on Con's face, Elsa closed her mouth and urged the mare down the path after Rob.

Elsa peered into the darkness behind her. The lights of the vigilantes shone nearer than before. Each time she glanced back, the movement of a darker shadow reassured her that Con followed.

But she could not see that shadow now.

Elsa faced forward to call out for Rob to stop, but he had already rounded the bend. She feared drawing attention with a shout. There seemed little to do but hope Con appeared soon. Whatever happened, she wouldn't abandon him.

She turned the mare off the path, dismounted, and led the horse beneath a patch of alders. She could see from here and still remain hidden in shadow. The path had moved away from Alder Creek, but she could hear its burbling and catch glimpses of silver through the shrubs.

Time passed, but Con did not emerge. Something rustled in the bushes.

Casting nervous glances about her, Elsa reached into her pocket and touched the hilt of the knife she'd taken from the cabin. The thought of using it, even in self-defense, sickened her.

Minutes went by without Con riding past. Elsa hesitated. Was she making a mistake by waiting here? If she didn't go soon, light from the vigilantes' lanterns would penetrate the shadows that hid her.

Arms slid around her all at once. A hand covered her mouth. "Quiet." Con's breath stirred her ear.

She nodded, and Con's hand slid away from her mouth. He pulled her backward, farther from the road. Hoofbeats filled the air. The lantern light increased. A horse nickered. Riders thundered by on the path.

Elsa sheltered against Con. He held her with one arm, his pistol in the other. His heartbeat thudded against her ear.

The riders continued on, and the lantern light faded. Elsa turned in Con's arms. "I thought I'd lost you."

"Not if I can help it." His lips pressed hers in a swift kiss. "A rabbit ran across my path and Archibald shied. I fell off, but not before I saw you turn aside. I left Shane's horse tied up behind the bushes and came after you. Come with me."

He led her onto the path a short distance, then turned onto an animal trail that cut through the underbrush. Shane's horse stood tethered to the shrubbery at the edge of a small clearing. His piebald coat gleamed in the moonlight.

Con untied Archibald and moved into position to climb onto the horse.

"I can help you into the saddle."

He shook his head. "That's not necessary."

Elsa resisted the urge to insist.

Con pulled himself halfway up, but then gasped and fell to the ground. He lay still while Archibald swung around and nuzzled his face.

Elsa rushed to him, her heart picking up its pace. She thought him unconscious, but he sat up. "Are you hurt?" She knelt beside him.

Con picked up his hat and dusted it off against his trouser

leg. "Only my pride."

"Let me help you." She rose and reached a hand down to him.

Con frowned. "I told you I don't need support."

"It's clear that you do," she answered lightly but firmly.

"Are you always this strong-minded?" Frustration edged Con's voice, but he let her steady him while he stood.

"Only when I'm right."

He tilted his head. "And I suppose that makes me—"

"Wrong."

He smiled. "I'd love to argue with you more. Truly, I would. But we'd better keep quiet. Hard telling who might be on the path tonight. The sooner we leave it behind, the better. It galls me to need assistance, but yes, you may give it."

Elsa tied the pack mare's reins around a bush while Con led Archibald into position. Con placed a hand on the pommel and a foot in the stirrup, then lifted himself. She hurried to push him higher.

He swung a leg over Archibald and straightened in the saddle. "Elsa?"

She turned from untying the pack mare. "Do you need something else?"

"Thank you."

She smiled. "You're welcome."

They backtracked along the path and passed Con's cabin on the way to the road. Once there, they turned right and crossed the bridge toward Nevada City. The dirt track took them through open bottomland threaded by waterways. The moon sailed upward, a glowing beacon in the night. A bird flew above them, its wings glinting.

Elsa sat straighter and forgot her weariness. "What was that?"

"A great horned owl, probably out hunting," Con replied from beside her.

She stifled a yawn. "When will we reach Nevada City?"

"It's not much farther. I only hope Rob and Shane kept ahead of that mob, and that we don't have a reception committee waiting for us."

Elsa shuddered at the thought. "When will this ordeal be over?"

"I'm sorry to drag you into my problems."

Elsa reined in her surprise. "I thought I was burdening you with mine."

Con laughed. "We seem to share the same knack for finding trouble."

The wind ruffled the horses' manes and tugged at Elsa's hair. She didn't mind. Lulled by the swaying of the pack horse, she might have slept had it not been so cold.

Con slowed. "Nevada City is just ahead."

"Where will we find Rob and Shane?"

"Rob wanted to meet on the far side of town. I'm sure they'll be watching for us from beside the road. But first, we have to make it past town." He urged Archibald forward with a glance over his shoulder. "Follow me."

Elsa's sleepiness evaporated. She turned off the road and down a slight incline behind Con. They traveled a small distance, then came out of a gulch and back onto the road.

Con waited for her to draw up beside him, and they continued together. "I'm not sure we needed to do that, since I didn't see the mob's lights, but I'd rather be safe than not."

"What if we've ridden too far and missed your brother and cousin?"

"I'm fairly certain they'd want to be farther out of town than this. For that matter, so do we." He clicked his tongue, and

Archibald picked up the pace.

Elsa pressed her horse to catch up. They rode together through barren land and a place where the river beside the road braided into channels.

Two men emerged from shrubbery lining the banks. Shane's wide-brimmed hat was easy to spot. Elsa hadn't known Rob long, but she recognized him.

"It's about time you made it." Rob scolded his brother with a smile.

"Yes, well"—Con grinned back at him—"I was delayed."

Shane's beamed at them, and his teeth glowed in the moonlight. "At least you had the good sense to keep Elsa with you."

Basking in their comradery, Elsa felt the tension leave her. She might have to sleep under the sky tonight, but the nightmarish journey had finally come to an end.

Rob took hold of the pack horse's bridle. "We'd better water the horses and be on our way. That mob won't be far behind."

CHAPTER EIGHTEEN

Con kicked a stone out of his way and sat down on a log beside Shane, who kept watch near the fire. He should be asleep, but first he had something to settle.

Shane glanced at his cousin with a questioning tilt to his head. "Something on your mind?"

"I've been thinking."

"Always a serious sign." Amusement lilted Shane's voice.

Con decided to come right out with it. "I've decided I should marry Elsa."

Shane poked at the embers with a stick. "Oh, really? What does *she* say about this idea?"

"I haven't taken it so far as to ask her, but I feel I should."

Shane cocked an eyebrow. "Any reason in particular?"

Con cleared his throat. "Well, yes."

"Care to elaborate?"

"When we were in Bannack, she spent the night in my cabin."

Shane stopped poking the fire. "Go on."

"It's not how it sounds. We didn't have much choice. You see, Miles had the staff at the hotel out looking for her."

Shane blew on the smoking end of his stick to make it glow. "Why would that be?"

"She'd run away and needed a place to hide, so I put her up in my cabin."

"Gallant of you."

"And then she stayed with us in Virginia City."

"Yes, but her reputation was already less than sterling at that point."

Con's lips twisted in a frown. "That was no fault of her own,"

"Of course not." Shane pitched the stick into the fire. "I was merely pointing out that the responsibility to shield her from gossip would not fall to you."

"I understand that, but I can't help feeling I should protect her, regardless."

Shane nodded. "That's admirable, but there are other ways than marriage to protect a woman."

"What, for instance?"

"You could offer her employment, help her move somewhere else, maybe send her back to Germany."

Con pushed a hand through his hair. He'd come to Shane with one decision to make. It had now become several. "What would *you* do?"

Shane smiled. "Between you and me, I was in a similar quandary over America."

"I see."

"No, you don't. Our situation wasn't 'like that' either. If anything, the whole thing made it harder to sort out because I loved America to distraction. That's why I wanted to marry her, not out of any duty to preserve her honor."

"Would you have done it, though?"

Shane picked up a new stick and went back to poking the fire. "Maybe. She didn't want me to marry her for that reason, though. It almost broke us apart."

"I've wondered what happened between the two of you."

"Well, now you know. I can tell you that marrying for duty doesn't hold a candle to marrying for love. If you only want to make an honest woman of Elsa out of duty, I'd suggest one of the other options I mentioned instead. But if you love Elsa, you should tie the knot." He grinned. "Assuming she'll have you. Do you know how you feel about her?"

Con stared into the embers, then glanced up. "I'm not entirely certain, to tell you the truth. Feeling duty-bound to wed her muddies the issue."

Shane nodded. "Give yourself time to make a decision you'll live with for a lifetime."

Elsa lay in her bedroll, staring up at the stars, weary beyond measure. It had been a hard ride. She wasn't used to spending so long in a saddle, and every muscle in her body ached. Now, all she wanted to do was sleep, but it had always been the same for her. Whenever she grew overtired, she had a hard time relaxing.

Con and Shane were talking at the fire, and the rumble of their voices drifted to her. It felt strange to travel with three men, live outdoors, and run from pursuers. If she was home in Germany, she would have her soft bed to sleep in and *Mutter* to wish her sweet dreams.

Tears burned Elsa's eyes, blurring the stars overhead. *How I wish I could go home.*

She sighed. Feeling sorry for herself was foolish. No one had forced her to come to America. She'd chased after a better life without realizing the value of the one she already led. She probably wouldn't have married Peter if she'd stayed, but that didn't matter.

In Germany, she could recognize the challenges she faced. She'd known how to earn money. The boundaries between people had been easy to navigate. In the West, she understood none of those things. She felt like a small child in need of a friend.

Elsa's chin quivered, and tears ran down her cheeks. Blaming God for her troubles would serve no purpose. She'd brought on these troubles by trying to improve her life without considering God's plan for her.

Now it was too late. Unless she found a way to return to Germany, she would never see her family again.

CHAPTER NINETEEN

In Bry's dream the odors of sweat mingled with grease and horse flesh hung heavy in the air. The war pony beneath Bry swung about, and her Cheyenne captor tightened his arm around her middle. Mules brayed and trampled the grasses. Painted warriors opened their throats in blood-curdling cries and plunged their ponies pell-mell around a crippled wagon.

Through a gap in the throng, Bry caught sight of Maisey weeping. Her husband sprawled on the ground beside her, an arrow protruding from his throat.

The world spun. Bry swallowed against the urge to retch.

Con darted from behind the wagon toward Maisey.

Bry's breath clogged in her throat. This couldn't be happening. Less than an hour before she'd been traveling in the wagon train, contemplating what to cook for dinner. Now she stared in horror while her brother placed himself in harm's way.

An arrow twanged and glinted. Con went down.

Bry whimpered. *Please, God. Don't let my brother be dead.*

The arm squeezed off her breath. Bry clawed at her captor. He hissed in a breath and released her. Bry fell from the pony. She scrambled to her feet and sprang away before the warrior could claim her again.

Bry pushed through the mounted warriors, hearing neither voices nor the stomping of hooves. She threw herself down beside Con and gasped.

Rob, staring with sightless eyes, lay in the grass where Con had fallen.

"No!" She grasped his chest. "Not you too."

Bry started awake. Sweat bathed her face. She sat up with the dream fading along with the sound of Indian warfare.

Nick pulled up in bed and curved his arm around her shoulder. "Are you all right?"

Bry shuddered. "I had a nightmare. Rob died."

Nick rubbed her back. "That's no surprise. You've been worrying about your brother ever since he left."

Still shaking, Bry clung to her husband. "I can't seem to move past the fear of losing him too."

"We don't know for certain that Con is dead, or have you forgotten that?"

"You're right. I should hold to faith. Something else troubles me, though."

Nick lay down and pulled Bry beside him, tucking her head under his chin. "Tell me."

"My dream took me to the time I saw Con shot. Whenever that happens, it's so real, I feel like I'm there all over again."

"It's natural to need time to recover from such a shock." He kissed her hair. "Your mind is trying to make sense of what happened."

With her husband's warmth soothing her, Bry let her eyelids drift shut. "That makes sense, I suppose."

"Have you considered releasing your brothers to God's care?" Nick's voice rumbled against her ear.

"That's easier said than done."

A chuckle shook his chest. "Did you at any time hear me say that trusting God is easy? Dear Heart, faith takes courage and the will to believe."

Elsa huddled at the fire, grateful for its warmth on an overcast day. Smoke curled upward to blend with the mist lowering through the pine branches.

She'd been too exhausted to notice much when they'd halted the journey in the early morning. Waking from a sound sleep, she found herself in a small valley. Surrounded by evergreen-clad hills and cut by a stream that cascaded from a gap between tumbled rocks, the valley seemed a sanctuary no evil could touch.

Con came to stand near where Elsa sat. "Did you sleep well?" He sipped coffee from a tin cup.

She looked up and nodded. "Once I fell asleep, I did."

"Were you awake while I was talking to Shane?"

Why did he sound startled? "I heard your voices."

"Oh." His expression revealed his relief.

What were he and Shane talking about? Elsa couldn't help but wonder if it had anything to do with her. When arriving in America with her hopes pinned to her sleeve, she'd never expected to become a burden to others. She should let Con know that she wouldn't intrude on him much longer.

"Where are we going?" She skirted the subject.

Con glanced at her and then away. "I want to take you to my ranch, if you'd care to accompany me there."

Elsa stared at him and searched for her voice. "I couldn't live with you."

"We wouldn't be alone." Con smiled. "My sister and her husband live at the ranch. I think you'd like Bryanna."

She sighed, hating to impose. "I suppose I must."

Con frowned. "I'm sorry you feel that way."

"Oh, no. I didn't mean—" She broke off, her face heating. "Thank you for your generosity."

"Well then, it's settled. Take all the time you need at the ranch. There's no hurry to decide your future."

"Thank you."

"We're packed and ready." Shane joined them. "Rob's with the horses. Time to go." He kicked out the fire.

"Such impatience, Cousin." Con smiled at Shane, then Elsa. "We should reach Deer Lodge before nightfall."

"Deer Lodge?"

"It's a town in a large valley by the same name. I learned to ranch there." Con started toward the horses.

Elsa fell into step beside him. "Why is it called that?"

"At the north end of the valley there's a large mound formed by a warm spring. The Snake Indians call it 'The White-tailed Deer Lodge' because so many of the creatures come to the salt deposits. The mound resembles an Indian lodge on a winter's morning, with steam rising like smoke above it."

Elsa tried to picture such a place and couldn't. "It must be a wonderful sight."

"I'll take you to see it, if there's time." Con stopped beside the pack horse. "I wish I could boost you into the saddle."

Elsa gave him a shy smile. "How are you feeling this morning?"

Con touched his side. "I'm aware that I have ribs, shall we say?"

"If you can tear yourself away from the pretty lady, brother of mine, we should be on our way." Rob grinned from atop his horse.

"That's a hard thing you ask." Con gave Elsa a smile that took her breath away before joining Shane beside the horses.

About to remark that he seemed to be moving better today, Elsa froze with the words on her lips. She scanned the underbrush. Had she heard a twig cracking beneath someone's foot?

Shane helped Con onto his horse.

Probably just a deer or other animal. Elsa grasped the pommel and put her foot in the stirrup.

The chink of metal cut through the air.

The men froze.

"Throw down your weapons," a man called from out of sight, "by order of Sheriff Alan Gerhart of Virginia City." The click of guns cocking reinforced his words. "Take it nice and slow."

Con's head snapped up. Shane peered about. Rob's hand inched toward his gun.

Elsa took her foot out of the stirrup. She waited, her pulse racing, for what would happen next.

Con tensed, then he reached for his gun with a feeling of utter defeat. He couldn't bring himself to look at Elsa, whom he had tried but failed to protect.

"Don't forget--make it slow and steady." The sheriff remained hidden, but his voice made his presence known. "In case you wondered, I have a rifle trained on your chest."

Con removed his weapon from its holster and tossed it on the ground. He didn't turn his head to look, but two more thuds told him that Shane and Rob had done the same.

Sheriff Gerhart and the other horsemen—all holding rifles—surrounded them on every side.

Con recognized the lawman who had intervened in his fight with Miles.

"Pick up their weapons." The sheriff pulled down his hat

brim to shade his eyes. Several men dismounted and rushed to obey.

Miles rode up beside Elsa. In his bowler hat and greatcoat, he looked like the perfect gentleman. The effect was somewhat diminished by the purple bruise ringing his eye.

Con stifled a grin at the beauty of his work.

Miles nodded to Con, and a slow smile spread across his face. "Lynch the murderer!"

"String him up," another man took up the call.

"Time for a necktie party," a third chimed in.

Rob's horse edged closer to Con. "Let's not be hasty, Sheriff."

"Stay put." Sheriff Gerhart raised his weapon. "As you can hear, this posse is eager to impart justice."

Rob's face assumed the innocent expression Con knew well from when he'd gotten into trouble as a child. "Would you blame me for a restless horse?"

"You'd better calm it down fast," the sheriff replied in a droll voice.

Shane took hold of Rob's bridle. "You wouldn't want to harm an innocent man, now would you?"

Miles's smile vanished. "Don't listen to their lies."

Rob glared at Miles before returning his attention to the sheriff. "What charges do you have against my brother?"

Sheriff Gerhart sat forward in the saddle, making the leather creak. "There's talk of kidnapping, and a report that he murdered a man."

"A report, *nothing*!" Miles rode out from the mob to Sheriff Gerhart's side. "There's a body buried on Con Walsh's claim."

The sheriff shot him an annoyed glance. "Mr. Peabody, I must ask you to quiet yourself."

Miles shook his head. "I won't be silent about this, Sheriff.

The preacher's guilty too. Atticus saw him bury the body."

"String them up!"

"Lynch the murderers."

The cries grew louder. The posse pressed forward.

Elsa cowered beside her horse.

Con turned his head toward the sheriff. "They're frightening the lady."

Sheriff Gerhart's rifle fired. Smoke poured from the barrel as the bullet launched skyward.

Silence fell.

"That's enough." Gerhart sat taller in the saddle. "While I'm sheriff, we won't hang anyone without a trial, and most certainly not in front of a woman." He glanced toward Elsa. "Are you all right, Miss?"

She nodded but kept her gaze cast downward. The urge to comfort her swept over Con.

The sheriff turned to Shane. "Well, preacher? Did you bury a body?"

Shane's head bobbed, his slouch hat skating shadows across his face. "Yes, I did, and I would again. It's part of my job as a preacher to give the dead decent burials. Even the miserable claim jumper who tried to kill my cousin has that right."

The sheriff narrowed his eyes. "That's a lot to do for someone you consider a scoundrel."

"God judges the souls of men, not I."

"Did you witness his death?"

"No, but I found my cousin in his own cabin, barely able to move from the bruising he'd received. He pulled his gun in self-defense when an intruder attacked him. It went off by accident in their struggle."

Miles snorted. "He'll say anything to clear his cousin."

Sheriff Gerhart sighed. "Save it for miners' court, Peabody."

He turned his horse about. "Arrest these men."

CHAPTER TWENTY

"Wait!" Elsa thrust herself forward before the sheriff could ride past. She had kept silent, overwhelmed by the crowd, but she could not stand by while those who had helped her toward freedom lost theirs. "There's been no crime."

The sheriff's face softened. "Miss Meier, if I may ask, have these men forced you to do anything against your will?"

Heat climbed up Elsa's neck. The sheriff's inference couldn't have been plainer. She held her head high. "Not at all. They have shown me only kindness. Reverend Hayes told you the truth, I promise you."

"How can you know that, Miss Meier?"

"Because . . ." Elsa swallowed. She didn't want to think how this might sound. "Because I was with him when he found his cousin."

The sheriff searched her face. "Were you forced to go with Reverend Hayes to Mr. Walsh's cabin?"

She sighed. "I went with him freely. We found Con—Mr. Walsh—gravely injured, just as Reverend Hayes described."

"Did Mr. Walsh say anything in your presence?"

"He expressed his sorrow that the intruder had died. He told me it was an accident."

The sheriff narrowed his eyes. "And you believed him?"

Elsa nodded. "It seemed clear that he'd spoken the truth."

"Forgive me, but I must ask. Why did you go to the cabin?"

Miles rode nearer to them. "What does this have to do with the murder?"

Sheriff Gerhart gave Miles a stern glance, then looked at Elsa. "Go on."

She wavered. How could she tell the horrible details of what had happened to her? She looked at Con. His gaze burned into hers, lending her courage, while the men handcuffed him.

How was it possible that Con could give her strength without saying a word? It had been the same on the stagecoach when they'd first met. Since then, the invisible tie that bound them together had somehow grown stronger.

What should I do? Elsa couldn't accuse Miles and Alicia of drugging her without providing proof. She had none.

Worse, she had traveled with them of her own volition, even if they'd made it hard to consider doing anything else. It would be her word against any testimony Atticus, Miles, and Alicia might give. She had no doubt they would reinforce one another's stories.

It would do no good to speak up, and it might create hardships for her. She'd have to testify if it went to trial and suffer the notoriety that ordeal would bring. It would probably be for nothing, since she was unlikely to win. What chance did she stand against a prominent citizen of Virginia City like Atticus?

She thought back to the time when Papa had caught her lying. He'd impressed on her in more than one way that she should always tell the truth. She sighed and took a deep breath. "While walking along Alder Creek, I fell over a boulder and hurt myself. Reverend Hayes came along and took me on his horse to Mr. Walsh's cabin, where he hoped to tend my injuries."

Sheriff Gerhart's forehead creased. "That doesn't sound like a man bent on concealing a murder."

"She's in it with them." Miles's voice rose to a nervous pitch. "Obviously."

"Keep interrupting, Peabody, and I'll ask why you're so interested in convicting these men."

"I know why," Elsa said softly.

Miles's face went white. "Elsa is not well."

Sheriff Gerhart nodded. "So you say. No need to pull out that letter. It hasn't changed from the last time you showed it to me. I'm not sure I believe it, anyway. What's to stop a person from forging such an item?"

Miles pursed his lips. "You're making a grave mistake if you believe Miss Meier's nonsense."

"If you ask me, the lady seems a sight more composed than you do at the moment." Sheriff Gerhart pointed to a large pine tree overshadowing the circled men. "Ride over there, will you? No point breathing down Miss Meier's neck."

Miles gave the sheriff a frustrated glance and Elsa a venomous glare, then retreated the requested distance.

Sheriff Gerhart moved closer to Elsa. "You want to tell me what you didn't say earlier?"

"I was kidnapped, but not by Con Walsh." She spoke barely above a whisper.

"Miles Peabody?"

She nodded swiftly. "Yes, but Atticus Merrick ordered it."

"Those are serious charges." The sheriff's eyes widened. "Do you have proof?"

"No. It would be my word against three others. That's why I didn't say anything before now."

Sheriff Gerhart rubbed the back of his neck, clearly mystified. "Something seems wrong here. I'm inclined to believe your story, Miss Meier, simply because of the way Peabody's acting." He turned to Shane. "Reverend, you claimed the deceased man tried to kill your cousins. Care to elaborate?"

Shane sat on his horse with his hands cuffed. "You already

know about Con's experience. I suggest you ask Rob about his."

"That claim jumper tried to kill me when I was staying in Con's cabin," Rob volunteered. "He beat me and left me for dead in the creek. Then he made off with my horse."

The sheriff turned to Elsa. "Do you believe Con Walsh told you the truth that night?"

She didn't hesitate. "I'd stake my life on it."

"She'd be making a good bet!" a voice called out.

"Who said that?" Sheriff Gerhart peered past the mob. "Let the man through."

The mob parted, and Cecil rode forward. "Good morning, sheriff." He touched his hat. "Ma'am."

"Cecil, what are you doing here?" The sheriff gave the crusty miner a baffled look.

"I've come to see justice served, same as the rest of you." Cecil reined in beside Elsa. "I might have a different idea of that than some of these fine men. You see, I was there when Tate Weatherby tried to kill Rob. I looked on Tate's face before Shane buried him. And I saw what Tate did to Con when he beat him up."

Sheriff Gerhart peered at him. "Would you attest to that?"

"Most assuredly."

The sheriff divided a glance between Con, Shane, and Rob. "Where were you headed today?"

"To my ranch in the Bitterroot Valley," Con answered.

"If you'll remain in that valley until after I've conducted my investigation, you're free to go."

Miles's face turned red. "You're making a mistake, sheriff."

Grumblings rose from some of the men.

Sheriff Gerhart pointed his gun at Miles. "If you or anyone else sees fit to challenge my authority, I have a jail cell waiting for you."

Oil sconces in gilt cages scattered light across the restaurant's gray carpet which was woven with lighter fan shapes. Con seated Elsa in a high-backed chair cushioned in dark leather, then claimed a place across from her. Shane opened his menu beside her. Rob sank down next to Con and glanced around the room.

Elsa leaned back in her chair with a sigh. This elegant restaurant was a far cry from the campfires they'd taken meals around while traveling to Deer Lodge.

Con was watching her from across the table, a somber expression on his face. The claim jumper's death must haunt him, or else his mood had something to do with her. Elsa frowned. Did he regret offering to take her to the ranch?

Shane glanced up from the menu. "After days of eating trail food, this all looks good."

Rob smiled. "I never claimed to know how to cook. Thankfully, Elsa took pity on me."

"I meant no insult to Elsa's cooking." Shane smiled.

"Only to mine?" Rob roared with laughter.

"Elsa, tell Rob and Shane what the doctor said about your ankle." Con's quiet voice cut through the merriment.

She smiled. "It's mending well."

"And you, Con?" Rob glanced at his brother. "What did the doctor say about your ribs?"

"They're bruised, but each remains intact. I suspected as much."

"It's good to be certain about these things." Shane returned to his menu. "I can't make up my mind."

"It's good to be certain, indeed." Con's gaze rested on Elsa. "Some decisions can't be rushed."

"Well, I'm hungry, so I'd better choose." Shane scanned the bill of fare, yet again. "I'm going to have the rib eye steak."

"Me too." Con laid his menu aside.

"Oh, really?" Shane raised an eyebrow. "I've never known you to follow anyone."

Con grinned. "I'm not."

"How can you say that when you never even opened your menu?"

"I didn't need to see it. A steak is what I want."

"Then you'll be glad to know there are several to choose from." Shane winked at Rob.

"That's not surprising, so close to the Kohrs ranch. I still want rib eye."

Elsa chuckled at their bantering. This was how being in a family felt. "What is the Kohrs ranch?"

"It's the original cattle holding in Deer Lodge Valley. Johnny Grant built the place, but he sold out to Conrad Kohrs last year. I worked there before striking out on my own." Con turned to Rob. "Did you find out when the stagecoach leaves for Liberty?"

"Day after tomorrow, but I won't be on it. There's a small matter of two horses to return, unless I want to forfeit the cost of reserving them."

Con tilted his head. "Which was?"

"A hundred dollars each, the price of replacements."

Con nodded. "That's not unusual. The charge protects the livery. No need to return the horses. Unless I've forgotten my financial details, I can afford to buy them."

"You already have, in a way. I used the profits from driving your cattle to the gold camps last year."

"Thank you for looking after the ranch that way. I'd say you earned the money fairly."

"I'd just as soon have gold than horses."

Con's eyebrows lifted. "I don't mind keeping them and paying you."

Rob frowned and said no more on the subject.

Con opened the door at a knock. Rob stood waiting in the hotel hallway. Con stepped back and waved him inside.

Rob sat in the winged-back chair by the fire. "The sky's clear tonight, and I suspect the weather tomorrow will be fine to take Elsa on an excursion, if you're so inclined."

"Wipe that grin off your face." Con chided him but could not suppress his own smile.

"Elsa would make a good wife."

"The thought has occurred to me." Con perched on the bed. "And what about you? Is there anyone special?"

"Maybe." Rob frowned. "I suppose nothing will come of it now."

"Why would you say that?"

"Because I am smitten with the chance to make something of myself in Virginia City," Rob said in a rush.

Con frowned. "Are you telling me that I've come home, only to lose my brother?"

"Try to understand this from my point of view. I have nothing but what you give me."

"You had little enough in the slum."

"True, but what I had was my own." Rob stood and paced before the fire. "I'm a man, Con. I need to earn my way."

"Do you think you wouldn't at the ranch?" Con snapped back.

"Of course not." Rob shook his head. "It's hard to explain . . . except that I'll not travel on another man's coattails, not even yours."

"That's it, I suppose. You've decided this without me."

"Yes, but I hoped for your blessing."

Con knew his approval mattered to his brother, but . . . "I'd give it gladly, if I thought going after gold was anything more than a fool's gamble."

"*You* did it."

"That should be enough to warn you."

Rob paused in his pacing. "I've always looked up to you, Con. I wanted to be like you -- that is until you left us."

"Sorry, Rob. I didn't intend for things to work out that way."

"Never mind." Rob sat down. "I was wrong to blame you. I can see that now, when I couldn't then. If you hadn't left, you wouldn't have returned to deliver us from that vile place."

Con closed his eyes and sat quietly.

"Forgive me, if you can, for what I said when you came back for me."

"I have."

"Thank you." Rob rose and headed for the door. When his hand grasped the doorknob, he glanced over his shoulder. "You were more of a brother to me than I knew."

"Wait!" Con shot up from the bed before the door closed. "You can work my claim in Virginia City until you establish your own."

Rob turned back into the room. "I appreciate that."

"My thoughts are muddied by what I feel, coming home after so long. I do understand and wish the best for you."

Rob offered a weak smile. "Say goodbye to Bry for me."

The restaurant sounded different in the morning, with dishes clattering and voices louder. Elsa found Con and Shane already at the table. She ordered coffee and an omelet. Breakfast arrived with gratifying swiftness.

"We'll be at loose ends for a day." Con buttered his toast.

Elsa put her fork down and gave him a puzzled glance. Why did he sound so happy about the delay?

Con smiled. "I promised Elsa the chance to see the Deer Lodge mound."

"I'm afraid I'll have to beg off." Shane lifted his coffee cup. "I'm having lunch with Brother Masters."

"With Rob gone, that leaves Elsa alone with me all day."

Shane frowned. "I wish your brother had talked with me before leaving."

"He did to *me*." Con bit into his toast.

Shane's brows rose. "And you approved?"

"Not exactly." Con swallowed his coffee. "But it was his choice."

"Much as I hate to admit it, Cousin, you're right."

The corners of Con's mouth tilted. "I'd love for you to repeat that."

Shane smiled. "Saying it once was bad enough. I've seen this coming with Rob for a long time, but I never imagined he'd leave so abruptly. Bry will be upset, and I hate to think how Maisey will react."

"Maisey?" Con frowned. "The name rings a bell."

"She is Bry's friend from the wagon train." Shane peered at

him. "Do you recall her?"

Con squinted. "I think so." His eyes widened. "She was kidnapped with Bry. What does she have to do with Rob?"

Shane glanced at Elsa. "Something was brewing between the two of them, or so I thought."

Con sipped from his coffee cup. "Rob admitted he was interested in a woman. Maybe he meant Maisey."

"I wouldn't doubt it."

Elsa frowned. She'd broken Peter's heart by going away, much as Rob would Maisey's.

"Elsa?"

She startled and stared at Con.

He smiled. "You were daydreaming, I suppose."

"I'm sorry."

"Don't be. The bewildered look on your face is utterly charming. I suppose you didn't hear anything I said?"

Elsa had been lost in thoughts of Peter, but there was no need to mention that. She sighed. "Please forgive me."

Con's eyes gleamed. "I asked if you would be willing to brave a buggy ride with me. I promise to behave like a gentleman."

The idea took Elsa's breath away, but she managed to nod.

Shane excused himself after breakfast, leaving them alone. Con walked Elsa to her room. "Bring your coat. It's warm now, but we'll be gone most of the day. This time of year you don't know when the weather will turn. I'll bring the buggy around."

After gathering her coat, reticule, and a blanket, Elsa hurried downstairs and outside. Con opened the buggy door and offered his hand to help her in.

Elsa hesitated, concerned about his ribs, but then accepted his assistance. She understood enough about men to know Con would not want her to coddle him. He joined her and took up the lines.

The buggy rolled down the street behind a pair of sleek black horses. Elsa settled against the leather backrest, happier than she'd been in a long time. With the buggy top down and the sun radiating warmth, it seemed nothing bad would happen to her ever again.

Elsa could hardly credit that mere days ago, she'd climbed out a window to escape a man bent on making her his prisoner. Tasting freedom made it all the more precious.

I will never surrender my freedom again.

She no longer felt under obligation to repay Miles. The cost of a ticket to America was a small price for what he'd put her through. He'd sold her to Atticus like livestock.

Con handled the lines with confidence, and the horses raced across the valley. Snow-clad mountains stood steadfast beneath a blue sky wisped by clouds. Ponds and streams shimmered against the grassy plain. Lines of geese arrowed overhead, honking.

With the wind in her face, Elsa laughed out loud for the sheer joy of living.

Con joined in, his eyes shining. "You are more beautiful in this moment than ever."

Elsa's face warmed. "Thank you."

"You should always laugh."

She smiled. "I would soon tire."

"Tell me, if you could have whatever you wanted in life, what would you choose?"

Her smile faltered. "To have my family near."

"I'm sorry. I didn't mean to make you sad."

Elsa bit her lip, then decided to speak. "I wonder . . . would you help me find a job?"

Con's eyes widened. "You won't need to work. I have

enough money to support you."

"I'm used to paying my own way."

Con sighed. "You and Rob are alike in some ways. Please allow me the joy of taking this burden from your shoulders."

"All right, for a *little* while, but at least let me help out around the ranch."

He took her hand. "What I would really like is for you to cook some of those delightful German meals you prepare so well."

Elsa broke into a smile. "Of course! That's easy."

"Then it's all settled. I'm sure Bry won't mind stepping aside from kitchen duty now and again."

"That will be all right for a couple of months, but then I must find a job." She shouldn't accept his charity for long.

"Why do you feel the need of one?"

"I can't impose on you forever, and a job will bring money for my passage to Germany." The words did not come easily, which made no sense. After being so homesick, why did she hesitate to speak of returning to her homeland?

"I wondered if you might put down roots in America, but it's clear where your heart lies." Con frowned. "Did you leave a sweetheart behind?"

"Not really. Peter was not my *Schatz*."

"Who is Peter?"

"Just a boy from my village." She shrugged. "Well, a man now. We grew up together. He had . . . certain hopes."

Con guided the horses around a curve. "How did he react to your going away?"

"He wasn't pleased." He had, in fact, ranted at her before stomping off.

"I can imagine. What about you?"

She glanced at him in surprise. "I'm not sure what you

mean."

"How did you react to leaving him? From what I understand, you felt obligated to go. Would things have turned out differently if you had stayed?"

"It doesn't matter anymore." She sighed. "I doubt Peter would want me now."

Con's scowl forbade further conversation.

Elsa rode beside him in silence. Con must think her foolish. She'd abandoned a suitor who might have married her to risk coming to America with nothing. She sat primly and yearned for the miles to pass.

CHAPTER TWENTY-ONE

SHANE CROSSED THE HOTEL RESTAURANT TO the table where Bishop David Masters stood smiling. Clean-shaven and wearing his usual black jacket, white shirt, and string tie, David offered a handshake. "It's been a while since we've talked, Shane."

"Nearly a year. It's good to see you."

David sat down. "It's gratifying to find you in a better state each time we meet."

Shane took the chair across from him. "Thanks to your guidance."

"You may credit our Lord with that. I am but His messenger. How is your lovely wife?"

"America blossoms in the midst of trials. I've never seen anything like it. I learn from her daily. It's amazing that I ever doubted my feelings for my wife. How could I have been so dense? I love her more than breath."

David broke into a smile. "God chooses a preacher's wife with care. So, what brings you to Deer Lodge?"

"A long and sorry tale, having to do with my cousin, Con."

David's face brightened. "Ah, yes. An intense young man."

"Con landed in trouble through no fault of his own and vanished for a year. It was hardest on Bry."

"I can well imagine."

"I found him alive, but the worse for a run-in with a claim jumper. That's a complicated story. What matters is that we're together and headed home." He picked up his glass and gulped water, then met David's gaze. "A posse chased us partway here, but the sheriff turned us loose."

"Why did they pursue you?"

"To charge Con with murder, but it was an accident. There are certain factions that want my cousin in jail. Do you remember Atticus Merrick?"

"How could I forget the man? He made target practice out of you."

Shane winced. "I'd prefer no reminder of that. I ran into Atticus in Bannack recently and found him a shrunken shadow of the man who terrorized me."

"That's the way of it when you're dealing with a bully." David's lips curved. "Once you confront a tormentor, you inevitably realize how weak he is."

"Yes! That was it exactly. What I felt couldn't have surprised me more."

David watched him without stirring.

"It was pity." Shane shook his head. "It startles me still."

David's lips curved in a tender smile. "Are you surprised to find the love of God growing in you? Think of it, Shane. We are like ants in His sight, and yet Almighty God sent His Son to die for our sins. That makes no sense in human terms, but God doesn't think like a man."

"He certainly does not think like this man. I've long wondered what I would do if I ran into Atticus again." Shane grimaced. "I had thoughts of pummeling him."

"Instead, God gave you the ability to forgive."

"That's a marvel."

"We must accept His love and mercy without trying to fathom them, for we cannot."

Shane sat forward in his chair. "Not here on Earth, but in Heaven we will understand. The Bible tells us so in first Corinthians. 'For now we see through a glass darkly, but then face to face. Now I know in part, but then shall I know even as also I am known.'"

"I always believed you'd make a fine preacher."

"There it is ahead." Con pointed out a rust-colored mound that rose higher and sat wider than Elsa had imagined from his description. Four men could stand on one another's shoulders and still not reach the top.

Con drew up the buggy and helped her down. She skirted bubbling pools at the base to touch the rock. "It's warm." She took a step, slipping a little in the dampness.

"Steady there." Con caught her by the waist. "The spring is quite hot. There's more steam in winter, but you can see a little now."

She nodded. "Why is the rock this color?"

"It's rusty from the iron within it."

She gazed up at him. "Thanks for bringing me today."

He smiled down at her. "It's my pleasure. Are you hungry?"

"I am."

His smile broadened. "All right, woman, I'll feed you."

Elsa caught herself staring at Con, captivated by his handsome features and shifting expressions. He stared right back in a way that made her want to lose herself in his arms again. She wrenched her gaze away.

Con touched her elbow and guided her to the buggy. He handed her a basket weighted with food and slung a blanket over his arm. "Do you favor a particular spot for our picnic?"

"We could sit in the shade by that tree."

Con spread the blanket in the place she indicated. Elsa

unpacked the basket, which contained fried chicken, biscuits, potato salad, and carrot cake. Con poured glasses of lemonade, and they began their feast.

Elsa had eaten many meals with Con by now, but never alone. This felt different. "Do you come to this place often?" She bit into a biscuit.

"Not anymore. One of the other wranglers at the ranch where I worked brought me to see it shortly after I relocated to Deer Lodge." He grinned. "I was pretty green back then. Now I know a thing or two about cattle."

"Do you like ranching?"

"Tending livestock comes naturally to me. Working at something I'm good at is better than drifting about. I did that for far too many years. It was high time for me to follow Shane's example and settle down."

His smile lit his eyes, turning them a color that reminded Elsa of a green pool shining in the sun. Distracted, she gazed into their depths.

Con's expression softened.

Realizing she was staring, Elsa looked away. "I used to take care of our milk cow. We called her *Pfirsiche.* That means 'peaches' in English."

"That's a strange name for a cow. I can probably guess how you came up with it."

"Whenever she went through the fence, we children always chased her out of the peach trees." Elsa laughed. "She loved them."

"I can picture you as a milkmaid." He touched her hair, which she'd worn partway down. "You'd have your hair in braids and a glow on your cheeks."

She should pull away from his touch instead of gaping at him like a love-struck schoolgirl.

Con dropped his hand and gave his attention to his food.

Elsa seemed to have lost her appetite, but she did her best to eat.

Con picked up his glass of lemonade. The cords of his neck flexed as he drank. He lowered his glass and turned to catch her staring again.

Whatever Elsa had been about to say vanished from her thoughts. Con leaned forward, and his mouth covered hers. His lips, cool and enticing, tasted of lemonade. Utterly beguiled, Elsa tipped her face at a better angle, and he obligingly deepened the kiss. Con held her lightly, with his hand at her back. Elsa slid her hands around his neck and felt the smooth texture of his hair between her fingers.

Con threaded his fingers through the hair at her nape and rubbed circles in her scalp while his mouth explored hers. Elsa clung to him for support, feeling like a leaf spinning out of control in a wild current.

Con gently withdrew. "I've forgotten my promise to behave."

She lowered her gaze. "Shane is right. We should be careful."

"It's up to me to ensure we do. I wouldn't wrong you for the world." He kissed her forehead, a simple gesture, but one that marked possession. "We should go back."

They packed the remainder of the food and shook out the blanket. Con held Elsa's hand on the way back to the buggy and kissed it before helping her inside.

Elsa watched him take up the lines, blinking away foolish tears. How could she have made such a mistake? Right when she'd made up her mind to earn her way home to Germany, she'd fallen in love with Con.

Elsa waved to Shane from the window as the stagecoach started off. He planned to follow more slowly on Archibald. Con pressed against Elsa, waving also, then fell back into the seat beside her. She was glad to leave Deer Lodge behind. The town was too close to Virginia City—and Atticus. Her nerves had troubled her the whole time they'd stayed here, and she'd noticed Con's vigilance. The stagecoach picked up speed on the road out of town, stirring dust in its wake. Outside the window, a herd of antelope bounded across the waving prairie. Elsa never tired of seeing the creatures with their dark noses, white tails, and short, curving horns. She watched until the herd dwindled out of sight.

The stage bucked across wagon ruts at a meeting of roads. Elsa held onto the leather strap beside the window to avoid sprawling across the mailbags on the floor, a feat two men had already performed. The coach veered westward onto a more even surface. The men climbed back onto the backless middle bench with apologies for the feet they trampled.

Elsa let go of the strap. "That was rough."

Con smiled. "The ride should stay smooth for a while. We're on the Mullan Road."

Elsa gave him a questioning look.

"The army built and now maintains this road to provide a better route west from Fort Benton. We'll follow it until we turn south at Hell Gate."

Elsa glanced at him in surprise. "That's a strange name for a town. Or is it another formation like the Deer Lodge mound?"

"I can see how you might wonder that. No, Hell Gate is a town. It received its name because French trappers found so many human remains in the canyons. They called it *Porte de l'Enfer*, which means Gate of Hell."

"What a terrible story." Elsa shuddered. "What happened there?"

"When the Bitterroot Salish tribe tried to reach their hunting grounds, the Blackfeet would ambush them."

"How sad. Wasn't there enough game for both tribes to hunt?"

"There was plenty of game."

Elsa frowned. "Then why do such a thing?"

Con took her hand. "I'm sorry I told you the tale. I should have realized it would upset you."

"Why must people be cruel?"

"Not everyone finds kindness easy, and there's the trouble."

Elsa had learned firsthand the truth of Con's statement. It would take a long time to put the injustices she'd suffered behind her.

Needing to withdraw, she gazed out at a blue ribbon of water that unfurled through the grasses.

"That's the Clark Fork River."

She nodded but said nothing further. Eventually, Con entered into a conversation with the fresh-faced youth on his other side. From the bits and pieces Elsa gleaned, the young man was on his way to join his family in the Bitterroot Valley.

The two passengers on the middle bench weren't much older than the youth. Across the stagecoach sat an elderly woman, a younger woman, and a little girl with bright eyes and a mischievous smile. She reminded Elsa of her youngest sister, Aileen.

The older woman was probably the little girl's grandmother. She gave Elsa a disapproving glance and turned her shoulder. She had glowered at Elsa ever since they'd introduced themselves. Short of lying, there had been no way for Elsa to hide that she was traveling alone with a man not her husband. The woman probably wouldn't understand that this compromising situation, like the others Elsa had endured, was no fault of her own.

She sighed. *What must it be like to have your life so ordered that you can control everything that happens to you?*

The rhythmic tick and sway of the stagecoach lulled Elsa into closing her eyes. After catching herself nodding off twice, she gave up and rested her head in the padded corner. Elsa longed to stretch out, but it was not possible in the cramped space. She drifted into a state between wakefulness and sleep, accomplishing neither.

Con half-listened to his young companion's chatter. Jamie Broderick had never been west of St. Louis. Despite this considerable handicap, he brimmed with tales, obviously gleaned from dime novels.

Oh, to be that age with all your prospects before you. Con had never been so young and carefree. His had not been a world of wonder such as Jamie's, but rather a struggle for survival in the slums of Manhattan. He did not begrudge young Jamie his enthusiasm, however. His own life had taught him to treasure such innocence.

He could not attend to every nuance of each story Jamie told. The youth rushed on in a one-sided dialogue, and Con realized his attention was not required. This freed him to steal glances at Elsa, who gave every appearance of being asleep. Curled in the corner, her sweet face relaxed in repose, she looked at once vulnerable and desirable. This stirred within him the longing to shelter her in his arms. He wished he had the right.

Con frowned. Elsa had spoken of Peter, who might even now be waiting in Germany. He shouldn't ask her to stay, not when she had clearly expressed the desire to return to her homeland.

He understood Elsa's wish to be near family, especially after he'd been separated from his own for so long. He had invited Rob to mine his claim partly so he would know where to find him. Con preferred to avoid Virginia City but would show his face from time to time to check on his brother's welfare.

Rob's apology meant a lot. Con had never planned to abandon his family, but it must have seemed that way. Regret pulled at Con. He'd hoped to establish a better relationship with his brother at the ranch. That dream had ridden off with Rob and might never find its way home.

Pauses appeared in Jamie's narrative, then silences of a longer nature. Jamie's head nodded and fell back against the button-leather upholstery. A glance around showed Con the other passengers in a similar state. The two men riding in the middle sat with heads together and backs turned. Con couldn't tell if their eyes were closed, but he suspected so. The child had fallen asleep across her drowsing mother's lap. The older woman rested against the younger's shoulder with her eyes closed.

The stagecoach rattled around a corner with more speed than caution, throwing Elsa into him. She opened her eyes briefly, but then her eyelids shut. She rested her head on his shoulder and nuzzled against his neck.

Con grinned and slid his arm around her. He couldn't recommend stagecoach travel, but it had its compensations.

A sudden shout from the driver signaled trouble.

Con shifted Elsa and craned out the window. Two armed men waited alongside the road ahead. His heart pounding, Con considered what to do. He should wake the others, certainly, and call them to arms.

Elsa lifted her face and blinked sleepy eyes. "What's wrong?"

Gunfire punched the air, and a body dropped past the window.

Elsa shrieked and clung to Con.

The other passengers cried out in alarm.

Con reached for his gun.

The stagecoach shuddered to a stop.

CHAPTER TWENTY-TWO

BRY OPENED THE DOOR AND SLIPPED into her brother's bedroom. Afternoon light penetrated the curtains at the window and painted patterns on the Persian rug. She crossed to the bed, a tall piece of furniture with a high headboard. The massive furniture served as a reminder that Con never did anything by half-measures.

She pictured Con lounging against the headboard and gazing out the window, deep in thought. He acted tough, but Bry knew her brother's soft heart. Con had been gone for over a year. Standing in his room brought him closer, and it felt to Bry that he might return any moment.

The closet door swung open beneath her hand. She ran her fingers through the garments Con had left behind. This jacket resembled the one he'd worn in Independence in the hotel restaurant. They had run into a couple—what were their names? Bry wrinkled her brow. She couldn't remember.

Whatever her name, the blonde woman had caught Con's interest, more was the pity. She pressed her lips together at the sudden memory of the woman dropping her handkerchief. Con should have let it lie. He'd been foolish enough to retrieve the lacy scrap, leading to all sorts of trouble.

Bry's lips curved upward at her brother's naivety. He hadn't suspected the woman of dropping the hankie on purpose. Her smile broadened. Of course he'd been flattered when Bry suggested she had.

Whatever the strange couple's story, Bry had sensed

something untoward going on. She was glad when they left them behind. In Bry's opinion, Con was well out of it. The woman had introduced the trouble, but the man seemed no better.

Tears stung Bry's eyes. If only she knew that her brother lived, she could endure his absence. Not knowing made the burden heavier. And now Rob had gone too. She couldn't bear the loss of a brother twice over.

Bry closed the closet door behind her and went to look out the window. The river was swelling its banks. Trees gusted by winds swayed above the water, like so many dancing girls with skirts flying. Smiling at the idea, she lowered herself into the chair by the window, where Con must have often sat and enjoyed the view as she did now. During those moments, had he thought of the sister he'd left behind and the younger brother who so desperately needed him?

Bry closed her eyes with a sigh and did what she'd come to do. Kneeling beside the chair, she bowed her head. "God, I don't have the ability to keep my brothers safe, but You do." A sob caught in her throat. "I release them into Your care."

Elsa lined up with the other passengers for the outlaws' inspection. She couldn't stop trembling. The stagecoach driver stood among his passengers, but the shotgun rider sprawled unmoving alongside the road.

More than anything, Elsa yearned for Con's reassuring touch. He was right beside her, but she dared not turn to him. A road agent wearing a blue hood cut with eye holes sashayed down the line, brandishing his pistols.

An outlaw in a black mask leveled a pair of six shooters at the passengers with more precision. "Relieve these folks of their bounty, Lonesome."

The other outlaw moved to obey. The youth, Jamie, held his arms high while Lonesome searched his pockets. "Hey, Gentleman! I found a roll of greenbacks," he hooted.

Gentleman pulled the brim of his hat down, shading his eyes. "Keep going down the line, Lonesome."

"Hey, that's private property." Jamie's protest ended with the sound of a fist smacking his mouth. He went down but stood quickly, nursing a cut lip and spitting blood. "You're filthy, yellow-bellied cowards."

"That so?" Lonesome pointed his pistol at Jamie's head and pulled back on the hammer.

Con tensed. "Leave him alone. He's only a kid who's read too many dime novels."

Lonesome roared with laughter. "He'd better mind his Ps and Qs if he wants to live to read another."

"Move on, or we'll be here all day." Gentleman pushed his fellow highwayman away from the youth. Gentleman turned and stared at Elsa but made no move to rob her.

Skin crawling, Elsa looked away. He seemed eerily familiar.

Lonesome pointed his pistol at one of the men from the stagecoach's middle seat. "Hand over your money."

"I have none."

"Don't give me that."

"I'll show you." He turned out his pockets, proving them empty. "I'm a miner down on his luck. I spent the last of my gold dust on stage fare and a bit of food for the journey."

"What, no money?" Lonesome chuckled. "Then you'll have to entertain us with a dance."

The miner looked at him blankly. "I . . . I don't understand."

"Oh, you will." Lonesome shot the ground near the miner's feet.

The miner yelped and jumped backward. Elsa screamed, and the other passengers raised protests.

A second shot pinged, then a third. The miner hopped away from each bullet. Laughing, Lonesome continued to lead him in a macabre dance.

"Enough!" Gentleman pointed one of his guns at the other road agent. "All I require is that you rob the passengers. Anything more is at your peril."

"Sorry." Lonesome moved to the next passenger.

Elsa dreaded her turn, for she had no money either. She searched her pockets with the foolish hope of finding a stray coin or bill.

Her fingers closed around the hilt of the knife she'd taken when they'd left Con's cabin. Acting quickly, Elsa pulled the blade out of her pocket and hid it within the folds of her coat. The weapon lent her courage, although she had no idea if she could use it to defend herself.

"Well, well, what have we here?" Lonesome approached the woman who was cradling her young daughter.

Elsa opened her mouth to protest. "Lea—"

"Quiet, woman." Gentleman stepped forward and pinched Elsa's face.

Con jerked.

"Don't," Elsa whispered. She could barely bring the words out past the fear clogging her throat. "They'll kill you."

"Take the lady's jewelry, but don't lay a hand on her in front of the child." Gentleman spoke to his companion, then returned his attention to Elsa.

A shiver ran through Elsa. She gripped her knife tighter.

Behind his black mask, the outlaw's eyes swept Elsa's face.

"Here's a beauty."

She tried to jerk away from him.

He chuckled. "A spirited woman too, I see. Well, my beauty, what can *you* give me?"

Elsa swallowed. "I have nothing."

"What? Nothing?" He rubbed a thumb over her cheek. "I would hate to mark this lovely face."

Elsa tamped down her panic.

"Leave her alone." Con's voice shook with rage. Other passengers murmured in agreement.

Gentleman glanced sideways at Con. "Utter another word, and it will be your last."

"Con, be careful for my sake." Elsa sobbed the words. *"Please."*

"Pipe down, all of you!" Lonesome waved his pistols.

"Perhaps I should charge a kiss." Gentleman laughed, clearly taken by his own humor. Before Elsa could blink, he cupped a hand behind her neck and drew her close. His lips hovered inches from hers.

In a flash, Elsa brought up the knife and pressed its point against Gentleman's chest. "Get away from me." She emphasized each word.

The outlaw's eyes widened, and he backed away. "You're a bit more than a spirited woman. You're a harpy." Quick as a snake, he grasped her wrist and twisted.

The knife dropped to the ground as Elsa cried out in pain.

Con flung himself at Lonesome and took him down. Lonesome's pistols discharged. Bullets ricocheted. The male passengers scrambled for the weapons they'd flung down.

Gentleman pulled away, his mask askew. He shoved it back into place, but not before Elsa recognized him. She didn't blurt his name but kept her face impassive. If he knew she'd seen him, he might shoot her.

He peppered the ground with bullets near the piled weapons, and the men stopped advancing. "Get back in line!" Gentleman looked down at Con and Lonesome, still flailing at one another in the dust. "Lonesome, you're embarrassing me."

Lonesome broke away from Con and shoved him to the ground before he could fire. The male passengers went for their guns.

Gentleman flicked his head. "Let's go. Now!"

The outlaws raced for their horses.

Con staggered to his feet and stumbled after them. The stagecoach driver stopped him with an arm around the shoulder. "Hold on there and let the others go after those two. You took a hard blow."

Elsa hurried to support Con.

He threw an arm around her. "I'm sorry I couldn't do anything sooner. Did that scoundrel hurt you?"

"Not really." She would have bruises and her nerves felt raw. However, all the passengers had survived the ordeal, and that's what counted.

Rob pocketed the gold he received for the two horses and turned away from Virginia City's livery. It wasn't much to start a life with, but it would have to do. He preferred his successes to be his own, and not from the hands of another, even a brother. Con couldn't see that, but Rob hoped he would understand in time.

It seemed strange to return to the place he had fled from, but Rob refused to be intimidated. He would find the cabin as they'd left it, although perhaps a little lonelier.

No matter. He must get used to living on his own. These were the sacrifices a man undertook to make his way in the world. He had Cecil's friendship, a dry place to sleep, and food in his belly. That was enough.

Rob rode the horse the claim jumper had stolen, now restored to him, down Wallace Street. He passed saloons and dance halls asleep in the afternoon warmth. Business would pick up soon enough, but by then he'd be on Con's claim, out of harm's way. Rob would not waste any gold he found on rotgut whiskey, as so many others did to their sorrow.

Like Con, Rob would save what he earned to buy a spread of his own. He'd discovered the knack for ranching while taking care of Con's property. In time, he would make the Bitterroot Valley his home, the same as Con and Shane.

Maisey's face appeared in his mind's eye, along with an ache he'd rather not feel. He should have given her a special goodbye. Maisey deserved that much from him. He wouldn't ask her to wait for him, though. That wouldn't be fair, since he didn't know how long he'd be gone.

Rob turned aside and entered the mercantile to pick up a few supplies. He would come back for more another time, when he wasn't so tired. He stowed his supplies in the saddle bags, untied his horse from the hitching post, and stepped into the saddle.

The hair on the back of his neck bristled.

Rob glanced around. Nothing moved in the street. The storefronts were quiet. Chalking the unnerving sensation up to exhaustion, he continued on his way.

Con turned over the man lying in the grass and felt for his pulse. "He's alive. There's a lot of blood, but it looks like the bullet passed clean through his arm. The fall must have knocked him out."

The driver knelt beside Con. "Gus! Can you hear me?"

The wounded man didn't stir.

The driver shook his head. "Poor fellow." He removed his belt and strapped it around Gus's arm. "He may lose that arm, but he'll keep his life if we get him to a doctor fast enough." He looked up at Con. "It wasn't Gentleman that shot him, I can tell you that. It must have been the other one."

"What makes you think so?"

"They say Gentleman robs stagecoaches for sport, but he never murders. When I ran up against him before, he gave a widow back her wedding ring. We'd better put Gus inside the coach. He sure can't ride outside. Hold on."

The driver hurried to the stagecoach and climbed up to the driver's box. He returned with a dusty blanket that had seen better days. "Gus needs this more than me." He spread the blanket beside the shotgun rider.

The driver lifted Gus by the shoulders while Con took his feet. Together, they rolled the wounded man onto the blanket. Using the blanket as a stretcher, they carried Gus to the stagecoach. A bit of manhandling put him inside the coach. They laid him on the middle bench, his legs canted and his feet resting on a mail sack so he'd fit.

"I'll figure out a way to strap him down." The driver hurried off.

Con searched for Elsa among the passengers discussing the robbery in agitated tones. He hadn't seen this much discourse between them since the trip began. Adversity made for fast friends, it seemed. He found Elsa talking to the mother, who was rubbing the back of the child in her arms.

Elsa turned when Con reached her, but he resisted the urge to put his arm around her. With the grandmother watching disapprovingly, Elsa would not welcome the attention. She leaned on him, however, when he escorted her to the stagecoach.

He helped her inside, then turned to assist others.

The younger woman walked toward him carrying her daughter. She accepted the hand he offered, but the grandmother held back.

The driver stepped in to help her. Afterwards, he pulled Con aside. "I find myself in need of a shotgun rider. How are you at aiming a rifle?"

Con buried his regret. He preferred to spend the remainder of the trip comforting Elsa, but with the wounded rider taking up space in the coach, two passengers would have to sit on top. One might as well be him. He'd serve Elsa better by keeping watch over the stage. "I'm not bad."

"You're hired." The driver turned to Jamie, who was about to climb into the coach. "I need someone to ride in one of the jump seats. Care to volunteer?"

"Would I!" A grin spread across the youth's face.

Con smiled. Dodging branches and playing lookout might satisfy Jamie's sense of adventure. It would certainly provide fodder for many tales to come. Con climbed up beside the driver and accepted the rifle from his hands.

"Git up!" The driver's cry rang out, and the horses pulled at the traces. The stagecoach picked up speed, barreling down a lane in dappled shade. Leaves rustled overhead, then the stage broke free into sunshine. The driver cracked his whip, and the horses thundered down the road.

Gripping the rifle while doing his best to remain seated, Con kept his eyes moving. Road agents, Indians, or other malcontents might lurk in every shadow.

All told, it would be a long ride.

CHAPTER TWENTY-THREE

ELSA TOOK THE HAND CON EXTENDED and stepped down from the stagecoach. The low-slung building before her displayed a sign that read "Liberty Stagecoach Station." The town proper seemed to consist of one main road. Besides the stage stop, it contained a general store, drug store, post office, livery, and farm supply store.

With the day advancing toward evening, neither horse nor wagon traveled the street. Elsa had a sneaking suspicion that traffic might always be light.

Con cupped Elsa's elbow and guided her along the street. The stage rumbled off.

She turned to watch it go. How strange that she might never again see her fellow passengers. After going through such a traumatic event, they'd formed strong alliances. She sighed. People came and went, and no one could turn back the clock.

"Come, Elsa." Con touched her elbow. "We're within walking distance of Shane's house."

She let him guide her, and the town soon fell away. Fields and pastures unfolded on either hand and birds flew into a sky wisped by high clouds. Elsa recognized geese and pheasants, but the other feathered creatures lay outside her experience.

She stumbled over a rut, and Con gripped her elbow. "Steady."

Elsa regained her balance, wincing a little at a twinge in her ankle. "Thank you."

Con released her elbow but tucked her hand into his arm.

Drained by the long journey, Elsa didn't protest. . She turned her face to the breeze and breathed deeply. Fresh and chill, it infused her with new strength. She picked up her pace.

Con tilted a glance sideways. "I'm certain you will enjoy Shane's wife, America."

She smiled. "I wouldn't be surprised, since I like Shane already."

"She'll make you welcome, have no doubt."

"That's reassuring since we're descending on her without warning."

"'Tis true. She won't be expecting us, especially not me."

She squeezed his hand. "I'm sure you'll be most welcome."

They turned aside at a path that took them to a garden arbor hung with climbing roses. A white house stood beyond it. Con swung open the gate beneath the arch and stepped aside while she went through. Elsa waited for him to latch the gate. She would not venture farther without him.

At Con's knock, a woman with red-blonde hair holding a boy of three or four opened the door. Her eyes widened, and she gasped. "*Con*! Where did you come from?"

Con laughed. "What kind of greeting is that for your long-lost cousin?"

Her face brightened. "Here's a better one." She flung her free arm around his neck. Con embraced her, and the child too.

The woman broke away and held Con at arms' length. "My, but you surprised me. Come in and tell me why you stayed away so long."

Con laughed. "Gladly. I hope I'm not too late for supper, and that you have enough to share with us."

The joy on their faces struck Elsa to the heart. Would *she* ever experience a homecoming like this?

America glanced at Elsa with a puzzled frown, then back at

Con. "Who have you brought with you?"

Elsa looked away, feeling awkward.

Con touched Elsa's back. "This is Elsa Meier. She's come under my protection. Elsa, this is Shane's wife, America. I told you about her."

"Oh, you did, did you?" America glinted a teasing smile at him.

"Yes, indeed. I mentioned that she will find a friend in you."

"Of course." America's smile broadened. "Anyone who can look that unharried after traveling with *you* has my admiration."

Elsa took the hand America extended. "I'm pleased to meet you."

America gazed searchingly past Con. "Have you brought my husband?"

"Shane's following on Archibald. We took the stage."

The young boy reached out to Con, who accepted his weight and held him close. "I've missed you, Seth."

America started. "I'm forgetting my manners. Won't you come in?" She stepped back. Her movement revealed a brown-haired woman standing behind her.

"Con?" The woman rushed forward. "I thought I heard your name. Is it really you?"

"It is indeed." Con embraced her. "Hello, Maisey. It's good to see you looking so well and happy."

Maisey's smile slipped. "Have you seen Rob? He set out searching for you weeks ago."

"I've seen him, yes." Con's voice held caution.

America glanced at him. "Shall we all go inside?"

Elsa followed her into the house. A hollow sensation fluttered in her stomach. Returning to her mother's home in Germany would feel this warmhearted. She didn't begrudge Con his happiness, but it reminded her of everything she'd lost.

America stopped on the pad of stones that served as an entryway. "Elsa, allow me to introduce you to Maisey Wilcox. She's practically a family member. Maisey, Elsa is Con's friend."

Maisey looked from Elsa to Con, and then back again. "I'd have said hello before this, but Con's sudden appearance blindsided me. My daughter . . ." She glanced about with a baffled air. "Phoebe is around here somewhere."

Con grinned. "I suppose that one still leads you a dance."

"Come into the kitchen while I make tea." America looked over her shoulder with a smile for Con. He was hanging Seth upside down, to the boy's delighted giggles. "He'll pester you to do that all the time now."

A parlor with comfortable-looking furniture lay to the right, but America continued through the open doorway. A kitchen table sat just beyond it. "I'm sure you must be thirsty. Are you hungry too?"

"Ravenous," Con answered without hesitation. "Whether you bring your own meals or purchase them at stops along the way, stagecoach travel does not offer the best food."

Maisey sat in one of the ladderback chairs at the table. "How long have you been on the road?"

"Two days."

"Goodness!" America waved a hand. "Sit down, and I'll feed you."

Elsa perched on a chair across from Maisey. Con took the spot beside her.

A little girl with blonde curls haloing her head and a mischievous smile peeked in at the doorway. An ache went through Elsa. The child looked much the same age as her littlest sister, Aileen.

"There's Phoebe." Maisey spoke with relief.

Phoebe ran to her mother and climbed into her lap, from

which shelter she gave Con bright glances.

Con smiled at the child. "I don't suppose you remember me."

Phoebe hid her face against her mother.

Maisey smoothed Phoebe's curls, but they sprang back with abandon. "How's Rob?" She spoke off-handedly, but Elsa could tell the answer meant a lot.

Con frowned. "Rob's decided to try his hand at mining in Virginia City."

Maisey stared at him. "Don't tell me he's moved there."

"I'm afraid so."

Her eyes lost their shine. "I see."

America paused with the gravy ladle above her plate. "Sometimes people have to find their way home again."

"I wish we knew that for certain about Rob." Con passed the mashed potatoes to Elsa. "My hard-headed brother will do as he sees fit."

"Stubbornness seems to be a family trait." America smiled.

The corners of Con's mouth tilted upward. "You have a gentle way of putting things."

America laughed. "Being a preacher's wife teaches a woman tact."

"Shane is a blessed man." Con grinned at her.

"Speaking of Shane, when can I expect my husband home?"

"In a day or two, I imagine."

"Hopefully, he won't run into trouble like we did." Elsa wished she could take back her words. She shouldn't have blurted out anything that would cause America worry.

"What happened?" America divided a glance between them.

"Nothing that should affect Shane." Con gave Elsa a quelling look. "Outlaws robbed our stage. The passengers gave them something to think about, and they made off. I doubt they'll try again anytime soon."

America frowned. "I'll be glad when my husband comes safely home."

Shane sat undecided on Archibald's back. The Mullan Road looked inviting at this hour, with the sun halfway behind the mountains and the clouds blushed pink. He would rather go on a little longer and arrive home sooner. But with the breeze scented of moisture and blowing ever more stiffly, he would risk a soaking.

The thought of America waiting for him at the end of his journey might be worth that cost. Perils lurked in a storm, however, and he'd promised to be careful.

Choosing the sensible course, Shane turned aside. He came to a grassy hollow, where trees broke the wind. He strung his rubber blanket over his bedroll, tying it between saplings that stood apart from the taller trees. He didn't want to lie beneath creaking branches, especially if the wind blew any harder.

The first crack of thunder preceded a deluge that pelted the rubber blanket sheltering him. It made Shane glad he'd stopped to make camp.

Morning dawned with a drizzle misting the trees. Last night's eagerness abandoned Shane, and he huddled in the warmth of his bedroll. Maybe he could wait out the weather.

A willow tree, leaves bedecked with springtime yellow, waved at the edge of the hollow. Shane squinted. Something moved behind the lacy limbs, he would swear to it. He sat up slowly and reached for his gun. If it was a bear, he'd let it pass—

unless it made trouble.

Another figure joined the first.

The hair on Shane's arms bristled. Bears did not whisper to one another in human accents. He spotted a fallen log to retreat behind and eased out of his bedroll.

The figures advanced, always behind the foliage. They were soon joined by more.

A glance about confirmed Shane's suspicions. Hiding behind the log would do no good. He was surrounded, with his only recourse to rely on God. Shane sent up a prayer for deliverance.

Indians brandishing knives and aiming arrows at him, rushed in from all sides. They slowed before reaching him and edged closer in an ever-tightening circle.

With a bloodcurdling cry, one of the Indians bore down on him. Shane held his fire. There was no point in killing the man, not when his own life was already forfeited. The Indian grasped Shane's hair and jerked his head backward. He pressed his blade against Shane's exposed neck.

The broad face, high forehead, and hooked nose covered by white war paint struck a familiar chord with Shane. He grasped for a name. "Little Elk."

The anger went out of the Indian's expression. "Preacher?"

"Yes," Shane answered in the Salish language. "Why have you come into my camp like this?"

Little Elk withdrew and sheathed his knife. "We have no fight with this man," he called to the others. "He is not like those who lie and take our land."

"He is from their nation." The throaty voice belonged to a warrior with a red circle painted around one eye. "We must drive *all* the settlers away."

Little Elk stood. "This man does good for the people. He is

like the black robes who live at the mission. Chief Victor would not want us to kill him."

"Chief Victor is old and seeks peace." A warrior with a black hand painted on the lower part of his face called out in bitter tones.

"Peace is not bad to want." The words, uttered by an Indian wearing a leather collar adorned with bear claws, sighed through the air.

The challenger with the red-circled eye shook his head. "*I will take his scalp.*"

Little Elk held his ground. "We will not harm this man who has been kind to us."

An Indian wearing a headdress with drooping feathers came to stand beside Little Elk. "The preacher gave my family blankets in the winter. I will not return death for life."

A third Indian joined the two shielding Shane. "He gave us medicine that saved my son."

The challenger turned away.

Shane breathed a thankful prayer.

Con pulled his jacket closer and followed the path from the house. The barn hunched in the drizzle like an old crone seeking the warmth of her shawl. He slipped inside. Hooves thudded against the stalls, and a nicker came softly. He picked up a pitchfork and wheelbarrow and went to the haymow.

He pitched hay into the wheelbarrow and pushed his way down the stalls, delivering breakfast. The rhythm of the chore soothed his mind. He spared a thought for the Fitzgeralds. How were they doing with him gone? He had contributed his share of work, but now it all fell on Finley. Con had no doubt that Finley, who knew how to apply himself to hard labor, could manage without him.

"I thought I saw you come in here." America's soft voice drifted from the entrance. A beam of light from a high window haloed her golden hair.

"You're up early." He set aside the pitchfork and dusted off his hands.

"I have to rise with the sun or I'd never finish my chores."

"Well, then, I'm glad to relieve you of a few of them. I've fed the horses. Have you anything else I can do?"

"If you wouldn't mind bringing in a load of firewood, I'd be thankful."

"Of course." Con expected her to leave, but she lingered, walking down the row of stalls.

She stopped beside him. "We lost all our horses while Shane was away."

"Oh?" He glanced down the aisle. The stalls were full.

"Indians broke in one night and took them."

Con tensed. "Did they come near the house?"

"Not the house, no. They went to the cabins." America sighed. "Emma, the schoolteacher, escaped, but they found Maisey hiding in the closet with Phoebe. They forced her to cook for them."

Con pictured Maisey's terror. "Were they content with that?"

"They never tasted the food. I broke in with Shane's rifle."

Con frowned. "I should speak to that cousin of mine about looking after his family better."

"You are always so straightforward."

He tilted his head. "Am I? Shane's absence from home might be more my fault than his. He came looking for me, after all."

"Sometimes things happen. No one's to blame." She started for the door.

He fell into step beside her. "So, how did you get your horses back?"

"That's the funny thing. They showed up in the barn one morning."

"Why take the horses, only to return them?"

America shrugged. "I can't figure it out, except to think that wiser heads in the tribe prevailed. From working with the Indians at the school, I've noticed that they are more conflicted than most settlers realize. They want to be friendly, but it's not easy."

"How can it be, when newcomers invade your land and show no respect for your way of life?"

Outside the barn, America put a hand on his arm. "Tell me about Elsa."

"Now, there's another mystery."

"How did she come under your protection?"

"That's a long story. I'm rescuing her from . . . a bad situation."

America searched his face but didn't ask him to elaborate. "She seems unhappy at times."

He looked away. "I know she's often homesick."

America's brow furrowed. "Will she go back home to Germany?"

Con frowned. "I wish I knew."

"The answer to that question clearly matters to you."

"Elsa has a way of growing on a person."

She gave him a knowing look. "If you should find that you love her, dear cousin, don't let anything come between you."

CHAPTER TWENTY-FOUR

WARMTH FROM THE DISHWATER SOOTHED AMERICA'S hands. Her fingers found the dishcloth, and she washed the first plate from the noon meal. Seth and Liberty squealed with delight from the parlor, where Con was giving them horsey rides. Elsa stood by with a dishtowel, ready to dry.

"Thank you for helping in the kitchen today." America slipped the clean plate into the rinse water.

"I'm happy to help." Elsa responded with the polite answer America expected, but her eyes glowed with genuine warmth.

"I can tell that you like to cook."

"I do. When I was small, my mother stood me on a stool and let me stir the *Streuselkuchen* batter." She laughed. "I was so proud when she served *my* cake after dinner."

"What is *Streuselkuchen*?" America drew her brows together. "Did I say that right?"

"It's a kind of cake that you cover with—" Elsa frowned. "I'm not sure what Americans call *Streusel*."

"Streusel." America grinned.

Elsa's eyes widened. "It's pleasant to find a little of my homeland here."

"I'm glad." America added a porcelain serving bowl to the dishwater. "Con mentioned that you might wish to go home." *America Liberty Hayes, you are a meddling woman.* Although she chided herself, America couldn't summon any guilt.

Elsa's expression went from happy to crestfallen, making America wonder if she'd said something amiss. "I'm sure he would like you to stay."

Elsa's brow cleared. She'd fallen behind in her kitchen duties but picked a plate from the rinse water and started drying.

America waited for her to catch up before washing more. The becoming shade of pink that stole into Elsa's cheeks told America all she needed to know about her feelings for Con. She glanced out the kitchen window, which gave onto the barn. "I wonder how Maisey is doing today."

Elsa fished another plate from the rinse tub. "Is she not well?"

With the back of her hand, America pushed a stray lock of hair out of her eyes. "Not in the sense you mean, but I think she's sad over Rob. They grew close when he helped build her cabin. I'm sure she misses him."

"Oh." The single word held a wealth of meaning. "Maybe he'll change his mind and come back."

"We can hope for that, but Maisey needs cheering now."

Elsa stared at the plate in her hands while dishes piled up in the wash tub. She finally looked up. "She needs company."

America washed a cup. "I'm sure you're right. I have to start supper, but why don't you take her one of the dried-apple pies we baked today? There's nothing like dessert to bring a little sweetness into life. Phoebe would love it too."

"I'd be happy to do that," Elsa chirped.

America smiled to herself. It never failed. Thinking of others brought people out of their own pain.

Elsa licked her lips, tasting their sweetness after a bite of dried-apple pie. The tea Maisey poured into a dainty cup painted with roses warmed her throat and comforted her stomach. Across the trestle table, Phoebe sat on her knees and stretched tall, pretending to sip from an empty cup. Elsa's lips curved at the memory of Aileen assuming the same posture to look older than her five years.

Maisey pulled up a ladder-back chair beside Phoebe. Her spoon tinked as she stirred lumps of sugar into the steaming amber liquid. She sipped with her eyes closed and released a sigh. Her lips spread in a smile. "It was nice of you to think of Phoebe and me."

Elsa set her cup on its saucer. "Honesty compels me to admit that America asked me to bring over the pie."

"Well, I'm glad you came, regardless. I wanted the chance to get to know you."

Elsa's tension eased. "Thank you. I feel the same."

Phoebe finished her "tea" and jumped down from her chair. She came to stand at Elsa's elbow. She tilted her head, her blond curls spilling backward.

Elsa gazed into her wide, blue eyes. "Did you enjoy your pie?" She asked the question, although the answer was smeared across the child's face.

Phoebe nodded. "You're pretty."

"Why, thank you." Elsa smiled. "I think *you're* beautiful."

Phoebe's face lit up, and she moved closer.

The urge to lift the child into her arms swept through Elsa, but it would feel too much like holding Aileen. She wasn't ready for the grief that might bring.

"Phoebe, go in your room and play a while."

The disappointed look on the little girl's face stirred Elsa's sympathies. Phoebe stood on tiptoe, and Elsa bent to catch her whisper. "Will you still be here later?"

"I won't leave without saying goodbye," Elsa promised.

Phoebe broke into a grin and raced from the room.

Maisey's lips curved in a smile. "I'm grateful for your kindness to my daughter."

"She's delightful." Elsa's hand trembled as she lifted her tea cup. "My little sister, Aileen, would enjoy playing with her."

"What a lovely idea. Is your family nearby?"

Elsa swallowed a mouthful of tea before answering. "They're in Germany."

Maisey's face softened. "You must miss them."

"I didn't fully understand what I gave up when I left my country." Elsa's voice quavered.

"I hope you won't mind my asking this." Maisey leaned forward. "How did you fall in with Con?"

Elsa cast about in her mind for a quick explanation but could find none. She settled on a simple but heartfelt answer. "He rescued me in the midst of trouble. I'll always be grateful."

"There's none better than Con. He's brought you among friends who will stand by you. I promise."

"Thank you." Elsa hesitated but then decided to speak. "Rob went to Virginia City because he wanted to earn his own way."

Maisey pressed her lips together, then nodded. "Thank you for telling me."

"Falling in love isn't easy." Elsa could testify to the truth of her own words.

"I'm not sure it's love." Maisey's eyes grew distant. "Rob was kind to me, and I came to rely on him. It's probably selfish, but I don't like the fact that he's gone." She leaned back in her chair. "He wanted freedom, and now he has it."

"Since coming to America, I've learned that freedom isn't so free."

Maisey lifted her tea cup. "There's always a cost, isn't there?"

"It seems that the wrong people have to pay it."

Maisey frowned. "That sounds more like sin than freedom. The two are often mistaken."

"I don't understand."

"Some believe they can take whatever they want from life, without regard to those they hurt." Maisey spoke with heat. "They turn liberty into a license."

Elsa thought of Miles, Alicia, and Atticus, and silently agreed.

Maisey's expression softened. "True freedom is gentle. It takes others into account and treats them kindly. It rises above every circumstance, bringing joy so deep nothing can move it. I learned this as a Cheyenne captive."

"You felt joy while living in captivity?" Elsa hoped her skepticism didn't show.

"It's hard to believe, but when God becomes your only hope, freedom lives *inside* you."

Elsa finished her slice of pie with Maisey's words echoing in her thoughts. Throughout her trials, she'd placed her hope in her own abilities, not necessarily in God. That had brought her to the edge of despair on a dark, lonely road, where Shane had found her.

The faith she saw in the preacher and Maisey called to her. Surrendering to God like they both had seemed an adventure.

Little Phoebe returned and leaned against Elsa's side. "Are you going to marry Uncle Con?"

Maisey's eyes gleamed. "Out of the mouths of babes . . ."

The lights shining into the darkness hurried Shane's footsteps on the path to his house. A whippoorwill opened its throat in the trees behind the barn, but otherwise silence shrouded the countryside. Daylight shrank from the land. The world paused, awaiting nightfall with breathless anticipation.

To avoid frightening anyone with unexpected sounds at the back door, Shane went around front. He knocked and waited.

The door opened, and America stood before him. "Shane! You're home." Emotion softened her voice.

The joy in her face brought a lump to Shane's throat. After three years of marriage, he still couldn't credit that such a woman would delight in his presence. She flew into his arms, and he embraced her. He buried his face in her hair and breathed in her scent.

Con and Elsa came into the entry through the parlor door. He kissed his wife in front of them, unashamed.

The children rushed in from the kitchen and tackled their father's knees. He gathered them into his arms. "I hope you've been good while I was away."

"Oh, we have, Pa." Liberty gave him a mischievous smile.

He tousled her hair. "Have you kept your Uncle Con out of mischief?" He asked the question with a serious face, but then winked at his cousin.

Con laughed. "A body can't get into much trouble chasing these two about."

"Supper's ready." America gave Shane an assessing look. "I hope you're hungry."

"I am."

Con grinned. "You timed your arrival well."

America took Shane's hand. "Come into the kitchen, and I'll lay another plate. Con, stop teasing your cousin. Go tell Maisey he's home, and that she and Phoebe should come to supper. There's plenty to spare."

A few minutes later, they all sat down to eat.

With loved ones around the table and a plate of roast beef before him, Shane bowed his head. He thanked God for providing for his family and for so much more. Today he had stared death in the face, and it had passed him by.

"We had rain last night and this morning." America passed the bowl of mashed potatoes to Con, seated on her right. "I thought of you, coming home in a downpour. Did you stay dry?"

Shane intercepted a roll from the bread basket. "For the most part. The local tribe invaded my camp this morning, which made it hard to worry about the weather."

America paused with the gravy ladle in her hands. "What happened?"

She furrowed her brow in the way Shane hated seeing, but he'd learned long ago not to shield her from the truth. "I'm pretty sure they thought I was trespassing. They have hard feelings over the Hell Gate Treaty and talked about being lied to."

"No wonder." Maisey glanced up from her plate. "Chief Victor signed the treaty believing it secured the Bitterroot Valley for his tribe. Unfortunately, it hasn't slowed settlement."

"The Salish are stirred up right now." America handed the gravy boat to Con.

Shane could attest to that. He'd have to consider what he could do to help the situation. Right now, he was too tired to think about anything but the food on his plate. He sliced into the roast beef and savored a mouthful.

"Hardly anyone attends the Indian school on Saturdays these days." Maisey brought up an uncomfortable fact.

Shane sighed. "We'll have to figure out whether to keep it going or abandon the project." After hearing the Salish people recite the blessings they'd received from him, he was not inclined to quit. Much remained out of his control, however. "God will show us what to do."

Con picked up his water glass. "I don't envy you such thankless work."

Shane smiled. "It has its moments."

Con drank then put down his glass. "I hope to drag you away from duty. I'll be off to the ranch soon, and I'd like you all to come along."

America sent Shane a beseeching look that meant she wanted to go along, and with him. They were agreed on that, then. He wouldn't miss Bry's reaction when she saw Con, nor the family celebration that would follow.

When the congregation knew Shane had returned, he'd be deluged by invitations and requests. It was gratifying to be wanted but facing his own mortality this morning had changed his perspective. He'd spent too many years planting his neighbor's crops while neglecting his own.

Shane would always serve his congregation, but not at the cost of his family. "We should go."

America gazed at him. "What about the congregation?"

He smiled at her bemusement. "No one needs to know I'm home yet, now do they?"

"Then it's settled," Con proclaimed joyfully.

"I'll stay here and look after the place." Maisey's voice cut through the merriment.

America frowned. "We can ask the neighbors to do that."

"You'll let out Shane's secret." Maisey's smile didn't reach her eyes.

"I don't really care if they know I'm home," Shane hastened

to reassure her. "You're welcome to go with us."

Maisey shook her head. "I don't want to intrude."

"That's not possible." Con gave her a charming smile.

"Won't you reconsider?" America urged in gentle tones.

Elsa, seated beside Maisey, turned to her. "It won't be the same without you."

Shane didn't like the sadness he saw in Maisey's face. *This had to do with Rob, of course.* Maisey needed to know she was welcome on her own account. "You're the same as family to us."

"But I'm *not* family," Maisey burst out. "And no amount of wishing can make it so."

The clopping of hooves, combined with the creak and rattle of a wagon, drew Bry to the kitchen window. A Conestoga made its way down the long driveway. The wagon stirred plenty of dust, reminding Bry that it had been a long time since she'd seen Shane and America. Since few other visitors made their way to the ranch, it probably belonged to them.

The driver wore a slouch hat like Shane's. The woman beside him had on a blue bonnet, just like the one Bry had given America for Christmas. She untied her apron and hurried to the front door, eager to welcome her guests. She'd already started a pot of Irish stew for supper. Stretching it with extra vegetables and more soda bread would be a simple task.

She paused briefly at the mirror in the entryway to tidy her hair. She'd spring-cleaned the library today, which meant she was wearing her drabbest clothing. Never mind. It couldn't be helped. Besides, Shane and America were family.

Bry stepped onto the porch and waved. Nick had gone

down to the river to check his fish traps and might not be back for some time. Shane probably wouldn't mind walking along the river to find him.

The wagon drew up, and Shane called out a greeting before alighting. He held up his arms, and America leaned into them. He swung his wife down from the driver's box.

Bry hurried down the steps. "This is a nice surprise!"

"Indeed it is." Shane gave the words more emphasis than seemed warranted. He disappeared behind the wagon. A few moments later, Liberty and Seth bounded toward her.

Bry bent to embrace the children, then glanced at America. "Where's Phoebe and Maisey?"

"Maisey's minding our home while we're away," Shane answered for his wife.

"That's disappointing." Bry straightened, ready to lead the way inside.

Con strode from behind the wagon.

Bry froze. She stared at her brother, robbed of speech. Tears sprang to her eyes. "*Con.*" She breathed his name but could say nothing more.

Her brother bounded up the steps and engulfed her in his embrace. She held on fiercely, shaken by laughter, and then tears.

When she could finally bring herself to let go, she stepped away. "Where have you been?"

A haunted look came over Con's face. "I lost my memory. That's why I didn't come home."

Bry's mouth dropped open. She snapped it shut and summoned the wit to speak. "What happened?"

"After I left Fort Sedgwick, I caught a ride in a freight wagon. The driver took a turn too fast, and it capsized. I was thrown clear but hit my head."

"How horrible!" Bry shuddered. "I'm thankful you weren't killed."

"I am also, as it happens." He smiled. "When I came to, I didn't know my own name, let alone anyone else's. The driver took me in."

"Thank the Lord he helped you."

"I'm grateful to Finley. I lived with his family all this time but never lost the longing to recall where I really belonged." He brightened. "You can be sure that as soon as I recovered my memory, I headed this way."

Tears fell to Bry's cheeks even as she smiled. "Never mind. You're home at last."

Con circled her with an arm and gazed around him. "I'm glad of that."

"Rob went after you." She clutched his vest. "Did you see him?"

He put his hand over hers. "Rob's safe. He decided to mine my claim in Virginia City."

"I suppose he has to try." Bry accepted the truth with a sigh of regret. She would rather have both brothers nearby.

"He may come back to us." Con released her.

"Nick and I were married last year. I wish you could have been there."

Con stared at her. "*What*?"

She lifted her chin. "Don't give me that look. You heard very well what I said."

"Maybe it's hard to credit that you would do something so rash."

"It wasn't at all. Nick and I gave a lot of thought to the consequences."

"And you decided to go through with it anyway?"

"We love each other." Bry spoke quietly.

Her words pierced Con like a knife. His sister's love for Nick had kept him from rejecting Nick entirely. Bry had seen enough misery. He hoped that marriage to Nick would make her happy, but he'd had his doubts. Con forced himself to speak more calmly. "And where is this husband of yours?"

She gave him a suspicious glance. "Why do you ask?"

"Don't worry. I only want to greet my new brother-in-law. Since you've already tied the knot, there's no point in my objecting. Besides, I owe him thanks for saving my life."

CHAPTER TWENTY-FIVE

NICK BENT OVER ONE OF THE fish traps he'd set up along the banks of the Bitterroot River. He added several trout to his bucket and flung one too small to eat into the river. He'd driven twigs into a shallow place along the shore to form a cage. Fish entered through a wider space between twigs, but then found it hard to find the exit.

Gleaming like blue silk, the water ran right up to the trees on the opposite bank. Cottonwoods tossed their heads behind willows that trailed their leaves in the water like women washing their hair. A log boomed against a boulder, the river burbled at his feet, and leaves hissed behind him.

Even so, Nick caught the tread of a footstep, too heavy to be Bry's. Nor could it belong to Turner, the hired hand who managed the place in Rob's absence. Turner had ridden over to the neighbor's spread and wouldn't be back today.

Nick scanned the grassy bank above him. No one appeared.

Moving swiftly, he retreated into shadow beneath a stand of cottonwood trees. A person couldn't be too careful these days.

A man strode over the top of the bank and down toward the fish trap. Recognizing Con, Nick came out of hiding. "Were you looking for me?"

Con changed course and met him. "I'm glad to see you." He extended his hand.

"Really?" Nick took Con's hand despite his doubts. "You weren't so happy about the prospect before."

"Yes, well." Con gave him a rueful smile. "I've changed

since then."

Nick nodded. "Maybe we both have."

Con summoned words that must be hard to say. "I haven't been fair to you."

"You were worried about Bry."

Con shook his head. "True, but that doesn't excuse my behavior. I made things harder than they needed to be for you and my sister. I hope you can forgive me."

Nick paused and let the words heal him. "I won't say it didn't hurt, but I forgave you long ago."

"Thank you." Con faced the river for a while, then turned to Nick. "I'm honored to call you brother."

"I feel the same way." Nick clasped a hand across Con's shoulder. "Let's go up to the house. You must be hungry, and I'm eager to learn where you've been keeping yourself."

When the others gathered in the parlor after supper, Elsa excused herself and slipped away. Con had shown her the library during a brief tour of the ranch house. Drawn to its air of quiet, and the mystery of the books on its shelves, she'd longed to return here all through supper.

Elsa loved books. Papa had often read to her when she was small. When she grew older, he allowed her to read near him in his office. That was in the big house, where they lived before a widow's poverty forced *Mutter* to move into tighter quarters.

Elsa pushed the door, already ajar, open wider and slipped inside the darkened room. She ran her hand along the wooden edge of the settee then along the spines of books stacked neatly on the shelves. If only Papa were alive and here with her now, she would ask him for advice.

Standing in a library full of books, printed in a language she struggled to read, why did she feel the desire to stay in this country? It would be easier to go home to Germany, where she could understand the written word.

Elsa turned away from the shelves and crossed to the window. From here she could see the river in the last gleam of daylight. Wild and beautiful, the land stretched to the mountains.

Con must love this place.

She returned to the settee and sank into a corner. If she made herself small enough, perhaps no one looking in would discover her. It was a childish trick, but it comforted her. She'd felt like a stranger at supper, sitting with the family while they celebrated Con's return. To her own family, Elsa was like Con. She had gone away but had not come home.

Muffled footsteps sounded on the hallway carpet. The door pushed inward, and Con stood on the threshold. "May I join you?"

Elsa had no right to tell Con he was not welcome in his own library, although she would rather be alone. "Of course."

Con took a seat in a wingback chair across from her. His eyes, gentle in the subdued light, watched her. "Tell me why you're sad."

"I'm sorry. I don't mean to dampen tonight's joy." Elsa gave way to her tears. "It makes me miss my family."

Con sank down beside her on the settee. "Don't cry, Elsa." He stroked her hair. "I'll pay your fare to Germany."

He was offering her all she wanted. She could be home within weeks!

Even as hope swelled, Elsa squelched it. "Thank you, but I can't accept such a gift. All I ask is that you help me find work."

Con watched her with darkened eyes. "I don't understand."

She heaved in a breath and dried her eyes. "Can't you see? This is *my* problem to make right. I need to pay my own way home."

"I don't understand. Why won't you let me help you?"

"Papa always took care of my family, but after he died we had to survive on our own. I needed to stand on my own feet and help *Mutter* provide for the little ones. Wishing things could be different landed me in trouble." She frowned. "Miles and Alicia promised that life would be better in America. I believed them because I so desperately wanted someone to take care of me." She straightened her spine. "I can't make that mistake again."

Cecil opened his cabin door at Rob's knock. "It's about time you came around to see me."

Rob blinked. "How did you know I was staying in the cabin?"

"I noticed you on the creek, panning for gold." He chuckled. "You were a mite busy."

Rob grinned. That was Cecil's polite way of saying that Rob had no idea what he was doing. "I've been back a while. My brother offered to let me mine his claim."

"That's one way to get started."

"I intend to earn my own way."

Cecil's face sobered. "There's nothing wrong with taking a hand, especially from your kin." He opened the door wider. "Want to come in? You can stay for supper."

"I was hoping you'd make that suggestion."

Cecil laughed. "Now I discover the reason for your visit. Eating your own cooking gets mighty lonely."

"Not to mention that I burn everything." Rob couldn't help being lonely, especially since today was his birthday. He didn't feel the need to tell the miner that fact, however.

Cecil gestured to a chair. "Sit you down, and I'll make coffee."

Rob pulled out a chair at the table.

The red-bearded miner spooned coffee grounds into a cast-iron kettle on the stove. "Last time we talked, you were bound and determined to commit suicide on the Bozeman Road. What happened to those plans?"

"I met a miner headed the other way. He set me straight."

"Oh did he?" Cecil's eyes widened. "I wonder what he said."

"He told me how I'd probably end up if I kept going." Rob looked Cecil square in the eyes. "You were right about everything."

"I'm glad you saw sense and turned around."

"It worked out for the best. I came across Con when I went back to his cabin."

"Why did you do that? After being attacked, I would have thought you'd steer clear of the place."

"I heard the posse talking about lynching someone for killing a man. I figured out they were after my brother. Thank you for riding after the posse."

"I'm glad Sheriff Gerhart has a good head on his shoulders." Cecil glanced sideways at him. "There's been a bit of news since then."

"Oh?"

Cecil lowered himself into the chair across the table. "Turns out Tate broke out of jail in Helena. He was convicted of murder and sentenced to hang."

Rob whistled. "That puts matters in a different light."

"I'd say so. Sheriff Gerhart came by to see me the other day."

"He did?" Rob waited for the miner to go on.

"Yep, he sure did." Cecil nodded. "I told him in detail what I saw. I think he took me at my word."

"I'm grateful."

Cecil narrowed his eyes. "There's folks in town who should move out if they don't want to act civilized." He jumped up and padded to the stove. He pulled a couple of tin cups from a shelf and picked up the cast iron coffee pot. Steam rose while he poured. He plunked Rob's cup down in front of him. "Careful, it's hot."

Rob thanked him and blew on the fragrant brew to cool it. "I'm no good at making coffee, either."

"Sounds like you should find yourself a wife." Cecil chuckled. "But that's easier said than done in these parts. Unmarried ladies have their pick of suitors."

An image of Maisey stirred Rob's thoughts. "I have hopes, but I'm not sure it will work out."

Cecil sipped his coffee. "What's holding you back?"

"I have nothing to offer her."

"Are you sure she wants anything? Some women get along fine with next to nothing."

"I don't want that for her." Rob snapped out the words.

Cecil raised an eyebrow. "Pardon me. I didn't realize you're more interested in what *you* want." Before Rob could voice a retort, Cecil lumbered to his feet. "Guess I'll make corn cakes to go with the chili in the warming oven." He set to work.

Supper was simple but hot. Afterward, Cecil trotted out more mining-camp tales. When Rob's eyelids began to droop, he pushed to his feet. "I'd better head back."

Cecil glanced out the window. "It's getting dark. Where's your lantern?"

"I'd have brought it if I'd known we would visit this long." He sighed. "I should have realized what would happen, the way we like to talk."

Cecil laughed. "You mean *I* like to talk, don't you? You'd better borrow my lantern to find your way home."

Rob accepted the light. "Thanks again for supper. It meant a lot."

Cecil's face sobered. "I know." He walked Rob out to the porch. "Stop by again."

"Thanks, I will. And you know where to find me." Rob left the warm cabin behind and turned down the darkening path. The lantern light reached forward then receded at his feet. After Cecil's enjoyable company, he walked with a lighter step.

Rob had not expected to suffer so much from loneliness. He found himself saving up little stories to tell Maisey, only to realize that the distance between them was too great.

What is she doing tonight? Rob pictured her tucking Phoebe into bed, then opening a book by the fire, as she liked to do. She borrowed from Con's library on a regular basis. What would it be like to sit beside her, reading interesting snippets aloud, or listening to the ones she shared with him?

He reached the dirt road as darkness fell. Fitful moonlight broken by clouds dappled leaves that hissed in the wind like angry snakes.

A chill skittered down Rob's spine, and the hair at the back of his neck bristled. A sense of uneasiness turned him around. Something heavy bludgeoned the back of his neck.

CHAPTER TWENTY-SIX

MAISEY WATCHED HER DAUGHTER BENDING OVER her slate at one of the schoolhouse desks. Phoebe clenched her tongue between her teeth, grimacing in concentration while her chubby hand formed letters.

Apart from Phoebe, the schoolroom stood empty.

Where were all her students? The Saturday Indian school had grown so much, giving Maisey an effective way to teach the native children. She'd helped them learn English, handwriting, and to better understand their pioneering neighbors. She'd hoped to foster more harmony between the two groups. The empty schoolroom mocked her efforts and accomplishments.

Maisey sighed. Maybe she was fooling herself into believing she could make a difference.

The clock above the teacher's desk ticked away the minutes, while the school's only student applied herself to her studies. Maisey pulled out the flour sack she'd turned into a dishtowel and set to work embroidering. She'd brought it along to fill the time she should have spent teaching. She'd almost given in this morning and kept the schoolhouse doors locked, but it seemed important to try. If no one came soon, she'd take Phoebe home.

The door creaked open, and America peeked in. "I thought you might like company."

Maisey awarded her a smile. America had returned home last night. "How kind of you to come by, but I'm sure you have a hundred things to catch up on after your trip."

"I don't mind." America shut the door behind her and

advanced down the aisle toward the desk. "I brought you and Phoebe some *Streuselkuchen* Elsa made."

Maisey accepted the cloth-covered dish. "What is it?"

"It's a delicious crumb cake."

"Thank you. How are Bry and Nick?"

America smiled. "They're blissful newlyweds."

Maisey tied off her thread. "If ever two people belong together, they do."

"I agree. Con's come around about Nick."

"I'm glad to hear it." Maisey snipped the thread. "He would only make himself unhappy if he tried to separate a husband and wife."

The schoolhouse door burst open. Maisey started and looked toward the entrance. America spun around.

Se'ułku, Maisey's Salish translator, whose name meant *water*, ventured into the building. She carried her daughter, Bluebird, in her arms. Behind her, Saka'am, named after the moon, brought her daughter, Rain. Both girls lay limply in their mothers' arms. A bumpy rash covered their faces.

Maisey jumped up. "What's wrong with them?" She set aside her sewing.

Tears streamed down Se'ułku's face. "Please help us, Teacher. Our daughters are dying."

"What sickness do they have?" America asked in sharp alarm.

Se'ułku took a shuddering breath. "Measles."

America took Phoebe's hand. "Come along, sweetie." She hurried the little girl outside.

Maisey followed. "What should I do for them?"

"They can stay here," America said. "The regular students aren't using the building in summer, anyway. I'll come back as soon as I send Shane for the doctor. We'll set up cots."

"You don't need to return. I'll set up the cots we offer those who travel for Sunday meetings."

"I'll bring food, then."

"Leave it outside and knock. There's no point exposing your household."

"But what about you?" America's voice throbbed with concern.

"Don't worry about me. I had measles as a child. People who have it once don't seem to catch it again." Maisey bent and kissed her daughter, then straightened briskly. "Would you please take Phoebe away from here?"

"Yes, of course. I'll look after her until this is over." America whispered to Phoebe then started for home.

Maisey hurried back inside and closed the door.

The river looked different each time Elsa saw it from the library window. This morning, mists hid the surface and curled in lazy spirals through the trees. Light fractured into beams from the sky, picking out the leaves of one cottonwood, while another tree huddled in shadow.

"Con said I might find you here." Bry stood in the doorway, an apron covering her brown-gingham dress.

Elsa stepped away from the window. "I hope you don't mind my spending time in here."

"Of course not. This is your home for however long you need it." Bry stepped into the room. "I came to ask if you'd like to help me in the kitchen."

"Yes, I would, thank you. I love to cook."

"I don't, but I love my family, so I do it."

Elsa smiled eagerly. "You should let me take over. Then we'd both be happy."

Bry laughed. "Con said you are easy to love, and I begin to see why."

Con's words sent a thrill through Elsa. "What would you like me to do?"

Bry started for the door. "We attend Sunday service in Liberty. It's a long day's journey, but we usually break it by camping partway. . Preparing food for the journey takes extra work, so I'm delighted you want to pitch in."

Elsa followed Bry from the library and along the hallway to the kitchen. Open sacks of flour and sugar, mixing bowls, knives, whisks, eggs in a wire basket, and assorted vegetables cluttered the counter. Breakfast dishes tilted precariously on the cupboards near the sink.

Elsa rolled up her sleeves. "What would you like me to do first?"

"Why don't we start with tea for the cooks? Pull up a stool, and I'll clear a spot for us on the counter."

Elsa remained standing. "I can scrape and rinse dishes while you make tea."

Bry smiled. "All right. I'll finish washing them afterwards. Then you can chop vegetables for tonight's soup. Aren't they lovely? The garden Rob planted this spring is already giving us turnips and greens." Her forehead puckered. "Too bad he's not here to enjoy the fruits of his labor."

Elsa stared at the metal pipes with knobs on their ends protruding from the wall above the sink. "What are these?"

Bry came to stand beside her. "My ambitious brother uses a windmill to pump water piped from the river into the house."

"Aren't you worried about finding fish among your dishes?"

Bry laughed. "The water passes through filters before we use it. Go ahead. Turn one of the knobs. Con calls them faucets. They're both cold right now, but he has ideas for bringing warm water through one of them." She shrugged. "If anyone can figure out how to do it, Con can."

Elsa turned one of the faucets, and water rushed into the sink. She immediately shut it off. "What wonder is this?"

"I prefer well water for drinking. Nick keeps a pail of it filled for me on the old wash table." Bry stepped out the back door.

Elsa watched her fill the tea kettle from the pail, using a dipper. When Bry returned, she put the kettle on to heat and pulled a tin of English Breakfast tea and sugar biscuits from the open cupboard.

Elsa went to work on the dirty dishes. She turned the faucet handle more slowly this time and began to rinse the scraped dishes.

She glanced up to find Bry watching her with an amused gleam in her eyes. "It's nice to have someone else in the kitchen with me again. Now that Maisey has gone to live with Shane and America, I'm stuck with all the cooking."

Elsa glanced at her in surprise. "Did Maisey live here before?"

"Yes." Bry retrieved a tea service, embellished with twining roses, from the open shelves below the cupboard. "She came home with me after an unfortunate incident."

"Maisey told me she was kidnapped by Cheyenne warriors."

Bry's eyes held the shadow of remembered sorrow. "We both were."

"How awful." Elsa could well imagine the women's fear and suffering at the hands of people foreign to them. "Your brother helped me escape from my own kidnappers."

"Is that what happened?" Bry's face softened. "Con wouldn't say."

"Those who held me captive were not Indians, but people who buy and sell women."

Bry gazed at Elsa with sympathy. "I'm so glad you escaped them. No wonder you're so terribly homesick and often draw away to be alone."

"I'm sorry. I don't mean to be ungrateful."

"Don't let it trouble you, Elsa." Bry gave her an encouraging smile. "Being in the company of others will become easier with time."

"Did you suffer in such a way?"

"I did. In some ways, our experiences have been the same."

The kettle came to a boil, and Bry hurried to the stove.

Elsa sat quietly, musing over Bry's last remark. Being kidnapped had changed her in ways she was only beginning to understand. Some were obvious. She jumped at noises that hadn't bothered her before, cried readily, and woke with nightmares.

Other, subtle changes were more positive. Elsa felt better able to stand up for herself. She viewed strangers with more caution than before. The resolve to be true to herself had strengthened. Her greatest improvement had led to all of these things. Driven to prayer, she'd surrendered her human frailty to God.

Elsa sat down on the kitchen stool to savor a cup of coffee. She breathed in the fragrant steam and swallowed a mouthful of the warm brew. The quiet settled around her like one of her mother's quilts. She'd slept well on her second night in the ranch house. No one else was about. That suited her fine. A moment alone gave her time to collect herself.

Bry wasn't hard to talk to, and Elsa was used to the men's company. Even so, living in Con's home required an adjustment. Seeing him at home with his family made her miss her own all the more. She took another sip of coffee and banished her uncomfortable reflections. What good did it do to pine? This morning she would think only of comforting things.

Elsa's coffee was nearly gone when Bry dragged into the kitchen. She was barely awake, from all appearances. Her eyes were at half-mast, and her movements reminded Elsa of a floundering fish.

"Good morning." Elsa greeted her. "Would you like coffee?"

Bry made a face. "Not this morning. I'm a little nauseous." She rummaged in the cupboard. "We have a tin of soda biscuits somewhere."

"Here." Elsa retrieved them for her. "Why don't you sit down? Perhaps a glass of water would help. I hope you're not coming down sick."

"The crackers should do the trick, but thank you." Bry lowered herself gingerly onto a stool at the counter. "You're up early."

"Birds singing in the trees outside the window woke me."

Bry smiled. "They like to do that."

"It will be an easy sound to grow used to." Elsa finished her coffee.

"You'll be happy to know that the ranch is full of birds. I favor the bluebirds. Their feathers are such a beautiful color."

"We have them in Germany too."

"We're going on a picnic by the river today. I hope you'll come along. There are plenty of birds to watch."

"I'd like that." Elsa discovered after uttering the polite response that she meant every word.

"Good. It will be more fun with another woman along."

"Do you think you'll be well enough to go?"

"I think so, yes. Fresh air should do me good."

A stomping sound came from outside the back door. Bry frowned in confusion, but then brightened. "That's Nick and Con at the washstand after feeding the livestock in the barn." She sat straighter.

The back door burst open, and Nick and Con clumped in.

Nick dropped a kiss on his wife's forehead. "Are you feeling better?"

Bry nodded. "Mostly, but I'll only have toast for breakfast. Speaking of which—" She stood up briskly. "You must be hungry."

Bry still looked a little green, so Elsa spoke up. "I can make breakfast, if you like, and prepare the picnic food."

"That would be wonderful." Bry smiled.

"You are very kind." Con rolled up his sleeves.

"What are you doing?" Elsa's cheeks burned at her reaction to the sight of his muscular forearms. She jerked her gaze up to his face.

"Taking my sister's place in the kitchen." He smiled as if well aware of the reason for her distraction. "You can't do all that alone."

Bry gazed at Con, a bemused expression on her face. "I've never known you to cook."

"If I hadn't learned, I'd have starved by now." He raised an eyebrow. "You do recall that apart from housing Shane occasionally, I lived alone for years. I don't have Elsa's skill, but

I know my way around a kitchen."

"Seeing is believing." Bry gave him an impudent grin. "I'll need to watch you in action."

"Nick, please remove my sister from the kitchen."

Nick chuckled. "Come, darling. You're not wanted here."

"If I must." Bry rose with an injured air, but her eyes gleamed. "Thanks for stepping up. I was going to make eggs and bacon. There's sourdough bread to toast and the wild strawberry preserve I made last week."

"Leave breakfast to us." Con shooed her from the kitchen.

Elsa spilled her coffee. She reached for the dishcloth to wipe the counter. Her spoon clattered to the floor.

Con picked up the spoon, smiling as if he guessed why she'd dropped it. "I'll start cooking the bacon."

Elsa cracked eggs into a bowl. The aroma of bacon sizzling in the cast iron frying pan wafted to her. She stole a glance at Con manning the stove. He looked incredibly attractive doing the humble chore. She reached for the whisk, sending it flying. She sighed. Why had she suddenly become clumsy?

Elsa grabbed the whisk at the same instant Con went after it. His hand grasped hers. She raised her head to find herself inches from Con, gazing into his eyes. They straightened together, Elsa still holding the whisk and Con's hand on hers. His gaze shifted to her mouth. "You'll burn the bacon." Her voice sounded breathy.

"We can't have that." Con released her and turned to the stove.

After breakfast, Elsa returned with Con to the kitchen. She set to work baking cornbread while Con opened the trap door that led into the cellar. He emerged a short time later carrying a box of brown bottles. "It's ginger ale, which I'll have you know originated in Ireland. I remembered about it last night."

"That sounds lovely."

They put together a picnic of fried chicken, a salad from the garden, Elsa's cornbread, and Con's ginger ale. The climbing heat sent Elsa to her room to change into one of the calico dresses Bry brought her. Chiding herself for vanity, she glanced in the mirror. Her green dress made her hazel eyes look the same hue. Elsa tucked stray wisps of her red-blonde hair behind her ear and put on the bonnet that matched the dress. Its protection would help her endure the sun.

She joined the others. Con carried the basket of food. Nick brought the box of ginger ale and a jug of water. Elsa fell into step beside Bry, who carried a worn quilt. "How do you feel?"

"I've recovered." Bry gave her a brilliant smile.

They skirted the garden and followed a path toward the river. Con called a halt on a small crest that gave a view of the river. Bry laid the quilt beneath a large cottonwood that spread welcome shade across the grass.

Elsa breathed deeply. The river shone, vivid blue, below them. Trees crowded in other places, but beyond the cottonwood, boulders tumbled into the river. Willows lining the opposite bank draped branches over the water. Shadows clustered in pools beneath the trees, dark places where a fish might hide. A bald eagle soaring above the river dove toward the surface and dipped its talons into the water. The eagle flapped upward, a dripping fish in its claws.

Elsa shielded her eyes and watched its flight. The eagle landed at the top of a tall cottonwood a short distance downriver. She turned to Bry. "Do you see its nest?"

Bry smiled. "It's well established. The same pair raised eaglets in that tree last year."

"As long as nothing disturbs them, eagles return to the same spot." Nick helped Bry lower herself onto the quilt, then sat beside her. "They build it the nest over time, every year making it grander."

Con laughed. "That reminds me of what people do." He set the basket down, then offered his hand to Elsa. She let him support her while she settled on the quilt, then thanked him with a smile. Con took a spot beside her and lifted the cloth covering the basket. Elsa helped him serve the food. Working beside Con like this seemed so right. She could almost pretend that she was mistress of the ranch house. How would it feel to be Con's wife? Her face heated at her thoughts. She gladly kept them to herself.

A familiar tapping came from the tree above them. "What is it?" Elsa pointed to a bird standing on the furrowed trunk. The feathered creature boasted a green head and back, red cheeks, a pale gray collar, and a blush-pink chest. "It stands like a woodpecker, but it doesn't have a crest."

Con peered upward. "You're right, Elsa. It's a Lewis's Woodpecker, named for Meriwether Lewis, the explorer who first reported it."

"It's so colorful! In my village, the woodpeckers are all black and have red crests."

"We have one like that, except with stripes of white that make it look like the bird is wearing a black eye band."

Throughout the meal, Elsa compared the birds she saw to the ones she'd known in Germany. Her companions supplied the names of unfamiliar birds. She would never remember them all. After they finished eating, Nick glanced at Con and Elsa before returning his attention to Bry. "Shall we take a walk beside the river, Dear Heart?"

"What a lovely idea." Bry gave her husband an eager look.

Elsa glanced away, feeling that watching them was intruding. What would it be like to possess the kind of love they shared? She wished she knew. Her parents had cherished one another with the same degree of devotion. Like her brothers and sisters, Elsa would pretend shock whenever her parents embraced, but their love had formed part of her security. The world could fall apart, and yet her family would remain safe. Her parents' love had sheltered them even when her father was taken ill.

After a final swallow of the fizzy ginger ale, Elsa helped Con pack the food away. Being alone with him felt far too intimate. "I'll be back." She scrambled to her feet. "I want to pick wildflowers."

"Elsa, wait." Con stood. "I have something to tell you."

"What is it?" Alarm tinged her voice. She'd never seen him unsure of himself.

"I've given thought to what you said last night."

Elsa tensed and made no reply.

"I still don't agree with you, but it is your decision. I'll help you find employment."

Moisture filled her eyes. "Thank you."

"I hope you'll remain my guest a little longer. You've been through a terrible experience and need rest." He brushed a tear from her cheek. "I'll admit that I find taking care of you pleasant."

"I'm glad to hear that." She smiled. "I thought I might be a bother."

"You're never that, Elsa." He shifted closer.

Elsa should step back, but she parted her lips and waited.

Con's kiss pushed aside her every defense. She didn't care. The scent of wildflowers, the song of the river, and feel of his mouth against hers were a heady ambrosia. They filled her senses and satisfied the yearnings of her heart. She held onto Con as her every argument faded to nothing.

Elsa broke off in confusion. What was she doing? She

wanted to go home to Germany, not stay here with Con.

"Elsa—"

"No." She backed away. "I can't do this."

CHAPTER TWENTY-SEVEN

MAISEY HANDED SE'UŁKU A FRESH GLASS of water. Her translator had fallen ill a little over a week ago with the same sickness that had taken her daughter, Bluebird, to the brink of death. The doctor had come and gone, leaving willow drops for the fever and a promise to return. Se'ulku had rallied of late.

"How is Bluebird?" Se'ułku lifted her head.

"She's sleeping peacefully. The doctor believes she's over the worst now."

Tears crowded Se'ułku's eyes. "Thank you."

Maisey smiled but frowned when she turned away. Bluebird was almost well, but little Rain grew weaker every day.

Maisey left the meeting room, where she had set up cots for the sick. Located up the stairs in the center of the building, this room had no windows to disturb their sleep. She found Saka'am in the gathering room. The Indian woman had not succumbed to measles. Maisey was trying to keep her and Rain separated but doing so broke the hearts of both the mother and daughter.

Saka'am stood on the balcony. When she saw Maisey, she ran to her. "What doctor say?"

"Rain is very ill. All we can do is wait."

"*Wait* is all he say?" The woman's face turned red.

Maisey stepped back. She could appreciate that Saka'am was grieving, but her criticism pierced to the core. She was, after all, going without sleep to care for this woman's daughter. She pushed at a lock of hair that fell into her eyes and fought for self-control. "I'm doing all I can."

Saka'am gripped her arm. "Save her, Teacher."

Maisey pulled away. "I'll try to bring her fever down again. Maybe that will help."

"I go to her."

"I've explained why that isn't a good idea."

"No!" Saka'am's eyes flashed, and her nostrils flared. "I go to her."

Maisey looked into her stricken face and shook her head. "All right."

She led Saka'am to the meeting room. Just before they entered, Maisey put a finger to her lips. They tiptoed past Se'ułku, who had fallen asleep at last. Maisey peeked at Bluebird. Her cheeks had regained their color.

Before they reached Rain's cot, Maisey knew something was wrong. The child lay in utter stillness, her face waxy. The covers over her chest did not rise and fall. No breath came through her parted lips.

Maisey gasped. Tears stung her eyes and spilled down her cheeks.

Saka'am's keening wail throbbed through the air. "You killed my daughter!" Her nostrils flared as she launched herself at Maisey.

Struggling to push Saka'am away, Maisey staggered backward.

Saka'am's fingernails dug into Maisey's cheek.

"Stop," Se'ulku called in a weak voice.

The force of rage drove Saka'am, but Maisey's strength came from desperation. Maisey gripped the woman's wrists and pulled her hands from her face.

Saka'am spewed spittle into Maisey's eyes. "You will suffer as I suffer."

Maisey peered into the small mirror she kept in the teacher desk. Red scratches stood out on her white face. The welts were still swollen this morning. They stung, but not nearly as badly as the words Saka'am had flung at her. The grieving mother had picked up her dead daughter and carried her out of the schoolhouse. She hadn't returned all night.

Maisey climbed the stairs and walked onto the gathering room balcony. Soft light greeted her. The day's heat would take over soon, but right now she breathed in the cool air of early morning. The road unfurled like a brown ribbon with hayfields beyond it. The trees south of the schoolhouse clung to shadow, as if loathe to let go of the night.

Maisey's patients had taken a long time to fall asleep. After Saka'am's outburst had revealed Rain's death, calming Bluebird proved difficult. Maisey gave her a mild sedative draught left by the doctor and sat behind Bluebird until her mouth slackened in slumber. Se'ułku also slept, so Maisey slipped from the room.

Exhausted, she crawled fully clothed into the cot set up for her in the gathering room. Her mind wouldn't rest, however. Rain's face in death kept flashing before her. Maisey had poured out her grief into her pillow.

Maisey shook back her hair, which she hadn't troubled to braid last night. She'd tried so hard to help the Salish tribe, but once again she'd failed. Taking in the sick girls was not a kindness if it brought strife between the tribe and local settlers. Maisey hoped that Saka'am would not make good her threat to bring suffering upon her. The consequences could be far-reaching.

She left the balcony door open to cool the upper floor. After a cup of coffee, Maisey felt better. She'd heard no sound yet from the meeting room where her patients slept.

Se'ułku stood up shakily. "I must leave you." She spoke in a quiet voice.

Maisey glanced at Bluebird, still sleeping. She guided Se'ułku from the room. "But you're still sick."

"I am almost better." Se'ułku gave her a quick smile.

"Come sit down, and I'll heat your breakfast. America left a basket of pancakes on the step this morning."

"Both of you and the preacher's wife have given me many blessings. I do not wish to harm you."

"I don't understand. How could you do that?"

"By staying with you. Saka'am will not be silent. Now that she goes back to the tribe, she will tell my husband that you killed Rain. He will come to take my daughter and me home, but he won't ride alone. Do you see why we can't stay?"

Maisey nodded. "I would prefer you to rest here longer, but I'd hate for there to be trouble. Since your rashes faded days ago, you're no longer contagious. You shouldn't walk far, though. I'll ask Shane to take you in his wagon."

"You are so kind." Se'ułku's almond eyes shone. "I am grateful to you for saving Bluebird's life."

"Give your thanks to God, not me." Maisey didn't feel responsible for Rain's death, but neither could she take credit for saving Bluebird.

Shane hitched the wagon and drove off with Se'ulku and Bluebird.

Maisey leaned against the doorframe and watched the wagon roll out of sight. Saka'am might curse her, but she had made a difference for Se'ułku and Bluebird.

She turned back into the schoolhouse and rolled up her sleeves. Time to scrub down every surface—twice .

Maisey pulled Phoebe closer and kissed the top of her head. How she had missed holding her sweet daughter. She'd wanted to do little else since their reunion yesterday. The whole episode with the sick Indians had thrown her normal routine off kilter. After more than a week spent catching sleep when she could, she needed time to recover.

Rain's death reminded her of what mattered most. Teaching at the Indian school had been a lot to add to her already busy life. Sometimes she had to ignore Phoebe simply to provide for her. Supper needed cooking or clothes wanted cleaning. She fell into bed at night exhausted and rose early to begin again. And yet, she wouldn't trade her role as Phoebe's mother.

A knock came at the door, and Maisey lowered Phoebe. Her daughter continued to cling to her, so Maisey picked her up and carried her along.

Emma Duncan, the schoolteacher who lived in the other cabin on the Hayes' property, stood on the porch. Blonde and delicate, she might make a better debutante. She held a covered baking dish. "I've caught you at home. I'm glad."

"Won't you come in?" Maisey stood back. She didn't really want company, but it would be impolite to turn her neighbor away. She closed the door.

"I brought you coffee cake." Emma lifted the cover on her dish. "It's apple-caramel."

Phoebe perked up. "Can we have some, please?"

"I should have asked before taking the lid off. I hope you don't mind."

Maisey smiled. "It's all right. Phoebe ate lunch earlier. Can I offer you coffee and a slice of cake?"

"Thank you, but I won't intrude. America told me what you went through at the schoolhouse. I'm sure you'd rather spend time with Phoebe. If you ever need help, I hope you won't hesitate to call upon me."

Elsa leaned down from the wagon and reached for Con. He caught her against him with strong arms. His smile quickened Elsa's pulse. For a wild moment, she thought he might kiss her. Instead, he lowered her to the ground and stepped back.

"Thank you." Her voice came out breathy.

Con gave Elsa a look that did nothing for her composure. "My pleasure."

Her face warmed, and she looked anywhere but at him. Wagons and tents filled the ground between the Hayes' house and the school.

"Folks come from far away to attend Sunday meeting." Con supplied the answer to her unspoken question. "They roll in once a month on Saturday, and camp through Monday morning."

Bry joined them. "It's a festive gathering, and a lot of work for America and Shane. But they would never turn anyone away."

"They'll need kitchen workers." Elsa sang out her thought. "There they are."

Shane and America, crossing the yard, waved in greeting.

"We must do our best to help them cope." Bry and Nick picked up their pace to meet them.

Con waited for Elsa, and they walked together down the path. How different this greeting felt. She was no longer among strangers.

"Come inside, all of you." America beamed.

Con held back. "I'd better see to the horses."

Nick perked up. "I'll give you a hand."

"Make that three." Shane fell into step beside Con.

America watched them go. "I bet they'll talk about politics, fishing, and guns." Her tone gave away her feelings on those topics.

"Never mind." Bry smiled. "They've given us the perfect opportunity to talk about *them*."

America laughed. "Not that we will. I'd rather hear what you've been doing at the ranch."

"Elsa has taken over the kitchen duties. I'm thankful that she loves to cook. She makes divine apple strudel." Bry sighed. "The only trouble is, I'm putting on weight."

"That sounds like a problem worth having." America held open the arbor gate. "Elsa, maybe you can teach Maisey to make strudel. Did she tell you that she likes to cook too?"

"She didn't mention it, but Bry told me."

"You and Maisey have a lot in common." America waited at the open door and waved them inside.

Elsa smiled as she passed. "I'd like to get to know her better."

America closed the door. "I'm sure Maisey feels the same. She went through a difficult time lately. Several women from the local tribe asked her for help when their daughters came down with measles."

"Goodness." Elsa shuddered. "That's such a terrible disease. I remember most of my village suffered from it. My household certainly did."

"Maisey quarantined the women and their daughters in the schoolhouse. She tended them for more than a week. I couldn't do more than watch Phoebe and leave meals for them on the step."

"I'm glad you took Phoebe." Bry glanced back from the doorway. "Hopefully no one around here will catch measles."

America held back for Elsa to go inside. "No one was exposed except Maisey, and she'd already had them."

"What about the schoolhouse?" Bry frowned. "Is it safe to hold Sunday meeting there?"

America led the way into the kitchen. "I'm sure of it. Maisey scrubbed down the place, and Emma went over it too. I've aired it out for the past two days." She turned to Elsa. "Maisey offered to let you stay with her and Phoebe tonight, so we set up a cot in her cabin. I hope that's all right."

"How nice of her. Yes, I'd like that."

"Then it's settled. Emma will also be there. She shifted from the schoolteacher's cabin to allow Bry, Nick, and Con to sleep there. Come into the kitchen, and I'll give you a glass of raspberry shrub. Are you hungry?"

"We ate the noon meal on the road, but shrub sounds lovely in this heat." Bry led the way into the kitchen. "What can we do to help you finish up in here?"

"I only have sugar cookies to make for tomorrow's potluck, and soda biscuits for supper. Everything else is ready."

"I'll wash the dishes." Bry rolled up her sleeves.

"I can make the *Plätzchen*." Elsa tied on one of the aprons hanging from a hook.

America laughed. "You make ordinary recipes sound special."

Bry smiled. "I've learned that when Elsa cooks, no recipe is ordinary."

"That's kind of you to say." Elsa soaped and rinsed her hands at the wash table, then dried them with a flour-sack towel.

She set to work making the cookies.

America poured glasses of raspberry-infused vinegar drink and carried them to her workers. Then she excused herself to check that those camping in the yard had all they needed.

"I honestly don't know how she does everything." Bry shook her head. "It's hard enough caring for a husband and young children, without adding a congregation."

Elsa looked up from measuring the flour. "I don't think she feels burdened by much."

"You are right, I'm sure. Here I was thinking how *I* would feel, but I'm not called to be a preacher's wife . . . thankfully."

The men came in from the barn and took up residence in the parlor. The rumble of their voices carried to Elsa as she mixed and rolled out the cookie dough. Pressing the heart-shaped cookie cutters into the dough reminded her of making cookies as a small child under her mother's guiding hand.

Once the cookies were baked and decorated with a simple frosting, Elsa admired her handiwork. The children, especially, would enjoy this treat.

"Thank you, ladies." America hugged Bry and Elsa in turn. "Rest a few minutes while I set the table."

At supper, Elsa relished the corned beef and vegetables America pulled from the warming oven. She enjoyed a second glass of the refreshing raspberry drink. More than the food, though, she enjoyed the company. She could almost believe she belonged.

America heated wash water on the stove while they ate. The large pots of water Shane had hefted onto the stove filled the kitchen with steam. Elsa pitched in to wash the dishes, which Bry dried and America put away.

Later, Shane brought in a washtub and placed it in a corner of the kitchen.

"It's time to bathe my children and lay out their clothes for the morning. Bry, you know where to find the schoolteacher's cabin. Elsa, Maisey is expecting you."

Con accompanied Elsa along the path. Just ahead, Nick and Bry strolled along, holding hands. The murmur of voices and shared laughter rose from the temporary encampment. Children tussled in the grass, giggling, while women called them to get ready for bed.

"You seem happy this evening." Con reached for Elsa's hand, and she let him take it.

"I am surrounded by wonderful people." Miles, Alicia, and Atticus lived very differently from this. Perhaps that was why they brought so much sorrow to others.

They turned aside at the barn. The trees met overhead, shutting out the stars. Con guided Elsa lightly by the elbow. "Be careful of roots on the path. I'm surprised America didn't send us off with a lantern."

"She had her hands busy." Elsa could see well enough, but she slowed her steps for safety's sake.

Nick and Bry broke free of the trees but then halted and stepped into shadow. Con held onto Elsa's arm more firmly and pulled her off the path. "What is it?" Con's question vibrated in the stillness.

"Something's wrong at Maisey's cabin." Nick's whisper stirred the air.

CHAPTER TWENTY-EIGHT

MAISEY HUDDLED BESIDE EMMA. SHE LONGED more than anything to hold Phoebe. Her daughter, held aloft by Saka'am's husband, looked so small. Beside Spukani stood two other warriors, their weapons at the ready. One pulled a bowstring taut. The other held a tomahawk.

"Why are you doing this?" Maisey asked in English without expecting to be understood. She already knew the answer, and it terrified her. She and Phoebe should not have to pay the price for Rain's death.

"You killed my child." Spukani answered in English.

"No!" Maisey shook her head. "I did all I could to save Rain."

He bared his teeth in a grimace. "Don't speak your lies. Saka'am told me what happened." His voice rose. "She brought Rain to you for healing, but you let our child die." He covered Phoebe's golden hair with his dark hand. "You must give up your own."

"No!" Maisey hauled in a breath. "If you take Phoebe, the soldiers will come to your village."

Saka'am's nostrils flared. "If they do, we will soak the ground with their blood." Phoebe wailed, and he pulled her close to his chest. "Your daughter is now *my* daughter."

Sorrow washed through Maisey, but also relief. Spukani wanted to adopt Phoebe, not murder her. She would take comfort in that knowledge until Shane helped her recover Phoebe. She had to believe that.

Maisey squared her shoulders. "Let me kiss my child goodbye." Her voice shook so badly, she could barely force out the words.

Spukani held Phoebe tighter against him. "You have no child."

"Don't let this happen." Emma clutched Maisey's arm. "If they take Phoebe, you may never get her back."

Phoebe's face crumpled. "I want my ma."

Spukani stalked to the door. It slammed open against the wall. The doorway gaped, empty. The other warriors backed toward the opening.

Tears blurred Maisey's vision. Avery had died, and now Phoebe was gone. The worst had happened. She had lost her family completely.

Con pulled Elsa closer and felt her tremble in his arms. He kissed her forehead. "Go warn the camp and tell Shane."

She nodded and slipped away. Bry joined her, and the two women hurried down the path in the fading light.

Nick's gaze met his. "I saw an Indian through the window."

The two men crept closer to Maisey's cabin. Raised voices reached Con from inside, and figures passed behind the panes. He saw Phoebe's shining curls catch the light, only to be covered by a dark hand.

Con's throat went dry. Surely, they would not harm one so young! He had heard horrifying tales of such happenings, but his mind rejected the idea. Nick reached the side of the cabin first. He motioned to Con. Together, they rounded the corner and edged their way toward the front porch.

The door swung open. A warrior wearing large, round shells in his ears and long braids on either side of his face burst through the opening. Phoebe, in his arms, wailed for her mother. The Indian started down the steps.

"Stop." Con stepped out from the shadows, his gun cocked.

Another warrior, his bow nocked and ready, emerged from the cabin.

Nick vaulted the porch railing and launched himself into the Indian. They toppled together. The bow flew from the warrior's hands and clattered against the porch boards.

With a throaty cry, a third warrior rushed through the doorway with his tomahawk raised. Con's gun went off, and one of the Indians fell.

Nick staggered to his feet, pistol in hand. He pushed the fallen Indians with his toe. Neither stirred.

Con spun. The warrior carrying Phoebe had taken advantage of the distraction. He was hurrying between the trees, toward the road. Con took off after him. Nick stayed close on his heels.

"Stop, or I'll shoot," Con called after the fleeing Indian. It was an empty threat. He would never risk Phoebe's life.

"If he doesn't stop, *I'll* shoot." Nick cocked his gun.

The warrior turned to face them. "Leave me alone. I only want what is mine."

Con watched for any sudden movements. "Phoebe does not belong to you."

"She's my daughter now."

"Can't you hear her bawling for her mother?" Indignation rang in Nick's voice.

The Indian's shoulders shook. Tears glistened on his cheeks. "The teacher took my daughter from her mother in death. That is why she must give up her own child."

Shane had told Con earlier about the measles outbreak and the little girl's death. He'd wondered then if something bad might happen as a result.

"Death comes, and none can stop it. Will you punish Maisey for what she could not change?" Con lowered his gun and held the grieving man's gaze. "Let Phoebe go."

The warrior bent over, weeping, and set Phoebe on her feet. She dashed to Con and flung herself against his knees.

The Indian broke and ran.

"Let him go." Con picked Phoebe up and cradled her. "There's been enough sorrow already."

Glad to be home, Con drew up in front of the ranch house. Elsa had remained quiet throughout the journey, but then, so had they all. He jumped down and came around the wagon to help her down. The trouble with holding her was that he didn't want to stop.

However, he swung her down from the wagon, briefly caressed her shoulders, and stepped away. Right now, he could tell she needed distance more than closeness.

In certain ways, so did he. It had been a long night at the Hayes' house. Shane had gathered the flock for a somber Sunday meeting. He'd kept the message brief before leading the congregation in prayer for Maisey, Phoebe, and the local tribes. Most folks packed up and left early the next morning, anxious to escape further trouble.

Shane loaded the two Indian prisoners in his wagon first thing and drove off to Hell Gate. Nick's bullet had passed through one of the intruder's arms. The other Indian had simply been knocked out.

Doc Bailey tended both men. Nick also needed care. He'd pulled a leg muscle during the fray. Bry immediately dedicated herself to comforting her husband.

Or possibly smothering him, Con noted with a silent chuckle. He returned to the wagon and lowered Bry to the ground.

Nick glared a warning when Con turned back for him. He grinned and delivered their luggage to the front porch, letting his brother-in-law alight on his own.

Con climbed back onto the driving box, rubbed a kink out of his neck, and took up the lines. The horses pricked their ears, clearly ready for their hay.

Nick started for the barn, no doubt to help, but Con waved him away. He needed to be alone. It had been hard to witness Maisey almost losing her daughter a second time. It brought back memories of the buffalo stampede Phoebe had wandered into, and of the fourteen-year-old girl who had lost her life rescuing her.

Life was fleeting, a fact Con should not forget. One of the reasons he had turned down Keira's invitation was the chance that he might already be married. That wasn't the case, but maybe he should make it so.

He'd stopped wandering. Settling down would give him time for a family of his own. He blew out a breath. What was he doing pining for Elsa? She had more than once expressed her desire to live on a different continent from him.

Con stopped the horses at the barn and hopped out to open the door. He drove inside, and the shadow of the barn closed over him. After parking the wagon in its usual space, he went to unhitch the horses.

"Don't move." A voice spoke behind him.

Con froze. "What do you want?"

"I'm here to make a deal with you."

The voice had a timbre Con recognized. He shifted slightly to use his side vision.

"I told you not to move." A gun clicked.

"Call me curious. Who are you?" Con forced a calm note into his voice.

"All you need to know about me is that I have your brother."

"Where?" *So much for sounding relaxed.*

"Somewhere no one will find him."

"Have you injured him?"

"He's well for now, but he misses his brother. I'm sure we can come up with a way to have this all end in a happy reunion."

"How much money do you want?"

"Give me Elsa Meier, and we'll call it even."

CHAPTER TWENTY-NINE

ROB STOMPED A RAT AWAY. THE creature's claws scrabbled on the rotting floorboards as it forged a trail through the dust and into a hole. He cringed. A snake might wriggle through that hole next. Even with his hands tied in front of him, rather than behind, there wasn't much he could do to protect himself without a weapon. The wall at his back yielded, groaning like a man in pain from the pressure of leaning his head against it.

I'd knock it down if my hands and feet weren't shackled.

A thick chain tethered Rob to an eye bolt embedded in a cement block sunk in the ground. He couldn't go far dragging that around, provided he could pull it up in the first place. The gaps between wall slats, where the tar paper had peeled, showed trees crowding the dilapidated shack.

Rob's abductor had hidden him well.

He counted yet again the cracks letting in light through the wall. Rob might have borne the humiliation of imprisonment better, if it wasn't for the utter futility of time dragging by. He would almost welcome a visit from his abductor. Almost.

That Miles was behind his kidnapping, he had no doubt. The person who brought him food wore a mask and didn't speak, but his stature and weight were consistent with Miles's. He might attempt to extract a ransom from Con or use Rob to lure his brother into danger.

Whatever the plan, Rob prayed the scoundrel was not successful.

The new life Rob wanted to create for himself in Virginia

City had not been going well, even before this interruption. Panning gold was back-breaking labor and not very rewarding, especially when someone didn't possess the necessary skills, which he clearly did not.

Plagued by loneliness, Rob had taken to talking to himself. He would never again judge those who did so. Even that simple pleasure had been stolen from him by the gag on his mouth.

His friends and family were too far distant to miss him. Cecil might notice him gone . . . or he might not. Besides Rob's abductor, no one knew where he was.

God knows. The truth resounded within him. *Lord, I trust myself to Your care.*

The footfalls outside the shack sounded lighter than the ones that had come before. The lock rattled, and the door squeaked open. A masked figure, too small to be Miles, stood outlined in the light pouring through the opening.

The person approached, carrying a basket over one arm and a jug of water in one hand. The free hand pointed a gun at his chest. "Try anything, and I'll shoot you."

Rob started. The voice belonged to a woman.

She moved behind him and untied his gag. "Eat."

Rob worked his jaw. The basket contained a couple of biscuits and a bowl of beans with chunks of salt pork. "How can I eat with my hands tied?" Miles had made him eat with his hands bound, but this unknown woman might not know that.

"Find a way." The eyes behind her mask reminded him of blue sapphires—cold and hard. She was more calculating than he'd given her credit for.

The next day when she arrived, Rob decided to try a different tactic. "Did he make you bring me food?"

She glared at him. "No one makes me do anything."

"Oh? I thought you smarter than this."

"Be quiet!"

Rejecting her suggestion, Rob went on. "How did you get mixed up in breaking the law?"

The door slammed behind her, shaking the building.

He was sleeping when she arrived again. He sat up, blinking as the doorway opening widened. She hurried in and thrust a jar at him.

"Thanks." He sipped at the bean and bacon soup.

She thumped down a water jug, picked up the empty one, and turned toward the doorway.

Rob couldn't let her go without making an effort. "A friend of mine is due to stop by my cabin."

"Who cares?"

"You might." Rob spoke quickly, before she could close the door. "He'll report me missing. Once he does, the sheriff is bound to find me."

"*Shut up*." Her voice shook with anger. The door thudded into place. A key grated in the lock.

She watched him from the doorway the following day, reluctance in her bearing. Rob hesitated. He had riled her. Maybe he should stop. She was, after all, feeding him.

Rob decided to take his chances. He'd set out to rattle her and had apparently succeeded. He gave her a pitying look. "Why don't you admit that you're in over your head?"

"Hold your tongue!" She stomped over to him and plopped the water jug onto the ground.

"Let me go, and I'll say nothing about this to anyone."

She made no reply.

"You're afraid, aren't you?" he goaded her.

"I've had about enough of you." She slammed the gun butt into the side of his neck, sending him sprawling. Then she hurled the basket across the shack. It thumped into the wall, and

Rob's supper flew out. The bowl crashed to the ground in a mess of glass shards, beans, and salt pork.

"I hope you starve," the masked woman hissed. She stomped out, slamming the door behind her. The lock rattled.

Rob pushed himself into a sitting position. She hadn't put his gag back on. He could shout for help to his heart's content.

Something told him that no one would hear.

Con struggled to sit up. Someone supported his back. Con's head ached, the warmth of blood trickled into one eye, and he fought the urge to retch.

"Steady." Nick's face swam into view. "Who did this to you?"

Con touched the tender place on his head and winced. "I don't know. I only had a glimpse, and the person wore a mask. He sounded like Miles. I wouldn't put something like this past him, either. That man hates me."

"Let me take a look." Nick inspected Con's wound. "Bry sent me out when you didn't come in right away. I think she was nervous about Indian trouble after what happened in Liberty."

"It's a good thing she did. Whoever beat me up has Rob. If we track him soon, he may lead us to my brother."

"We'd better patch you and alert the women before we go."

"All right, but do it quickly. We don't want to lose his trail."

Nick's lips quirked into a smile. "You forget you are talking to the son of a tracker."

Con nodded, then wished he hadn't. "That's convenient."

Nick extended a hand to him. "Can you get up?"

"I think so." He managed to gain his feet.

"Throw an arm over my shoulder."

Con obliged him. "I don't want to lean on you too much, not with your injured muscle."

"You'll find that I can handle the strain."

Con felt certain Nick could. He was learning a great deal about his new brother-in-law, most of it good.

By the time they reached the house, Con was walking on his own. It took a concerted effort, but he determined not to let the pain show. They entered the kitchen by the back door. No use upsetting the women.

Elsa looked up from stacking dishes. Her eyes widened. "Are you all right?".

"I had an accident—"

"Con was attacked in the barn." Nick stepped around him.

Con flashed a pointed glance at Nick, who displayed no qualms about frightening the women. Mentioning an assailant on the property seemed a bad idea.

Elsa's gaze shifted between Nick and Con.

Who does she believe? Con didn't want to guess. It was better to distract her. "I need a little attention. It's nothing that iodine and a bandage can't improve."

Nick rummaged in a cupboard. "I thought I saw it here."

Elsa pulled a tin box from a shelf. "Let's patch you up." She sent Nick after a washcloth.

"Don't worry," Con said when they were alone. "My assailant left. He's gone."

Elsa's hazel gaze watched him with a frank appraisal. "Are you sure about that?"

"I believe so."

"Was it someone you know?"

Con hesitated. "Maybe."

"Who?"

"I don't want to say until I'm certain. Nick and I will ride out tonight to track him."

Elsa's forehead furrowed. She retrieved the washbasin from the stand and rolled up her sleeves before replying. "I hope he's worth the trouble."

"I'd say so." Con spoke carefully, guarding his tongue. Elsa had a keen mind. She could pick up on his slightest inference. It was one of the things he loved about her.

Once the forbidden word slipped into Con's mind, it refused to leave. He could admit he loved Elsa, but where would that get him unless she felt the same about him?

Nick returned with a washcloth, interrupting Con's musing. Bry came in also and hurried to her brother's side. "What have you done to yourself this time?" Concern warmed her eyes, despite her chiding.

Elsa wrung out the cloth above the steaming washbasin and brought it to Con's grazed jaw.

"Nothing serious," Con assured his sister. He closed his eyes and gritted his teeth. Elsa bathed his face with gentle hands. . If it wasn't for the pain, he'd enjoy her ministrations.

Nick chuckled. "I can see I'm not needed here. I'll saddle the horses."

"You're not planning on going tonight?" Bry gave her husband a pleading look.

"Sorry, Bry, but we have to. There's a life at stake."

Elsa started. "What's going on?"

"Whose life?" Bry snapped out.

"Rob's in danger." Nick put an arm around her.

Con gave Nick a pointed glance. "We'll take every precaution," Con hastened to assure his sister.

Bry swept a glance from Nick to Con. "I can see you're united in this decision. I don't like it, but I won't hold you back."

Con doubted she could have stopped them, anyway, but he didn't tell her that.

Nick kissed his wife. "Stay inside. Lock the doors while we're gone. If we're not back by tomorrow, take the manager along and go tell Shane we need help." He paused. "And you know where the gun case is."

Bry brought her chin up. "Yes."

Con kissed his sister's cheek. "We'll be home before you know it."

Elsa was watching him with darkened eyes. After his recent thoughts about her, he simply nodded and turned away.

The sun hung low in the sky. The Morgans that had pulled the wagon crunched hay in their stalls. Two quarter horses, one dark and the other a buckskin, stood saddled and waiting.

Nick gave Con an uncertain glance. "Are you able to ride?"

"Don't concern yourself. I qualify as hardheaded, from what my sister tells me. I think you'd have more trouble with that bad leg."

Nick laughed. "Listen to us. We're the halt leading the lame."

Con smiled for the first time all day.

There were still a couple of hours of sunlight remaining, and fast, fresh horses could carry them a ways. Ignoring his dizziness, Con climbed onto Blackie and gathered the reins.

Nick lifted himself into Buck's saddle. "I found a fresh trail leading away from behind the barn. I assume that's the culprit."

"It seems likely."

Nick led the way. He took them along the river bank before striking out across open countryside. The trail curved back toward the river and reached a clearing just as the sun hovered above the mountains.

"What's this?" Nick dismounted and examined the tracks.

"It makes no sense, unless—" He pressed his lips together.

"Say it." Con felt sick to his stomach.

"I suspect he's doubled back." Nick shook his head. "We may have fallen for a ruse."

"Why would he do such a thing?" Con knew the answer before he finished asking the question.

Elsa gazed out the library window toward the river, which glimmered in the last rays of the sun. The crescent moon hung in a clear sky. Con would sleep under the stars tonight.

Bry looked in from the doorway. "Are you hungry? I can heat the soup America sent home with us."

"I'm not, but thank you." Elsa couldn't think of eating when the men might be in peril.

Bry came to stand behind Elsa at the window. "I'd feel better if the ranch manager was here."

Elsa stared at her, thunderstruck. "You mean we're alone on the ranch?"

"Turner didn't answer my knock, and his horse is gone. He must be out on the range with the cattle. Who knows when he'll return?" Bry wrapped her arms around herself. "I doubt Nick and Con would have gone had they known."

Elsa let the curtain fall across the window. "Let's hope theycome back soon."

Bry stood with her back to the unlit fireplace. "I have an uneasy feeling about them rushing off like that. I don't think they gave it much thought." She went to the door. "I'll eat in the kitchen then turn in. I'm getting sleepy. There's no point sitting up fretting."

Bry had a good idea, Elsa decided. She left the library and climbed the stairs to her bedroom. Tired though she was, Elsa couldn't sleep. Catastrophes that could befall Con and Nick tortured her mind. Trying to turn her thoughts down happier pathways, she counted the many kindnesses Con had shown her. If only she had thanked him more.

"What will I do if he doesn't come back?" she whispered. "Please, God, let Con be all right." *Let them both be all right.*

The prayer soothed Elsa's nerves. A familiar sensation of drowsiness stole over her, and she drifted into sleep.

The tread of footsteps outside her door startled Elsa awake. How long had she been asleep? She sat up in bed, holding her breath while she listened.

She exhaled in a rush. It was only Bry, coming to bed. She lowered herself onto her pillow and rolled onto her side.

Elsa woke with footsteps pacing down the hallway. Her heartbeat picked up, but then Bry's loud yawn reached her.

Elsa sighed in relief. Bry must have forgotten something she'd left downstairs earlier. Or maybe the house settling had sounded like footsteps. Either way, it was nothing to worry about. She needed to stop letting every sound alarm her.

As a child, Elsa had awakened more than once with a bad dream. Afterwards, she'd been unable to go back to sleep. Hearing her cries, *Mutter* had come in and taught her to give her fears to God.

Praying wasn't a bad idea right now. She composed her thoughts.

A soft footfall broke into Elsa's concentration. She sat up in confusion. This sound came from much closer—someone was in her room!

A hand slid over her mouth. "Hello, Elsa." Miles's whisper stirred the air near her ear. "Atticus wants you back."

CHAPTER THIRTY

CON LEAPED FROM THE BACK OF his horse and took the ranch house steps two at a time. Pain throbbed in his head with each step. Nick came more slowly, favoring his leg.

The door burst open before Con reached it. Bry rushed onto the porch. Her haunted expression confirmed his fears. "Elsa's gone."

Con grasped his sister by the shoulders. "What happened? Tell me everything."

Bry wrung her hands. "She didn't come down for breakfast this morning. When I checked her room, she wasn't there. The lamp by her bed had been overturned, but her window was shut and locked."

Nick glanced up at the windows. "Did you check the rest of the house?"

Bry nodded. "After I went to the gun case." Spots of color flared in her cheeks. "I found the bolt on the kitchen door broken."

Con swung toward Nick. "It has to be Miles. He's taking her back to Atticus. They can't be far away."

"Sorry, Con. I can't leave Bry by herself."

"No, Nick. You have to go with him." Bry touched her husband's arm. "I can beg a bed from the neighbors if I have to. I'll be all right. Go after Elsa."

Nick slanted an admiring look at her. "You're a brave and generous woman, Bryanna Laramie, and I love you for it. I'll take you to the neighbors before we go."

Con fretted at the delay, but he agreed with Nick's decision. "Lorne and Mary will take Bry in. I'll ask Lorne to ride out and find Turner. He can send word to Shane. We may need his help. Bry, how fast can you pack?"

Elsa shifted uncomfortably under the bedroll Miles had tossed over her. The smell of sweaty horse blankets wafted in her nostrils, but she couldn't do anything about the stink. Rope bound and chafed her wrists and ankles.

She groaned. The horrible nightmare had come true. Miles was taking her back to Atticus.

Footsteps crunched near her head. "So, you're awake." Miles stood over her.

Elsa put her back to him. "Go away."

He chuckled. "You're sassy this morning. I'd ask if you slept well, but obviously you didn't." He pulled back the bedroll and slit the rope tying her wrists and ankles.

Elsa staggered to her feet and rubbed her sore wrists. "Don't pretend you care anything about me. I know you don't. All I am to you is money."

"Spending time with Connor Walsh hasn't improved your disposition." He moved closer and slid a hand along her jawbone. "Try a little honey and see what it gets you."

"Don't touch me." She jerked away. "You're a parasite who preys on women."

Miles's eyes narrowed, and his nostrils flared. His palm slapped Elsa's face with stinging force.

Elsa's head snapped to the side, and she fell at his feet. Dirt ground into her palms. She pushed to her hands and knees. "I'm sorry I ever met you!"

"That feeling, dear Elsa, is mutual."

She glared up at him. "Touch me again, and I'll tell Atticus."

Miles snorted. "You've made that threat before."

Elsa scrambled to her feet and squared her shoulders. "This time I'm not afraid to carry it out."

His eyes flared wider. "You've changed, little mouse."

"Maybe I've learned that you're more a prisoner than I am."

Miles flinched, and his mask of elegance slipped. "Don't worry. I won't do it again. There's no need to tell Atticus anything."

Elsa stood taller. How had she missed seeing that this man, who had terrorized her so badly, was only a paper tiger? Miles hid his crudeness behind smooth manners and a charming smile. His domineering behavior covered the uncertainty of a lost soul. She would never fear him again.

The day hovered at the edge of darkness, a time that favored surprise attacks. Con nodded to Nick, who waited beside him in the shadow of an aspen grove. The rushing leaves covered Con's quiet footsteps as he circled Miles's camp. He hid in a spot where thick underbrush would not keep him from springing out quickly.

Con waited for Nick's bird call, the agreed-upon signal to coordinate tonight's rescue. Con didn't want to take the chance of Elsa being caught in crossfire.

After his episode with the claim jumper, he wanted nothing more to do with killing. He preferred not to shoot Miles, although the man richly deserved justice for his misdeeds.

Con peered through the bushes and clenched his jaw to hold his temper. Miles lounged by the fire, watching Elsa clean dishes with her hands strung together by a rope. Her shoulders were slumped in hopelessness. The sight brought a lump to Con's throat.

"That's enough," Miles growled. After flinging coffee grounds from his tin cup, he stretched in the firelight. The man was obviously at ease, expecting no interference.

The hooting trill of a screech owl reverberated through the trees.

Con gripped his gun and stepped into the camp. "Put your hands up, Miles."

Miles stiffened and raised his hands. "Hello, Con. I've been expecting you."

"Have you indeed?" Con asked to distract him.

Nick crept up behind Miles and relieved him of his gun. "But maybe not me."

Miles twisted toward Nick.

"Face forward." Con snapped.

Miles obeyed with a shrug. "I've given thought to your offer to pay for your brother's release."

Con's mouth quirked into a wry smile. Miles could be counted on to take money-making endeavors to heart. "And?"

"I've decided to accept."

"Don't pay him anything." Elsa, who had watched in silence, advanced toward Miles.

Con might have restrained her, but she stopped just out of the man's reach.

Elsa lifted her head in a magnificent gesture. "I didn't press charges before because I couldn't prove you'd done anything wrong. You and I know the truth, though, don't we? Well that's changed, now that Nick and Con can also testify against you."

Con could have kissed her for finding the courage to stand up to Miles. "Believe me"—he dragged out every word--"I welcome the chance to testify. Folks around here don't take kindly to a woman being kidnapped. They'll put you behind bars for quite a while."

"I'm willing to tell the sheriff what you did," Nick added. "But show mercy, and I might also." He raised his pistol. "Lead Con to his brother."

Shane helped Bry down from his wagon. He'd picked her up from the neighbors' house after Lorne sent word of the situation. She'd wanted to come home so she'd know the instant Nick and Con returned. He didn't blame her, although it meant he'd have to stay longer to look out for her. He opened the ranch house door and stepped onto the porch with Bry following close behind. She touched the corners of her eyes. "Thank God you're back safely."

A dirt-smeared Elsa climbed the porch with the slow steps of exhaustion. She smiled weakly.

Nick stood holding their horses' reins.

"I'm glad to see you've brought Elsa back." Shane glanced down the drive. "Where's Con?"

"He and Miles went to Virginia City." Nick embraced Bry, who had gone down the steps to greet him.

"Miles?" Shane's tone gave his opinion of that idea. "He seems a strange traveling companion for Con."

Nick glanced at Bry. "I'll explain when I come in. Thanks for coming, by the way."

"I felt compelled, after such an intriguing summons. I need

to keep track of what my cousins are up to, now don't I?"

"You might say we went snake hunting."

"Oh, did you?" The lift of Shane's head revealed his quick understanding. "I hope you had happy results."

"Yes, but there's more to come." Nick lifted the reins. "You should help me with the horses."

Shane smiled. "The thought occurred to me." He fell into step beside Nick.

"Poor Elsa, you look exhausted." Bry's voice drifted to him from the porch. "Come inside and sit down. Would you like me to heat water for a bath?"

Shane waited until the horses were lipping water at the trough before he spoke. "Tell me about this hunting expedition."

Nick's face shadowed. "We caught Miles making off with Elsa."

"Did he harm her?"

"She says he slapped her but didn't touch her otherwise."

"Thank the Lord for that." Shane pushed his hat back on his head. "I'm missing something, though. Why is Con on his way to Virginia City?"

"Rob's being held in a shack on the outskirts of town."

"Why?"

"From what Con told me, Miles hoped to exchange Rob for Elsa. When Con refused, Miles changed tactics." Nick clucked to the horses. "He led us on a merry chase to get us out of the house so he could break in and take Elsa."

Shane shook his head. "I'm sorry he did that."

"I think he may be too now. His actions gave Elsa the proof to press charges against him. Hoping to avoid the law, Miles has given us directions to Rob's location."

"Everything makes sense now." Shane's eyes glinted. "When do we leave?"

Nick smiled. "I'm glad you want to go, but I'd feel better if you stayed here. With our manager on the range, I don't like leaving the women alone. Bry can handle a gun, although I'd prefer she had no reason to fire one."

"Don't worry about Bry and Elsa. They won't be on their own." Shane squinted against the sunlight. "Turner came and got me after Lorne found him. He's back in his cabin."

"That takes a load off my mind." Nick picked up a curry comb and flicked a glance at Shane. "We should leave at first light."

The ticking clock punctuated the scritch of Phoebe's pencil on the slate board. Maisey watched her daughter with soft joy in her heart but also a touch of fear. She hadn't wanted to risk bringing her to the schoolhouse after what had happened, but it was important to remain open, if possible.

Spukani was grieving, or she doubted he'd have attempted to take Phoebe. She had known both Spukani and Saka'am since the Indian school began. They had always seemed to appreciate her efforts to teach their daughter. She hoped Spukani would not return to cause more trouble. If he did, she would call upon the gun hidden in the teacher's desk.

The day ticked on. Whining that she was bored, Phoebe came to sit with her, something she'd done more frequently since the attack.

Maisey took her daughter's sweet weight into her arms and held her closely. She smoothed the golden curls from Phoebe's brow and kissed her forehead. God had been merciful. Maisey had lost Avery, but in his child she would always have a part of her husband.

America looked in at the door. "Has no one come today?"

"No." Maisey put Phoebe down and stood, but her daughter clung to her skirt. "I should close now."

America walked down the aisle between the rows of desks. "It's not your fault, Maisey. It's the way things are right now. I wish it wasn't so, but we live in a chaotic time."

"I know, but I can't help but wonder if the entire tribe blames me for Rain's death. Maybe they would come back if I wasn't here."

America took Maisey's hands. "You mustn't think like that."

"It's hard not to." Maisey brushed away a tear. "Maybe I should leave."

America gazed at her. "Is that what you want to do?"

"I don't know anymore." Maisey picked up Phoebe. "I can't keep taking your charity when I'm not earning my way."

America cupped Maisey's face in her hands. "Don't worry about that. You and Phoebe have come to mean a great deal to Shane and me, and our children love you both."

Maisey's tears fell in earnest. "It was important to open the school today, whether anyone came or not. If only God had not laid a burden on my heart to help the local tribes, I wouldn't have to face this rejection."

America put an arm around her. "I'm glad He did. Whatever happens with the Indian school, you'll know you tried."

Maisey sniffed. "Thank you for saying that."

Phoebe put out a hand and caught one of her mother's tears. Maisey hiccupped on a laugh.

America gave her a quick squeeze. "Count your blessings, and you'll pull through."

Maisey nodded but made no reply. Whether anyone came

to the school or not, God had not released her from the call to reach the local tribes. She didn't know what that would look like in the future, only that it would not be easy. She put Phoebe down and guided her toward the door. America followed.

Maisey closed and locked the schoolhouse and went home to the cabin Rob had helped build. She sighed. Whatever Rob was doing right now, she hoped he was well and happy.

Rob's female captor had not returned in four long days, apparently intent on fulfilling her promise to let him starve. Lack of water would kill him before that event, so he rationed the supply in the jug she had abandoned.

Rationing became exceedingly difficult as the temperature climbed. The exposed gaps in the tar-paper shack cooled him with breezes at night but let in heat during the day. He counted the cracks again, although their number was forever imprinted on his mind.

Night crept in, bringing a blustery wind. Rob leaned his head against the wall and breathed in its vigor. The gusts seemed the very breath of God, sent to restore him. His mind eased, along with his body.

Maisey crept into his thoughts like a gentle rain moistening a barren landscape. He escaped into his imagination, where he could hold her hand and stroll with her on the road to Liberty. A scene from the past seemed very real.

He watched as a stag burst from the brush near them. Maisey fell against him with a startled cry. He caught her, preventing a nasty fall. The deer leaped across the road and vanished into the undergrowth. Maisey turned in his arms and gazed up at him with her lips parted. She needed kissing, and he was the one for the job.

The memory faded, and Rob shook his head. He'd let the moment pass.

Maybe one day he could be worthy of someone like Maisey. She didn't need a man who had escaped the slum on the back of another. All the more reason to prove he had the same gumption that had lifted his brother out of poverty.

First, he had to survive his present circumstances.

Rob strained to pull the block from the ground and felt it yield. He collapsed and lay panting. Regret assailed him. He shouldn't have wasted his strength on a pointless task. Shouting endlessly had not brought him rescue. He could only conclude that no one dwelt nearby.

What good would it do to leave the shack, which provided, however scantily, protection from the elements? Even if he figured out which way to go, dragging a heavy weight meant he would probably perish before he reached help.

Only God could save him now.

CHAPTER THIRTY-ONE

C ON REINED HIS HORSE AND GAZED at the tall building hung with a balcony. It stood in relief against the blue sky. He glanced at Miles, sitting on his horse beside him. "You'd better be telling the truth."

"That's just it, isn't it?" A slow smile spread over Miles's face. "You don't know."

During the past couple of days, Con had been tempted on more than one occasion to strike his companion. This was one of them. "I thought you said Rob was being held in Virginia City, not Robbers Roost."

"We moved him closer to swap him for Elsa."

"*We*?" Con fixed a piercing gaze on him. "Who else is in this with you?"

"No one important," Miles answered with another maddening smile.

Strolling into a notorious roadhouse like Robbers Roost would be foolhardy. Con considered his options. He could trust Miles and be right, in which case his brother would be restored to him. He could trust Miles and be wrong, reaping the rewards of stupidity.

Or he could refuse to believe Miles and save his own hide, based on his growing suspicion that this was a trap. But if he did that—and later discovered Rob had been here—he'd never be able to live with himself.

He turned his head and caught Miles watching him, like a cat stalking a mouse. The irritating man knew he had won. Con sighed. "Lead on."

They dismounted and tied their horses to hitching posts in front of the building. Con kept a lookout for shady characters who might emerge onto the balcony or travel down the path and through the wooden turnstile. Bypassing the main entrance, Miles led Con along the side of the building and past a wooden well. They crossed the grass to a footbridge that leaped a narrow waterway.

A low-slung cabin stood just beyond the water. Miles knocked on the door.

Con strained his ears. Did he hear voices whispering inside or was that the wind swishing?

The door creaked open. An arm reached out. Miles yelped as he was dragged inside.

Atticus Merrick appeared in the doorway. A black mask hung around his neck, and he wore the same clothes as Gentleman during the stagecoach robbery. He pointed a pistol at Con's chest. "Nice to see you again, Walsh. Maybe now we can finish that game of cards."

"I'd rather not, if it's all the same to you."

"Inside." Atticus gestured with his head. His gun hand remained steady.

Con walked past him and into the cabin. Cards and glasses of spirits scattered the battered table in one corner. A door opened into a second room. A brown-haired man in rough clothes was pressing Miles against the wall. He turned his head when Atticus entered. "Shall I beat him up?"

"I'm tempted to let you, but that would make a mess." Atticus pushed Con's face against the wall and removed his gun from its holster. "He hasn't done anything wrong except fail to bring my woman back."

"Con wouldn't give her up, so I brought *him* instead," Miles spoke in a rush.

Atticus searched Con, then stepped back. "You can turn around now."

Con faced him. "Elsa has never been *your woman.*"

Atticus backhanded him, snapping Con's head sideways. "Elsa is mine, and you'd do well to remember it. You were a fool to refuse my offer. Your brother will suffer the consequences."

"What have you done with him?" Con touched his mouth and winced. Blood trickled from his split lip.

"Your devotion to family is admirable. Rob is tucked away in a grand hotel, soon to enjoy supper."

The gleam in Atticus's eyes told Con the opposite. He drew in a painful breath. "I'll give you money, if that's what you want."

"You know what I want, and it's not money."

Con leaned his head against the wall. "Do you honestly believe I would turn over an innocent woman to you for any price?"

Atticus's eyes darkened. "You wound me. Elsa will be well cared for and cherished. She'll have everything money can give her."

"Except her freedom."

"That's a small price to pay for a life of luxury."

"She doesn't want you."

"She will in time." Atticus straddled a chair but kept his gun trained on Con. "You are more like Shane than I knew."

"Thank you. I consider that a compliment."

"Lonesome." Atticus kept his gaze on Con.

"Yes?"

"Tie them both up and be sure to use gags."

"What are you going to do?" Miles's voice rose in pitch.

"I haven't made up my mind yet." Atticus narrowed his

eyes "But the possibilities intrigue me."

Maisey woke in a fresh state of mind. Her exhaustion yesterday had added to her discouragement. God would make things better. She needed to believe that He would put her life right in time.

Meanwhile, she should take America's suggestion and count her blessings. Phoebe never failed to make her smile. She had friends nearby. Even sharing breakfast with someone was a delight.

Phoebe had not yet wakened. This gave Maisey undisturbed time to relish her morning coffee. Being without a husband made for a busy life, and it was nice to have moments to herself. She spent extra time reading the Good Book this fine Sunday morning. When Phoebe woke, she would read to her from one of the parables.

Coffee in hand, Maisey stepped outside and onto the porch to greet a perfect morning. Light danced in the trees. The grass looked soft and new. It shone vibrant green in these fleeting days before summer dried it golden. The grass was dotted by delicate bitterroot blossoms in shades of pink and white. She would bring Phoebe out later this morning to play in the grass.

Not far away, Emma hailed her from the porch of the schoolteacher's cabin. She pointed to a tin measuring cup in her hand. "Have you any sugar?"

"Yes, and you're welcome to some."

Slender and fair-haired, Emma reminded Maisey of a flower. She climbed the steps, and Maisey held the door open. "Come inside. Would you like coffee?"

"Thank you, but I've had mine." Emma's smile softened her refusal. "I made apple cake yesterday. Would you like a couple of slices?"

"Phoebe would love that, and so would I."

Emma glanced around. "Where is she?"

"Still sleeping." Maisey pulled out a sack of sugar. "Help yourself."

"Thank you." Emma dipped her measuring cup into the sugar. "I've been putting off going into town to buy more."

"I'll shop with you tomorrow, if you'd like company."

"That would be nice." Emma gave Maisey an apologetic look. "I'm sorry to have kept to myself so much. I've been grieving my father. He died right before I accepted my teaching position."

"I'm sorry."

Emma's eyes clouded. "I miss him terribly." She dashed moisture from her cheeks. "I'd better get back. Thanks for the sugar."

Maisey walked her out to the porch. "Stop by when you have more time to visit."

"I will." Emma turned at the top of the steps. "How is Phoebe coping after her scare the other day?"

"She's clinging quite a bit."

"That's normal after a trauma. There's nothing harder for little children than being separated from their mothers. Keep giving her extra attention right now. That will help a lot."

"Thanks for the advice. I can tell you have a fondness for children."

Emma smiled. "That's why I'm a schoolteacher. Say hello to your darling girl for me."

Maisey bid Emma goodbye and went inside. *Phoebe should be up by now.* She opened the door to her daughter's room but stopped short of the bed, gripped by an uneasy feeling.

Phoebe lay sprawled across the feather tick in a posture of utter exhaustion. Her red-stained cheeks glistened with moisture. Maisey felt her daughter's forehead. Phoebe was burning with fever.

Her daughter moaned but didn't wake.

Maisey's heart pounded. *What's wrong with —*

She caught her breath at the memory of Phoebe in the schoolroom when Saka'am and Se'ułku brought their measles-ridden daughters. That had been three weeks ago. Maisey had heard of measles showing up that long after exposure, but Phoebe had only been in the schoolroom a short time. Could she have caught the disease so quickly?

Maisey turned and rushed outside. Thankfully, Emma was still on the path. "Wait!"

Emma turned around.

"Phoebe has a fever, and it may be measles. Would you please ask America to fetch the doctor?"

"Goodness, yes! Let me put the sugar down, and I'll run right over."

Maisey hurried back to rouse her daughter. She held a glass of water to Phoebe's lips. After only a few sips, Phoebe whimpered and pushed it away.

"I'll be right back, sweetie." Maisey filled a wash basin with cool water and hurried back to bathe her daughter's forehead.

Phoebe was wandering about, speaking nonsense and crying. Maisey put her back to bed. After Phoebe calmed and fell into sleep once more, Maisey sank to her knees beside the bed.

Please God, don't let my daughter die.

"Are you sure about this?" Shane asked as Nick turned toward Robbers Roost.

Nick looked over his shoulder. "It's where the tracks lead."

Shane tamped down his nervousness and followed his brother-in-law. "Be careful."

"I'll do my best."

Shane thought of America and his children. What would become of them if this situation turned out badly? He sent up a prayer to improve their chances. He also prayed for Miles, in the hope that he would change his ways. God had love to spare, even for such a wayward soul.

They reined in and tied their horses to hitching posts. Several men sat smoking on the balcony, but no one challenged them. Shane started through the wooden turnstile, but Nick pulled him back. "We should listen around the buildings before we go inside."

"I suppose that's a better plan than busting in and demanding my cousin's return," Shane reluctantly agreed.

"It might come to that, but we first need an idea of what we're getting ourselves into. Let's water the horses. We won't want them flagging if we need a quick getaway."

Nick nodded toward a different hitching post. "That's Con's horse, and I'm sure the one beside it belongs to Miles. They look bad-off, as if they've been tied up a while. I'll take them with our own horses to the creek. Hopefully, the management won't mind. We should probably stay away from the livery."

At Shane's nod, Nick untied the two horses and led them with their own to the creek. Shane brought the horses they'd rented from the livery in Bannack. He had left Archibald behind to rest. His horse had carried him a long way in a short time. Come to think of it, he'd taken advantage of Archibald's goodwill far too often of late. He sighed. His life wouldn't settle down until his cousins did.

He snapped his head toward a familiar voice from the cabin across the creek.

Atticus showed his presence in many locations, but Robbers Roost seemed a strange place to find him. Shane held a finger to his lips to warn Nick. Leaving the horses chomping the lush grass, he jumped the narrow creek and stole toward the sound.

Shane, with Nick following behind him like a shadow, headed behind the building. No one from the roadhouse or livery would see them there. Shane crept to a window on the rear wall.

A man's voice drifted through the open window, and Shane easily made out his words. "What are you planning?"

"I have the advantage." Excitement sharpened Atticus's voice. "With both Con and Rob in my possession, there's nothing to stop me from holding them both hostage. Con refused to cooperate, but Elsa might agree to save them."

He might have known Atticus was up to no good. The man excelled at playing people, one against the other." Shane clenched his jaw. This time he wouldn't get the chance.

Risking a glance through the window revealed Con and Miles bound, gagged, and propped against the wall. The open doorway beyond them gave glimpses of Atticus seated at a table with another man.

Any fear Shane might have felt fled before his wrath. He drew his gun and motioned to Nick, who did the same. Together they charged around the cabin. Shane slowed before reaching the front, and Nick came up behind him. Together, they kicked open the door.

Surprised faces turned toward them.

"Hands in the air!" Shane barked before anyone could

move.

Atticus and the other man leaped to their feet. When Atticus saw Shane, a smile spread across his face. "You're not going to shoot anyone, *Saint Preacher*. You were always too soft."

Shane met his stare without flinching. "You don't want to try me."

Atticus raised his hands.

"I'll take their weapons." Nick handed his gun to Shane.

Shane leveled Nick's pistol along with his own and kept careful watch.

Nick removed five guns and several knives from the men. He went to work securing them to their chairs with rope he found in a corner. After gagging them, he disappeared into the other room.

Nick returned a short while later with Con beside him.

Shane hurried to his cousin. "Are you all right?"

Con touched his swollen lip. "I'll recover." He glared at Atticus. "He deserves to spend time behind bars."

"My thoughts exactly." Shane glanced at Nick. "Looks like we're taking them in."

Nick started for the door. "I'd better gather the horses plus rent two more."

"We should wait until after dark to leave." Con found his gun and slipped it into his holster. "Handing this bunch over to the sheriff in Virginia City will be a delight. I'd like to personally escort Miles into his jail cell."

Shane nodded his approval. "Sheriff Gerhart will likely extract Rob's location from them."

"If not, there's another member of this ring to ask." Con's gaze shifted to Atticus. "Given the right motivation, I suspect Alicia will let on. Maybe you'd better think about coming clean. Tell us where you're holding Rob, and we'll put in a good word with the sheriff for you."

Maisey pulled Phoebe's door partway closed and followed Doc Bailey into the front room. Doc Bailey had stopped by to check on Phoebe each day of her illness. "She's getting better, isn't she?" Maisey asked.

The seams in Doc Bailey's face deepened. "I wish I could tell you that."

Her throat went dry. "What *can* you tell me?"

He sighed. "Your daughter is gravely ill. I'm not certain it's measles, but that is possible. Keep her fever down, give her plenty of water, and pray. If she makes it through the night, I believe she'll begin to recover. That's not a promise, mind you."

Maisey closed her eyes and released her breath on a sigh. "May God help us."

"I hope He will, Mrs. Wilcox." He put on his bowler hat and tucked his medical bag under his arm. "At this juncture, He's the only One who can."

"If it's measles, when will the rash appear?"

He squinted. "She's been sick four days. It should have shown up by now. That doesn't mean it won't, but if you don't see it tonight or tomorrow, I suspect it's influenza and not measles." He started for the door. "If Phoebe takes a turn for the worse, call me. Otherwise, it's a matter of letting nature take its course."

She followed the doctor onto the porch. "Thank you for coming by."

He touched the brim of his hat. "Good day, Mrs. Wilcox."

Maisey watched the doctor climb into his buggy and trot

away. She hurried through the doorway, anxious to watch over Phoebe.

"Wait!" Emma's voice followed her inside.

"What is it?" Maisey poked her head around the door frame.

Emma hurried down the path between the cabins, carrying a covered dish. She climbed the porch. "My chicken soup might help Phoebe."

Tears blurred Maisey's vision. "Thank you. But I'm afraid Phoebe won't eat. She needs far more than chicken soup to heal her."

"Oh, I'm sorry to hear that. Is there anything I can do?"

"Pray."

"I will, and I'm sure America is already. She can't come by because of the risk of bringing back measles to her children, but I've had them already." Emma gave her an encouraging smile. "I hope you'll take some nourishment."

"Thank you." Maisey wasn't sure she could swallow anything, but she accepted Emma's gift. She placed the covered dish in her stove's warmer oven before pushing open Phoebe's door. Her daughter muttered in her sleep and flung out her arm. Maisey touched her forehead. Phoebe frowned and turned away.

Maisey rinsed the washcloth in a basin of cool water and laid the cloth on her daughter's forehead. Phoebe thrashed, but then went so still that Maisey's heart pounded. She laid a shaking hand on her child's chest, which faintly rose and fell. Her daughter still breathed! Relief shuddered through Maisey. She sank on shaky legs into the chair at Phoebe's bedside, determined not to budge until the crisis passed.

Phoebe woke several hours later with a coughing fit. Maisey bent over her. "I'm right here, sweetheart."

"My throat hurts." Her little girl burst into tears.

Maisey kissed her, thankful she was lucid, a sign her fever had gone down. "Drink some water."

Phoebe turned her head away, but Maisey insisted. Phoebe protested but finally swallowed a few sips. Maisey filled a spoon with honey-onion syrup. "Here, take this for your throat."

The syrup seemed to ease Phoebe. She lay quietly for a while, only to wake again. Each time, Maisey gave Phoebe water and syrup, then bathed her brow. In the middle of the night, the coughing fits left Phoebe strangling. Maisey rubbed her chest with menthol salve and covered it with warm cloths.

Tears rolled down Maisey's cheeks. *I have failed Phoebe.* She'd been so involved in helping the Indian children that she neglected her own daughter's safety. *I should have looked after her better.* "God, please give me another chance. I promise to do better."

Maisey woke with her head on the table and a soft light pouring through the window. She jerked her head up. *Phoebe!*

Her daughter lay with her face turned away. Was her chest moving? Maisey put a finger under Phoebe's nose and sagged in relief.

Tears flooded Maisey's eyes, and she whispered a prayer of thanksgiving. Her hands gentle, she pushed her daughter's night clothes aside and checked her upper back. The pale skin gleamed but showed no mottling. A check of Phoebe's legs and stomach revealed no sign of the measles rash. Through the day it failed to appear, and Phoebe's fever gradually reduced. Her heart full, Maisey tiptoed out of the room, leaving her daughter peacefully sleeping.

Maisey sank into a chair at the table and propped her head in her hands. *Thank you, God, for giving me a second chance.*

"Hello, Miss Peabody." Con greeted Alicia in the doorway. They'd ridden away from Robbers Roost at first light. Sparing themselves little had brought them to Virginia City by noon. Con had left Shane and Nick handing over the prisoners to the sheriff and ridden straight to Atticus's home.

Dressed in an elegant gown of watered silk, with pearls at her throat, Alicia ran an assessing gaze over him "What are you doing here?"

"We need to talk."

"I'm otherwise occupied." She swung the door closed, but it didn't shut. She glanced down. "Remove your foot."

Con ignored her command. "I thought you should know that Miles and Atticus are in custody."

A shocked expression covered Alicia's face, but it smoothed over quickly. She was harder to fluster than Miles, he'd give her that. "Are you going to invite me in?"

She opened the door, scowling. Con strode past her into the parlor and helped himself to an overstuffed chair. She followed, her stiff posture betraying her discomfort.

"Have a seat." Con gestured toward the settee.

She remained standing. "Let's get this over with."

"Careful, or you'll wound my masculine pride." Con put a hand over his heart in mock despair. "I can recall a time when you showed interest in me."

A faint smile curved Alicia's lips. "I was merely amusing myself at your expense. I admit you're easy on the eyes, but my affections belong elsewhere."

"It's obvious you're Miles's mistress, if that's what you're hinting at."

"I find this conversation extremely boring." She adopted a languid air but her quickened breathing betrayed her.

"Then let's talk about a topic nearer to your heart. Can I interest you in your personal liberty?"

She looked away. "Say what you mean."

"From what I know of Miles, he'd betray you for a pardon. I wouldn't put it past Atticus to do the same."

Alicia swallowed and glanced at Con from the corner of her eyes. "For that to happen, there would need to be a crime."

"They aren't in jail for no reason. Let's talk about my brother Rob."

She blinked. "I don't know anything about him."

"That's too bad." Con shrugged. "Because if you knew where they hid my brother, I'd speak to the sheriff on your behalf."

She gave a quick shake of her head without looking at him. "I told you . . . *I don't know.*"

"I doubt that." Con stood to leave. "Be aware of one thing, Miss Peabody. If my brother dies, I won't rest until justice is served."

CHAPTER THIRTY-TWO

ROB TIPPED THE JUG TO HIS lips and tried to coax a few drops out. No use. He threw the jug across the room, refusing to let despair fill his mind. He'd held a faint hope that his female captor, struck by some glimmer of humanity, would return. Or maybe Miles hadn't completely abandoned him.

Neither appeared. Perhaps they'd both skipped town. Why should they free someone who could testify against them anyway?

Rob leaned his head against the wall. He should not spend his final hours, if that's what they became, pondering such intricacies. His mind reached for Maisey, as it always did when he was in need of rest. She'd suffered greatly since Avery's death. It was nice to see her settled among friends and happy in her work.

Thoughts of Maisey gave him the restless urge to escape. Waiting around for death to claim him didn't come naturally. Rob decided to try once more, come what may. He grasped the chain binding him to the eye bolt and heaved with all his might. All at once, the concrete block gave way and rolled out of the hole.

Rob fell back, panting and more than a little surprised at his success. His earlier tries must have loosened it.

Hooves beat outside the shack. Rob had listened for that sound but now wished it gone. A visit from his captors was the last thing he needed while trying to escape. He blew out his breath and pushed to his feet. Harnessing the strength of desperation, he dragged the block behind him and moved into position. Whoever it was wouldn't expect to find him lurking beside the doorway.

He tightened the chain binding his hands together.

Footsteps neared. A key rattled the lock, and the door creaked open. A figure entered.

Rob sprang. The chain caught around the intruder's neck. Two others crouched beyond the opening, their guns drawn.

Light from the doorway fell across the person Rob had captured. "Sheriff Gerhart!" Rob released him. "Sorry about that."

The sheriff rubbed his neck. "No harm done."

The other men straightened as sunlight flashed from their deputy badges. One gave a low whistle. "They trussed you like a calf ready for branding."

"Don't worry, Rob. We'll bust you lose." Sheriff Gerhart turned to his deputy. "Davis, hunt down a sledgehammer and come right back. Corey and I will wait here."

"I don't like leaving you."

"Atticus and Miles are in jail right now, so it should be all right."

"I believe there's a woman involved," Rob felt compelled to point out. "I doubt she'll show up, though."

"Go on, Davis." The sheriff jerked his head. "Corey and I can handle whoever comes along."

Davis vanished through the doorway.

Sheriff Gerhart eyed Rob. "How are you?"

"Hungry enough to eat a bear, and thirsty too." He grinned. "I sure am glad to see you."

"I bet you are. Let me get you something." He disappeared through the door but returned a few minutes later with a canteen and a box of soda crackers.

Rob wetted his chapped lips and drank deeply.

The sheriff tapped his arm. "Slow down, or you'll make yourself sick."

Rob inserted the plug and wiped his mouth, then tore into the box of crackers. "How did you find me?"

"Miles told me where he'd hidden you."

"Why would he do such a thing?" Rob spoke around a full mouth.

The sheriff's lips quirked. "He wanted to betray Atticus, before Atticus could betray him."

Rob snorted his amusement. "I'm glad to keep him on the right side of the law."

"So, who's the woman you mentioned?"

"I don't know for certain, but I can guess."

Sheriff Gerhart nodded. "We'd better bring Alicia Peabody in for questioning."

Rob should have been glad to hear that after she'd left him for dead. But somehow, all he felt was sadness at the waste of a life.

The crunch of footsteps on the path outside his cabin sent Con to the window. Out of the shade beneath the large cottonwood strode a familiar figure. Rob's here!" He shouted to Nick and Shane, just rising from the table. Con threw open the door and ran to meet his brother on the path along Alder Creek. Rob had grown leaner, for certain. Hs clothes were filthy, and strain marked his face.

Con held onto his brother for a long time. "I was worried about you."

"Yes, well. That's how I felt too."

He kept an arm around Rob's shoulders as they walked to the cabin. "Where did they keep you?"

Rob shook his head. "In a place I'd rather forget."

Nick and Shane were crowding the doorway. Shane grinned. "It's good to see you, Cousin."

"I'm thankful to say the same." Rob embraced him.

Nick clapped him on the shoulder. "We'll give you a hearty serving of Shane's stew and an early bed tonight."

Rob smiled. "Sounds good."

They went inside. Shane held up the coffee pot with a questioning glance.

Rob sank down at the table. "Thanks, but Sheriff Gerhart gave me plenty of the stuff when he took my testimony."

Con pulled out a chair across from Rob. "How did you escape?"

"That was the sheriff's doing. Miles struck a deal with him to betray Atticus. He confessed to kidnapping me and told them where I was in exchange for getting out of jail. He's supposed to stay in Virginia City to testify against Atticus, but I doubt he will." Rob shook his head. "I'm glad to have my freedom back, but I hate what it cost."

Shane moved to stand behind Con. "Maybe Miles will learn from his mistakes and become a better man."

"One of my captors was a woman. The sheriff went after Alicia Peabody."

That struck Con as no surprise. "Did he arrest her?"

"She's vanished, along with Atticus's carriage." Rob clasped his hands and rested them on the table. His sleeves fell back, exposing the bruises on his wrists.

Con's jaw tightened. "This is my fault. I must have warned Alicia when I questioned her about your location."

"Alicia knew it, all right." Rob spoke bitterly. "She left me to rot in that miserable shack."

"Never mind." Shane sat down between them. "Miles and Alicia Peabody won't avoid the higher judgment to come."

Con eased his grip on the table edge. "I can always trust you to think in lofty terms, Cousin. I have a more practical bent." He leaned back in his chair. "A little satisfaction in the here and now wouldn't go amiss."

"I won't ask you in." Maisey called down to America from her front porch. "The doctor isn't sure what Phoebe has, but we're not past the contagious period if it's measles. I don't want to risk infecting your household."

America stopped at the bottom of the steps. A basket dangled from her arm. "I won't come any closer, but I couldn't stay away. We're all wondering how Phoebe is doing."

Maisey gripped the railing. "She's a sick little girl, but I think she's out of the woods."

"I'm so glad." America set the basket down on the bottom step. "I brought a jar of elderberry syrup and some of Phoebe's favorite foods."

"Thank you for your kindness." Tears sprang to Maisey's eyes.

America smiled. "It's no bother. Let me know if you need anything else. Anything at all."

"I will."

America turned away.

"Wait." Maisey stepped off the porch. "After Phoebe is better, I'll find work in a larger town."

America faced her. "What about the Indian school?"

Yes, what about it? Maisey had struggled with this question ever since making her decision to move. It wasn't fair to abandon her students, not if she thought the school could continue. She picked up the basket from the step and hooked it over her arm. "I think we need to admit that the school has closed for good. It doesn't exist anymore."

America shook her head. "I'm not sure that's true. The school might yet recover."

"I wish I had your faith."

"I'm not surprised you're discouraged, what with everything you've had to deal with lately. I don't know if the school will go on or not. Either way, you're welcome to stay on with us."

"That wouldn't work." Maisey climbed the steps.

"Tell me why."

She leaned on the railing. "Sitting up with Phoebe the other night, I figured out how foolish I've been. While caring for the Indians, I forgot to protect my daughter. I aim to be a better mother."

"I don't see why you can't do that and live here."

"I won't impose on you any longer. It's high time I earned my own way in the world."

America frowned. "You remind me of Rob. He was quick to leave friends and family, not realizing he already had all he needed. Con would have given him a chance at independence. Sometimes, you need to let others help you."

"Yes, but there's also a point when it's best to help yourself."

"What will you do?"

"I sew pretty well. Maybe a tailor or seamstress would hire me."

America gave her a steady appraisal. "You've thought this out. Well, I won't hold you back, but please think this over a little longer. Decisions made during a crisis are usually guided by emotion more than logic. If you find that you truly want to go, I'm sure Shane would be willing to help you get situated."

"What can I do for you, Con?" Sheriff Gerhart looked up from his desk. With his handlebar moustache neatly trimmed and an immaculate white shirt under his leather vest, he appeared to never stray outside his office.

Con knew better. He took one of the chairs across from the sheriff and frowned. "I understand Miles went free."

Sheriff Gerhart sighed. "I don't like it either, Con, but I had to do it. Striking a deal with Miles probably saved your brother's life. He wouldn't have lasted much longer in the heat without water."

"Thank you for rescuing Rob." Con sighed. "At least Atticus is still on the hook."

An uneasy expression crossed the sheriff's face.

Con stiffened. "What's wrong?"

"Atticus escaped last night."

"What? How?"

"When one of my deputies brought supper, Atticus tricked him into coming into his cell. Atticus left him out cold and escaped on his horse."

"That's horrible." Con's thoughts turned to Bry and Elsa at the ranch. He jumped up. "I need to start for home right away."

The sheriff rose. "We'll find him in time."

"I hope so." A wealthy man like Atticus would have money

for bribery and lots of places to hide. Con drew a deep breath. "I actually stopped by about another matter."

"Oh?" Gerhart sat back. "Go on."

Con lowered himself into his chair. "Elsa Meier stands ready to press charges against Miles for kidnapping her."

"When did this happen?"

"Last week. Nick and I would also be willing to testify. Elsa went missing from my ranch, and we found her tied up in Miles's camp."

"That puts a new face on things. Where is Miss Meier now?"

"She's staying at my ranch."

"Is that so?" The sheriff gave him an inquisitive glance.

"My sister enjoys her company."

Sheriff Gerhart smiled. "Seems to me you do too."

Con grinned. "I won't deny that."

"You haven't asked my advice, but if I were you, I'd stake my claim. A woman like that doesn't come along often."

"I'll bear that in mind."

The sheriff cleared his throat. "Now, down to business. Where can I find you and Nick?"

"At my place. Nick and I will leave at first light."

"I'll be in touch." Sheriff Gerhart stood and offered a handshake "Have a safe journey home."

Con walked through his Bannack cabin, wondering who had put the place to rights. It had been a shambles after his beating.

Nick scraped back a chair at the scarred oak table. "Rob must have stopped here on his way to Virginia City."

"That must be it." Con dropped his saddlebags on the

kitchen board. "I'll have to thank him when he and Shane join us at the ranch."

"I hope he recovers enough to make the journey soon."

Con clenched his fists. "When I think of how they treated him—"

"Let's hope justice will be served."

After a quick supper of corn cakes and beans, Con climbed into his bed. An owl hooted outside his window, and grasshoppers sent up a nighttime chorus.

Con's thoughts turned to Elsa, as they always did in idle moments. Sheriff Gerhart had a point. If he planned to claim her, he should do so soon. A woman as desirable as Elsa would not stay single long. In the West, too many lonely men were starved for female companionship.

He wished he knew what Elsa wanted.

He woke before Nick and wandered outside. He had seen Bannack's moods in other seasons, but the town showed its best face on a clear morning in early summer. The grass that clothed the hills was turning gold in the sun. Grasshopper Creek glinted in shades of blue and brown, and the wide sky covered it all.

Con's steps carried him to Chrisman's store. This early, only a few men speaking in quiet tones gathered beside the fireplace. Chrisman glanced at him over his spectacles. "How are you Con?"

"Pleased to be traveling home."

"I suppose you've heard about the murder."

"Murder?"

Chrisman stepped out from behind the counter. "Miles and Alicia Peabody were found dead in the Merrick Hotel yesterday. They were shot at close range."

Con sucked in a breath. "That's terrible. Do they know who did it?"

"No one ventures an opinion, but I think we can all take a guess."

"Thank you for the information." Con didn't linger. Shaken beyond measure, he left the store without purchasing anything. In the guise of a road agent, Atticus refused to kill. And yet, he seemed to have committed murder.

Anyone could figure out that Atticus Merrick had gone after the man who had betrayed him. Alicia must have simply been in the way. What a sad ending, to be a side note in someone else's murder.

He walked to the cabin with quickened steps. If Nick wasn't up by now, he'd wake him. They needed to leave right away. Reaching Bannack from Virginia City took two days and traveling to the ranch needed another two. Con chafed at the thought of what might happen before he reached Elsa. *God, I'm relying on you to keep the women safe.*

CHAPTER THIRTY-THREE

ELSA BENT IN THE GARDEN AND pulled up an onion for the *Brotsuppe* she planned to make for the noon meal. She would cook the bread soup with the rest of the day's food this morning to avoid working in the kitchen during the day's heat.

She had willingly taken over the garden Rob had started. As she worked, she remembered the one she'd tended in Germany. She dug out a garlic head and cut spinach leaves to use for tonight's supper. A butterfly with gold and black wings darted past, and Elsa lost herself in watching its flight. At a moment like this, with birds warbling and the sun waking the land, she could almost believe she'd found a home.

A shadow rippled over her, cast by an eagle on its way to fish the river. She stood with a hand shielding her eyes. How much better it would be to fly than to walk, as humans must. She smiled at her thoughts and picked up her basket.

A hand covered her mouth and nose, cutting off her air. A body pressed against hers. "I have you at last, Elsa," Atticus murmured in her ear.

Elsa jerked her head sideways but could not break his hold. Twisting only made his grip tighten. Her lungs burned for air, but none came. Blackness crowded her vision, and she fell into its depths . . .

She woke with trees passing overhead. Clasped by strong arms, she lay on her back. Her head lolled with her captor's every step. How had this happened again?

Atticus swung her down. "Sorry, but I was afraid you'd

scream." He held Elsa tightly, keeping her from crumpling to the ground.

Giving up the battle, she sank to her knees. "I would have screamed to save myself from being carried off against my will. Why do you insist on tormenting me? I want nothing to do with you."

Atticus's eyes went flat, but then a new spark lit their depths. "You will feel differently in time."

"I promise you, I will not." Elsa didn't care any longer if Atticus might not like this truth. She'd pretended before, to put him off-guard. That was a mistake she would not repeat. It was better to tell the truth and take the consequences.

"Don't contradict me, Elsa." He lifted her to stand before him. "You don't know what you want right now, but I'll teach you." He dragged her closer until his face hovered inches from hers. "I killed for you, and I'd do it again."

"Who did you kill?" The words wrenched from Elsa. Images of Con sprawled on the ground, bleeding, filled her mind.

"Miles called you a . . . certain name, and Alicia laughed." He stroked her cheek. "They won't trouble you any longer."

"*What*?" She stared at him. "Have you done away with them?"

"Why didn't you tell me they were mistreating you? I would have shot them sooner."

Elsa's thoughts reeled. How could Atticus discuss murdering people in the calm voice he might use to order breakfast? "Atticus, please listen to me." Elsa clutched the hand holding hers. "You need help. I think you have lost your reason."

Confusion traveled across Atticus's face for a moment, and then a blank expression settled over his features. "Don't try to trick me." He slapped her, hard, on her cheek. "You're just like Ada, after all."

Elsa ignored the stinging pain and opened her mouth to reason with him. "Please, Atti—"

"Ada pretended to love me. She flirted with me, but it was all a lie." He twisted Elsa's arm behind her back. "You'd better not toy with me."

"Let her go." Bry's sharp tones cut the air. "I have a rifle, and I won't hesitate to use it."

Atticus yanked Elsa in front of him like a shield. He whipped out a pistol and pressed the barrel against her temple. "If you come any nearer, I'll fire."

"Don't tempt me to pull this trigger."

Atticus's arm gripped Elsa so tightly she could barely breathe. He continued talking, but his words drifted to her sporadically. If he hadn't been holding her, she would have slid to the ground. She felt like a drowning person, ready to grasp anything that would pull her into the air. There was nothing to hold onto.

A gun fired, and Atticus spun away. Elsa dropped into darkness.

Elsa woke in her bedroom and sat up. *How did I get here?*

Bry knocked and came in. "I heard you stirring." She sank into a chair beside the bed. "How are you feeling?"

"I'm all right." Elsa tried to gauge the time of day by seeing the light slanting through the window. She couldn't. "What time is it?"

It felt late. Vague images returned to Elsa's memory—the sunny garden, Atticus carrying her, a gun at her head. Atticus falling. She shuddered. Atticus had been shot. She'd been standing between him and Bry. How had it happened?

"It's two o'clock in the afternoon. I let you sleep as long as you wanted."

"How is Atticus?"

"Turner shot him. He glimpsed Atticus making off with you and circled around behind him."

Elsa had forgotten all about the ranch manager. He lived in a cabin on the property, did his job, and mostly kept to himself. "I must thank him—and you—for defending me."

"I was in the kitchen making coffee. I looked out to say good morning and saw him hauling you off. I grabbed the rifle Rob keeps over the back door and went after you."

"Is Atticus—"

"He's dead, Elsa. He'll never hurt you again."

Relief washed through Elsa. She was finally free of him. Guilt at welcoming someone's death niggled her. Atticus had been a broken person. His mind clearly had not reasoned well.

Like a shattered mirror, the shards that had been Atticus revealed not only his wickedness, but also the man he *might* have been. He had restrained Elsa unlawfully but had not violated her. As Gentleman, he'd robbed but never killed. And yet, when the soul merchants he'd hired to abduct Elsa dared to disrespect her, he'd shot them.

His actions obviously showed the breakdown of his thinking. What a sad progression.

From outside came the pounding of horses' hooves. Bry peeked out the window. "Con and Nick are home."

Elsa threw back the covers. She was fully clothed, but Bry must have unbuttoned her bodice and loosened her corset. She restored order to her clothing and went to the washstand mirror to tidy her hair. She winced. A bruise the size of Atticus's hand stained one cheek.

Bry waited for her at the door, and they went downstairs together.

When they reached the porch, Bry hurried down the steps to meet Con and Nick on the driveway. From her gesturing and the two men's rapt attention, Elsa guessed Bry was telling them about Atticus.

Elsa waited on the porch, reluctant to recount the event that continued to torment her with vivid flashbacks.

Nick leaped from his horse and engulfed his wife in his arms. Con dismounted below the porch. He took off his hat and climbed the steps two at a time. He cupped Elsa's bruised cheek with his hand. "I'm so sorry, Elsa."

Words tangled in her mind, preventing speech. She gazed at Con, filling herself with the sight of him. Days of travel had lent Con a certain roughness. She yearned to thread her fingers through his rumpled hair. Her palms itched to touch the stubble on his face. His air of exhaustion brought out an urge to comfort him.

Con pulled her into his arms, and the world receded. There was only now, this moment, and the embrace of the man she loved.

After a long while, he released her. They stood alone on the porch. The horses were gone, and the barn door hung open. Bry must have slipped past them to go inside.

Con ran his thumb over her mouth, making her yearn for another kiss. His lips curved in a tender smile. "We need to talk, but another day." He walked away and joined Nick in the barn.

Elsa clasped her arms about herself. She could guess what Con had in mind. He would tell her that they shouldn't continue like this. She knew that as well as he did.

It wasn't fair to let him hold her, caress her, and kiss her when she wasn't ready to give up her family in Germany. She had disappointed Peter out of thoughtlessness. She didn't want to repeat the same mistake with Con. She sighed and accepted the truth. Leaving him would break her own heart.

Elsa found Bry in the kitchen making tea. Elsa cut slices of the *Bienenstich* she'd baked for yesterday's dessert. Bry was partial to the bee-sting cake, with its brioche dough, cream filling, and honeyed-almond topping.

Bry turned to Elsa, the tea tray in her hands. "Aren't you coming? We'll be in the parlor."

Elsa shook her head briefly. "I should start supper."

"Don't you want to catch up with the men? I told Nick to hurry in."

Elsa touched her aching forehead. The bruise on her cheek throbbed. "I don't feel up to it."

Bry scanned her face. "You're pale."

"My head is spinning."

"Maybe you should go back to bed. Don't worry about making supper. I'll manage."

"Thank you." Elsa climbed the stairs with slow steps. In her bedroom, she loosened her corset, hoping to alleviate her dizziness, and stretched out on the bed. Sleep dragged her down at once.

"Supper's ready." Bry's concerned face swam into view.

Elsa moaned.

"Sorry, but do you want to come down?"

"I'm too tired." Elsa rolled over.

"Elsa?" It was Con's voice. He touched her forehead. "You have a fever. How are you feeling?"

"My throat hurts."

"I hope she hasn't caught measles. They're going around."

"Stay with her, Bry." Con's voice seemed far away. "I'm going for the doctor."

CHAPTER THIRTY-FOUR

MAISEY HELD HER DAUGHTER AND GENTLY rocked her. A week had gone by since Phoebe's crisis, and she strengthened daily.

Thank you, God. She kissed Phoebe's brow and, finding her asleep, carried her to bed. Maisey tiptoed from the room and pulled the door partially closed. Going into the kitchen, she sat down at the table, where paper and a quill pen in a pot of ink awaited her.

Dear Rob,

Maisey gazed at the wall and considered what to write next. There lay her difficulty. She had no idea how to form her swirling thoughts into words. Rob had left without saying goodbye. Why did she feel the need to do otherwise? She sighed. Until she understood her reasons, she couldn't write the letter.

A soft knock came at the door. Maisey stood, her heart racing. When would she stop jumping at every sound? Hopefully soon.

Bolstering herself with the thought that an intruder wouldn't knock, she peeked out from the kitchen window.

Rob stood on the porch, hat under his arm.

Why was he here? In her fevered state, Maisey could almost believe her thoughts had summoned him. She squared her shoulders and opened the door.

"Hello, Maisey."

Rob seemed quieter and looked leaner than normal. Was he feeding himself well enough? She snapped her thoughts into line. Whether Rob nourished himself was no concern of hers.

"You've come back." She stood aside and let him enter.

"Only for a visit."

She shouldn't feel rejected by his quick assurance, and yet she did. "Phoebe's sleeping."

"I came to see *you*."

Maisey hid her surprise. "Won't you sit down?" She made the offer out of polite habit. She assumed he would go into the main room, but he headed for the table. She swept up the letter emblazoned with his name and turned it face down on the far counter.

Rob tilted his head quizzically. "Writing a letter to me?"

Face flaming, Maisey nodded but couldn't bring herself to speak.

He leaned closer. "I'm right here to talk with."

She couldn't meet his eyes.

He drew back. "I can tell that I've hurt you. I'm sorry, Maisey. I shouldn't have gone away without a word. You mean more to me than that."

She crossed her arms. "I won't say it didn't hurt me. I was foolish enough to think that . . . well, never mind. It doesn't matter anymore."

Rob's silence told Maisey all she needed to know. The fact that he didn't press her to explain meant he wasn't interested. He pulled out a chair and sat down at the table. "I've missed you and Phoebe. How have you been?"

A lot had happened since he'd left. She chose the most important news. "Phoebe's been ill with a bad case of influenza."

"Oh, no."

"Don't worry, she's no longer contagious."

He sighed. "I was thinking of Phoebe. How is she?"

"She's getting better." Maisey willed herself to stop lashing out at him. He couldn't help not wanting her.

He shook his head. "I wish I'd been here to help you with her."

Maisey arched an eyebrow. "That's not your responsibility."

"I don't like thinking of you caring for her all alone."

"Well, I *am* alone, aren't I?" She sat down across from him. "We need to stop pretending that you and I are family."

"Is it pretending to care about you?" His eyes pleaded with her.

Maisey hardened her heart. "Can't you see? That's what we were doing. Maybe it eased our loneliness, but it hurt Phoebe. She asks for you, but I can tell her nothing."

Sorrow spasmed his face. "I never meant to hurt Phoebe."

She softened. "It's not your fault alone. I shouldn't have let her become so attached to you. I do have relatives, but they live back East and want nothing to do with me. I wanted to belong, if only for a little while. It was so easy to adopt your family as my own. But wishing won't make it true."

Rob gazed at her, his eyes sorrowful. "I didn't realize how much I hurt you. I hope you can bring yourself to forgive me."

"I'll try." Maisey rose and picked up the letter she'd begun. "I was having trouble writing to you, but I didn't want to leave without saying goodbye."

Rob's eyes widened. "You're leaving? Where will you go?"

She couldn't look at him. "I don't know yet, but somewhere else."

Rob took the letter out of her hands. "You've told me now, so there's no need to write."

She flinched. "No, I suppose not."

Rob pulled Maisey into his arms and lowered his mouth to hers. She whimpered and kissed him with all the passion she'd held inside. He released her abruptly and stepped away. "I shouldn't have done that. Maisey, I—" He shook his head.

"What were you going to say?"

"Never mind." He shoved a hand through his hair. "Can I look in on Phoebe? I won't wake her."

Maisey nodded. Trembling, she waited in the kitchen while Rob went into Phoebe's room. If she watched him bending over her daughter, she'd never hold back her tears.

Rob returned and picked up his hat from the table. "Tell Phoebe I stopped by."

"I will." She walked out to the porch with him. A breeze stirred the trees while a whippoorwill lamented and starlight shone down from the heavens.

Rob tilted his head and gazed into her up-tilted face. "Goodbye, Maisey." His voice caressed her.

For a moment, she thought he might kiss her.

She swallowed. "Goodbye, Rob."

He walked down the stairs and along the path toward the road.

Maisey gripped the railing as tears ran down her cheeks.

At the edge of the trees, he turned and waved.

She slipped inside her cabin and closed the door between them.

Elsa sat up, muttering in her fever. She ended with a coughing fit.

Con lowered her back to the bed. "You're all right, darling." He wrung out a washcloth and laid it on her fevered brow.

Sighing, she settled against her pillow. Her face took on a look of peace.

The door swung inward and Bry entered. "What did the doctor say?"

He stood up. "It's measles. I thought he would have told you."

"Nick saw him out on his way to talk to Turner. He hasn't come back yet, so I thought I'd ask you. I had measles as a child, but I can't remember you ever coming down with them. Did you?"

Con's eyes twinkled. "Yes, Bry, before you were born. What about Nick?"

She went to the window, twitched back the curtain, and looked out. "I don't believe he's had it."

Con glanced at Elsa. She'd started coughing again. "Then it's up to me to take care of her."

"Don't you trust me to do it?"

"It's not that." He shook his head. "I don't want you to carry the illness to Nick."

Her eyes rounded. "That didn't even occur to me."

"No, it wouldn't, but it can happen."

"Did the doctor say when she'll get better?"

Con looked away from her. "It can take a while."

She took a step toward him. "What aren't you saying?"

He moved closer and lowered his voice. "Some people don't recover."

Bry nodded. "I know. We'll have to help Elsa through it, that's all. I'll make a batch of licorice and honey syrup for that cough."

"Thanks, Bry. Leave the syrup and anything else you bring outside the door."

She touched his arm. "Try not to fret." She pulled the door to behind her.

Con returned to the chair beside Elsa's bed. His reaction to her illness told him what he had known for quite some time, that he had fallen in love with Elsa. He would not willingly part from her for any reason.

He picked up her hand. "Get better, darling."

Elsa's fingers curled around his.

"Come in, Shane." Maisey held open the door. "Can I offer you a cup of coffee?"

Shane strode past her into the cabin. "Not for me, thanks."

"Won't you sit down?" She gestured into the front room.

"Thank you." He took one of the wingback chairs beside the fireplace.

Phoebe peeked around the corner from her bedroom. She ran to Shane. She was bouncing back quickly from her illness. Less than a week ago, she had lain unresponsive in her bed. Shane propped her on his knee and looked over her head at Maisey. "I won't keep you long, but I wanted to talk with you about the Indian school. America tells me you're having doubts about your involvement."

"Just a moment." She peeled Phoebe off Shane and set her daughter down on a chair at the kitchen table with a slice of Emma's carrot cake. Maisey returned to the front room and took the chair across from Shane's. "It's more than doubts. I've decided to move away."

Shane studied her. "Have you taken this to prayer? You were certain of your direction when you moved here."

Maisey clasped her hands together and laid them in her lap. "It's three weeks since any students showed up. After Rain's death, I doubt any will."

"I can't blame you for being discouraged." Shane sighed. "I've been praying about the Indian school."

"Have you had an answer?"

"I don't feel compelled to close it." He lifted a brow. "The opposite, in fact."

Maisey jumped up to pace about the room. "How can you say that? From every appearance, the Indian school is dead. We need to accept that truth."

Shane watched her with a steady gaze. "'Faith is the substance of things hoped for, the evidence of things not seen.' That's a quote from the Bible, as I'm sure you know. What are you putting your faith in, Maisey?"

She shook her head. "I don't know anymore. All I can think is that I've made a mistake. Surely, God wouldn't thrust me into the middle of something He didn't intend to finish."

"That's my point exactly."

Maisey sat down again. "Shane, I feel the need to take better care of my daughter."

"America and I can help you."

"I appreciate that, but it's not your responsibility. We're not family."

"Being a family involves more than a blood relationship. When the family we're born into fails us, God fills those gaps in other ways. I've seen it time and again, in my own life, and in the lives of others. It's a matter of noticing His hand at work and being willing to accept the results."

"I'll pray." Now that Maisey thought about it, she'd neglected to ask God to reveal what He wanted for the Indian school. She'd been too busy worrying about Phoebe.

Shane rose and picked up his hat. "Whatever you decide, America and I will support you. I hope you'll give this decision the time it deserves. I'd hate to see you throw away something you believe in so deeply." He smiled at her. "I'll head home now."

"Thank you for stopping by." Maisey stepped outside to see him off.

Shane started down the steps, but then turned back. "You have visitors."

Se'ułku was walking beside her daughter Bluebird on the path beneath the trees. Several others with children who had attended the Indian school, paced toward Maisey. They stopped below the porch.

Se'ułku tilted her head to gaze up at Maisey. "Teacher, we came for school."

Maisey stared at her. "What did you say?"

"It's Saturday. Why is the schoolhouse locked?"

Maisey hurried down the steps past Shane and stood before the small crowd. "I don't understand. Why are you here?"

Se'ułku gave her gentle smile. "We are sorry for what happened with Spukani. We don't share his ideas. You helped save my daughter's life, and I will always be grateful."

Her gesture included them all. "There is so much we need to know in order to live in freedom. Some of *The People* don't believe this is possible, but you have shown us we can. Please open the school. We want you to teach us."

Elsa came back to the world from far away. Her body ached, but the heavy cloud oppressing her had finally dissipated. She tried to sit up but found she couldn't. A moan escaped her.

Arms enfolded her. "Lie down, darling."

Con's whisper soothed her, and she drifted into sleep.

The next time Elsa woke, the sun was shining brightly through her bedroom window. She opened her eyes and gazed on Con's sleeping face. He'd slumped over in the bedside chair and lay with his head on her pillow.

How uncomfortable he looked. How long had Con stayed with her? She remembered waking many times to find him there. Elsa pulled more upright, trying not to disturb him.

Con lifted his head and blinked sleepy eyes at her. "I must have dozed off." He stretched. "How are you feeling?"

She made a face. "My throat aches, I'm thirsty, and my head hurts."

He touched her brow. "You've cooled down, thankfully."

"I'm sorry to be so much trouble."

His face softened. "Dear Elsa, when will you learn that you are a delight, not a burden? I must apply myself to changing your view of my opinion."

The heat in his gaze left her in no doubt of his feelings. Cast into confusion, she ducked her head. A woman should not receive such interest from a man while on her sickbed.

Bry came in balancing a tray laden with a tureen of soup, two bowls, a plate of soda crackers, and beverages in tall glasses. "The noon meal has arrived." She smiled and placed the tray on the bedside table. "It's good to see you sitting up, Elsa."

Con filled one of the bowls and offered it to Elsa. "Can you manage on your own?"

Her face heated at memories of him spoon-feeding her. "Yes."

Bry touched her brother's arm. "Come away." She winked at Elsa. "I couldn't persuade him to leave you for long."

Elsa looked up in surprise. "Thank you."

Bry tapped her foot. "Go on, Con. You'll be in the way while I bathe Elsa."

"Oh, yes. Of course." Con lurched to his feet.

Was that a blush on his cheeks? Elsa hid a smile.

Con pushed a hand through his hair. "Perhaps I should seek my own bed."

Elsa held back a laugh. "That would be best, rather than sleeping on my pillow."

Bry gave her brother a stern glance, but her eyes sparkled. "If you've compromised this woman, brother of mine, you'd better marry her."

CHAPTER THIRTY-FIVE

MAISEY'S BOOTS TAPPED ON THE FLOORBOARDS as she navigated the schoolroom. She touched the worn wooden surface of her desk, then lowered herself into the chair behind it. Folding her hands, she looked out as she'd done so many times in the past. Gone were the rows of faces gazing at her with trust.

Her work had not been in vain. She had touched their lives. She had taught the children to the best of her ability. Now they were gone. She'd sent them away today along with their mothers, telling them she needed time to make a decision. Calling them back would be easy, if she wished to do so. They had promised to come. Shane and America would support the school. She could go on exactly as before.

And yet, she couldn't.

Maisey had learned something during Phoebe's illness, something so important that she could not set it aside. As Phoebe's only parent, she needed to take better care of her sweet daughter.

Staying here would eventually throw her back into Rob's company. The heartache of that, especially if he brought home a wife, would crush her.

Maisey had helped Shane and America open the school. She'd had high hopes, but perhaps God's purpose for her in this place was at an end. If true, though, why had parents from the tribe requested that the school continue?

So much remained a mystery.

Maisey rose from her teacher chair and walked about,

touching surfaces. If she rejected her role at the school and earned a living sewing, would she feel whole? She made her way outside to the balcony and stood at the railing.

The sky glowed a vivid blue. The scent of sun-warmed grass wafted to her. In the distance, a flock of geese lifted above the river. *God, I surrendered my life to You long ago. I won't take it back again. What do You want me to do?*

Se'ułku's words returned to her in memory. *There is so much we need to know in order to live in freedom.*

The knowledge she could give the Indian children would free them to live in peace. Their world was changing forever. They could never go back to the old ways. Maisey stood as a small shield against the forces bent on destroying them. She could help them, as she herself had hoped for rescue when she was a captive. The cords of sinew that had confined Maisey were not unlike the prejudice and ignorance that caged the tribes.

It would be easier to run away than to try again, but she couldn't ignore their plight.

Remaining would require her to surrender to the inner prompting she wanted to ignore. God's plan for her life mattered more than her own. It might lead her to face the heartbreak of seeing Rob again, but out of love for others she would accept even that sorrow.

Maisey returned to the schoolhouse with a purposeful step. She had a lot to do before next Saturday.

Bry caught sight of Nick carrying a basket of cleaned and scaled fish. She hurried to meet him at the kitchen door. "You're not coming in with those muddy feet."

"Is that all the thanks you can give a man for providing your supper?" He gave her a wounded look, but then betrayed it by smiling.

She relieved him of the basket. "You well know I'm grateful. That still doesn't give you the right to tramp mud all over the floor."

He gave her a brilliant smile. "Come walk with me."

She peeked into the basket. "I need to deal with these."

"The fish will keep."

Bry wavered. If she waited, Elsa would come in to start supper and find the fish. Elsa's fish in mustard cream was a delight, but it wasn't fair to expect her to cook right now. She'd recovered from her illness, but her strength hadn't completely returned.

Nick gave Bry his most beguiling look, and she lost the battle. "All right, but only for a short while." She would come back and help Elsa cook.

Her husband deserved to know the truth she'd hidden for the past month. Her stomach fluttered at the thought. How would Nick react?

Bry slid the basket onto the counter, reached to untie her apron, and opened the screen door. She took the hand Nick held out. His grin made it clear that he felt the same joy that leaped in her chest.

They took the path toward the river and stopped on the small crest above the water. A cottonwood spread its branches overhead. The tree's furrowed bark stood out against its silken blooms. Bry smiled. How like life's rough patches and moments of beauty that seemed.

Nick turned and pulled her into his arms. "You're beautiful when your face lights up."

"After cleaning the stove, I'm a mess."

"I like you like this." He threaded his fingers through her hair. The pins gave way, and Bry's hair cascaded about her face.

"Now look what you've done." She tried to sound stern, but the breathiness of her voice gave away her feelings.

Nick laughed, clearly unrepentant. He lowered his head and covered her lips with his own.

Bry wound her arms around her husband's neck and returned the caresses of his mouth.

He lifted his head and kissed her forehead. "I've wanted to do that, Mrs. Laramie, since you scolded me at the back door."

"And rightfully so, mind you." She flashed a mischievous smile at him. "I've cleaned up after your boots a time or two."

"Your memory is too good." He tightened his arms around her. "You must need more kissing."

"Wait." Desire had deepened her voice, but she pressed a hand on his chest to hold him back. "I have something to tell you."

"Yes?" He nibbled her fingers.

She pulled her hand away. "Stop that or I'll never collect my thoughts."

"I'm glad to hear it. Now tell me what's on your mind."

Now that it came down to revealing her secret, Bry couldn't think how to begin. Her carefully-rehearsed speech fled her mind. "I'm with child," she blurted out at last.

A surprised look came over Nick's face. "You're sure?"

She nodded.

Nick's forehead creased. "I hope we did right by getting married."

Bry gazed at her husband in faint alarm. That wasn't how she'd expected him to react. "I hoped you'd be pleased."

"I am, of course. It's just that—" He turned his head away.

"What is it?"

He looked back to her. "I wonder if we have the right to bring a mixed-blood child into the world."

"Nick." She touched his face, and stubble scratched her palm. "We went all through that before we married. We agreed that we shouldn't let the prejudice of others keep us from happiness. Have you changed your mind about that?"

"No." He turned his face and kissed her palm. "Forgive me for losing faith. I thought I'd conquered my fears." He sighed. "I guess it will take more time."

"You can't expect to instantly overcome long-held beliefs." She embraced him, then leaned back and gazed into his eyes. "We have love enough to give our child. That's all that matters."

"It's the most important thing." He kissed her forehead and gave her a tender smile. "We'll want a home of our own. Con plans to help me build one on the ranch, if we'd like. I don't mind staying on, helping out, and learning the cattle business. What do you think?"

"That sounds wonderful." Bry's eyes gleamed. "We'll have a place to raise a family. I can picture our children around us at the table."

Nick's frown gave way to a grin. "I guess you're hoping for a big dining room, Mrs. Laramie."

Elsa breathed in the fresh air scented by river water. The sweet bitterroot blossoms tangled with the blue spikes of camas lilies along the grassy banks. Water splashed and burbled. The rain-washed sky promised sunshine, despite scattered clouds.

Con walked beside Elsa, his hand at her elbow. "I've been wanting to take you on a walk for some time now." A smile lilted his voice. "I hope you are recovered enough."

"I feel stronger every day."

"Soon you'll run rings around me."

"I'm looking forward to cooking supper again."

He laughed. "Not every woman shares your feelings about that task."

"I want to make a special meal, to thank you and Bry for taking such good care of me."

Con stopped her with a gentle press of her arm. "No thanks are necessary, Elsa. I cared for you because I wanted to. I'm sure Bry would say the same."

"Nevertheless, I'm grateful. You and Bry must allow me to show my gratitude."

He grinned. "You are a stubborn woman. However, since you insist, you are at liberty to feed me. I have a question for you. Rob telegraphed to say that he believes Sheriff Gerhart has found a hurdy-gurdy at Atticus's house. He believes it may belong to you."

Elsa caught her breath. To have her father's precious gift restored to her seemed a blessing beyond measure. "I'm sure it is mine. I had to leave it when I climbed out the window."

"I'll let him know." They walked on, watching the jumping fish send ripples across the river's surface. Elsa stumbled over a root, and Con tucked her hand in his elbow. "You're tiring. We should turn back soon."

She pulled on his arm. "Can't we go a little farther? Please?"

Con's smile broadened. "I'll have to harden my heart a little, or I'll wind up bending to your every whim." He faced her. "I've given thought to your wish to join your family."

"Yes?" She gazed at him, her heart breaking. *He's going to send me home.*

"What if they came to live near here?"

Elsa sighed. "I would love that, but I can't afford my own ticket, let alone passage for my family."

He tilted her chin. "I'm offering to pay."

"I can't let you do that." She turned away and continued walking.

He followed her. "I insist."

"You are a stubborn man." Elsa kept going.

Con caught up to her, grinning. "That makes us a perfect match."

Elsa stared at him, hardly crediting her ears. "What did you say?"

His arms encircled her. "Perhaps you missed that I proposed marriage."

"That was a proposal?" No, she hadn't realized what Con was saying.

"You're not shaking your head at the thought of marrying me, I hope."

She gave him a look that answered his question.

Con tightened his arms around her. "Elsa, I love you beyond reason, and I want to spend the rest of my life with you. Please honor me by becoming my wife." He gazed at her in a way that made her heart race. "Is that better?"

Tears of joy sprang to Elsa's eyes. "Yes, Con."

His brows drew together. "Yes, it's better or yes, you accept?"

Elsa ginned. "Yes, I'll marry you. I love you with all my heart."

He beamed. "You won't be sorry."

"What makes you think I would ever be sorry?"

"I wasn't trying to pick an argument."

She laughed. "Then I won't give you one. I only hope spending your life with me will be a blessing."

Con captured her hand and brought it to his lips. "Elsa, my darling, it cannot fail to be." He lowered his mouth to hers in a lingering caress. Waves of desire left her breathless. Her hands found their way behind his head, and her fingers explored the crisp locks at his nape. Con threaded his fingers through her hair, sending her pins flying. He pulled her closer to deepen the kiss. Elsa clung to him, caught by desire and the certainty that she had never belonged to anyone more.

Con broke away and set her from him with gentle hands and a final kiss. He tilted her face to the light. "You have the most beautiful, changing eyes. Sometimes they look green, other times brown, but right now they've turned to gold. I can never quite decide what color they are. I'm sure it will take a lifetime to figure out."

Author Notes

During my research for the Montana Gold series, I learned something that gave me a new perspective on the dance hall girls of the Wild West. Starting in the 1820's, poverty-stricken German farmers and their workers supplemented their income by brooms and fly-whisks they made by hand. To draw a crowd and increase sales, pretty young girls played the hurdy-gurdy (a stringed instrument) and danced. The hurdy-gurdy girls' fame captured the attention of unscrupulous Americans who put the girls under contract with the promise of a better life in America. In exchange, each girl agreed to entertain in western mining towns. Many hurdy-gurdy girls came, like Elsa, from the part of Germany known as Hesse. Parents were willing to send their daughters away to secure a better future for them and to ease the burden of their upkeep. The girls often went in order to send money back home.

Some hurdy-gurdy girls were expected to do no more than dance with miners for a fee (usually a dollar a dance plus the purchase of a beverage). Unfortunately, others were mistreated and fell ill. Some became prostitutes.

The plight of the hurdy-gurdy girls wouldn't leave my mind or heart. I could picture the vulnerable and frightened young girl who became Elsa in the pages of this book. I know firsthand how disorienting travel to a foreign country can be. How would it feel to leave your home in the hope of a better life elsewhere, only to discover you'd been tricked into going there by people who meant you harm?

Throughout her adventures, Elsa has to let go of her dreams and every ounce of her own strength before she can find true freedom. It's a journey we all must take. Only by allowing God to manifest His miracles in our lives can we strike true gold.

Factual Historical Events in this Book

Young girls who danced and played the hurdy-gurdy did come to the dancehalls of the American West, as described above.

The sheriff's office in Bannack was actually located in the back of the general store. I saw them when I walked through George Chrisman's store, the hub of news and social activity for the men of Bannack.

Deputy Donald H. Dillingham of Bannack was murdered in Virginia City as I've described. Historical accounts state that he was an honest man who paid the ultimate price when he fell afoul of fellow deputies. His death added to the outrage that led to formation of the vigilance committee in Virginia City.

Locals remained divided on the morality of the vigilantes' actions. The miners' committee in Bannack eventually demanded that the vigilantes leave town with the promise to repay five deaths for every life they took.

Alicia's description of traveling West on an Orphan Train is based on true events in American history. Between 1855 and 1875, the Children's Aid Society transported thousands of orphans and homeless children westward by train. Some of the homeless children were separated unwillingly from their living parents, usually poor immigrants. The children were adopted out at stops along the way. The approval process for adoptive parents was not well-monitored. In all, 200,000 children were removed from crowded Eastern cities before the Orphan Trains stopped running.

In conversation, Atticus and Miles referred to Thomas Meagher, an Irishman who served briefly as Montana's Territorial governor. He was a fascinating figure who died under mysterious circumstances that were probably politically-motivated.

Red Cloud's War took place between 1866 and 1868. The Bozeman Trail was the most direct route from Fort Laramie and the Oregon Trail into the gold fields of Montana. However, it cut through hunting grounds used by the Cheyenne, Arapaho, and Lakota. Red Cloud's War cost many lives. The Fetterman Massacre and Hayfield and Wagon Box fights were part of Red Cloud's War. It ended after the Treaty of Fort Laramie.

Deer Lodge Valley's namesake feature, the 40' high geo-thermal formation Elsa and Con visit, was a major landmark. The steam which gave the appearance of smoke rising from a medicine lodge no longer rises from the dome. The warm spring has been capped and a kiosk sits atop the mound.

The ambush of the Bitterroot Salish by the Blackfoot tribe gave Hell Gate Canyon its name.

Robbers Roost was a roadhouse situated between Bannack and Virginia City in Montana's Ruby Valley. During my research, I received permission to explore the building and surrounding area. The experience brought me face-to-face with history. The main building, wooden entrance turnstile, livery, and well still stand.

Read more stories behind the story. Enjoy reader bonuses. Try recipes from the book. Subscribe to Janalyn Voigt's email list. Visit the author at http://janalynvoigt.com.

Book Club Discussion Questions

1. Were Elsa's reasons for leaving her family and coming to America valid?

2. Miles has a habit of not looking at Elsa directly. Have you ever avoided acknowledging someone's existence by avoiding eye contact? If so, why? Has anyone ever done that to you?

3. If you lost your memory like Con, how would you feel?

4. Con and Elsa make a powerful connection when they meet on the stagecoach. What factors do you think contributed to them forging a bond so quickly?

5. When Elsa escapes from Atticus, she leaves her hurdy-gurdy behind. What did the instrument represent to her? How did losing it change her prospects?

6. Was Rob's decision to make his own way in the world wise or foolish?

7. Why did the local tribe approach Shane when he camped overnight in the clearing, but then decide to leave him alone?

8. What circumstances caused Elsa's homesickness to intensify?

9. Should Maisey have turned away the sick Salish children whose mother brought them to the schoolhouse? What risks did she take by helping them?

10. Which events led Con to propose to Elsa and for her to accept him? What changed for them both?

Now, A Sneak Peek at Book Four
THE FOREVER SKY

CHAPTER ONE

Liberty, Montana Territory, May 1870

"I SHOULDN'T LINGER, THERE'S SO MUCH to do." Maisey Wilcox sipped the last of the amber liquid in her tea cup but made no move to leave.

"I'll make another pot of tea." America Hayes smiled, correctly discerning that Maisey wasn't going anywhere.

She should go home and bake bread before the day warmed, see to her neglected mending, and put together lessons for the local tribe's children when they came to the Indian school on Saturday. Maisey sank against the backrest of her chair. Those tasks could wait a little longer.

Whoops drifted in the window from Seth and Liam, the Hayes's young boys. High-pitched chatter mingled with giggles from her daughter Phoebe and America's Liberty drifted in from the parlor. At eight, Phoebe was two years older than Liberty, but the girls played well together. Phoebe's playfulness contrasted against Liberty's serious nature sometimes made her seem the younger of the two. Maisey's lips curved in a soft smile. She wouldn't want to change a thing about her lively, mischievous, adorable daughter.

A shadow fell across the floorboards. America's husband, Shane, filled the open doorway. He grinned at Maisey, then sneaked up on his wife, at the counter measuring tea into a blue willow pot. She must have heard him at the last instant, for she started to turn. Shane slipped his arms around his wife and landed a kiss on her cheek.

"I'm surprised at you, Reverend Hayes, ambushing an unsuspecting woman." America's dancing eyes belied her protest.

Maisey glanced away from the loving couple and tried not to mind that she sat alone at the table. She didn't begrudge Shane and America their happiness, but it sometimes reminded her of all she'd lost. Maisey sighed. Five years had gone by since her husband had drowned while fording the Laramie River. The memories of her life before were fading. One day she might forget how it felt to be cherished by a man who adored her.

"'Tis a fair day, and no mistake." Shane caught hold of his wife's hand and twirled her gently about. "What do you say to a picnic, Mrs. Hayes?"

America fell against him, laughing breathlessly. "You're after fried chicken and apple pie, no doubt."

"It's the cook I want, and I'll eat beans to prove it." His hands slid to her thickened waist. "Come away. We can't have you working too hard with the new baby on the way."

America's face turned pink. "All right, you rogue. Take yourself out of here or I'll never get ready."

"The children will be pleased." He pecked her lips and turned to leave.

Maisey stood. "I should be going."

Shane looked back from the doorway. "There's no need. You and Phoebe are welcome to join us."

"Yes, do." America's eyes lit.

Maisey hesitated. She'd prefer to go home and console herself in private, but that wasn't fair to her daughter.

"Then it's settled." Shane bestowed a beatific smile on Maisey.

"Don't rush the woman, Shane." America frowned at her husband but used a gentle voice. She poured hot water from the cast iron kettle into the teapot. "You will come, won't you, Maisey? It won't be as fun without you."

Maisey's reluctance melted. "All right."

"Wonderful. I'll let the children know." Shane sauntered from the room.

"The children will be pleased." Shane sauntered from the room.

"What shall I bring?" Maisey frowned. The contents of her larder were sparse at the moment. She needed to take a trip to town for supplies and also do the week's baking.

"Nothing." America carried the tea tray to the table. "There's enough food left over from yesterday to feed five families."

Maisey nodded. Members of the congregation often gave food left over from the monthly Sunday meeting to the preacher's family. "I'd still like to contribute something."

"You can if you'd like. More tea?"

"Yes, please." Maisey watched a steaming amber stream pour into her cup. "I know. I saved part of the saltwater taffy Emma gave me for my birthday. Shall I bring it for a treat?"

"The children would love that, I'm sure. Only, don't let on or they won't want to eat anything else." Her forehead puckered. "I have half a mind to invite Emma also. Do you think she's up to it?"

Maisey shook her head. "That was a nasty cold she caught. I took over a pot of soup last night. Her color looked better, but she needs time to rest."

America exhaled. "I'm glad she's on the mend."

"I'll look in on her before we leave."

"That would ease my mind. I'll ask Shane to let the neighbors know we'll be away from home. I doubt we'll go far."

America poured tea into her own cup but didn't sit down again. Instead, she hurried to the shelves lining the wall. Standing on tiptoe, she reached upward. Her fingers brushed the wicker picnic basket above her but failed to dislodge it. The basket wobbled and seemed ready to fall.

"You shouldn't do that." Maisey pushed back her chair. "Let me."

America shifted out of the way. "I almost had it."

"I'm taller." Maisey stood on tiptoe and retrieved the basket. "Is there anything else I can fetch before I leave?"

"I'll manage, thanks."

Maisey left by the back door. After the cold of winter, the sunshine bathing the path felt like a touch from heaven. A few tattered clouds scurried across the pale sky. Bitterroot flowers threaded the grass, their purple faces gay. She rounded a corner of the barn but stopped short at the clopping of hooves. Maisey backed into the shadow beside the building. Traffic on the road wasn't unusual, but using caution never hurt. A man on horseback turned into the barnyard. The sunlight picked out features she knew all too well. Rob Walsh sat tall in the saddle with an air of confidence he'd once lacked.

Maisey swallowed against the lump in her throat. Tears pricked, and she drew a shaky breath. She'd known this moment would come when deciding to stay on in Liberty, but that didn't make bearing it any easier. She hadn't seen Rob Walsh since he'd left her with a kiss on her lips three years ago. She'd convinced them both that their futures lay apart, but that hadn't kept her from yearning for the impossible. The old feelings came rushing back.

If only she'd left for home a little earlier or waited longer, she wouldn't have faced Rob alone. Maybe she should wait for him to go into the barn, then cut around behind the building. The stand of trees between the Hayes's house and the schoolteachers' cabins made going that way difficult. Besides, she was no coward.

Maisey stepped out of shadow and into the light. "Hello, Rob."

Rob tensed and reined in his horse. Finding Maisey still living on his Cousin Shane's property twisted his gut. She'd told him she was moving away. What had changed to make her stay? The three years since he'd seen her last must have treated her well. Her deep brown eyes lacked the haunted look they'd so often held before. She wore a simple dress of gold calico and a shawl woven in brown hues. Her chestnut hair swept backward in gleaming wings and wound in a braided roll behind her head. Desire kicked through Rob like a stubborn mule that refused to be tamed. The impulse to leap from his horse, pull her into his arms, and kiss away the pucker between her brows took possession of him. He tipped his hat instead. "Maisey."

"You've come back." She curved her lips into a smile that didn't include her eyes. Those remained wary.

She might wonder, as he did, how they would make it through this awkward encounter. A sudden urge to shelter her swarmed over him. He smiled. "For a little while." Knowing she'd have to endure his nearness only so long might comfort her.

Her smile faltered. "I suppose you've made your fortune in

gold."

He nodded. "I've done well for myself, but it's time to move on to new challenges."

Surprise swept her face.

He dismounted to hide his confusion. Had she thought he would continue to mine his brother's claim and never strike out on his own? Didn't she know him better than that? But then, he hardly understood himself. She'd been right to accuse him of pretending they were family when it wasn't true. He'd never meant to hurt her and disappoint Phoebe. His dreams had simply exceeded his grasp. Now that he possessed the right to claim what he wanted, he couldn't. He'd carried Maisey's memory with him all this time, but it was hopeless. She had roundly rejected him, and judging by the scowl on her face, she felt no different now.

Rob's horse stomped and snorted, making it plain that stopping short of the barn was less than satisfactory. Maisey stood poised, as if ready to flee. He should go into the barn and put them all out of their misery. "Why didn't you leave?" Rob asked the question against his better judgment. But otherwise, he might always wonder what she would have said.

"Members of the local tribe asked me to continue teaching their children." Her face lit. "I couldn't refuse."

"Of course not." He'd been a fool to hope she'd waited for his return. He needed to accept that their bridges were thoroughly burned. All that remained was to get over this woman, if possible. He'd planned to visit Shane and America a while. Instead, he would spend the night and remove himself farther down the Bitterroot Valley to his brother's ranch. Meanwhile, avoiding Maisey seemed best. He touched the brim of his hat. "Don't let me keep you."

She flinched, ever so slightly.

Rob frowned. Maybe he shouldn't have dismissed her like that. He always seemed to wound Maisey while trying to spare her. It was too late to fix his gaffe, even if he knew how. He retreated to the barn but paused at the door. Maisey walked down the path without looking back. That was just as well, or she'd have caught him watching. He didn't care. It might be his last sight of the woman he loved, and he wanted to cherish it.

Maisey shut the door rather firmly behind her. She cast herself into the wingback chair by the fire, her mind racing. The picnic would be impossible with Rob along. Shane and America were sure to invite him. Shane had already told Phoebe, and Maisey refused to disappoint her child. Besides, this might be the last time they saw Rob. Down with measles, Phoebe had been unable to say goodbye to him before he rode away. She'd asked often about him ever since. Maisey couldn't bring herself to deprive her daughter of the chance to say goodbye to the man she'd made into something of a father. As for herself, well… Maisey pressed a hand to her temple, where a headache throbbed.

Even in the sanctuary of her home, Rob surrounded her. He'd helped Shane build her cabin. She'd looked forward to his reports on their progress for more than one reason. After she moved in, he'd spent a lot of time under this roof. He would sit in the chair across from her, holding Phoebe while she cried as often as when she giggled. They'd laughed and talked over many suppers. He'd kissed her while she stood right there.

Maybe she could beg off herself but send Phoebe. No, she couldn't do that. It would be a different picnic for Phoebe if her mother didn't come. She worked hard as a parent alone to give

Phoebe all she needed. Maisey pushed herself to her feet. She'd better get back. In the kitchen, she climbed on a stool and retrieved the box of saltwater taffy from the high shelf where she'd hidden it. She'd knock lightly on the door of the cabin next door so as not to wake Emma if she was asleep.

She started for the door, which burst open before she reached it. An Indian stood in the doorway, his hand on the knob. Round shells hung from his ear lobes and laddered in ropes across his chest. Fur wraps secured his long braids. Behind him stood two other Indians. One gazed at her from bright eyes above a long nose. The other wore twin braids on either side of his fleshy face.

Maisey gasped but held her ground, bolstered by the absence of war paint. "Spukani, why have you come?" He'd tried to steal Phoebe three years ago but had been persuaded to release her. He'd stayed away ever since, and Maisey had let herself believe he'd given up on punishing her. He obviously continued to hold a grudge against her for his daughter's death from measles while under her care.

Spukani thrust out his chin. "You come with us, Teacher."

Maisey hauled in air. "I can't today." He was only asking, not forcing her to go, but that was hard to remember while pinned by his glare. "The other teacher is sick and needs my help." She realized her mistake as the words left her mouth.

The cords of Spukani's neck stood out, and his face turned angry red. "You bad medicine!" He spoke so forcefully that spittle flew.

"All right." She spoke quickly. Any moment he might reach for her. "Let me tell the preacher and his wife."

His nostrils flared. "You come!"

"Where are you taking me?"

He blinked, obviously taken aback by the calm tone she

mustered. "New chief ask for you."

"I have heard of Chief Charlo." Maisey paused for effect. "He wants peace, like his father before him."

Spukani gritted his teeth but fell back from the doorway. He waved his companions forward. "Bring her."

Watch for this book releasing December 1, 2019.

www.ingramcontent.com/pod-product-compliance
Lightning Source LLC
Chambersburg PA
CBHW051628180726
48284CB00006B/1650